P9-DOB-947

PENGUIN TWENTIETH-CENTURY CLASSICS

LADY CHATTERLEY'S LOVER
A PROPOS OF 'LADY CHATTERLEY'S LOVER'

David Herbert Lawrence was born into a miner's family in Eastwood, Nottinghamshire, in 1885, the fourth of five children. He attended Beauvale Board School and Nottingham High School, and trained as an elementary schoolteacher at Nottingham University College. He taught in Croydon from 1908. His first novel, *The White Peacock*, was published in 1911, just a few weeks after the death of his mother, to whom he had been extraordinarily close. His career as a schoolteacher was ended by serious illness at the end of 1911.

In 1912 Lawrence went to Germany with Frieda Weekley, the German wife of the Professor of Modern Languages at the University College of Nottingham. They were married on their return to England in 1914. Lawrence had published *Sons and Lovers* in 1913; but *The Rainbow*, completed in 1915, was suppressed, and for three years he could not find a publisher for *Women in Love*, completed in 1917.

After the war Lawrence lived abroad, and sought a more fulfilling mode of life than he had so far experienced. With Frieda, he lived in Sicily, Sri Lanka, Australia, New Mexico and Mexico. They returned to Europe in 1925. His last novel, *Lady Chatterley's Lover*, was published in 1928, but was banned in England and America. In 1930 he died in Vence, in the south of France, at the age of forty-four.

Lawrence's life may have been short, but he lived it intensely. He also produced an amazing body of work: novels, stories, poems, plays, essays, travel books, translations, paintings and letters (over five thousand of which survive). After his death Frieda wrote, 'What he had seen and felt and known he gave in his writing to his fellow men, the splendour of living, the hope of more and more life . . . a heroic and immeasurable gift.'

Michael Squires gained his doctorate from the University of Maryland in 1969 and is currently Head of the English Department at Virginia Polytechnic Institute and State University. His books include *The Pastoral Novel* (1974), *The Creation of Lady Chatterley's Lover* (1983) and *D. H. Lawrence's Manuscripts* (1991). He has published essays on Dickens, George Eliot and Hardy. Together with his wife, Lynn K. Talbot, he is now collecting the letters of Frieda Lawrence. They live in Blacksburg, Virginia, with their son Andrew.

John Worthen is advisory editor for the works of D. H. Lawrence in Penguin Twentieth-Century Classics. Currently Professor of D. H. Lawrence Studies at the University of Nottingham, he has published widely on Lawrence; his acclaimed biography, *D. H. Lawrence: The Early Years 1885–1912*, was published in 1991. He has also edited a number of volumes in the authoritative Cambridge Lawrence Edition whose texts Penguin Twentieth-Century Classics are reproducing.

D. H. LAWRENCE

LADY CHATTERLEY'S LOVER

A PROPOS OF 'LADY CHATTERLEY'S LOVER'

EDITED WITH AN INTRODUCTION AND
NOTES BY MICHAEL SQUIRES

PENGUIN BOOKS

PENGUIN BOOKS

Published by the Penguin Group
Penguin Books Ltd, 80 Strand, London WC2R 0RL, England
Penguin Putnam Inc., 375 Hudson Street, New York, New York 10014, USA
Penguin Books Australia Ltd, 250 Camberwell Road, Camberwell, Victoria 3124, Australia
Penguin Books Canada Ltd, 10 Alcorn Avenue, Toronto, Ontario, Canada M4V 3B2
Penguin Books India (P) Ltd, 11 Community Centre, Panchsheel Park, New Delhi – 110 017, India
Penguin Books (NZ) Ltd, Cnr Rosedale and Airborne Roads, Albany, Auckland, New Zealand
Penguin Books (South Africa) (Pty) Ltd, 24 Sturdee Avenue, Rosebank 2196, South Africa

Penguin Books Ltd, Registered Offices: 80 Strand, London WC2R 0RL, England

www.penguin.com

First published 1928
Cambridge University Press edition first published 1993
Published with new editorial matter in Penguin Books 1994

13

Copyright © the Estate of Frieda Lawrence Ravagli, 1993
Introduction and Notes copyright © Michael Squires, 1994
Chronology copyright © John Worthen, 1994
All rights reserved

The moral right of the editor has been asserted

Filmset by Datix International Limited, Bungay, Suffolk
Printed in England by Clays Ltd, St Ives plc

Contents

Note on the Penguin Lawrence Edition

D. H. Lawrence stands in the very front rank of English writers this century; unlike some other famous writers, however, he has always appealed to a large popular audience as well as to students of literature, and his work still arouses passionate loyalties and fervent disagreements. The available texts of his books have, nevertheless, been notoriously inaccurate. The Penguin Lawrence Edition uses the authoritative texts of Lawrence's work established by an international team of scholars engaged on the *Cambridge Edition of the Works of D. H. Lawrence* under its General Editors, Professor James T. Boulton and Professor Warren Roberts. Through rigorous study of surviving manuscripts, typescripts, proofs and early printings the Cambridge editors have provided texts as close as possible to those which Lawrence himself would have expected to see printed. Deletions deliberately made by printers, publishers or their editors, accidentally by typists and printers – at times removing whole pages of text – have been restored; while house-styling introduced by printers is removed as far as is possible. The Penguin Lawrence Edition thus offers both general readers and students the only texts of Lawrence which have any claim to be the authentic productions of his genius.

Chronology

1885   David Herbert Richards Lawrence (hereafter DHL) born in Eastwood, Nottinghamshire, the fourth child of Arthur John Lawrence, collier, and Lydia, née Beardsall, daughter of a pensioned-off engine fitter.

1891–8   Attends Beauvale Board School.

1898–1901   Becomes first boy from Eastwood to win a County Council scholarship to Nottingham High School, which he attends until July 1901.

1901   Works three months as a clerk at Haywood's surgical appliances factory in Nottingham; severe attack of pneumonia.

1902   Begins frequent visits to the Chambers family at Haggs Farm, Underwood, and starts his friendship with Jessie Chambers.

1902–5   Pupil-teacher at the British School, Eastwood; sits the King's Scholarship exam in December 1904 and is placed in the first division of the first class.

1905–6   Works as uncertificated teacher at the British School: writes his first poems and starts his first novel *Laetitia* (later *The White Peacock*, 1911).

1906–8   Student at Nottingham University College following the normal course leading to a teacher's certificate; qualifies in July 1908. Wins *Nottinghamshire Guardian* Christmas 1907 short-story competition with 'A Prelude' (submitted under name of Jessie Chambers); writes second version of *Laetitia*.

1908–11   Elementary teacher at Davidson Road School, Croydon.

1909   Meets Ford Madox Hueffer (later Ford), who begins to publish his poems and stories in the *English Review* and recommends rewritten version of *The White Peacock* (1911) to William Heinemann; DHL writes *A Collier's Friday Night* (1934) and first version of 'Odour of Chrysanthemums' (1911); friendship with Agnes Holt.

1910   Writes *The Saga of Siegmund* (first version of *The Tres-passer*, 1912), based on the experiences of his friend, the Croydon teacher Helen Corke; starts affair with Jessie Chambers; writes first version of *The Widowing of Mrs. Holroyd* (1914); ends affair with Jessie Chambers but continues friendship; starts to write *Paul Morel* (later *Sons and Lovers*, 1913); death of Lydia Lawrence in December; gets engaged to his old friend Louie Burrows.

1911   Fails to finish *Paul Morel*; strongly attracted to Helen Corke; starts affair with Alice Dax, wife of an Eastwood chemist; meets Edward Garnett, publisher's reader for Duckworth, who advises him on writing and publication. In November falls seriously ill with pneumonia and has to give up school-teaching; *The Saga* accepted by Duck-worth; DHL commences its revision as *The Trespasser*.

1912   Convalesces in Bournemouth; breaks off engagement to Louie; returns to Eastwood; works on *Paul Morel*; in March meets Frieda Weekley, wife of Ernest, Professor at the University College of Nottingham; ends affair with Alice Dax; goes to Germany on a visit to his relations on 3 May; travels, however, with Frieda to Metz. After many vicissitudes, some memorialized in *Look! We Have Come Through!* (1917), Frieda gives up her marriage and her children for DHL; in August they journey over the Alps to Italy and settle at Gargnano, where DHL writes the final version of *Sons and Lovers*.

1913   *Love Poems* published; writes *The Daughter-in-law* (1965) and 200 pp. of *The Insurrection of Miss Houghton* (aban-doned); begins *The Sisters*, eventually to be split into *The Rainbow* (1915) and *Women in Love* (1920). DHL and Frieda spend some days at San Gaudenzio, then stay at Irschenhausen in Bavaria; DHL writes first versions of 'The Prussian Officer' and 'The Thorn in the Flesh' (1914); *Sons and Lovers* published in May. DHL and Frieda return to England in June, meet John Middleton Murry and Katherine Mansfield. They return to Italy (Fiascherino, near Spezia) in September; DHL revises *The Widowing of Mrs. Holroyd*; resumes work on *The Sisters*.

1914   Rewrites *The Sisters* (now called *The Wedding Ring*) yet again; agrees for Methuen to publish it; takes J. B. Pinker as agent. DHL and Frieda return to England in June, marry on 13 July. DHL meets Catherine Carswell and S. S. Koteliansky; compiles short-story collection *The Prussian Officer* (1914). Outbreak of war prevents DHL and Frieda returning to Italy; at Chesham he first writes *Study of Thomas Hardy* (1936) and then begins *The Rainbow*; starts important friendships with Ottoline Morrell, Cynthia Asquith, Bertrand Russell and E. M. Forster; grows increasingly desperate and angry about the war.

1915   Finishes *The Rainbow* in Greatham in March; plans lecture course with Russell; they quarrel in June. DHL and Frieda move to Hampstead in August; he and Murry bring out *The Signature* (magazine, three issues only). *The Rainbow* published by Methuen in September, suppressed at the end of October, prosecuted and banned in November. DHL meets painters Dorothy Brett and Mark Gertler; he and Frieda plan to leave England for Florida; decide to move to Cornwall instead.

1916   Writes *Women in Love* between April and October; publishes *Twilight in Italy* and *Amores*.

1917   *Women in Love* rejected by publishers; DHL continues to revise it. Makes unsuccessful attempts to go to America. Begins *Studies in Classic American Literature* (1923); publishes *Look! We Have Come Through!* In October he and Frieda evicted from Cornwall on suspicion of spying; in London he begins *Aaron's Rod* (1922).

1918   DHL and Frieda move to Hermitage, Berkshire, then to Middleton-by-Wirksworth; he publishes *New Poems*; writes *Movements in European History* (1921), *Touch and Go* (1920) and the first version of 'The Fox' (1920).

1919   Seriously ill with influenza; moves back to Hermitage; publishes *Bay*. In the autumn, Frieda goes to Germany and then joins DHL in Florence; they visit Picinisco and settle in Capri.

1920   Writes *Psychoanalysis and the Unconscious* (1921). He and Frieda move to Taormina, Sicily; DHL writes *The Lost Girl* (1920), *Mr Noon* (1984), continues with *Aaron's Rod*; on summer visit to Florence has affair with Rosalind Baynes; writes many poems from *Birds, Beasts and Flowers* (1923). *Women in Love* published.

1921   DHL and Frieda visit Sardinia and he writes *Sea and Sardinia* (1921); meets Earl and Achsah Brewster; finishes *Aaron's Rod* in the summer and writes *Fantasia of the Unconscious* (1922) and 'The Captain's Doll' (1923); plans to leave Europe and visit USA; puts together collection of stories *England, My England* (1922) and group of short novels *The Ladybird, The Fox* and *The Captain's Doll* (1923).

1922   DHL and Frieda leave for Ceylon, stay with Brewsters, then travel to Australia; he translates Verga. In Western Australia meets Mollie Skinner; at Thirroul, near Sydney, he writes *Kangaroo* (1923) in six weeks. Between August and September, he and Frieda travel to California via South Sea islands, and meet Witter Bynner and Willard Johnson; settle in Taos, New Mexico, at invitation of Mabel Dodge (later Luhan). In December, move up to Del Monte ranch, near Taos; DHL rewrites *Studies in Classic American Literature* (1923).

1923   Finishes *Birds, Beasts and Flowers*. He and Frieda spend summer at Chapala in Mexico where he writes *Quetzalcoatl* (first version of *The Plumed Serpent*, 1926). Frieda returns to Europe in August after serious quarrel with DHL; he journeys in USA and Mexico, rewrites Mollie Skinner's *The House of Ellis* as *The Boy in the Bush* (1924); arrives back in England in December.

1924   At dinner in Café Royal, DHL invites his friends to come to New Mexico; Dorothy Brett accepts and accompanies him and Frieda in March. Mabel Luhan gives Lobo (later renamed Kiowa) Ranch to Frieda; DHL gives her *Sons and Lovers* manuscript in return. During summer on ranch he writes *St. Mawr* (1925), 'The Woman Who Rode Away' (1925) and 'The Princess' (1925); in August, suffers his first bronchial haemorrhage. His father dies in September; in October, he, Frieda and Brett move to Oaxaca, Mexico, where he starts *The Plumed Serpent* and writes most of *Mornings in Mexico* (1927).

1925   Finishes *The Plumed Serpent*, falls ill and almost dies of typhoid and pneumonia in February; in March diagnosed as suffering from tuberculosis. Recuperates at Kiowa ranch, writes *David* (1926) and compiles *Reflections on the*

	Death of a Porcupine (1925). He and Frieda return to Europe in September, spend a month in England and settle at Spotorno, Italy; DHL writes first version of *Sun* (1926); Frieda meets Angelo Ravagli.
1926	Writes *The Virgin and the Gypsy* (1930); serious quarrel with Frieda during visit from DHL's sister Ada. DHL visits Brewsters and Brett; has affair with Brett. Reconciled, DHL and Frieda move to Villa Mirenda, near Florence, in May and visit England (his last visit) in late summer. On return to Italy in October, he writes first version of *Lady Chatterley's Lover* (1944); starts second version in November. Friendship with Aldous and Maria Huxley; DHL starts to paint.
1927	Finishes second version of *Lady Chatterley's Lover* (1972); visits Etruscan sites with Earl Brewster; writes *Sketches of Etruscan Places* (1932) and the first part of *The Escaped Cock* (1928). In November, after meetings with Michael Arlen and Norman Douglas, works out scheme for private publication with Pino Orioli, and starts final version of *Lady Chatterley's Lover* (1928).
1928	Finishes *Lady Chatterley's Lover* and arranges for its printing and publication in Florence; fights many battles to ensure its despatch to subscribers in Britain and USA. In June writes second part of *The Escaped Cock* (1929). He and Frieda travel to Switzerland (Gsteig) and the island of Port Cros, then settle in Bandol, in the south of France. He writes many of the poems in *Pansies* (1929); *Lady Chatterley's Lover* pirated in Europe and USA.
1929	Visits Paris to arrange for cheap edition of *Lady Chatterley's Lover* (1929); unexpurgated typescript of *Pansies* seized by police; exhibition of his paintings in London raided by police. He and Frieda visit Majorca, France and Bavaria, returning to Bandol for the winter. He writes *Nettles* (1930), *Apocalypse* (1931) and *Last Poems* (1932); sees much of Brewsters and Huxleys.
1930	Goes into Ad Astra sanatorium in Vence at start of February; discharges himself on 1 March; dies at Villa Robermond, Vence, on Sunday 2 March; buried on 4 March.

1935   Frieda sends Angelo Ravagli (now living with her at
        Kiowa Ranch – they marry in 1950) to Vence to have
        DHL exhumed, cremated, and his ashes brought back to
        the ranch.
1956   Frieda dies and is buried at Kiowa Ranch.

John Worthen, 1994

Introduction

Lady Chatterley's Lover is D. H. Lawrence's most famous novel, at one time banned in both the USA and Britain. Although critics have long differed about its literary merits, the novel has endured not only because of its peculiar status as a sexually explicit work but also because, like a camera, it succeeded in photographing a series of moments in the particular history of a society. To understand the novel's complex genetic and literary history – and to appreciate its enduring qualities as well as its particular distinction – it is necessary first to spend a short time exploring the novel's origins and development across three complete versions.

THE NOVEL'S ORIGINS

Although D. H. Lawrence had rarely left the Midlands of England until he was twenty-three, he spent much of his adult life travelling the world with his wife Frieda, whom he married in 1914. Italy had, however, long been a favourite place – 'I like it best here,'[1] he remarked in 1926. Returning to Europe from a lengthy stay in New Mexico and then Mexico, where he had written his novel *The Plumed Serpent* (1926), Lawrence went first to Spotorno on the Italian Riviera. Then, in May 1926, he moved to Florence, where for a little over two years he and Frieda rented a country villa, seven miles from the city and named – after its owner – the Mirenda. Increasingly troubled by the inroads of tuberculosis and depressed by his visit in the summer of 1926 to the English Midlands – where miners had begun by taking part in the General Strike but were now, isolated, on strike against a lengthened working day – Lawrence professed himself disinclined to write when he returned to the Villa Mirenda. 'I feel how nice it is, in the soft, sunny days . . . just leisurely to drift one's way,'[2] he wrote on 18 October: he could watch the local grape harvest, with the peasants still ferrying grapes on wagons drawn by white oxen. But his detachment from his native land could never be as final as he wished. When the weather cooled about 22 October, he suddenly began writing what he first thought would be a short novel, set – unlike his two previous novels – in England. He wrote very fast, and around 25 November he had finished the first version of what had grown to be a full-length novel. But Lawrence often rewrote a work until he was satisfied, and at the beginning of December he apparently began a complete rewriting. This time he composed more slowly, the new version emerging from the 'bottomless pools'[3] of his imagination – yet it was also becoming, he sensed, '*absolutely* improper':[4] he hardly knew what to do with it. In February 1927 he laid it aside, then in March decided to 'go over it again'.[5] The summer drowse stilled him for a while; and then, having been seriously ill in July with bronchial haemorrhages, he needed a long convalescence in Frieda's native Germany, after which he wrote to a London friend, 'I don't want to work – don't want to do a thing – all the life gone out of me'.[6]

Once he recovered, Lawrence recognized two things. First, that he needed money: the income from his writing came in 'slowly, much more than anybody would imagine', he confessed on 8 November.[7] Second, that although his usual English and American publishers would baulk at the novel's sexual explicitness, he might be able to publish the book privately, in Florence, with the help of his bookseller friend, Giuseppe ('Pino') Orioli. Together they 'could easily do all the work' and production would be cheap.[8] With a potential publishing plan, Lawrence began the novel's third and final version about 26 November 1927.[9] He first mentioned it on 8 December: 'My novel I'm writing all over again'.[10] With amazing speed, and in spite of bouts of illness, he completed the final version in about forty-four days, working steadily through December and finishing on 8 January 1928: it was now, he believed, 'a very pure and tender novel', but also 'the most improper novel in the world!'[11]

Trouble loomed. The first typist he approached – Nellie Morrison, a novelist friend in Florence – refused to go beyond Chapter Five. But Catherine Carswell, an old ally in London, agreed to recruit several friends to type batches from Lawrence's handwritten notebook; and Maria Huxley, wife of the novelist Aldous Huxley, agreed to type the last seven chapters while the Lawrences and Huxleys enjoyed a holiday together in Les Diablerets, Switzerland. Lawrence spent the mornings correcting batches of typescript as they arrived, but he also expurgated two duplicate copies for his regular publishers

Martin Secker in London and Alfred Knopf in New York, in case commercial publication proved feasible (it did not).

The big moment came on 9 March 1928, when Lawrence and Orioli carried the unexpurgated typescript to the Tipografia Giuntina, an old-fashioned printshop in Florence where the workers still set type by hand. On 1 April, Orioli brought the first proofs out to the Villa Mirenda. They were thick with error. Understanding no English, the printers had set 'dind't, didn't, dnid't, dind't, din'dt, didn't like a Bach fugue', Lawrence told Aldous Huxley;[12] the words 'danced weird and macabre' (334:27). The Giuntina, possessing only enough type to set half the novel, had to print the text in two stages. In May the shop printed 1,000 copies of the first stage on specially made paper, and 200 more on ordinary paper, then worked quickly to set and print the novel's second half. By 4 June Lawrence had finished correcting all the proofs; by 7 June he had signed and numbered sheets for the limited edition; he then departed with Frieda for the cool mountains of Switzerland. On 28 June he received his copy, 'handsome and dignified'.[13]

For months Lawrence and Orioli had been sending announcements and order-forms to prospective purchasers in Britain and the USA. As copies came from the binder – about twenty a day – Orioli mailed them via registered book post. Some booksellers, however, when they examined the contents, declined to accept the copies they had ordered; Lawrence's London friends collected them, as did the faithful Enid Hilton (1896–1992), who retrieved seventy-two copies from one bookseller and then delivered some of them herself to English purchasers.

By contrast, copies mailed to American subscribers were often confiscated by the customs authorities; by August 1928 Lawrence concluded that it was *'useless* to mail copies to America'.[14] But in Europe copies sold fast. By September Lawrence had netted nearly £700: he would have been pleased to make half that sum from a novel published in the usual way.

In 1928, books judged indecent could not be protected by international copyright. Pirates could therefore steal the text of Lawrence's novel, photograph or reset it, then sell it as authentic. In December Lawrence lamented to Orioli, 'If only, if only we had 2000 of the cheap edition [instead of 200] . . . to cut out the pirates!'[15] With pirated editions now available to buyers, Lawrence wrote on 28 December, 'I am at my wits end . . . trying to get out quickly a Paris edition at about 100 frs. to put on the market and nip them if I can.'[16] Finally, in March, he located a bookseller named Edward R. Titus, who soon printed 3,000 copies, in paper covers, to be sold at only 60 francs: a tenth of what the pirates could charge, and only a little more than a normal hardback novel.

For the Paris edition Lawrence wrote, between 26 March and 3 April 1929, a foreword that exposed the pirates' fraud; later, probably in October, he expanded the essay into 'a sort of key to the whole novel',[17] which he called *A Propos of 'Lady Chatterley's Lover'*. Reprinted in this edition, it offers Lawrence's final thoughts on male–female relationships in the modern world.

THE NOVEL IN THREE VERSIONS

Because Lawrence wrote – and kept – three complete versions of *Lady Chatterley's Lover*, we have an unparalleled opportunity to study his creative processes and can ask why Lawrence rewrote and what directions his rewriting took.

Having recently visited his native English Midlands (once in 1925 and again in 1926) Lawrence was struck by how different it felt: 'not pleasant at all'.[18] The coal strike had altered his feelings about the people of the region; but returning home had also reawakened his interest in local material. He had created gamekeepers before in his fiction – Annable in *The White Peacock* (1911) and Arthur Pilbeam in 'The Shades of Spring' (1914). In *Lady Chatterley's Lover* he was ready now to explore a more complex figure: one who is simultaneously in touch with nature, yet educated; vulnerable, yet wise; female in sensitivity, yet male in strength and attitude. In his earlier fiction Lawrence had also created more than one woman like Connie Chatterley – a woman with a social 'position' who is drawn to an outsider of a lower class, then yields to her instinctive desire for him – in works like 'Daughters of the Vicar' (1914), *The Lost Girl* (1920) and *The Virgin and the Gipsy* (written 1926). There, class differences wither in the fire of physical attraction; the male body joins with (and empowers) the female's in fulfilment, and the woman can be reborn into a new kind of life.

When Lawrence began the novel's first version, he approached it as a short novel of the kind he had written earlier in the 1920s, such as *The Fox*, *St. Mawr* and *The Princess*. In rewriting *Lady Chatterley's Lover* twice more, Lawrence created for himself the possibility

Introduction

of rethinking the significance of scenes and reworking their narrative proportions in order to discover what had been latent in them. We can usefully imagine each version of the novel as starting with a section of *negation*, followed by a section of *regeneration*, and concluding with a section of *resolution and escape*. These three sections correspond in the final version (printed here) to chapters one to nine, ten to sixteen and seventeen to nineteen. In all three versions, the *negation* section takes Connie Chatterley to the point where, responding to a failed marriage, she finds refuge in the gamekeeper's hut. The long *regeneration* section begins when the keeper, having given Connie a key to his hut, becomes her lover. The final section, *resolution and escape*, varies considerably between versions, but in each case begins when Connie leaves Wragby Hall for a long holiday.

With each rewriting Lawrence greatly expanded the *negation* section, from 51 to 160 and finally to 277 manuscript pages. The oppressive atmosphere of Wragby, her husband Clifford's estate, becomes dominant. Connie's father – a character added to version two – advises his daughter to meet people and advises Clifford to help her do so. Condensing this material in version three, Lawrence introduced another new character, the playwright Michaelis, who offers Connie a sexual experience radically different from her fulfilment later in the novel. At the same time, by showing how Clifford and his Cambridge friends intellectualize sexual experience, and by exposing Michaelis's emotional egotism and dislike of women, Lawrence reveals this society's wilful misuse of sexuality. After Michaelis, Connie's 'whole sexual feeling . . . collapsed' (54:37–8).

Many early scenes – Connie encountering the keeper and his daughter, Connie taking a message to the keeper, Connie scrutinizing her body in the mirror – follow Lawrence's usual pattern of composition: statement in version one, expansion in version two, then both condensation *and* expansion to create version three. Within this pattern Lawrence gradually alters the novel's texture and tone. In the scene where Connie escapes to the wood (Chapter Six), for instance, he adds to version three a seventeen-paragraph segment beginning at 62:7 ('Connie went slowly home . . .') in which she meditates on her entrapment; the narrator's newly sardonic tone darkens Connie's plight while facilitating his more forceful stand on the links between the Chatterley story and the values which the reader is assumed to hold. Those values the narrator will challenge. In the scene where Connie takes a message to the keeper (also in

Chapter Six), Lawrence gradually devotes more space to the keeper (named 'Parkin' in versions one and two) and then, in Chapter Seven, sharpens the material new to version three: 'The mental life! Suddenly she hated it with a rushing fury, the swindle!' (71:3–4). Connie matures with each version, so that the many realizations she reaches in version three, reflecting her greater despair, naturally focus more criticism on her world.

Just as Lawrence unifies the early scenes in order to explore the constraints of society as Connie perceives them, so too does he suggest a counterforce of tenderness – as when she becomes aware of the daffodils in the wood, 'rustling and fluttering and shivering so bright and alive' (86:20–21). But a sensual awakening is still only a possibility when she stumbles into the keeper's secret clearing, itself a 'little sanctuary' from Wragby Hall nearby (Chapter Eight). Although the first section is thus almost complete, Lawrence before dramatizing Connie's regeneration added to versions two and three the narrator's searing indictment of corrupt forms of power (Chapter Nine), creating a cultural nadir to parallel Connie's personal nadir with Michaelis. With Chapter Nine the novel plumbs its deepest moral and spiritual depression.

The regenerative section, which opens just before Connie and the keeper become lovers and closes with their final love-making in the wood, constitutes the novel's longest and most stable section, comprising only a third of version one but about half of the later versions. Whereas Lawrence progressively expanded the introductory *negation* section, he developed the regenerative section more variously: he eliminated or condensed some scenes, kept or enlarged others, and created some which were altogether new. While rewriting version one, Lawrence discovered an organizational strategy of advancing the relationship between Connie and Mellors in carefully controlled 'stages . . . of passion' (247:8–9). The first stage leads Connie to a spontaneous orgasm; the middle stage sets her sexual awakening against Clifford's sterility, Teamdashes Tevershall's ugliness and Mrs Bolton's poignant memories of passion, culminating in Connie's rapturous sexual fulfilment at the hut (173–5); and the final stage advances the lovers beyond daytime love to a night of passion and then to a night-time episode of anal intercourse, narrated at a distance, which leads Connie to expose 'her ultimate nakedness' to Mellors (247:26). In the expression of the lovers' full sexual range, the regenerative sequence is complete.

In this section Lawrence typically makes a statement, gradually enlarges it, then vigorously reshapes it, as in the powerful scene in Chapter Thirteen where Connie and Clifford (he in his motorized chair) visit the wood. In version one Clifford readily educates Connie about the obligations of the governing classes – in case the miners strike; the disagreements of husband and wife remain civil. In version two, however, where Connie openly challenges Clifford, provoking his irritation, their mask of propriety slips; and whereas in version one Connie simply walks behind Clifford's broken machine, in version two she touches the keeper's hand as they push the heavy chair. Sharper in tone, version three increases both Clifford's vehemence and Connie's obstinacy, the word 'but' regularly used to index their conflict. Lawrence intensifies the final version in order to distance the reader from Clifford and to enhance sympathy for Connie and Mellors. Each version of *Lady Chatterley's Lover* makes Connie's escape from her marriage more difficult while it makes her need to escape more imperative.

The final section, of resolution and escape, puts the earlier sections into perspective and is divided into Connie's departure from Wragby for a holiday – which remains unchanged – and her return to England, which changes greatly. Away from Wragby, Connie can reassess her commitment to the keeper, while their liaison, exposed as a scandal, prevents them from returning to Wragby. In unfolding the scandal Lawrence gradually mutes the keeper's lower-class origins, empowering him verbally, then implicates Connie in the scandal, barring her return as Lady Chatterley. In the early versions Lawrence leads Connie only to the borders of a break with Clifford, but in the final version her firmer commitment to the keeper justifies both her plea for a divorce and their eventual hope of living together on a 'small farm of their own' (298:4). Once Lawrence imagines Mellors outside the constraints of a particular social class, the novel's central struggle is no longer between Connie and the keeper but between their commitment to each other and the forces hostile to their relationship. The class struggle in versions one and two yields to a divorce struggle in version three.

The novel's final scenes are wholly transformed. The first version is uncertain and slightly episodic; the second is anguished and truncated; whereas the third absorbs both the motifs of version one – such as the need for human contact – and the exchange of letters in version two. For example, Lawrence chooses the scene in version one where Connie informs Clifford of her pregnancy, then effectively reworks it so that, in version three, she confronts Clifford with the surprise that she loves not her alibi, Duncan Forbes, but her husband's gamekeeper. By concluding the final version with an eloquent letter from Mellors to Connie,[19] Lawrence shapes the novel's opening and closing alike into long, distancing perspectives. The concluding letter, tentative yet hopeful, uses Mellors's social critique as a way to position the lovers at the margins of constructive activity.

THE NOVEL'S THEMES

Having seen how Lawrence patiently derived version three out of his earlier materials, we can isolate now some of the novel's central themes: transformations of the self, binary oppositions, silence and the search for security.

Stepping back a generation in the development of the English novel takes us to Thomas Hardy (1840–1928 – he died the year *Lady Chatterley's Lover* was published). Hardy was fascinated by characters who become enmeshed in a destiny they cannot control, are ensnared by social convention and let guilt sap their energy. Lawrence found Hardy his most useful teacher, in the way that good students absorb, then question, then usually disagree with what they are taught. In his 'Study of Thomas Hardy' written in 1914 (but published posthumously), Lawrence wrote that Hardy's 'passionate, individual, wilful' characters find conventional security a walled prison and die, either from lack of strength to bear their isolation or from their community's revenge on them.[20] Tess Durbeyfield, for example, having 'sided with the community's condemnation of her', 'has become inert'. But whereas Hardy's characters usually acquiesce, yield, submit or succumb, Lawrence's rarely do: they struggle. Although they themselves are tender, pliant, soft – or ill, forlorn and lonely – they are not complaisant, but capable of decisive action, moral decision, and sometimes great courage. Like seeds waiting to be transformed by air, water and earth, they are alive on the 'inside', vital, full of unused energy.

When readers first see Connie Chatterley, they do so through the narrator's lens: it is he who explains that she, though well-off and married to a baronet, is unhappy, unfulfilled – almost as paralysed inwardly as her husband Clifford is paralysed below the waist. Only her keen intuition reveals to her a core of despair that is unassuaged by either Clifford or his clever Cambridge friends. A Sleeping Beauty, she has not awakened to life.

Although Oliver Mellors is like Connie in feeling acutely his own inner despair, he is presented to readers rather differently, not in narrated monologue (in which the narrator mixes his own perspective with that of his character), but first objectively (saluting Clifford and Connie, carrying a gun, using broad dialect) and through the filter of Connie's own awareness of him. This is important. Whereas the narrator presents us with Connie's initial perspective, Mellors provides much of his own. Ten years older than Connie, Mellors has already begun to transform himself: in the army he has seen the world, has rejected its values, and for a while welcomes his separateness – being 'alone' (47:3) so that he can heal 'a big wound from old contacts' (88:35). His incompleteness is not intellectual but social and emotional. Like Connie (like all of us!), he seeks to end his incompleteness.

Curiously, Sir Clifford Chatterley also seeks (though perversely) to transform himself, from a passive writer of malicious stories that are bait to the media, to an economic activist, a coal magnate like Gerald Crich in Lawrence's earlier *Women in Love* (1920), who successfully conceals his pulpy inner self and its vulnerability in order to embrace the work of hiring an engineer, descending into a coal mine, exploiting technology – becoming *mechanically* absorbed. Clifford seeks to understand 'the chemical possibilities of coal' (107:37), then to convert coal into 'electric power' (149:39) or 'into oil' (214:19). Unlike Connie and Mellors he needs another person not as sexual fulfilment or social completion, but as support, crutch, moral prop: to make him 'burn' as efficiently as his new-found fuel. That person, Mrs Ivy Bolton, a native of Tevershall and a keen observer of the local people, helps him comprehend his role of rousing others – managers and miners alike – to manipulate the earth's natural resources:

> Power! He felt a new sense of power flowing through him: power over all these men, over the hundreds and hundreds of colliers. He was finding out: and he was getting things into his grip.
>
> And he seemed verily to be re-born. *Now* life came into him! He had been gradually dying, with Connie, in the isolated private life of the artist and the conscious being. Now let all that go. Let it sleep. He simply felt life rush into him out of the coal, out of the pit. The

very stale air of the colliery was better than oxygen to him. It gave
him a sense of power, power. He was doing something: and he was
going to do something. He was going to win, to win: not as he had
won with his stories, mere publicity, amid a whole yapping of envy
and malice. But a man's victory, over the coal, over the very dirt of
Tevershall pit. (108:15–27)

Mrs Bolton satisfies Clifford's need because, as his social inferior
and nurse-companion, she demands no reciprocity; he remains her
Master. Like Clifford, she abandons her inner emotional self (it
clings to her dead husband, Ted, killed in the mines twenty-three
years earlier); now she can embrace Clifford's goal of reinvigorating
his mines. Her transformation is not political or emotional, but
social: 'She was coming bit by bit into possession of all that the
gentry knew, all that made them upper class' (100:6–8). And Mrs
Bolton would say to herself, 'My word, he'd never have got on like
this with Lady Chatterley. She was not the one to put a man
forward' (292:4–6). Antinomies are central, even celebrated, in Lawrence's novel. Moving forward is also moving backward; growth
harbours atrophy; dependence breeds bondage. Even commitment
stirs resistance.

These various transformations of the self occur in a larger artistic
context of binary tensions. These tensions set nature against culture,
wood against Wragby, flesh against intellect, frankness against ma-
nipulation, tenderness against insentience, renewal against sterility.
Lawrence has been criticized for so strongly opposing such tensions
in *Lady Chatterley's Lover*. A well-known essay by Stephen Gill
impugns Lawrence's rigid oppositions. Other critics (e.g. Eliseo
Vivas, Ian Gregor, R. E. Pritchard) have agreed.[21]

Yet Lawrence is not simplifying his novel: we have seen how
carefully he enriched it by rewriting. Nor is he composing 'a frankly
didactic tale'.[22] Rather, he concentrates these oppositions more
potently than his contemporaries would have done. Hence a second
major theme of the novel is the struggle not only to transform the
self but to discriminate among the immensely powerful forces to
which human beings must respond. Distilling a long novel into a
relatively short space, Lawrence highlights those forces and the
opposing responses they compel from us. Like Charles Dickens
before him, he skilfully explores clusters of oppositions. Structurally,
the novel moves back and forth between Wragby and the wood:

Wragby coming to represent sterility and spiritual emaciation, will and mental control; the wood coming to represent the free play of instinct and sensual awareness, tenderness and otherness. The two cannot mix. Clifford spoils the wood's flowers with the intrusion of his mechanical chair; Mellors is an intruder and in both 'senses an outsider at Wragby Hall. Connie, caught between the two of them, performs her wifely duty to Clifford at Wragby while pursuing her relationship with Mellors in the wood.

The novel's structural oppositions are reified in the way characters themselves balance each other in a kind of symmetry. Clifford invites and relishes the company of his Cambridge friends; Mellors sets the pheasant eggs and protects the young chicks. Mrs Bolton's gossip empowers Clifford to act; Connie's warmth empowers Mellors to begin his 'life' again (118:7). Clifford is paralysed; Mellors is frail and troubled by a cough. In the war Clifford lost the use of his legs (5:19); Mellors lost the devotion of his beloved Colonel (216:28–9). Clifford is overbearing with his servants; Mellors is arrogant with Duncan Forbes. Similarly, at Wragby, Michaelis wounds Connie with his selfish complaint, 'You keep on for hours after I've gone off' (54:4–5); in the wood, Mellors recalls how his wife Bertha Coutts 'sort of got harder and harder to bring off, and she'd sort of tear at me down there, as if it was a beak' (202:7–8). Michaelis reappears in Venice; Bertha reappears at the cottage after Connie departs. Connie's father advises Clifford early, Mellors late.

Yet Lawrence sets up these oppositions only to begin dismantling them. Behind the contrasts we are forced to recognize similarities. Clifford is assertive and wilful (99:12), but so is the narrator: for example, in the diatribe against contemporary mores (97:15–29). Clifford is verbally articulate; but so is Mellors in his final letter to Connie. Mrs Bolton is subservient to Clifford, but so is Connie to Mellors in the passage, often discussed, where 'She had to be a passive, consenting thing, like a slave' (247:3–4). Connie may liberate herself from convention, but her sister Hilda accuses her of having 'a slave nature' (253:20). To 'deconstruct' the novel in this way is to reveal its fascinating inner complexity, and the way its energy is directed sometimes with, sometimes against, the novel's thematic unfolding.

Perhaps the most interesting opposition sets silence against talk, mystery against clarity, stasis against kinesis. As Connie and Mellors retreat from the 'outer world of chaos' (10:26) into the protected 'sanctuary' of the wood (20:13), Lawrence stresses silence and still-ness. The novel's central action is internal, its motion is emotional, its kinetic energy lies in feelings. Finally, the characters seek safety rather than ecstasy: they are fugitives.

The novel insists on enclosures – a hut, a secret clearing, a cottage, a private wood, an enclosed yard, a bedroom shielded from entry, a woman's secret body – all offering protection not only from intrusion but also from psychological pain. The admired characters seek such protection in actual physical enclosures, in protective circles created by the imagination, or, in Mellors's case, in the linguistic barrier of the local dialect, which he wields to 'excess' (94:32). Mellors is 'afraid of society' (120:9), and Connie too recoils from the 'insanity of the whole civilised species' (110:16–17).

At first she can only flee, like one pursued, 'up to her room: or out of doors, to the wood' (110:15). For Connie the wood is 'her one refuge' (20:14); for Mellors, recoiling in horror from the outer world, 'his last refuge was this wood. To hide himself there!' (88:37–8). As Connie and Mellors retreat, they discover smaller and smaller en-closures as shields against the laceration of their spirits. The lovely wood is a hospital in nature, a sacred place, a sanctuary, silent and healing, where his essential 'stillness' touches even her 'womb' (89:15–17) but where his silence also remains 'unfathomable' (175:24). Protection offers the characters equilibrium, stasis, peace. At the end of version two, Connie clings to Mellors 'in an intense and healing stillness, that was passion itself, in its pure silence'.[23] Connie and Mellors yearn for pure silence, quiescence, even anonym-ity; they almost never call each other by name. Indeed, sexuality leads less to excitement than to relief, less to pleasure than to recovery.

But the protective enclosures they discover and the equilib-rium they achieve are fragile, perishable. The lights and hooters of the mines invade the ancient wood, let in the malevolence. Threat-ened by the encroaching forces of 'mechanised greed' (119:20), the wood awaits destruction. When thunder crashes outside the keeper's cottage, Connie and Mellors feel they are 'in a little ark in the Flood' (216:33), at risk of annihilation. This threat makes especially compel-ling the forms of safety which they crave.

Mirroring the progressive inward movement of the novel, from the outer world of chaos to an inner world of fulfilment, the threatened physical enclosure gradually becomes the threatened enclosure of the mind. Mellors, hearing the hooters at Stacks Gate, shivers, then presses Connie's 'soft breasts up over his ears, to deafen him' (211:22). The protective enclosure is now only the human body, in which Mellors, entering Connie, discovers 'the moment of pure peace' (116:33). Together, they locate themselves, enclosed and encircled, within the 'phallic body' (Lawrence's special language for the achieved sexual relationship), away from danger – until memory, like a wound, opens to recall their dual history outside the magic circle of their bond. Enriched, released from the confines of their earlier loneliness, having eased their spiritual isolation, Connie and Mellors must move at last into the matrix of historical pressures, of the 'intricacy of mechanism' (281:7–8), where redirection is the first mandate of a life negotiated beyond enclosures.

THE NOVEL'S ACCOMPLISHMENT

When critic Lytton Strachey read the novel soon after it was published, he complained of Lawrence's 'creative powers thrown away'.[24] We now recognize that Lawrence, like James Joyce and Virginia Woolf, was writing in literary forms unfamiliar to contemporaries like Strachey. In *Lady Chatterley's Lover* Lawrence is particularly innovative at projecting *voices*, which range from external to internal and encompass a wide narrative space. I shall examine three, and negotiate the issues they raise.

Providing a wide and authoritative angle of cultural vision, the narrator, although often close to Lawrence as author, always preserves a separate voice.[25] The narrator's tone varies from sympathetic and compassionate, to wry and amused, to pungently sardonic. A passage from Chapter One illustrates the skill and authority of this voice. To frame the sexual initiation of Connie and her sister Hilda, the narrator uses, throughout the opening chapter, the *least* intimate of his voices. In the following passage notice the sentence fragments and the shift, after the words 'a bit jeering', to yet another voice:

> In the actual sex-thrill within the body, the sisters nearly succumbed to the strange male power. But quickly they recovered themselves, took the sex-thrill as a sensation, and remained free. Whereas the men, in gratitude to the woman for the sex experience, let their souls go out to her. And afterwards, looked rather as if they had lost a shilling and found sixpence. Connie's man could be a bit sulky, and Hilda's a bit jeering. But that is how men are! Ungrateful, and never satisfied. When you don't have them, they hate you because you

won't. And when you do have them, they hate you again, for some other reason. Or for no reason at all, except that they are discontented children, and can't be satisfied whatever they get, let a woman do what she may. (9:10–21)

The narrator stands apart, olympian, speaking not with compassion or intimacy but with irony; detached from the experience, sententious. The offhand fragment 'And afterwards, looked rather as if they had lost a shilling and found sixpence' employs a cliché to signal the empty rhetoric – all of this very much like the opening of *St. Mawr*, Lawrence's novella of 1925, where readers are also satirized.[26]

The passage's major shift, in 'But that is how men are!', reveals Lawrence's complexity of tone; it also raises the issue of the novel's sexual politics. For whom are the last five sentences written? They might be written for an inexperienced young woman wondering about the knowledge of men that a male narrator might offer; or they might be written for an intimate friend by a sophisticated older *woman* who, as narrator, distills her experience into a generalized 'you'. Despite its portentous certainty, the passage glistens with delicate mockery, half scolding and half sardonic, which is almost eclipsed by a jaunty contempt. The ironic tone helps to expose the moral 'veneer', which the novel must patiently strip and out of which a disembodied experience merges into abstraction. Yet that merger comes, finally, very close to the 'clever, rather spiteful' stories (16:19–20) which Clifford, shorn of his potency, writes. At one remove Clifford's voice is slyly reinscribed into the narrator's.

There is more. Readers, pondering phrases such as 'nearly succumbed to the strange male power', have worried that, from the outset, the novel engages in a sexual politics that specially empowers males. In 1969 Kate Millett complained of Lawrence's 'transformation of masculine ascendancy into a mystical religion' that celebrates 'the penis'.[27] Sheila MacLeod laments Lawrence's 'growing sexist bias'.[28] Others have agreed. To them, narrative voices matter less than the privileging of male dominance – expressed, for example, when Mellors forcibly 'takes' Connie in the woods (133:21–134:12, 222:1–3); when she finds his erect phallus 'so lordly' (210:4); and when later she 'let him have his way' (247:2) and submits to his 'phallic hunting out' (247:33), her enthralled appreciation of his lust arguably devaluing her own importance. It can be said that

Lawrence, when he identifies sexuality with the phallus, privileges patriarchal codes of entitlement. These codes arise from various textual sources, and to lump all of the novel's voices together is to miss the essential way in which *Lady Chatterley's Lover* is a *collective* of voices, its polemic conducted largely by the narrator. As Wayne Booth has pointed out:

> Lawrence was experimenting radically with what it means for a novelist to lose his own distinct voice in the voices of his characters, especially in their inner voices. In his practice, all rules about point of view are abrogated: the borderlines between author's voice and character's voice are deliberately blurred, and only the criticism of the whole tale will offer any sort of clarity to the reader seeking to sort out opinions.[29]

An attentive reader must always be ready to negotiate the novel's voices as they shift. Although Connie's voice readily yields to the narrator's, the narrator always protects Connie from the reader's criticism. Her voice is not muzzled, but shaped so that a significance is provided for her more often than she can provide it for herself. There is nothing patronizing about this: the voice that describes Mellors's 'strange potency of manhood' (174:36) is not the voice that sees his penis as 'proud' and 'lovely' (210:4–5). The challenge to Connie's voice is never the same as the challenge to her values: her values (including her life choices) are open to the reader's criticism; her voice is not – she possesses the voice of an agent becoming free, shaping an identity very different from the narrator's. Although her voice is framed by the narrator's, she speaks for herself. She dashes spontaneously into the rain, not to give Mellors an opportunity to 'take her' but to assert her independence and to express her own 'sudden desire' (221:10).

It is rarely acknowledged that, again and again, Connie breaks free of constraints; she resolves emotional dilemmas, escapes oppression. The novel's male figures – Clifford, Tommy Dukes, Mellors – have ideas; Connie acts on them. She reaches revelations that propel her forward on her own terms. Her ultimate act of freedom is to separate herself physically from the two men she has cared for: at the close she is living with her sister, Hilda, in Scotland, anticipating reunion with Mellors, but still empowered by rank, £20,000 of capital and a strong female ally.[30] Connie's freedom is only outlined by the narrator's rhetoric, which, to a surprising degree, remains external to her decision-making processes. The novel's final paradox is that Connie, though pregnant and preparing for marriage, remains free.

Whereas the novel's initial narrative voice remains external, beyond the characters' consciousness, the novel also develops voices that are internal. For example, as the narrator progresses inward to explore Mellors's character, he moves into – but not *fully* into – Mellors's idiom. The passage below, from Chapter Ten, is a dialogue between the voices of Mellors and the narrator: Mellors's voice is clipped and laconic and serrated with bitterness, the narrator's voice is more colloquial and gnomic and sometimes sentimental:

> He thought with infinite tenderness of the woman. Poor forlorn thing, she was nicer than she knew, and oh, so much too nice for the tough lot she was in contact with! Poor thing, she too had some of the vulnerability of the wild hyacinths, she wasn't all tough rubber-goods-and-platinum, like the modern girl. And they would do her in! As sure as life, they would do her in, as they do in all naturally tender life. Tender! Somewhere she was tender, tender with a tenderness of the growing hyacinths, something that has gone out of the celluloid women of today. But he would protect her with his heart for a little while. For a little while, before the insentient iron world and the Mammon of mechanised greed did them both in, her as well as him.
> (119:25–36)

This passage encapsulates Lawrence's later style: not a juxtaposition, not a counterpoint, but a fusion of lighter and darker voices – of tenderness with gloom, of pity with hopelessness, as, for instance, when the third sentence modulates from Mellors's 'Poor thing' to the narrator's 'all tough rubber-goods-and-platinum'. Graham Holderness writes that Lawrence 'has kept the rhetoric of his people';[31] yet it must be said that Lawrence continually *transforms* such rhetoric by embracing banality as a major ironic tone. These competing 'registers' within paragraphs subtly manipulate the oppositions I described earlier, and imbue the novel with a unique colour and texture.

Whereas the voices of Mellors and the narrator are contemporary in their use of experimental idioms, another voice is more traditional – and, to many readers, radiantly successful. It renders the vital, sensitive, fluid expression of female consciousness. As early as 1932, Anaïs Nin proclaimed Lawrence's gift of rendering a distinctively female consciousness: 'He had a complete realization of the feelings of women.'[32] And as recently as 1991, Carol Siegel has articulated the context of sexual difference out of which Lawrence promised, in

1912, to 'do my work for women, better than the suffrage'.[33] Although cited less often than the splendid passage that captures Connie Chatterley's enthralled sexual response (see 173:22–174:20), the following brief excerpt illustrates how the narrator intimately explores Connie's sensibility, revealing the range of her sensations, the depth of her sexual passion, and the power of feeling to change the self:

> Then as he began to move in the sudden helpless orgasm, there awoke in her new strange thrills rippling inside her, rippling, rippling, like a flapping overlapping of soft flames, soft as feathers, running to points of brilliance, exquisite, exquisite, and melting her all molten inside. It was like bells, rippling up and up to a culmination. She lay unconscious of the wild little cries she uttered at the last . . .

> She clung to him unconscious in passion, and he never quite slipped from her. And she felt the soft bud of him within her stirring and in strange rhythms flushing up into her, with a strange, rhythmic growing motion, swelling and swelling till it filled all her cleaving consciousness. And then began again the unspeakable motion that was not really motion, but pure deepening whirlpools of sensation, swirling deeper and deeper through all her tissue and consciousness, till she was one perfect concentric fluid of feeling. And she lay there crying in unconscious, inarticulate cries, the voice out of the uttermost night, the life-exclamation. (133:24–30, 133:40–134:9)

This fine passage invites two points. First, the stripping away of Connie's consciousness, mentioned twice, is reflected in the stripping away of the narrator's overt presence. The simplicity of rich feeling finds its equivalent in the lyrical elegance of Lawrence's flowing participles and repetitions, untinged with irony. Intimacy urges simplicity. It is therefore too easy to say that Connie, as she 'lay there', succumbs to the phallic power of her lover. Indeed, the passage requires readers to understand that her sexual response derives from a diffuse, unlocalized agent: not *he* awoke in her but 'there awoke in her strange new thrills'. The agent, though manifest as male, is cosmic – as it was for Ursula Brangwen in *The Rainbow*, Lawrence's novel of 1915. Skilfully, compassionately, Mellors (we infer) arouses himself from his post-coital quietude in order patiently to arouse Connie to a second orgasm, more resplendent, even more empowering emotionally and spiritually, becoming the 'uttermost' expression of passion. At the emotional centre of their encounter is a reciprocity that dismantles their sexual politics: 'And they lay, and knew nothing, not even of each other, both lost' (134:13). His physical power is transformed inside her as sexual response. They are human complements.

Second, although the tradition of such exact probing of female sensibility extends back to Samuel Richardson, Jane Austen and George Eliot, Lawrence develops it. He modifies Hardy's conception of Alec's seduction of Tess Durbeyfield, where 'the coarse appropriates the finer';[34] he discards Hardy's judgement in order to represent the *experience* rather than its moral implications. Sexual experience burdens Tess, frees Connie; Tess is violated, Connie is made triumphant. Lawrence penetrates a sexual stratum untouched by his predecessors (save by James Joyce in *Ulysses*, 1922), but – unlike Joyce – locates in sexuality the life force that animates the cosmos. He writes in *A Propos of 'Lady Chatterley's Lover'*, 'Sex is the balance of male and female in the universe' (323:17), 'the deepest of all communions' (325:1). Sex leads Connie to be 'reborn' and Mellors to be broken open, and both of them to be connected in 'vivid and nourishing relation to the cosmos and the universe' (329:30–31). Sex is the act that most fully integrates a man and a woman into the rhythm of the universe. Its inexplicable power of renewal is attuned to day, season, year – to all the natural cycles of renewal.

Connie's cries yield at last a 'life-exclamation', an affirmation, a vindication – not of psychological mastery, not of economic individualism, but of the human value of opening oneself to the unknown, unexpected, unleashed forces that roil unconquerable in the self. These forces drive the self toward renewal and away from mechanical deadness. Lawrence works to awaken and direct the reader's sympathies (a goal articulated at 101:13–23) without turning the novel into a tract. He succeeds because he roots his characters in recognizable forms of human interaction, rejoices in their peculiar forms of experience, and directs his own voice (as filtered through the narrator) to form one *layer* in the rich amalgam of the novel's voices.

During 1926–8, Lawrence was driven to keep illness at bay – and to overcome a profound despair of England – by an extraordinary investment of energy and concentration in the writing of three separate versions of *Lady Chatterley's Lover*. In each subsequent version the characters are better able to construct a fully human self out of the possibilities around them. Connie and Mellors have an enduring significance in twentieth-century culture because they shape their code of morality not *out* of their culture's materials but *apart* from them; they are hostile to impediments, averse to what is counterfeit, appalled by what is cheap, whether of body or mind. At the same time they retain their humanity and their personal integrity by demanding to be re-rooted in the most regenerative experience possible – the sexual. The novel's oppositions insist on the potential of that experience, separating the forces which erode from those which enable; and the novel's voices carry forward Lawrence's eloquent defence of the forces of renewal, these forces shaping a kind of moral fable. Lawrence's enduring accomplishment is to reveal a society to itself, to question its deepest assumptions and to awaken a counterforce of honesty and courage. *Lady Chatterley's Lover*, his last major prose work, uniquely combines energy with elegy, pungency with delight, tradition with experiment. It ranks among the twentieth century's most extraordinary literary achievements.

NOTES ON THE INTRODUCTION

1. James T. Boulton and Lindeth Vasey, eds., *The Letters of D. H. Lawrence*, volume V (Cambridge University Press, 1989), 490. (Hereafter referred to as *Letters*, v.)
2. *Letters*, v. 559.
3. *Letters*, v. 605.
4. *Letters*, v. 638.
5. James T. Boulton and Margaret H. Boulton, with Gerald M. Lacy, eds., *The Letters of D. H. Lawrence*, volume VI (Cambridge University Press, 1991), 21. (Hereafter referred to as *Letters*, vi.)
6. *Letters*, vi. 204.
7. *Letters*, vi. 209.
8. *Letters*, vi. 222.
9. The Cambridge Edition of *Lady Chatterley's Lover*, cited in Further Reading, offers a full account of the novel's genesis.
10. *Letters*, vi. 223.
11. *Letters*, vi. 238.
12. *Letters*, vi. 353.
13. *Letters*, vi. 440.
14. *Letters*, vi. 525.
15. Keith Sagar and James T. Boulton, eds., *The Letters of D. H. Lawrence*, volume VII (Cambridge University Press, 1993), 56. (Hereafter referred to as *Letters*, vii.)
16. *Letters*, vii. 105.

17. *Letters*, vii. 531.
18. *Letters*, v. 536.
19. An early draft of the letter is printed in Michael Squires, *The Creation of 'Lady Chatterley's Lover'*, pp. 217–20 (cited in Further Reading).
20. D. H. Lawrence, 'Study of Thomas Hardy', in *Study of Thomas Hardy and Other Essays*, ed. Bruce Steele (Cambridge University Press, 1985), p. 21. The quotations in the next sentence come, in sequence, from pp. 50 and 95.
21. Stephen Gill, 'The Composite World: Two Versions of *Lady Chatterley's Lover*', *Essays in Criticism* 21 (1971): 347–64. Eliseo Vivas, *D. H. Lawrence: The Failure and the Triumph of Art* (Northwestern University Press, 1960), pp. 119–47. Ian Gregor, 'The Novel as Prophecy: *Lady Chatterley's Lover*', in Ian Gregor and Brian Nicholas, *The Moral and the Story* (Faber and Faber, 1962), pp. 217–48. R. E. Pritchard, *D. H. Lawrence: Body of Darkness* (University of Pittsburgh Press, 1971), pp. 187–95.
22. Michael Bell, *D. H. Lawrence: Language and Being* (Cambridge University Press, 1992), p. 209.
23. D. H. Lawrence, *John Thomas and Lady Jane* (Viking, 1972), p. 330.
24. Quoted in Michael Holroyd, *Lytton Strachey*, volume 2 (Holt, Rinehart, & Winston, 1968), p. 571.
25. For decades critics have mistakenly assumed that Lawrence and Mellors share a voice, that Mellors is a mouthpiece for the author. See, for example, Stephen Gill (pp. 359–64); Graham Hough, *The Dark Sun: A Study of D. H. Lawrence* (1956; reprinted Gerald Duckworth, 1968), pp. 148–66; David Cavitch, *D. H. Lawrence and the New World* (Oxford University Press, 1969), p. 200.
26. D. H. Lawrence, *St. Mawr and Other Stories*, ed. Brian Finney (Cambridge University Press, 1983). For a discussion of Lawrence's audience, see John Worthen, *D. H. Lawrence and the Idea of the Novel* (Macmillan, 1979), pp. 175–82, and Michael Bell, *D. H. Lawrence*, pp. 217–24.
27. Kate Millett, *Sexual Politics* (1969; reprinted Avon Books, 1971), pp. 316–17.
28. Sheila MacLeod, *Lawrence's Men and Women* (Heinemann, 1985), p. 202. MacLeod observes that, in her experience, 'It is surely homosexual men rather than women who are fascinated or indeed obsessed by the penis rather than by the whole man' (p. 220).
29. Wayne C. Booth, 'Confessions of a Lukewarm Lawrentian', *The Challenge of D. H. Lawrence*, ed. Michael Squires and Keith Cushman (University of Wisconsin Press, 1990), p. 16.
30. In a letter written after the novel was published, Lawrence speculated, about Mellors, whether Connie might 'just have had him and put him down again', *Letters*, vii. 179.

31. Graham Holderness, *D. H. Lawrence: History, Ideology, and Fiction* (Gill & Macmillan, 1982), p. 135.
32. Anaïs Nin, *D. H. Lawrence: An Unprofessional Study* (1932; reprinted Alan Swallow, 1964), p. 57.
33. Carol Siegel, *Lawrence Among the Women: Wavering Boundaries in Women's Literary Traditions* (University Press of Virginia, 1991). Lawrence's quotation is from James T. Boulton, ed., *The Letters of D. H. Lawrence*, volume I (Cambridge University Press, 1979), 490. (Hereafter referred to as *Letters*, i.)
34. Thomas Hardy, *Tess of the d'Urbervilles*, ed. Scott Elledge, 3rd edn (Norton, 1991), p. 57. Originally published 1891.

Note on the Texts

LADY CHATTERLEY'S LOVER

D. H. Lawrence completed the manuscript (MS) of *Lady Chatter-ley's Lover* from which three copies of the typescript (TS) were prepared early in 1928. From one copy of TS, the Florence edition (F) was printed and, in July 1928, privately published in Florence, Italy.

The base-texts for the Penguin edition are four. (1) For Chapters One to Five, MS is emended with those revisions of TS that Lawrence corrected which also reappear in the Florence edition, so that at 28:23, for instance, 'begrudges' replaced 'envies for'. (2) For Chapters Six to Twelve, MS is emended with the substantive and accidental variants found in F, unless they are obvious compositor's errors or probable instances of eye-skip, as when, for instance, at 101:9 the compositor substituted 'know' for 'knew'; except that (3) for pages 254–62 of TS, which conclude Chapter Twelve, F has been emended with ten MS variants. (4) For Chapters Thirteen to Nineteen, MS is emended with the substantive variants found in F and with the accidental variants introduced into F that do not reflect inadvertent compositor's error, so that at 182:14–15, for instance, Connie's words 'They live the life of your coal-mine' are now included. Some textual choices required judgement. At 261:20, for instance, Lawrence's 'sea-baths' (MS) was altered by his typist to 'sea-bathe' (TS), which Lawrence then revised to 'sea-bathing'. But his revision was almost certainly stimulated by a typist's error and is therefore rejected. Again at 18:21–3 Lawrence's typist altered 'this vague life' to 'their vague life', perhaps causing Lawrence to revise his sentence, so that his MS reading 'Connie had been now nearly two years at Wragby, living this vague life of absorption in Clifford and his needing her, and his work, especially his work' (MS) has in the Florence edition a plural subject and a condensed predicate: 'Connie and Clifford had been now nearly two years at Wragby, living their vague life of absorption in Clifford and his work' (F). When interference likely caused revision, the Florence edition's readings were rejected.

Note on the Texts

A PROPOS OF 'LADY CHATTERLEY'S LOVER'

For this essay Lawrence wrote two manuscripts: they are the base-texts for the Penguin edition. He completed the first part, called 'My Skirmish with Jolly Roger', by 3 April 1929, from which a typescript was made. He then extended this part, completing his handwritten extension by mid-October 1929. Eight emendations have been adopted from the typescript and from the first English edition, published by the Mandrake Press on 24 June 1930. Included are variants that updated Lawrence's essay, such as, at 305:3, 'I brought out in 1929' rather than 'I now bring out', or at 305:15, 'produced in New York or Philadelphia' rather than 'produced in New York'. Rejected are variants that may have been introduced by a printer or publisher, e.g. at 309:17 the omission of 'young' from 'It is better to give all young girls this book . . .'

Advisory Editor's Note

I would like to thank Professor James T. Boulton and Professor F. Warren Roberts, General Editors of the *Cambridge Edition of the Works of D. H. Lawrence*, for their advice and planning in the preparation of this edition.

John Worthen, 1994

LADY CHATTERLEY'S LOVER

BY

D. H. LAWRENCE

PRIVATELY PRINTED

1928

CHAPTER I.

Ours is essentially a tragic age, so we refuse to take it tragically. The cataclysm has happened, we are among the ruins, we start to build up new little habitats, to have new little hopes. It is rather hard work: there is now no smooth road into the future: but we go round, or scramble over the obstacles. We've got to live, no matter how many skies have fallen.

This was more or less Constance Chatterley's position. The war had brought the roof down over her head. And she had realised that one must live and learn.

She married Clifford Chatterley in 1917, when he was home for a month on leave. They had a month's honeymoon. Then he went back to Flanders. To be shipped over to England again six months later, more or less in bits. Constance, his wife, was then twenty-three years old, and he was twenty-nine.

His hold on life was marvellous. He didn't die and the bits seemed to grow together again. For two years he remained in the doctor's hands. Then he was pronounced a cure, and could return to life again, with the lower half of his body, from the hips down, paralysed for ever.

This was 1920. They returned, Clifford and Constance, to his home, Wragby Hall, the family "seat." His father had died, Clifford was now a baronet, Sir Clifford, and Constance was Lady Chatterley. They came to start housekeeping and married life in the rather forlorn home of the Chatterleys, on a rather inadequate income. Clifford had a sister, but she had departed. Otherwise there were no near relatives. The elder brother was dead in the war. Crippled for ever, knowing he could never have any children, Clifford came home to the smoky Midlands to keep the Chatterley name alive while he could.

He was not really downcast. He could wheel himself about in a wheeled chair, and he had a bath-chair with a small motor attachment, so he could drive himself slowly round the garden and into the fine, melancholy park of which he was really so proud, though he pretended to be flippant about it.

Having suffered so much, the capacity for suffering had to some extent left him. He remained strange and bright and cheerful, almost, one might say, chirpy, with his ruddy, healthy-looking face and his pale-blue, challenging bright eyes. His shoulders were broad and strong, his hands were very strong. He was expensively tailored in London, and wore handsome neckties from Bond Street. Yet still in his face one saw the watchful look, the slight vacancy too, of a cripple.

He had so very nearly lost his life, that what remained to him was inordinately precious to him. It was obvious in the anxious bright-ness of his eyes, how proud he was, after the great shock, of being alive. But he had been so much hurt, something inside him had perished, some of his feelings were gone. There was a blank of insentience.

Constance, his wife, was a ruddy, country-looking girl with soft brown hair and sturdy body and slow movements full of unused energy. She had big, wondering blue eyes and a soft, mild voice, and seemed just to have come from her native village.

It was not so at all. Her father was the once well-known R. A., old Sir Malcolm Reid. Her mother had been one of the cultured Fabians in the palmy, rather pre-Raphaelite days. Between artists and cultured socialists, Constance and her sister Hilda had had what might be called an aesthetically unconventional upbringing. They had been taken to Paris and Florence and Rome, to breathe in art, and they had been taken in the other direction, to the Hague and Berlin, to great socialist conventions, where the speakers spoke in every civilised tongue, and no-one was abashed.

The two girls, therefore, from an early age were not in the least daunted either by art or ideal politics. It was their natural atmo-sphere. They were at once cosmopolitan and provincial, with the cosmopolitan provincialism of art that goes with pure social ideals.

They had been sent to Dresden at the age of fifteen, for music among other things. And they had had a good time there. They lived freely among the students, they argued with the men over philo-sophical and sociological and artistic matters, they were just as good as men themselves: only better, because they were women. And they tramped off to the forests with sturdy youths bearing guitars, twang-twang!—they sang the Wandervogel songs, and they were free. Free! That was the great word. Out in the open world, out in the forests of the morning, with lusty and splendid throated young fellows, free to do as they liked, and, above all, to say what they liked. It was the talk that mattered supremely: the impassioned interchange of talk. Love was only a minor accompaniment.

Both Hilda and Constance had had their tentative love affairs, by the time they were eighteen. The young men with whom they talked so passionately and sang so lustily and camped under the trees in such freedom wanted, of course, the love-connection. The girls were doubtful, but then the thing was so much talked about, it was supposed to be so important. And the men were so humble and craving. Why couldn't a girl be queenly, and give the gift of herself?

So they had given the gift of themselves each to the youth with whom she had the most intimate and subtle arguments. The arguments, the discussions were the great thing: the love-making and connection was only a sort of primitive reversion, and a bit of an anti-climax. One was less in love with the boy afterwards, and a little inclined to hate him, as if he had trespassed on one's privacy and inner freedom. For of course, being a girl, one's whole dignity and meaning in life consisted in the achievement of an absolute, a perfect, a pure and royal freedom. What else did a girl's life mean? To shake off the old and sordid connections and subjections.

And however one might sentimentalise it, this sex business was one of the most ancient sordid connections and subjections. Poets who glorified it were mostly men. Women had always known there was something better, something higher. And now they knew it more definitely than ever. The beautiful pure freedom of a woman was infinitely more wonderful than any sexual love. The only unfortunate thing was that men lagged so far behind women in the matter. They insisted on the sex thing like dogs.

And a woman had to yield. A man was like a child, with his appetites. A woman had to yield him what he wanted, or like a child he would probably turn nasty and flounce away and spoil what was a very pleasant connection. But a woman could yield to a man without yielding her inner, free self. That the poets and talkers about sex did not seem to have taken sufficiently into account. A woman could take a man, without really giving herself away. Certainly she could take him without giving herself into his power. Rather she could use this sex thing to have power over him. For she had only to hold herself back, in the sexual intercourse, and let him finish and expend himself without herself coming to the crisis; and then she could prolong the connection and achieve her orgasm and her crisis while he was merely a tool.

Both sisters had had their love experiences by the time the war came and they were hurried home. Neither was ever in love with a young man unless he and she were verbally very near: that is, unless they were profoundly interested, *talking* to one another. The amazing, the profound, the unbelievable thrill there was, in passionately talking to some really clever young man, by the hour, resuming day after day for months—this they had never realised till it happened. The paradisal promise: Thou shalt have men to talk to! had never been uttered. It was fulfilled before they knew what a promise it was.

And if, after the roused intimacy of these vivid and soul-enlightening discussions, the sex thing became more or less inevitable, then let it. It marked the end of a chapter. It had a thrill of its own too: a queer vibrating thrill inside the body, a final spasm of self-assertion, like the last word, exciting, and very like the row of asterisks that can be put to show the end of a paragraph, and a break in the theme.

When the girls came home for the summer holiday of 1913, when Hilda was twenty and Connie eighteen, their father could see plainly that they had had the love experience. L'amour avait passé par là, as somebody puts it. But he was a man of experience himself, and let life take its course. As for the mother, a nervous invalid in the last months of her life, she only wanted her girls to be "free" and to "fulfil themselves." She herself had never been able to be altogether herself: it had been denied her. Heaven knows why, for she was a woman who had her own income and her own way. She blamed her husband. But as a matter of fact, it was some old impression of authority on her mind or soul that she could not get rid of. It had nothing to do with Sir Malcolm, who left his nervously hostile, highly-spiritual wife to rule her own roost, while he went his own way.

So the girls were "free," and went back to Dresden and their music and the university and the young men. They loved their respective young men, and their respective young men loved them, with all the passion of mental attraction. All the wonderful things the young men thought and expressed and wrote, they thought and expressed and wrote for their young women. Connie's young man was musical, Hilda's was technical. But they simply lived for their young women. In their minds and their mental excitement, that is.

Somewhere else they were a little rebuffed, though they did not know it.

It was obvious in them too that love had gone through them: that is, the physical experience. It is curious what a subtle but unmistakeable transmutation it makes, both in the body of man and woman: the woman more blooming, more subtly rounded, her young angularities softened, and her expression either anxious or triumphant: and the man much quieter, more inward, the very shapes of his shoulders and his buttocks less assertive, more hesitant.

In the actual sex-thrill within the body, the sisters nearly succumbed to the strange male power. But quickly they recovered themselves, took the sex-thrill as a sensation, and remained free. Whereas the men, in gratitude to the woman for the sex experience, let their souls go out to her. And afterwards, looked rather as if they had lost a shilling and found sixpence. Connie's man could be a bit sulky, and Hilda's a bit jeering. But that is how men are! Ungrateful, and never satisfied. When you don't have them, they hate you because you won't. And when you do have them, they hate you again, for some other reason. Or for no reason at all, except that they are discontented children, and can't be satisfied whatever they get, let a woman do what she may.

However, came the war, Hilda and Connie were rushed home again—after having been home already in May, to their mother's funeral. Before the Christmas of 1914 both their German young men were dead: whereupon the sisters wept and loved the young men passionately, but underneath, forgot them. They didn't exist any more.

Both sisters lived in their father's—really their mother's— Kensington house, and mixed with the young Cambridge group, the group that stood for "freedom" and flannel trousers, and soft shirts open at the neck, and a well-bred sort of emotional anarchy, and a whispering, murmuring sort of voice, and an ultra-sensitive sort of manner. Hilda, however, suddenly married a man ten years older than herself, an elder member of the same Cambridge group, a man with a fair amount of money and a comfortable family job in the government: he also wrote philosophical essays. She lived with him in a smallish house in Westminster, and moved in that good sort of society of people in the government who are not tip-toppers but who are, or would be, the *real* intelligent power in the nation: people who know what they're talking about: or talk as if they did.

Connie did a mild form of war-work, and consorted with the flannel-trousers Cambridge intransigeants who gently mocked at everything, so far. Her "friend" was a Clifford Chatterley, a young man of twenty-two who had hurried home from Bonn, where he was studying the technicalities of coal-mining. He had previously spent two years at Cambridge. Now he had become a first lieutenant in a smart regiment, so he could mock at everything still more becomingly, in uniform.

Clifford Chatterley was more upper-class than Connie. Connie was the well-to-do intelligentsia, but he was aristocracy. Not the big sort, but still, it. His father was a baronet, and his mother had been a viscount's daughter.

But Clifford, while he was better-bred than Connie, and more "society," was in his own way more provincial and more timid. He was at his ease in the narrow "great world"—that is, landed-aristocracy society—but he was shy and nervous of all that other big world which consists of the vast hordes of the middle and lower classes, and foreigners. If the truth must be told, he was just a bit frightened of the vast hordes of middle and lower-class humanity, and of foreigners not of his own class. He was, in some paralysing way, conscious of his own defencelessness: though he had all the defences of privilege. Which is curious, but a phenomenon of our day.

Therefore the peculiar soft assurance of a girl like Constance Reid fascinated him. She was so much more mistress of herself in that outer world of chaos, than he was master of himself.

Nevertheless, he too was a rebel: rebelling even against his class. Or perhaps rebel is too strong a word; far too strong. He was only caught in the general, popular recoil of the young against convention and against any sort of real authority. Fathers were ridiculous: his own obstinate one, supremely so. And governments were ridiculous: our own wait-and-see sort especially so. And armies were ridiculous, and old buffers of generals altogether: the red-faced Kitchener supremely. Even the war was really ridiculous, though it did kill rather a lot of people.

In fact, everything was a little ridiculous, or very ridiculous: certainly everything connected with authority, whether it were in the government or in the army or in the universities, was ridiculous to a degree. And as far as the governing classes made any pretensions to govern, they were ridiculous too. Sir Geoffrey, Clifford's father, was intensely ridiculous, chopping down his trees and weeding men out of his colliery, to shove them into the war; and himself being so safe and patriotic; but also, spending more money on his country than he'd got.

When Miss Chatterley—Emma—came down to London from the Midlands, to do some nursing work, she was very witty in a quiet way about Sir Geoffrey and his determined patriotism. Herbert, the elder brother and heir, laughed outright, though it was his trees that were falling for trench-props. But Clifford only smiled a little uneasily. Everything was ridiculous, quite true. But when it came too close, and oneself became ridiculous too— —? At least people of a different class, like Connie, were earnest about *something*. They believed in something.

They were rather earnest about the Tommies, and the threat of conscription, and the shortage of sugar and toffee for the children. In all these things, of course, the authorities were ridiculously at fault. But Clifford could not take it to heart. To him, the authorities were ridiculous *ab ovo*, not because of toffee or Tommies.

And the authorities felt ridiculous, and behaved in a rather ridiculous fashion, and it was all a mad hatter's tea-party, for a while. Till things developed over there, and Lloyd George came to save the situation over here. And this surpassed even ridicule. The flippant young laughed no more.

In 1916 Herbert Chatterley was killed, so Clifford became heir. He was terrified even of this. His importance as son of Sir Geoffrey and child of Wragby, the family house, was so ingrained in him, he could never escape it. And yet he knew that this, too, in the eyes of the vast seething world, was ridiculous. Now he was heir, and responsible for Wragby, old Wragby. Was that not terrible! and also splendid, splendid! and at the same time, perhaps, purely absurd.

Sir Geoffrey would have none of the absurdity. He was pale and tense, withdrawn in himself, and obstinately determined to save his country and his own position, let it be Lloyd George or who it might. So cut off he was, so divorced from the England that was really England, so utterly incapable, that he even thought well of Horatio Bottomley. He stood for England and Lloyd George, as his fore-bears had stood for England and St. George: and he never knew there was a difference. So Sir Geoffrey felled timber and stood for Lloyd George and England, England and Lloyd George.

And he wanted Clifford to marry and produce an heir. Clifford felt his father was a hopeless anachronism. But wherein was he himself any further ahead, except in a wincing sense of the ridiculousness of everything, and the paramount ridiculousness of his own position? For willy nilly, he took his baronetcy and Wragby with the last seriousness.

The gay excitement had gone out of the war—dead. Too much death and horror. A man needed support and comfort. A man needed to have an anchor in the safe world. A man needed a wife.

The Chatterleys, two brothers and a sister, had lived curiously isolated, shut in with one another at Wragby, in spite of all their connections. A sense of isolation intensified the family tie, a sense of the weakness of their position, a sense of defencelessness, in spite of, or perhaps because of the title and the land. They were cut off from that industrial Midlands in which they passed their lives. And they were cut off from their own class by the brooding, obstinate, shut-up nature of Sir Geoffrey their father, whom they ridiculed, but whom they were so sensitive about.

The three had said they would all live together, always. But now Herbert was dead, and Sir Geoffrey wanted Clifford to marry. Sir Geoffrey barely mentioned it: he spoke very little. But his silent, brooding insistence that it should be so was hard for Clifford to bear up against.

But Emma said No! She was ten years older than Clifford, and she felt his marrying would be a desertion and a betrayal of what the young ones of the family had stood for.

Clifford married Connie, nevertheless, and had his month's honeymoon with her. It was the terrible year 1917, and they were intimate as two people who stand together on a sinking ship. He had been virgin when he married: and the sex part did not mean much to him. They were so close, he and she, apart from that. And Connie exulted a little in this intimacy which was beyond sex and a man's "satisfaction." Clifford anyhow was not just keen on his "satisfaction," as so many men seemed to be. No, the intimacy was deeper, more personal than that. And sex was merely an accident, or an adjunct: one of the curious obsolete organic processes which persisted in its own clumsiness, but was not really necessary. Though Connie *did* want children: if only to fortify her against her sister-in-law Emma.

But early in 1918 Clifford was shipped home smashed, and there was no child. And Sir Geoffrey died of chagrin.

CHAPTER II.

Connie and Clifford came home to Wragby in the autumn of 1920. Miss Chatterley, still disgusted at her brother's defection, had departed and was living in a little flat in London.

Wragby was a long, low old house in brown stone, begun about the middle of the eighteenth century, and added on to, till it was a warren of a place without much distinction. It stood on an eminence in a rather fine old park of oak trees: but alas, one could see in the near distance the chimney of Tevershall pit with its clouds of steam and smoke, and on the damp, hazy distance of the hill the raw straggle of Tevershall village—a village which began almost at the park gates, and trailed in utter hopeless ugliness for a long and gruesome mile: houses, rows of wretched, small begrimed brick houses with black slate roofs for lids, sharp angles and wilful blank dreariness.

Connie was accustomed to Kensington or the Scotch hills or the Sussex downs: that was her England. With the stoicism of the young she took in the utter soulless ugliness of the coal-and-iron Midlands at a glance, and left it at what it was: unbelievable, and not to be thought about. From the rather dismal rooms of Wragby she heard the rattle-rattle of the screens at the pit, the puff of the winding-engine, the clink-clink of shunting trucks and the hoarse little whistle of the colliery locomotives. Tevershall pit-bank was burning, had been burning for years, and it would cost thousands to put it out. So it had to burn. And when the wind was that way, which was often, the house was full of the stench of this sulphureous combustion of the earth's excrement. But even on windless days, the air always smelled of something under-earth: sulphur, coal, iron, or acid. And even on the Christmas roses the smuts settled persistently, incredible, like black manna from skies of doom.

Well, there it was: fated, like the rest of things! It was rather awful, but why kick? You couldn't kick it away. It just went on. Oneself also went on. Life, like all the rest! On the low dark ceiling of cloud at night red blotches burned and quavered, dappling and swelling and contracting like burns that give pain. It was the furnaces. At first they fascinated Connie with a sort of horror: she felt she was living underground. Then she got used to them. And in the morning it rained.

Clifford professed to like Wragby better than London. This country had a grim will of its own, and the people had guts. Connie wondered what else they had: certainly neither eyes nor minds. The people were as shapeless, haggard, and dreary as the countryside, and as unfriendly. Only there was something in their deep-mouthed slurring of the dialect, and the thresh-thresh of their hob-nailed pit-boots as they trailed home in gangs on the asphalt, from work, that was terrible and a bit mysterious.

There had been no welcome home for the young squire—no festivities, no deputation, not even a single flower. Only a dank ride in a motor-car up a dark, damp drive burrowing through gloomy trees, out to the slope of the park where grey damp sheep were feeding, to the knoll where the house spread its dark-brown façade, and the house-keeper and her husband were hovering, like unsure tenants on the face of the earth, ready to stammer a welcome.

There was no communication between Wragby Hall and Tevershall village—none. No caps were touched, no curtseys bobbed. The colliers merely stared: the tradesmen lifted their caps to Connie as to an acquaintance, and nodded awkwardly to Clifford: that was all. Gulf impassable, and a quiet sort of resentment on either side. At first Connie suffered from the steady drizzle of resentment that came from the village. Then she hardened herself to it, and it was a sort of tonic, something to live up against. It was not that she and Clifford were unpopular—they merely belonged to another species altogether from the colliers. Gulf impassable, breach indescribable, such as is perhaps non-existent south of the Trent. But in the Midlands and the industrial North, gulf impassable, across which no communion could take place.—You stick to your side, I'll stick to mine!—A strange denial of the common pulse of humanity.

Yet the village sympathised with Clifford and Connie, in the abstract. In the flesh, it was—You leave me alone!—on either side.

The Rector was a nice man of about sixty, full of his duty, and reduced, personally, almost to a nonentity by the silent—You leave me alone!—of the village. The miners' wives were nearly all Methodists. The miners were nothing. But even so much official uniform as the clergyman wore was enough to obscure entirely the fact that he was a man like any other man. No, he was Mester Ashby, a sort of automatic preaching and praying concern.

This stubborn, instinctive—We think ourselves as good as you, if you *are* Lady Chatterley!—puzzled and baffled Connie at first extremely. The curious suspicious, false amiability with which the miners' wives met her overtures, the curiously offensive tinge of—Oh dear me! I *am* somebody now, with Lady Chatterley talking to me! But she needn't think I'm not as good as her, for all that!—which she always heard twanging in the women's half-fawning voices, was impossible. There was no getting past it. It was hopelessly and offensively nonconformist.

Clifford left them alone, and she learnt to do the same: she just went by without looking at them, and they stared as if she were a walking wax figure. When he had to deal with them, Clifford was rather haughty and contemptuous—one could no longer afford to be friendly. In fact, he was altogether rather supercilious, and contemptuous of anyone not in his own class. He stood his ground without any attempt at conciliation. And he was neither liked nor disliked by the people: he was just part of things, like the pit-bank and Wragby itself.

But Clifford was really extremely shy and self-conscious now he was lamed. He hated seeing anyone except just the personal servants. For he had to sit in a wheeled chair, or a sort of bath-chair. Nevertheless he was just as carefully dressed as ever, by his expensive London tailors, and he wore the careful Bond Street neck-ties just as before, and from the top he looked just as smart and impressive as ever. He had never been one of the modern ladylike young gentlemen: rather bucolic, even, with his ruddy face and broad shoulders. But his very quiet, hesitating voice, and his eyes, at the same time bold and frightened, assured and uncertain, revealed his nature. His manner was often offensively supercilious; and then again, modest and self-effacing, almost tremulous.

Connie and he were attached to one another, in the rather aloof modern way. He was much too hurt in himself, the great shock of his maiming, to be easy and flippant. He was a hurt thing. And as such, Connie stuck to him passionately.

But she could not help feeling how little connection he really had with people. The miners were, in a sense, his own men: but he saw them as objects rather than men, parts of the pit rather than as parts of life, and crude raw phenomena rather than human beings along with him. He was in some way afraid of them, he could not bear to have them look at him now he was lame. And they had a queer crude manhood which to him was unnatural as hedgehogs.

He was remotely interested: but like a man looking down a microscope, or up a telescope. He was not in touch. He was not in actual touch with anything or anybody; save traditionally, with Wragby, and through the close bond of family defence, with Emma. Beyond this, nothing really touched him. Connie felt that she herself didn't really, not really touch him. She had never finally got at him: perhaps there was nothing to get at, ultimately: just a negation of human contact.

Yet he was absolutely dependent on her—he needed her every moment. Big and strong as he was, he was helpless. He could wheel himself about in a wheeled chair, and he had a sort of bath-chair with a motor attachment, in which he could puff slowly round the park. But alone he was like a lost thing. He needed Connie to be there, to assure him that he existed at all.

Still he was ambitious. He had taken to writing stories, curious, very personal stories about people he had known, clever, rather spiteful, and yet in some mysterious way, meaningless. The observation was extraordinary and peculiar. But there was no touch, no actual contact. It was as if the whole thing took place on an artificial earth.—And since the field of life is largely an artificially-lighted stage today, the stories were curiously true to modern life—to the modern psychology, that is.

Clifford was almost morbidly sensitive to these stories. He wanted everyone to think them good, of the best, *ne plus ultra*. They appeared in the most modern magazines, and were praised and blamed, as usual. But to Clifford the blame was torture, like knives goading him. It was as if the whole of his being were in his stories.

Connie helped him all she could. At first she was thrilled. He talked everything over with her monotonously, insistently, persistently, and she had to respond with all her might. It was as if her whole soul and body and sex had to rouse up and pass into these stories of his. This thrilled her, and absorbed her.

Of physical life they lived very little. She had to superintend the house. But the housekeeper had served Sir Geoffrey for many years, and the dried, elderly, superlatively correct female—you could hardly call her a parlour-maid, or even a woman—who waited at table had been in the house for forty years. Even the very housemaids were no longer young. It was awful! What could you do with such a place, but leave it alone! All those endless rooms that nobody used, all the Midlands routine, the mechanical cleanliness and the mechanical order! Clifford had insisted on a new cook, an experienced woman who had served him in his rooms in London. For the rest, the place seemed like a methodical anarchy. Everything went on in pretty good order, strict cleanliness, and strict punctuality: even pretty strict honesty. And yet, to Connie, it was a methodical anarchy. No warmth of feeling united it organically. The house seemed as dreary as a disused street.

What could she do but leave it alone! So she left it alone. Miss Chatterley came sometimes, and triumphed, from her aristocratic thin face, finding nothing altered. She would never forgive Connie for ousting her from her unison in consciousness with her brother. It was she, Emma, who should be bringing forth these stories, these books with him: the Chatterley stories, something new in the world. That was all that mattered: something new in the world, that *they*, the Chatterleys, had put there. There was no other standard. There was no organic connection with the thought and expression which had gone before. Only something new in the world: the Chatterley books: entirely personal.

Connie's father, when he paid a flying visit to Wragby, said in private to his daughter: As for Clifford's writing, it's smart, but there's nothing in it. It won't last!—Connie looked at the burly Scottish knight who had done himself well all his life, and her eyes, her big, still wondering blue eyes, became vague. Nothing in it! What did he mean by *nothing in it*? If the critics praised it, and Clifford's name was almost famous, and it even brought in money: what did her father mean by saying there was nothing in Clifford's writing? What else could there be?

For Connie had adopted the standard of the young: what there was in the moment, was everything. And moments followed one another without necessarily belonging to one another.

It was in her second winter at Wragby her father said to her:

"I hope, Connie, you won't let circumstances force you into being a demi-vierge."

"A demi-vierge!" replied Connie vaguely. "Why? Why not?"

"Unless you like it, of course!" said her father hastily.

To Clifford he said the same, when the two men were alone:

"I'm afraid it doesn't quite suit Connie to be a *demi-vierge*."

"A half-virgin!" replied Clifford, translating the phrase, to be sure of it.

He thought for a moment, then flushed very red. He was angry and offended.

"In what way doesn't it suit her?" he asked stiffly.

"She's getting thin—angular. It's not her style. She's not the pilchard sort of little fish of a girl. She's a bonny Scotch trout."

"Without the spots, of course!" said Clifford.

He wanted to say something, later, to Connie about the demi-vierge business—the half-virgin state of her affairs. But he could not bring himself to it. He was at once too intimate with her, and not intimate enough. He was so very much at one with her, in his mind and hers. But bodily they were non-existent to one another, and neither could bear to drag in the *corpus delicti*. They were so intimate, and utterly out of touch.

Connie, however, guessed that her father had said something, and that something was in Clifford's mind. She knew that he didn't mind whether she were demi-vierge or demi-monde, so long as he absolutely didn't know and wasn't made to see. What the eye doesn't see, and the mind doesn't know, doesn't exist.

Connie had been now nearly two years at Wragby, living this vague life of absorption in Clifford and his needing her, and his work, especially his work. Their interests had never ceased to flow together, over his work. They talked and wrestled in the throes of composition, and felt as if something were happening, really, in the void.

And thus far, it was a life: in the void. For the rest, it was non-existence. Wragby was there, the servants; but spectral, not really existing. Connie went for walks in the park and in the woods that joined the park, and enjoyed the solitude and the mystery, kicked the brown leaves of autumn and picked the primroses of spring. But it was all like a dream: or rather, it was like the simulacrum of reality. The oak-leaves to her were like oak-leaves seen ruffling in a mirror, she herself was a figure somebody had read about, picking primroses that were only shadows, or memories, or words. No substance to her or anything—no touch, no contact. Only this life with Clifford, this endless spinning of webs of yarn, of the minutiae of consciousness, these stories, of which Sir Malcolm said there was nothing in them and they wouldn't last. Why should there be anything in them, why should they last? Sufficient unto the day is the evil thereof. Sufficient unto the moment is the *appearance* of reality.

Clifford had quite a number of friends, acquaintances really, and he invited them to Wragby. He invited all sorts of people, critics and writers, people who would help to praise his books. And they were flattered at being asked to Wragby, and they praised. Connie understood it all perfectly. But why not? This was one of the fleeting patterns in the mirror. What was wrong with it?

She was hostess to these people—mostly men. She was hostess also to Clifford's occasional aristocratic relations. Being a soft, ruddy, country-looking girl inclined to freckle, with big blue eyes and curling brown hair and a soft voice, and rather strong, female loins she was considered a little old-fashioned and "womanly." She was not a little pilchard sort of fish, like a boy, with a boy's flat breast and little buttocks. She was too feminine to be quite smart.

So the men, especially those no longer so young, were very nice to her indeed. But, knowing what tortures poor Clifford would feel at the slightest sign of flirting on her part, she gave them no encouragement whatever. She was quiet and vague, she had no contact with them, and intended to have none. Clifford was extraordinarily proud of himself.

His relatives treated her quite kindly. She knew that the kindliness indicated a lack of fear—and that these people had no respect for you unless you could frighten them a little. But again, she had no contact. She let them go on. She let them be kindly and disdainful, she let them feel they had no need to draw their steel in readiness. She had no real connection with them.

Time went on. Whatever happened, nothing happened, because she was so beautifully out of contact. She and Clifford lived in their ideas and his books. She entertained—there were always people in the house. Time went on as the clock does, half-past eight instead of half-past seven.

CHAPTER III.

Connie, however, was aware of a growing restlessness. Out of her disconnection, a restlessness was taking possession of her like a madness. It twitched her limbs when she didn't want to twitch them, it jerked her spine when she did not want to jerk upright, but preferred to rest comfortably. It thrilled inside her body, in her womb, somewhere, till she felt she must jump into water and swim, to get away from it: a mad restlessness. It made her heart beat violently, for no reason. And she was getting thinner.

It was just restlessness. She would rush off across the park and abandon Clifford, and lie prone in the bracken. To get away from the house—she must get away from the house and everybody. The wood was her one refuge, her sanctuary.

But it was not really a refuge, a sanctuary, because she had no connection with it. It was only a place where she could get *away* from the rest. She never really touched the spirit of the wood itself—if it had any such nonsensical thing.

Vaguely, she knew herself that she was going to pieces in some way. Vaguely, she knew she was out of connection: she had lost touch with the substantial and vital world. Only Clifford and his books, which did not exist—which had nothing in them! Void to void. Vaguely, she knew. But it was like beating her head against a stone.

Her father warned her again: Why don't you find yourself a *beau*, Connie? Do you all the good in the world!—

That winter Michaelis came for a few days. He was a young Irishman who had already made a large fortune in America by his plays. He had been taken up quite enthusiastically for a time by smart society in London, for he wrote smart society plays. Then gradually smart society realised that it had been made ridiculous at the hands of a down-at-heel Dublin street-rat, and the revulsion came. Michaelis was the last word in what was caddish and bounderish. He was discovered to be anti-English, and to the class that made the discovery this was worse than the dirtiest crime. He was cut dead and his corpse thrown into the refuse can.

Nevertheless, Michaelis had his apartment in Mayfair and walked down Bond Street the image of a gentleman, for you cannot get even the best tailors to cut their low-down customers, when the customers pay.

Clifford was inviting the young man of thirty at an inauspicious moment in that young man's career. Yet Clifford did not hesitate. Michaelis had the ear of a few million people, probably: and being a hopeless outsider, he would no doubt be grateful to be asked down to Wragby at this juncture, when the rest of the smart world was cutting him. Being grateful, he would no doubt do Clifford "good" over there in America. Kudos! A man gets a lot of kudos, whatever that may be, by being talked about in the right way, especially "over there." Clifford was a coming man: and it was remarkable what a sound publicity instinct he had. In the end Michaelis did him most nobly in a play, and Clifford was a sort of popular hero. Till the reaction, when he found he had been made ridiculous.

Connie wondered a little over Clifford's blind, imperious necessity to become known: known, that is, to the vast amorphous world he did not himself know, and of which he was uneasily afraid: known as a writer, a first-class modern writer. Connie was aware, from successful old hearty, bluffing Sir Malcolm, that artists did advertise themselves, and exert themselves to put their goods over. But her father used channels ready-made, used by all the other R. A.'s who sold their pictures. Whereas Clifford discovered new channels of publicity, all kinds. He had all kinds of people at Wragby—without exactly lowering himself. But, determined to build himself a monument of a reputation quickly, he used any handy rubble for the making.

Michaelis arrived duly, in a very neat car, with a chauffeur and a manservant. He was absolutely Bond Street: but at sight of him something in Clifford's "county" soul recoiled. He wasn't exactly—not exactly—in fact, he wasn't at all—well, what his appearance intended to imply. To Clifford it was final, and enough. Yet he was very polite to the man: to the amazing success in him. The bitch-goddess, as she is called, of Success, roamed snarling and protective round the half-humble, half-defiant Michaelis' heels, and intimidated Clifford completely: for he wanted to prostitute himself to the bitch-goddess Success also, if only she would have him.

Michaelis obviously wasn't an Englishman, in spite of all the tailors, hatters, barbers, and booters of the very best quarter of

London. No no, he obviously wasn't an Englishman: the wrong sort of flattish pale face and bearing; and the wrong sort of grievance. He had a grudge and a grievance: that was obvious to any true-born English gentleman, who would scorn to let such a thing appear blatant in his own demeanour. Poor Michaelis had been much kicked, so that he had a slightly tail-between-the-legs look even now. He had pushed his way by sheer instinct and sheerer effrontery on to the stage and to the front of it: with his plays. He had caught the public. And he had thought the kicking days were over. Alas, they weren't—they never would be. For he, in a sense, asked to be kicked. He pined to be where he didn't belong—among the English upper classes. And how they enjoyed the various kicks they got at him! And how he hated them!

Nevertheless, he travelled with his manservant and his very neat car, this Dublin mongrel.

There was something about him Connie liked. He didn't put on airs to himself: he had no illusions about himself. He talked to Clifford sensibly, briefly, practically about all the things Clifford wanted to know. He didn't expand or let himself go. He knew he had been asked down to Wragby to be made use of, and like an old, shrewd, almost indifferent business-man, or big-business-man, he let himself be asked questions, and he answered with as little waste of feeling as possible.

"Money!" he said. "Money is a sort of instinct. It's a sort of property of nature in a man, to make money. It's nothing you *do*. It's no trick you play. It's a sort of permanent accident of your own nature: once you start you make money, and you go on: up to a point I supppose—"

"But you've got to begin," said Clifford.

"Oh quite! You've got to get *in*: you can do nothing if you're kept outside. You've got to beat your way in. Once you've done that, you can't help it."

"But could you have made money except by plays?" asked Clifford.

"Oh, probably not! I may be a good writer or I may be a bad one, but a writer, and a writer of plays is what I am, and I've got to be. There's no question of that."

"And you think it's a writer of popular plays that you've got to be?" asked Connie.

"There, exactly!" he said, turning to her in a sudden flash.

"There's nothing in it! There's nothing in popularity. There's nothing in the public, if it comes to that. There's nothing really in my plays to *make* them popular. It's not that. They just are—like the weather—the sort that will *have* to be—for the time being—"

He turned his slow, rather full eyes, that had been drowned in such fathomless disillusion, on Connie, and she trembled a little. He seemed so old—endlessly old, built up of layers of disillusion, going down in him generation after generation like geological strata; and at the same time he was forlorn like a child. An outcast, in a certain sense; but with the desperate bravery of his rat-like existence.

"At least, it's wonderful what you've done, at your time of life," said Clifford contemplatively.

"I'm thirty—yes, I'm thirty!" said Michaelis sharply and suddenly, with a curious laugh, hollow, triumphant, and bitter.

"And are you alone?" asked Connie.

"How do you mean? Do I live alone? I've got my servant. If a man doesn't have a wife he must have a servant. He's a Greek, so he says, and quite incompetent. But I keep him.—And I'm going to marry. Oh yes, I must marry."

"It sounds like going to have your hair cut," laughed Connie. "Will it be an effort?"

He looked at her admiringly.

"Well, Lady Chatterley—somehow it will! I find—excuse me—I find I can't marry an Englishwoman, not even an Irishwoman—"

"Try an American," said Clifford.

"Oh, American!"—he laughed a hollow laugh. "No, I've asked my man if he'll find me a Turk or something—something nearer to the Oriental—"

Connie really wondered at this queer melancholy specimen of extraordinary success: it was said he had an income of fifty thousand dollars a year from America alone. Sometimes he was handsome: sometimes as he looked sideways, downwards, and the light fell on him, he had the silent, enduring beauty of a carved ivory negro mask, with his rather full eyes and the strong, queerly arched brows, the immobile, compressed mouth; that momentary but revealed immobility, an immobility, a timelessness which the Buddha aims at, and which the negroes express sometimes without ever aiming at it: somethin, old, old, and acquiescent in the race! Aeons of acquiescence in a race destiny, instead of our individual resistance. And then a swimming through, like rats in a dark river.—Connie felt a sudden strange leap of sympathy for him, a leap mingled with compassion and tinged with repulsion, amounting almost to love. The outsider! The outsider! And they called him a bounder! How much more bounderish and assertive Clifford looked! How much stupider!

Michaelis knew at once he had made an impression on her. He turned his full, hazel, slightly prominent eyes on her in a look of pure detachment. He was estimating her, and the extent of the impression he had made. With the English, nothing would save him from being the eternal outsider, not even love. Yet women sometimes fell for him, Englishwomen too.

He knew just where he was with Clifford. They were two alien dogs which would have liked to snarl at one another, but which smiled instead, perforce. But with the woman he was not quite so sure.

Breakfast was served in the bedrooms: Clifford never appeared before lunch, and the dining-room was a little dreary. After coffee Michaelis, restless and ill-sitting soul, wondered what he should do. It was a fine November day—fine for Wragby. He looked over the melancholy park. My God! What a place!

He sent a servant to ask, could he be of any service to Lady Chatterley: he thought of driving into Sheffield. The answer came, would he care to go up to Lady Chatterley's sitting-room.

Connie had a sitting-room on the third floor, the top floor of the central portion of the house. Clifford's rooms were on the ground floor, of course. Michaelis was flattered by being asked up to Lady Chatterley's own parlour. He followed blindly after the servant—he never noticed things, or had contact with his surroundings. In her room, he did glance vaguely round at the fine German reproductions of Renoir and Cézanne.

"It's very pleasant up here!" he said, with his queer smile as if it hurt him to smile, showing his teeth. "You are wise to get to the top."

"Yes, I think so," she said.

Her room was the only gay, modern room in the house, the only spot in Wragby where her personality was at all revealed. Clifford had never seen it—and she asked very few people up.

Now she and Michaelis sat on opposite sides of the fire, and talked. She asked him about himself, his mother, his father, his brothers—other people were always somewhat of a wonder to her, and when her sympathy was awake, she was quite devoid of class

---

feeling. Michaelis talked frankly about himself, quite without affectation, simply, revealing his bitter, indifferent, stray-dog's soul, then showing a gleam of revengeful pride in his success.

"But why are you such a lonely bird?" Connie asked him, and again he looked at her with his full, searching, hazel look.

"Some birds *are* that way," he replied. Then, with a touch of familiar irony: "But look here, what about yourself? Aren't you by way of being a lonely bird yourself?"

Connie, a little startled, thought about it for a few moments, then she said:

"Only in a way! Not altogether, like you!"

"Am I altogether a lonely bird?" he asked with his queer grin of a smile, that looked almost as if he had toothache, it was so wry, and his eyes were so perfectly unchangingly melancholy or stoical, or disillusioned, or afraid.

"Why?" she said, a little breathless as she looked at him. "You are, aren't you?"

She felt a terrible appeal coming to her from him, that made her almost lose her balance.

"Oh, you're quite right!" he said, turning his head away and looking sideways downwards with that strange sudden immobility of an old race that is hardly here in our present day. It was that that made Connie really lose her power to see him detached from herself.

He looked up at her with the full glance that saw everything, registered everything. At the same time, the infant crying in the night was crying out of his breast to her, in a way that affected her very womb.

"It's awfully nice of you to think of me!" he said, laconic.

"Why shouldn't I think of you?" she exclaimed, with hardly breath to utter it.

He gave the quick wry hiss of a laugh.

"Oh, in that way!—May I hold your hand for a minute?" he asked suddenly, fixing his eyes on her with almost hypnotic power, and sending out an appeal that affected her direct in her womb.

She stared at him dazed and transfixed, and he went over and kneeled beside her, and took her two feet close in his two hands, and buried his face in her lap, remaining motionless. She was perfectly dim and dazed, looking down in a sort of amazement at the rather tender nape of his neck, feeling his face pressing her thighs. In all her burning dismay, she could not help putting her hand with tenderness and compassion on the defenceless nape of his neck, and he trembled in a sudden shudder.

Then he looked up at her with that awful, awful appeal in his full, glowing eyes. She was utterly incapable of resisting it. From her breast flowed the answering immense yearning over him: she must give him anything, anything.

He was a curious and very gentle lover, very gentle with the woman, trembling uncontrollably, and yet at the same time detached, aware, aware of every sound outside.

To her it meant nothing except that she gave herself to him. And at length he ceased to quiver any more, and lay quite still, quite quite still. Then with dim, compassionate fingers she stroked her fingers over his head, that lay on her breast.

When he rose, he kissed both her hands, then both her feet in their suède slippers, and in silence went away to the end of the room, where he stood with his back to her. There was silence for some minutes.

Then he turned and came to her again, as she sat in her old place by the fire.

"And now I suppose you'll hate me!" he said in a quiet, inevitable way.

She looked up at him quickly.

"Why should I?" she said.

"They mostly do," he said, then caught himself up. "I mean—a woman is supposed to."

"This is the last moment when I ought to hate you," she said, resentfully.

"I know! I know! It should be so! You're *frightfully* good to me—" he cried, miserably.

She wondered why he should be miserable.

"Won't you sit down?" she said.

He glanced at the door.

"Sir Clifford—!" he said. "Won't he—won't he be—?"

She paused a moment to consider.

"Perhaps!" she said. And she looked up at him. "I don't want Clifford to know—not even to suspect. It would hurt him so. But I don't think it is wrong—do you?"

"Wrong! Good God no! You're only too infinitely good to me—I can hardly bear it."

He turned aside, and she saw that in another moment he would be sobbing.

"But we needn't let Clifford know, need we?" she pleaded. "It *would* hurt him so. And if he never knows, never suspects, it hurts nobody."

"Me!" he said, almost fiercely. "He'll know nothing from me! You see if he does! *Me* give myself away! ha—ha!" he laughed hollowly, cynical at such an idea.

She watched him in wonder. He said to her:

"May I kiss your hand and go? I'll run into Sheffield I think. I'll lunch there, if I may, and be back to tea. May I do anything for you? May I be sure you don't hate me?—and that you *won't*—?—" He ended with a faint note of desperate cynicism.

"No, I don't hate you!" she said. "I think you're nice."

"Ah!" he said to her fiercely. "I'd rather you said that, than said you loved me! It means such a lot more!—Till afternoon, then—I've plenty to think about till then—"

He kissed her hands humbly, and was gone.

"I don't think I can stand that young man," said Clifford at lunch.

"Why?" asked Connie.

"He's just a bounder, underneath his veneer—just waiting to bounce us."

"I think people have been so unkind to him," said Connie.

"Do you wonder! And do you think he spends his shining hours doing deeds of kindness?"

"I think he has a certain sort of generosity."

"Towards whom?"

"I don't quite know."

"Naturally you don't. I'm afraid you mistake unscrupulousness for generosity."

Connie paused. Did she? It was just possible. Yet the unscrupulousness of Michaelis had a certain fascination for her. He went whole lengths, where Clifford crept a few timid paces. In his way, he had conquered the world: which was what Clifford wanted to do. Ways and means—? Were those of Michaelis more despicable than those of Clifford? Was the way the poor outsider had shoved and bounced himself forward, in person and by the back doors, any worse than Clifford's way of advertising himself into prominence. The bitch-goddess Success was trailed by thousands of gasping dogs with lolling tongues. The one that got her first was the real dog among dogs. If you go by success! So Michaelis could keep his tail up.

The queer thing was, he didn't. He came back towards tea-time with a large handful of violets and lilies, and the same forlorn hang-dog expression. Connie wondered sometimes if it were a sort of mask, to disarm opposition. Because it was almost too fixed. Was he really such a sad dog?

His sad dog sort of extinguished self persisted all evening, though through it Clifford felt the inner effrontery. Connie didn't feel it: perhaps because it was not directed against women, only against men and their presumption and assumptions. That indestructible inward effrontery in the meagre fellow was what made men so down on Michaelis. His very presence was an affront to a man of society, cloak it as he might in an assumed good manner.

Connie was in love with him. But she managed to sit with her embroidery and let the men talk, and not give herself away. As for Michaelis, he was perfect: exactly the same melancholic, attentive, aloof young fellow of the previous evening, millions of degrees remote from his hosts, but laconically playing up to them to the required amount, and never coming forth to them for a moment. Connie felt he must have forgotten the morning. He had not forgotten. But he knew where he was—in the same old place outside, where the born outsiders were. He didn't take the love-making altogether personally. He knew it would not change him from an ownerless dog whom everybody begrudges his golden collar, into a comfortable society dog.

The final fact being that at the very bottom of his soul he *was* an outsider, and anti-social, and he accepted the fact inwardly, no matter how Bond-streety he was on the outside. His isolation was a necessity to him: just as the *appearance* of conformity and mixing-in with the smart people was also a necessity.

But occasional love, as a comfort and soothing, was also a good thing, and he was not ungrateful. On the contrary, he was burningly, poignantly grateful for a bit of natural spontaneous kindness: almost to tears. Beneath his pale, immobile, disillusioned face his child's soul was sobbing with gratitude to the woman, and burning to come to her again: just as his outcast soul was knowing he would keep *really* clear of her.

He found an opportunity to say to her, as they were lighting the candles in the hall:

"May I come?"

"I'll come to you," she said.

"Oh good!"

He waited for her a long time—but she came. He was the trembling, excited sort of lover whose crisis soon came, and was finished. There was something curiously childlike and defenceless about his naked body: as children are naked. His defences were all in his wits and his cunning, his very instincts of cunning, and when these were in abeyance, he seemed so doubly naked and like a child, of unfinished, tender flesh, and somehow, struggling helplessly.

He roused in the woman a wild sort of compassion and yearning, and a wild, craving physical desire. This physical desire he did not satisfy in her: he was always come, and finished, so quickly: then shrinking down on her breast, and recovering somewhat his effrontery, while she lay dazed, disappointed, lost.

But then she learnt soon to hold him, to keep him there inside her when his crisis was over. And there he was generous and curiously potent: he stayed firm inside her, given to her, while she was active, wildly, passionately active, coming to her own crisis. And as he felt the frenzy of her achieving her own orgiastic satisfaction from his hard, erect passivity, he had a curious sense of pride and satisfaction.

"Ah, how good!" she whispered tremulously: and she became quite still, clinging to him. And he lay there in his own isolation, but somehow, proud.

He stayed that time only the three days, and to Clifford was exactly the same as on the first evening, to Connie also. There was no breaking down his external man.

He wrote to Connie, with the same plaintive melancholy note as ever, sometimes witty, and touched with a queer sexless affection. A kind of hopeless affection he seemed to feel for her: and the essential remoteness remained the same. He was hopeless at the very core of him, and he wanted to be hopeless. He rather hated hope. "Une immense espérance a traversé la terre," he read somewhere, and his comment was: "and it's darned-well drowned everything worth having."

Connie never understood him. But in her way, she loved him. And all the time she felt the reflection of his hopelessness in her. She couldn't quite, quite love in hopelessness. And he, being hopeless, couldn't ever quite love at all.

So they went on for quite a time, writing, and meeting occasionally in London. She still wanted the physical, sexual thrill she could get with him, by her own activity, his little orgasm being over. And he still wanted to give it her. Which was enough to keep them connected.

And enough to give her a subtle sort of self-assurance, something blind and a little arrogant. It was an almost mechanical confidence in her own prowess, and went with a great cheerfulness.

She was terrifically cheerful at Wragby. And she used all her roused alertness and satisfaction to stimulate Clifford, so that he wrote his best at this time, and was almost happy, in his queer blind way. He really reaped the fruits of the sensual satisfaction she got out of Michaelis' male passivity erect inside her. But of course, he never knew it, and if he had, he wouldn't have said thank-you!

Yet when those days of her grand joyful cheerfulness and stimulus were gone, quite gone, and she was depressed or irritable, how Clifford longed for them again! Perhaps if he'd known, he might even have wished to get her and Michaelis together again.

CHAPTER IV.

Connie always had a foreboding of the hopelessness of her affair with Mick, as people called him. Yet other men seemed to mean nothing to her. She was attached to Clifford. He wanted a good deal of her life, and she gave it him. But she wanted a good deal from the life of a man, and this Clifford did not give her: could not. There were occasional spasms of Michaelis. But, as she knew by foreboding, that would come to an end. Mick *couldn't* keep anything up. It was part of his very being, that he must break off any connection, and be loose, isolated, absolutely lone dog again. It was his major necessity: even though he always said: She turned me down!

The world is supposed to be full of possibilities, but they narrow down to pretty few, in most personal experience. There's lots of good fish in the sea—maybe! But the vast masses seem to be mackerel or herring, and if you're not mackerel or herring yourself, you are inclined to find very few good fish in the sea.

Clifford was making strides into fame: and even money. People came to see him. Connie nearly always had somebody at Wragby. But if they weren't mackerel they were herring, with an occasional cat-fish or conger eel.

But there were a few regular men, constants: men who had been at Cambridge with Clifford. There was Tommy Dukes, who had remained in the army, and was a Brigadier-General. "The army leaves me time to think, and saves me from having to face the battle of life," he said. There was Charles May, an Irishman, who wrote scientifically about stars. There was Hammond, another writer. All were about the same age as Clifford, the young intellectuals of the day. They all believed in the life of the mind, and keeping pure the integrity of the mind. What you did apart from that was your private affair, and didn't much matter. No one thinks of enquiring of another person, at what hour he retires to the privy. It isn't interesting to anyone but the person concerned.

And so with most of the matters of ordinary life—how you make your money, or whether you love your wife, or if you have "affairs."

All these matters concern only the person concerned, and, like going to the privy, have no interest for anybody else.

"The whole point about the sexual problem," said Hammond, who was a tall thin fellow with a wife and two children, but much more closely connected with a type-writer, "is that there is no point to it. Strictly, there is no problem. We don't want to follow a man into the W. C. So why should we want to follow him into bed with a woman? And therein lies the problem. If we took no more notice of the one thing than the other, there'd *be* no problem. It's all utterly senseless and pointless: a matter of misplaced curiosity."

"Quite, Hammond, quite! But if some-one starts making love to Julia, you begin to simmer; and if he goes on, you are soon at boiling-point."—Julia was Hammond's wife.

"Why exactly! So I should be if he began to urinate in a corner of my drawing-room. There's a place for all these things."

"You mean you wouldn't mind if he made love to Julia in some discreet alcove?"

Charlie May was slightly satirical, for he had flirted a very little with Julia, and Hammond had cut up very rough.

"Of course I should mind. Sex is a private thing between me and Julia: of course I mind anyone else trying to mix in."

"As a matter of fact," said the lean and freckled Tommy Dukes: he looked much more Irish than May, who was pale and father fat: "As a matter of fact, Hammond, you have a strong property instinct, and a strong will to self-assertion, and you want success. Since I've been in the army, definitely, I've got out of the way of the world, and now I see how inordinately strong the craving for self-assertion and success is in men. It is enormously overdeveloped. All our individuality has run that way. And of course men like you think you'll get through better with a woman's backing. That's why you're so jealous. That's what sex is to you—a vital little dynamo between you and Julia, to bring success. If you began to be unsuccessful you'd begin to flirt—like Charlie, who isn't successful. Married people like you and Julia have labels on you, like a traveller's trunk. Julia is labelled *Mrs Arnold B. Hammond*—just like a trunk on the railway that belongs to somebody. And you are labelled: *Arnold B. Hammond c/o Mrs Arnold B. Hammond.*—Oh, you're quite right, you're quite right! The life of the mind needs a comfortable house and decent cooking. You're quite right. It even needs posterity. But it all hinges on the instinct for success. That is the pivot on which all things turn."

Hammond looked rather piqued. He was rather proud of the integrity of his mind, and of his *not* being a time-server. None the less, he did want success.

"It's quite true, you can't live without cash," said May. "You've got to have a certain amount of it, to be able to live and get along—even to be free to *think*, you must have a certain *amount* of money, or your stomach stops you.—But it seems to me, you might leave the labels off sex. We're free to talk to anybody: so why shouldn't we be free to make love to any woman who inclines us that way?"

"There speaks the lascivious Celt," said Clifford.

"Lascivious! well, why not? I can't see I do a woman any more harm by sleeping with her than by dancing with her—or even talking to her about the weather. It's just an interchange of sensation instead of ideas—so why not?"

"Be as promiscuous as the rabbits!" said Hammond.

"Why not? What's wrong with rabbits? Are they any worse than a neurotic, revolutionary humanity full of nervous hate?"

"But we are not rabbits, even then," said Hammond.

"Precisely! I have my mind: I have certain calculations to make in certain astronomical matters that concern me almost more than life and death. Sometimes, indigestion interferes with me. Hunger would interfere with me disastrously. In the same way, starved sex interferes with me. What then?"

"I should have thought sexual indigestion from surfeit would have interfered with you more seriously," said Hammond satirically.

"Not it! I don't over-eat myself, and I don't over-fuck myself. One has a choice about eating too much. But you would absolutely starve me."

"Not at all! You can marry."

"How do you know I can? It may not suit the processes of my mind. Marriage might—and would—stultify my mental processes. I'm not property-pivoted that way.—And so I must be chained in a kennel like a monk?—All rot, and funk, my boy. I must live and do my calculations. I need women sometimes. I refuse to make a mountain of it, and I refuse anybody's moral condemnation or prohibition. I'd be ashamed to see a woman walking round with my name-label on her, address and railway station, like a wardrobe trunk—"

These two men had not forgiven each other about the Julia flirtation.

"It's an amusing idea, Charlie," said Dukes, "that sex is just another form of talk, where you act the words instead of saying them.—I suppose it's quite true. I suppose we might exchange as many sensations and emotions with women as we do ideas about the weather and so on. Sex might be a sort of normal physical conversation between a man and a woman. You don't talk to a woman unless you've ideas in common: that is, you don't talk with any interest. And the same way, unless you had some emotion or sympathy in common with a woman, you wouldn't sleep with her. But if you *had*—"

"If you *have* the proper sort of emotion or sympathy with a woman, you *ought* to sleep with her," said May. "It's the only decent thing, to go to bed with her. Just as, when you are interested talking to a woman, the only decent thing is to have the talk out. You don't prudishly put your tongue between your teeth and bite it. You just say out your say.—And the same the other way."

"No," said Hammond. "It's wrong. You, for example, May, you squander half your force with women. You'll never really do what you should do, with a fine mind such as yours. Too much of you goes the other way."

"Maybe it does.—And too *little* of you goes that way, Hammond my boy, married or not. You can keep the purity and integrity of your mind, but it's going damned dry. Your pure mind is going as dry as fiddlesticks, from what I see of it. You're simply salting it down."

Tommy Dukes burst into a laugh.

"Go it, you two minds!" he said. "Look at me—I don't do any high and pure mental work, nothing but jot down a few ideas. And yet I neither marry nor run after women. I think Charlie's quite right: if he wants to run after the women, he's quite free not to run too fast nor too often: but I wouldn't prohibit him from running. As for Hammond, he's got a property instinct, so naturally the straight road and the narrow gate are right for him. You'll see he'll be an English man of letters before he's done, A B C from top to toe. Then there's me, I'm nothing: just a squib. And what about you, Clifford? Do you think sex is a dynamo to help a man on to success in the world?"

Clifford rarely talked much at these times. He never held forth: his ideas were not vital enough to him, he was really too confused and emotional. Now he blushed and looked uncomfortable.

"Well!" he said. "Being myself *hors de combat*, I don't see I've anything to say on the matter."

"Not at all!" said Dukes. "The top of you's by no means *hors de combat*. You've got the life of the mind, sound and intact. So let us hear your idea."

"Well!" stammered Clifford. "Even then, I don't suppose I have much idea.—I suppose marry-and-have-done-with-it would pretty well stand for what I think. Though of course, between a man and a woman who care for one another, it is a great thing."

"What sort of a great thing?" said Tommy.

"Oh—it perfects the intimacy," said Clifford, uneasy as a woman in such talk.

"Well, Charlie and I believe that sex is a sort of communication like speech, and should be as free as speech. Let any woman start a sexual conversation with me, and it's natural for me to go to bed with her, to finish it: all in due season.—Unfortunately no woman makes any particular start with me, so I go to bed by myself; and am none the worse for it—I hope so, anyhow, for how should I know? Anyhow I've no starry calculations to be interfered with, and no immortal works to write. I'm merely a fellow skulking in the army—"

Silence fell. The four men smoked. And Connie sat there and put another stitch in her sewing.—Yes, she sat there! She had to sit mum. She had to be quiet as a mouse, not to interfere with the immensely important speculations of these highly-mental gentlemen. But she had to be there. They didn't get on so well without her. Their ideas didn't flow so freely. Clifford was much more hedgey and nervous, he got cold feet much quicker, in Connie's absence, and the talk didn't run. Tommy Dukes came off best. He was a little inspired by her presence. Hammond she didn't really like: he seemed so selfish in a mental way. And Charles May, though she liked something about him, seemed a little distasteful and messy, in spite of his stars.

How many evenings had Connie sat and listened to the manifestations of these four men: these and one or two others! That they never seemed to get anywhere didn't trouble her deeply. She liked to hear what they had to say, especially when Tommy was there. It was fun. Instead of men kissing you and touching you with their bodies, they revealed their minds to you. It was great fun. But what cold minds!

And also, it was a little irritating. She had more respect for Michaelis, on whose name they all poured such withering contempt, as a little mongrel *arriviste* and uneducated bounder of the worst sort. Mongrel and bounder or not, he jumped to his own conclusions. He didn't merely walk round them with millions of words, in the parade of the life of the mind.

Connie quite liked the life of the mind, and got a great thrill out of it. But she did think it overdid itself a little. She loved being there amid the tobacco-smoke of those famous evenings of the cronies, as she called them privately to herself. She was infinitely amused and proud too, that even their talking they couldn't do without her silent presence. She had an immense respect for thought—and these men at least tried to think honestly. But somehow, there was a cat and it wouldn't jump. They all alike balked at something: though what it was, for the life of her she couldn't say. It was something that Mick didn't clear, either.

But then Mick wasn't trying to do anything but just get through his life and put as much over other people as they tried to put over him. He was really anti-social. Which was what Clifford and his cronies had against him. Clifford and his cronies were not anti-social: they were more or less bent on saving mankind: or on *instructing* it, to say the least.

There was a gorgeous talk on Sunday evening, when the conversation drifted again to love.

" 'Blest be the tie that binds

Our hearts in kindred something-or-other,' "
said Tommy Dukes. "I'd like to know what the tie is!—The tie that binds *us* just now, is mental friction on one another: and apart from that, there's damned little tie between us. We bust apart and say spiteful things about one another, like all the other damned intellectuals in the world. Damned everybodies, as far as that goes, for they all do it. Or else we bust apart and cover up the spiteful things we feel against one another by saying false sugaries. It's a curious thing, that the mental life seems to flourish with its roots in spite, ineffable and fathomless spite. Always has been so! Look at Socrates in Plato, and his bunch round him! The sheer spite of it all, just sheer joy in pulling somebody else to pieces—Protagoras or whoever it was! And Alcibiades and all the other little disciple dogs joining in the fray! I must say, it makes one prefer Buddha quietly sitting under a bho-tree, or Jesus telling his disciples little Sunday stories, peacefully and without any mental fireworks. No, there's something wrong with the mental life, radically. It's rooted in spite and envy, envy and spite. Ye shall know the tree by its fruit."

"I don't think we're altogether so spiteful," protested Clifford.

"My dear Clifford, *think* of the way we talk each other over—*all* of us. I'm rather worse than anybody else, myself. Because I infinitely prefer the spontaneous spite to the concocted sugaries: now they *are* poison: when I begin saying what a fine fellow Clifford is, etc. etc. then poor Clifford is to be pitied. For God's sake, all of you, say spiteful things about me, then I shall know I mean something to you. Don't say sugaries, or I'm done."

"Oh, but I *do* think we honestly like one another," protested Hammond.

"I tell you—we must! We say such spiteful things to one another about one another, behind our backs! I'm the worst."

"And I do think you confuse the mental life with the critical activity. I agree with you, Socrates started the critical activity with a grand start. But he did more than that," said Charlie May rather magisterially. The cronies had such a curious pomposity under their assumed modesty. It was all so *ex cathedra*, and it all pretended to be so humble.

Dukes refused to be drawn about Socrates.

"That's quite true, criticism and knowledge are not the same thing," said Hammond.

"They aren't, of course," chimed in Berry, a brown, shy young man who had called to see Dukes, and was staying the night.

They all looked at him as if the ass had spoken.

"I wasn't talking about knowledge—I was talking about the mental life," laughed Dukes. "Real knowledge comes out of the whole corpus of the consciousness, out of your belly and your penis as much as out of your brain or mind. The mind can only analyse and rationalise.—Set the mind and the reason to cock it over the rest, and all they can do is to criticise and make a deadness. I say *all* they can do. It is vastly important. My God, the world needs criticising today—criticising to death. Therefore let's live the mental life and glory in our spite, and strip the rotten old show.—But mind you, it's like this. While you *live* your life, you are in some way an organic whole with all life. But once you start the mental life, you pluck the apple. You've severed the connection between the apple and the tree: the organic connection. And if you've got nothing in your life *but* the mental life, then you yourself are a plucked apple, you've fallen off the tree. And then it is a logical necessity to be spiteful, just as it's a natural necessity for a plucked apple to go bad."

Clifford made big eyes; it was all stuff to him. Connie secretly laughed to herself.

"Well, then we're all plucked apples," said Hammond, rather acidly and petulantly.

"So let's make cider of ourselves," said Charlie.

"But what do you think of bolshevism?" put in the brown Berry, as if everything had led up to it.

"Bravo!" roared Charlie May. "What do you think of bolshevism?"

"Come on, let's make hay of bolshevism—!" said Dukes.

"I'm afraid bolshevism is a large question," said Hammond, shaking his head seriously.

"Bolshevism, it seems to me," said Charlie, "is just a superlative hatred of the thing they call the bourgeois: and what the bourgeois is, isn't quite defined. It is Capitalism, among other things. Feelings and emotions also are so decidedly bourgeois that you have to invent a man without them. Then the individual, especially the *personal* man, is bourgeois: so he must be suppressed. You must submerge yourselves in the greater thing, the soviet-social thing. Even an organism is bourgeois: so the ideal must be mechanical. The only thing that is a unit, non-organic, composed of many different yet equally-essential parts, is the machine. Each man a machine-part, and the driving power of the machine, hate: hate of the bourgeois! That, to me, is bolshevism."

"Absolutely!" said Tommy. "But also, it seems to me a perfect description of the whole of the industrial ideal. It's the factory-owner's ideal in a nutshell: except that he would deny that the driving power was hate. Hate it is, all the same: hate of life itself. Just look at these Midlands, if it isn't plainly written up.—But it's all part of the life of the mind—it is a logical development."

"I deny that bolshevism is logical, it rejects the biggest part of the premisses," said Hammond.

"My dear man, it allows the material premiss. So does the pure mind—exclusively."

"At least bolshevism has got down to rock bottom," said Charlie.

"Rock bottom! The bottom that has no bottom! The bolshevists will have the finest army in the world, in a very short time, with the finest mechanical equipment."

"But this thing can't go on—this hate business. There *must* be a reaction—" said Hammond.

"Well—we've been waiting ten years—we can wait longer. Hate's a growing thing like anything else. It's the inevitable outcome of forcing ideas on to life, of forcing one's deepest instincts. Our deepest instincts, our deepest feelings we force according to certain ideas. We drive ourselves with a formula, like a machine. The logical mind pretends to rule the roost, and the roost turns into pure hate. We're all bolshevists, only we are hypocrites. The Russians are bolshevists without hypocrisy."

"But there are many other ways," said Hammond, "than the Soviet way. The bolshevists aren't really intelligent."

"Of course not. But sometimes it's intelligent to be half-witted: if you want to make your end. Personally, I consider bolshevism half-witted. But so I consider our social life in the west: half-witted. So I even consider our far-famed mental life: half-witted. We're all as cold as cretins: we're all as passionless as idiots.—We're all of us bolshevists—only we give it another name. We think we're gods—men like gods! It's just the same as bolshevism. One has to be human, and have a heart and a penis, if one is going to escape being either a god or a bolshevist—for they are the same thing: they're both too good to be true."

Out of the disapproving silence came Berry's anxious question:

"You do believe in love, then, Tommy, don't you?"

"You lovely lad!" said Tommy. "No, my cherub, nine times out of ten, no! Love's another of those half-witted performances, today. Fellows with swaying waists fucking little jazz girls with small boy buttocks like two collar-studs? Do you mean that sort of love? Or the joint-property, make-a-success-of-it, my-husband, my-wife sort of love? No my fine fellow, I don't believe in it at all!"

"But you do believe in something."

"Me! Oh, intellectually, I believe in having a good heart, a chirpy penis, a lively intelligence, and the courage to say shit! in front of a lady."

"Well, you've got them all," said Berry.

Tommy Dukes roared with laughter.

"You angel boy! If only I had! If only I had! No, my heart's as numb as a potato, my penis droops and never lifts his head up, I dare rather cut him clean off than say shit! in front of my mother or my aunt—they are *real* ladies, mind you; and I'm not really intelligent, I'm only a mental-lifer. It would be wonderful to be intelligent: then one would be alive in all the parts mentioned and unmentionable.

The penis rouses his head and says: How do you do! to any really intelligent person. Renoir said he painted his pictures with his penis—he did too, lovely pictures. I wish I did something with mine. God, when one can only talk! another torture added to Hades! And Socrates started it."

"There are nice women in the world," said Connie, lifting her head up and speaking at last.

The men resented it: she should have pretended to hear nothing. They hated her admitting she had attended closely to such talk.

"My God! If they be not nice to me
        What care I how nice they be!—
No, it's hopeless! I just simply can't vibrate in unison with a woman. There's no woman I can really want, when I'm faced with her. And I'm not going to start forcing myself to it—my God! I'll remain as I am, and live the mental life. It's the only honest thing I can do. I can be quite happy *talking* to women: I like women: but it is all pure, hopelessly pure. Hopelessly pure!—What do you say, Hildebrand my chicken?"

"It's much less complicated if one stays pure," said Berry.

"Yes! Life is all too simple!"

CHAPTER V.

On a frosty morning with a little February sun Clifford and Connie went for a walk across the park to the wood. That is, Clifford chuffed in his motor-chair, and Connie walked beside him.

The hard air was still sulphureous, but they were both used to it. Round the near horizon went the haze, opalescent with frost and smoke, and on top lay the small blue sky: so that it was like being inside an enclosure, always inside. Life either a dream or a frenzy, inside an enclosure.

The sheep coughed in the rough sere grass of the park, where frost lay bluish in the sockets of the tufts. Across the park ran a path to the wood gate, a fine ribbon of pink. Clifford had had it newly gravelled with sifted gravel from the pit-bank. When the rock and refuse of the underworld had burned and given off its sulphur, it turned bright pink, shrimp-coloured on dry days, darker, crab-coloured on wet. Now it was pale shrimp colour, with a bluish-white hoar of frost. It always pleased Connie, this underfoot of sifted bright pink.—It's an ill wind that brings no-body any good.

Clifford steered cautiously down the slope of the knoll from the hall, and Connie kept her hand on the chair. In front lay the wood, the hazel thicket nearest, the purplish density of oaks beyond. From the wood's edge rabbits bobbed and nibbled. Rooks suddenly rose in a black train, and went trailing off over the little sky.

Connie opened the wood gate, and Clifford puffed slowly through, into the broad riding that ran up an incline between the clean-whipped thickets of the hazel. The wood was a remnant from the great forest where Robin Hood hunted, and this riding was an old, old thoroughfare coming across-country. But now, of course, it was only a riding through the private wood. The road from Mansfield swerved round to the north.

In the wood, everything was motionless, the old leaves on the ground keeping the frost on their under-side. A jay called harshly; many little birds fluttered. But there was no game—no pheasants. They had been killed off during the war, and the wood had been left unprotected, till now Clifford had got his gamekeeper again.

Clifford loved the wood. He loved the old oak trees. He felt they were his own through generations. He wanted to protect them. He wanted this place inviolate, shut off from the world.

The chair chuffed slowly up the incline, rocking and jolting on the frozen clods. And suddenly on the left came a clearing, where was nothing but a ravel of dead bracken, a thin and spindly sapling leaning ricketty here and there, big sawn stumps showing their tops and their grasping roots, lifeless: and patches of blackness where the woodmen had burned the brushwood and rubbish.

This was one of the places that Sir Geoffrey had cut during the war, for trench timber. The whole knoll, which rose softly on the right of the riding, was denuded and strangely forlorn. On the crown of the knoll where the oaks had stood, now was bareness: and from there you could look out over the trees, to the colliery railway and the new works at Stacks Gate. Connie had stood and looked: it was a breach in the pure seclusion of the wood. It let in the world. But she didn't tell Clifford.

This denuded place always made Clifford curiously angry. He had been through the war, had seen what it meant. But he didn't get really angry till he saw this bare hill. He was having it re-planted. But it made him hate Sir Geoffrey.

Clifford sat with a fixed face, as the chair slowly mounted. When they came to the top of the rise he stopped: he would not risk the long and very jolty down-slope. He sat looking at the greenish sweep of the riding downwards, a clear way through the bracken and oaks. It swerved at the bottom of the hill, and disappeared. But it had such a lovely easy curve, of knights riding and ladies on palfreys.

"I consider this is really the heart of England," said Clifford to Connie, as he sat there in the dim February sunshine.

"Do you!" she said, seating herself in her blue knitted dress on a stump by the path.

"I do! This is the old England, the heart of it: and I intend to keep it intact."

"Oh yes!" said Connie. But as she said it, she heard the eleven-o'clock blower at Stacks Gate colliery. Clifford was too used to the sound to notice.

"I want this wood perfect—untouched. I want *nobody* to trespass in it," said Clifford.

There was a certain pathos. The wood still had some of the mystery of wild old England. But Sir Geoffrey's cuttings during the war had given it a blow. How still the trees were, with their crinkly innumerable twigs against the sky, and their grey, hoary, obstinate trunks rising from the brown bracken. How safely the birds flitted among them! And once there had been deer, and archers: and monks padding along on asses. The place remembered, still remembered.

Clifford sat in the pale sun, with the light on his smooth, rather blond hair, his reddish full face inscrutable.

"I mind more, not having a son, when I come here, than any other time," he said.

"But the wood is older than your family," said Connie gently.

It was. Chatterleys were only two hundred years at Wragby.

"Quite!" said Clifford. "But we've preserved it. But for us, it would go: it would be gone already, like the rest of the forest. One *must* preserve some of the old England!"

"Must one!" said Connie. "If it has to be preserved, and preserved against the new England? It's sad, I know."

"If some of the old England isn't preserved, there'll be no England at all," said Clifford. "And we who have this kind of property, and the feeling for it, must preserve it."

There was a sad pause.

"Yes, for a little while," said Connie.

"For a little while! It is all we can do. We can only do our bit. I feel every man of my family has done his bit, here, since we've had the place. One may go against convention, but one must keep up the tradition."

Again there was a pause.

"What tradition?" said Connie.

"The tradition of England! Of this!"

"Yes!" she said slowly.

"That's why having a son helps. One is only a link in a chain," he said.

Connie was not keen on chains, but she said nothing. She was thinking of the curious impersonality of his desire for a son.

"I'm sorry we can't have a son," she said.

He looked at her slowly, with his full, pale-blue eyes.

"It would almost be a good thing if you had a child by another man," he said. "If we brought it up at Wragby, it would belong to us and to the place. I don't believe very intensely in fatherhood. If we had the child to rear, it would be our own. And it would carry on. Don't you think it's worth considering?"

Connie looked up at him at last. The child, her child, was just an "it" to him. It—it—it!

"But what about the other man?" she asked.

"*Does* it matter very much? Do those things really affect us very deeply?—You had that lover in Germany—what is it now? Nothing, almost! It seems to me it isn't these little acts and little connections we make in our lives, that matter so very much. They pass away, and where are they? Where are the snows of yesteryear?—It is what endures through one's life, that matters: my own life matters to me, in its long continuance and development. But what do the occasional connections matter? And the occasional sexual connections especially! If people don't exaggerate them ridiculously, they pass like the mating of birds. And so they should. What does it matter! It's the life-long companionship that matters. It's the living together from day to day, not the sleeping together once or twice. You and I are married, no matter what happens to us. We have the habit of each other. And habit, to my thinking, is more vital than any occasional excitement. The long, slow, enduring thing—that's what we live by—not any occasional spasm of any sort. Little by little, living together, two people fall into a sort of unison, they vibrate so intricately on one another. That's the real secret of marriage, not sex: at least, not the simple function of sex. You and I are interwoven in a marriage. If we stick to that, we ought to be able to arrange this sex thing as we arrange going to the dentist: since fate has given us a check-mate physically there."

Connie sat and listened in a sort of wonder, and a sort of fear. She did not know if he was right or not. There was Michaelis, whom she loved: so she said to herself. But her love was somehow only an excursion from her marriage with Clifford: the long slow habit of intimacy formed through five years of suffering and patience. Perhaps the human soul needs excursions, and must not be denied them. But the point of an excursion is that you come home again.

"And wouldn't you mind *what* man's child I had?" she asked.

"Why Connie, I should trust your natural instinct of decency and selection. You just wouldn't let the wrong sort of fellow touch you."

She thought of Michaelis! He was absolutely Clifford's idea of the wrong sort of fellow.

"But men and women may have different feelings about the wrong sort of fellow," she said.

"No," he replied. "You cared for me. I don't believe you'd ever care for a man who was purely antipathetic to me. Your rhythm wouldn't let you."

She was silent. Logic might be unanswerable, because it was so absolutely wrong.

"And should you expect me to tell you?" she asked, glancing up at him almost furtively.

"Not at all. I'd better not know.—But you do agree with me, don't you, that the casual sex thing is nothing, compared to a long life lived together? Don't you think one can just subordinate the sex thing to the necessities of a long life. Just use it, since that's what we're driven to? After all, *do* these temporary excitements matter? Isn't the whole problem of life the slow building up of an integral personality through the years? living an integrated life? There's no point in a disintegrated life. If lack of sex is going to disintegrate you, then go out and have a love affair. If lack of a child is going to disintegrate you, then have a child if you possibly can. But you only do these things so that you may have an integrated life, that makes a long harmonious thing. And you and I can do that together—don't you think?—if we adapt ourselves to the necessities and at the same time weave the adaptation together into a piece with our steadily-lived life. Don't you agree?"

Connie was a little overwhelmed with his words. She knew he was right, theoretically. But when she actually touched her steadily-lived life with him, she—hesitated. Was it actually her destiny to go on weaving herself into his life all the rest of her life? Nothing else?

Was it just that? She was to be content to weave a steady life with him, all one fabric, but perhaps brocaded with an occasional coloured flower of an adventure.—But how could she know how she would feel next year? How could one ever know? How could one say yes! for years and years? The little yes!, gone on a breath! Why should one be pinned down by that butterfly word? Of course it had to flutter away, and be gone, to be followed by other yeses! and no's! Like the straying of butterflies.

"I think you're right, Clifford. And as far as I can see I agree with you. Only life may turn quite a new face on it all."

"But until life turns a new face on it all, you do agree?"

"Oh, yes! I think I do—really!"

She was watching a brown spaniel that had run out of a side-path, and was looking towards them with lifted nose, making a soft, fluffy bark. A man with a gun strode swiftly, softly out after the dog, facing their way, as if about to attack them; then stopped instead, saluted, and was turning downhill. It was only the new gamekeeper, but he had frightened Connie, he seemed to emerge with such a swift menace. That was how she had seen him, like a sudden rush of a threat out of nowhere.

He was a man in dark green velveteens and gaiters—the old style—with a red face and red moustache, and distant eyes. He was going quickly downhill.

"Mellors!" said Clifford.

The man faced lightly round, and saluted with a swift little gesture: a soldier!

"Will you turn the chair round and get it started. That makes it easier," said Clifford.

The man at once slung his gun over his shoulder, and came forward, with the same curious swift, yet soft movements, as if keeping invisible. He was moderately tall, and lean; and silent. He did not look at Connie, only at the chair.

"Connie, this is the new gamekeeper Mellors. You haven't spoken to her ladyship yet, Mellors?"

"No Sir!" came the ready, neutral words.

The man lifted his hat as he stood, showing his thick, almost fair hair. He was almost handsome without a hat. He stared straight into Connie's eyes with a perfectly fearless, impersonal look, as if he wanted to see what she was like. He made her feel shy. She bent her head to him shyly, and he changed his hat to his left hand, and made her a slight bow, like a gentleman; but he said nothing at all. He remained for a moment still with his hat in his hand.

"But you've been here some time, haven't you?" Connie said to him.

"Eight months, Madam—your ladyship!" he corrected himself calmly.

"And do you like it?"

She looked him in the eyes. His eyes narrowed a little, with irony, perhaps with impudence.

"Why yes, thank you, your ladyship! I was reared here—"

He gave another slight bow, turned, put his hat on, and strode to take hold of the chair. His voice, on the last words, had fallen into the heavy broad drag of the dialect—perhaps also in mockery, because there had been no trace of dialect before. He might almost be a gentleman. Anyhow he was a curious, quick, separate fellow, alone but sure of himself.

Clifford started the little engine, the man carefully turned the chair and set it nose-forwards to the incline that curved gently to the dark hazel thicket.

"Is that all then, Sir Clifford?" said the man.

"No! You'd better come along, for fear she sticks. The engine isn't really strong enough for the uphill work."

The man glanced round for his dog—a quick, thoughtful glance. The spaniel looked at him and faintly moved her tail. A little smile, mocking or teasing her, yet gentle, came into his eyes for a moment, then faded away and his face was expressionless. They went fairly quickly down the slope, the man with his hand on the rail of the chair, steadying it. He looked like a free soldier rather than a servant. And something about him reminded Connie of Tommy Dukes.

When they came to the hazel grove Connie suddenly ran forward and opened the gate into the park. As she stood holding it, the two men looked at her in passing, Clifford critically, the other man with a curious cool wonder: impersonally wanting to see what she looked like. And she saw in his blue, impersonal eyes a look of suffering and detachment, yet a certain warmth. But why was he so aloof, apart?

Clifford stopped the chair, once through the gate, and the man came quickly, courteously, to close it.

"Why did you run to open?" said Clifford, in his quiet calm voice that showed he was displeased. "Mellors would have done it."

"I thought you could go straight ahead," said Connie.

"And leave you to run after us?" said Clifford.

"Oh well, I like to run sometimes!"

Mellors took the chair again, looking perfectly unheeding. Yet Connie felt he noted everything. As he pushed the chair up the steepish rise of the knoll in the park, he breathed rather quickly through parted lips. He was rather frail, really. Curiously full of vitality, but a little frail, and quenched. Her woman's instinct sensed it.

Connie fell back, let the chair go on. The day had greyed over: the small blue sky that had poised low on its circular rims of haze was closed in again, the lid was down, there was a raw coldness. It was going to snow. All grey, all grey! The world looked worn out.

The chair waited at the top of the pink path. Clifford looked round for Connie.

"Not tired, are you?" he asked.

"Oh no!" she said.

But she was. A strange, weary yearning, a dissatisfaction had started in her. Clifford did not notice: those were not things he was aware of. But the stranger knew. To Connie, everything in her world and life seemed worn out, and her dissatisfaction was older than the hills.

They came to the house, and round to the back, where there were no steps. Clifford managed to swing himself over on to a low, wheeled house-chair: he was very strong and agile with his arms. Then Connie lifted his burden of dead legs after him.

The keeper, waiting at attention to be dismissed, watched everything narrowly, missing nothing. He went pale, with a sort of fear, when he saw Connie lifting the inert legs of the man in her arms, into the other chair, Clifford pivoting round as she did so. He was frightened.

"Thanks then for the help, Mellors," said Clifford casually, as he began to wheel down the passage through the servants' quarters.

"Nothing else, Sir?" came the neutral voice, like one in a dream.

"Nothing. Good morning."

"Good-morning Sir."

"Good morning! It was kind of you to push the chair up that hill—I hope it wasn't heavy for you," said Connie, looking back at the keeper outside the door.

His eyes came to hers in an instant, as if he wakened up. He was aware of her.

"Oh no, not heavy!" he said quickly. Then his voice dropped again into the broad sound of the vernacular: "Good mornin' to your ladyship!"

"Who is your gamekeeper?" Connie asked at lunch.

"Mellors! You saw him," said Clifford.

"Yes! But where did he come from?"

"Nowhere! He was a Tevershall boy—son of a collier, I believe."

"And was he a collier himself?"

"Blacksmith on the pit-bank, I believe: overhead smith. But he was keeper here for two years before the war—before he joined up. My father always had a good opinion of him, so when he came back and went to the pit for a blacksmith's job, I just took him back here as keeper. I was really very glad to get him—it's almost impossible to find a good man round here, for a gamekeeper—and it needs a man who knows the people."

"And isn't he married?"

"He was! But the wife went off with—with various men—but finally with a collier at Stacks Gate, and I believe she's living there still."

"So this man is alone?"

"More or less! He has a mother in the village—and a child, I believe."

Clifford looked at Connie with his pale, slightly prominent blue eyes, in which a certain vagueness was coming. He seemed alert in the foreground, but the background was like the Midlands atmosphere, haze, smoky mist. And the haze seemed to be creeping forward. So when he stared at Connie in his peculiar way, giving her his peculiarly precise information, she felt all the background of his mind filling up with mist, with nothingness. And it frightened her. It made him seem impersonal almost to idiocy.

And dimly she realised one of the great laws of the human soul: that when the emotional soul receives a wounding shock, which does not kill the body, the soul seems to recover as the body recovers. But this is only appearance. It is, really, only the mechanism of re-assumed habit. Slowly, slowly the wound to the soul begins to make itself felt, like a bruise which only slowly deepens its terrible ache, till it fills all the psyche. And when we think we have recovered and forgotten, it is then that the terrible after-effects have to be encountered at their worst.

So it was with Clifford. Once he was "well," once he was back at Wragby, and writing his stories and feeling sure of life in spite of all, he seemed to forget, and to have recovered all his equanimity. But now, as the years went by, slowly, slowly Connie felt the bruise of fear and horror coming up and spreading in him. For a time it had been so deep as to be numb, as it were, non-existent. Now slowly it began to assert itself, in a spread of fear, almost paralysis. Mentally, he still was alert. But the paralysis, the bruise of the too-great shock was gradually spreading in his affective self.

And as it spread in him, Connie felt it spread in her. An inward dread, an emptiness, an indifference to everything gradually spread in her soul. When Clifford was roused, he could still talk brilliantly and, as it were, command the future: as when, in the wood, he talked about her having a child and giving him an heir to Wragby. But the day after, all the brilliant words seemed like dead leaves, crumpling up and turning to powder, meaning really nothing, blown away on any gust of wind. They were not the leafy words of an effective life, young with energy and belonging to the tree. They were the hosts of fallen leaves of a life that is ineffectual.

So it seemed to her everywhere. The colliers at Tevershall were talking again of a strike. And it seemed to Connie there again, it was not a manifestation of energy, it was the bruise of the war, that had been in abeyance, slowly rising to the surface and creating the great ache of unrest, the stupor of discontent. The bruise was deep, deep, deep—the bruise of the false and inhuman war. It would take many years for the living blood of the generations to dissolve the vast black clot of bruised blood, deep inside their souls and bodies. And it would need a new hope.

Poor Connie! As the years drew on, it was the fear of nothingness in her life that affected her. Clifford's mental life, and hers—gradually it began to feel like nothingness. Their marriage, their integrated life based on a habit of intimacy, that he talked about: there were days when it all became utterly blank and nothing. It was words, just so many words. The only reality was nothingness, and over it, a hypocrisy of words.

There was Clifford's success: the bitch-goddess! It was true, he was almost famous, and his last book brought him in a thousand pounds. His photograph appeared everywhere. There was a bust of him in one of the galleries, and a portrait of him in two galleries. His seemed the most modern of modern voices, with his uncanny, lame instinct for publicity he had become, in four or five years, one of the best-known of the young "intellectuals." Where the intellect came in, Connie did not quite see. Clifford was really clever at that slightly humorous analysis of people and motives which leaves everything in bits at the end. But it was rather like puppies tearing the sofa-cushions to bits: except that it was not young and playful, but curiously old, and almost obscenely conceited. It was weird: and it was nothing. This was the feeling that echoed and re-echoed at the bottom of Connie's soul: it was all nothing, a wonderful display of nothingness. At the same time, a display. A display, a display, a display!

Michaelis had seized upon the figure of Clifford as a central figure for a play: already he had sketched in the plot, and written the first act. For Michaelis was even better than Clifford at making a display of nothingness. It was the last bit of passion left in these men: the passion for making a display. Sexually, they were passionless, even dead. And now it was not money that Michaelis was after. Clifford had never been primarily out for money: though he made it where he could, for money is the seal and stamp of success. And success was what they wanted. They wanted, both of them, to make a real display—*their* display—a man's own very display, of himself, that should capture for the time the vast populace.

It was strange—the prostitution to the bitch-goddess. To Connie, since she was really outside of it, and since she had grown numb to the thrill of it, it was again nothingness. Even the prostitution to the bitch-goddess was nothingness, though the men prostituted themselves innumerable times. Nothingness even that.

Michaelis wrote to Clifford about the play. Of course Connie knew about it long ago. And Clifford was again thrilled. He was going to be displayed again: this time, somebody was going to display him, and to advantage. He invited Michaelis down to Wragby, with Act I.

Michaelis came: in summer, in a pale-coloured suit and white suède gloves, with mauve orchids for Connie, very lovely, and Act I. The reading of Act I. was a great success. Even Connie was thrilled—thrilled to what bit of marrow she had left. And Michaelis, thrilled by his power to thrill, was really wonderful—and quite beautiful, in Connie's eyes. She saw in him that ancient motionlessness of a race that can't be disillusioned any more, an extreme, perhaps, of impurity that is pure. On the far side of his supreme prostitution to the bitch-goddess, he seemed pure, pure as an African ivory mask that dreams impurity into purity, in its ivory curves and planes.

His moment of sheer thrill with the two Chatterleys, when he simply carried Connie and Clifford away, was one of the supreme moments of Michaelis' life. He had succeeded: he had carried them away. Even Clifford was momentarily in love with him—if that is the way one can put it.

So next morning Mick was more uneasy than ever: restless, devoured, with his hands restless in his trousers pockets. Connie had not visited him in the night—and he had not known where to find her. Coquetry!—at his moment of triumph.

He went up to her sitting-room in the morning. She knew he

would come. And his restlessness was evident. He asked her about his play—did she think it good? He *had* to hear it praised: that affected him with the last thin thrills of passion, beyond any sexual orgasm. And she praised it rapturously. Yet all the while, at the bottom of her soul, she knew it was nothing—the bitch-goddess!

"Look here!" he said suddenly at last. "Why don't you and I make a clean thing of it? Why don't we marry?"

"But I am married!" she said, amazed, and yet feeling nothing.

"Oh that!—he'll divorce you all right.—Why don't you and I marry? I *want* to marry. I know it would be the best thing for me—marry and lead a regular life. I lead the deuce of a life, simply tearing myself to pieces. Look here, you and I, we're made for one another—hand and glove. Why don't we marry? Do you see any reason why we shouldn't?"

Connie looked at him amazed: and yet she felt nothing. These men, they were all alike, they left everything out. They just went off from the top of their heads, like squibs, and expected you to be carried heavenwards along with their own thin sticks.

"But I am married already," she said. "I can't leave Clifford, you know."

"But why not? why not?" he cried. "He'll hardly know you've gone, after six months. He doesn't know that anybody exists, except himself. Why the man has no use for you at all, as far as I can see: he's entirely wrapped up in himself."

Connie felt that this was true. But she also felt that Mick was hardly making a display of selflessness.

"Aren't all men wrapped up in themselves?" she asked.

"Oh, more or less, I allow. A man's *got* to be, to get through. But that's not the point. The point is, what sort of a time can a man give a woman? Can he give her a darn good time, or can't he? If he can't, he's no right to the woman—" He paused and gazed at her with his full, hazel eyes, almost hypnotic. "Now I consider," he added, "I can give a woman the darndest good time she can ask for. I think I can guarantee myself."

"But what sort of a good time?" asked Connie, gazing on him still in a sort of amazement that looked like thrill, and underneath feeling nothing at all.

"Every sort, darn it, every sort! Dress, jewels up to a point, any night club you like, know anybody you want to know, live the pace—travel—and be somebody wherever you go—Darn it, *every* sort of a good time!"

He spoke it almost in a brilliance of triumph, and Connie looked at him as if dazzled, and really feeling nothing at all. Hardly even the surface of her mind was tickled by the glowing prospects he offered her. Hardly even her most outside self responded, that at any other time would have thrilled. She just got no feeling off it all, she couldn't "go off." She just sat and stared, and looked dazzled, and felt nothing. Only somewhere she smelt the extremely unpleasant smell of the bitch-goddess.

Mick sat on tenterhooks, leaning forwards in his chair, glaring at her almost hysterically: and whether he was more anxious, out of vanity, for her to say yes! Or whether he was more panic-stricken for fear she *should* say yes! who can tell?

"I should have to think about it," she said. "I couldn't say now. It may seem to you Clifford doesn't count—but he does. When you think how disabled he is—"

"Oh damn it all, if a fellow's going to trade on his disabilities!—I might begin to say how lonely I am, and always have been, and all the rest of the my-eye-Betty-Martin sob-stuff! Damn it all, if a fellow's got nothing but disabilities to recommend him—"

He turned aside, working his hands furiously in his trousers pockets.

That evening he said to her:

"You're coming round to my room tonight, aren't you? I don't darned know where your room is."

"All right!" she said.

He was a more excited lover that night, with his strange, small-boy's excitement and his small-boy's frail nakedness. Connie found it impossible to come to her crisis before he had really finished his. And he roused a certain craving passion in her, with his little boy's nakedness and softness, she had to go on after he had finished, in the wild tumult and heaving of her loins, while he heroically kept himself up and present in her, with all his will and self-offering, till she brought about her own wild crisis, with weird little cries.

When at last he drew away from her, he said, in a bitter, almost sneering little voice:

"You couldn't go off at the same time as a man, could you? You'd have to bring yourself off! You'd have to run the show!"

This little speech, at that moment, was one of the shocks of her

life. Because that passive sort of giving himself was so obviously his
only real mode of intercourse.

"What do you mean?" she said.

"You know what I mean. You keep on for hours after I've gone
off—and I have to hang on with my teeth till you bring yourself off,
by your own exertions."

She was stunned by this unexpected piece of brutality, at that
moment when she was glowing with a sort of pleasure beyond words,
and a sort of love of him. Because after all, like so many modern men,
he was finished almost before he had begun. And that forced the
woman to be active.

"But you *want* me to go on, to get my own satisfaction?" she said.

He laughed in a hollow little way.

"*I* want it!" he said. "That's good. I want to hang on with my teeth
clenched, while you go for me!"

"But *don't* you?" she insisted.

He avoided the question.

"All the darned women are like that," he said. "Either they don't
go off at all, as if they were dead in there—or else they wait till a
chap's really done, then they start in to bring themselves off, and a
chap's got to hang on. I never had a woman yet who went off just at
the same moment as I did."

Connie only half heard this piece of novel masculine information.
She was only stunned by his feeling against her—his incomprehensible brutality. She felt so innocent.

"But you want me to have my satisfaction too, don't you?" she
repeated.

"Oh, all right! I'm quite willing. But I'm darned if hanging on
waiting for a woman to go off is much of a game for a man—"

This speech was one of the crucial blows of Connie's life. It killed
something in her. She had not been so very keen on Michaelis. Till
he started it, she did not want him. It was as if she never positively
wanted him. But once he had started her, it seemed only natural for
her to come to her own crisis, with him. Almost she had loved him for
it—almost, that night, she loved him and wanted to marry him.

Perhaps instinctively he knew it, and that was why he had to bring
down the whole show with a smash: the house of cards. Her whole
sexual feeling for him or for any man collapsed that night. Her life
fell apart from his as completely as if he had never existed.

And she went through the days drearily, wearily. There was

nothing now but this empty treadmill of what Clifford called the integrated life, the long living together of two people who are in the habit of being in the same house with one another.

Nothingness! To accept the great nothingness of life seemed to be the one end of living. All the many busy and important little things that make up the grand sum-total of nothingness!

CHAPTER VI.

"Why don't men and women really like one another, nowadays?" Connie asked Tommy Dukes, who was more or less her oracle.

"Oh but they do! I don't think, since the human species was invented, there has ever been a time when men and women have liked one another as much as they do today. Genuine liking! Take myself—I really *like* women better than men—they are braver—one can be more frank with them."

Connie pondered this.

"Ah yes, but you never have anything to do with them!" she said.

"I? What am I doing but talking perfectly sincerely to a woman at this moment?"

"Yes—talking—"

"And what more could I do if you were a man, than talk perfectly sincerely to you?"

"Nothing, perhaps—But a woman—"

"A woman wants you to like her, and talk to her—and at the same time love her, and desire her—and it seems to me the two things are mutually exclusive."

"But they shouldn't be."

"No doubt water ought not to be so wet as it is: it overdoes it, in wetness. But there it is!—I like women, and talk to them. And therefore I don't love them and desire them. The two things don't happen at the same time, in me."

"I think they ought to."

"All right.—The fact that things *ought* to be something else than what they are, is not my department."

Connie pondered this.

"It isn't true," she said. "Men can love women and talk to them. I don't see how they can love them *without* talking and being friendly and intimate: How can they?"

"Well!" he said. "I don't know. What's the use of my generalising? I only know my own case. I like women—but I don't desire them. I like talking to them—but talking to them, though it makes me intimate in one direction, sets me poles apart from them, as far as kissing is concerned.—So there you are! But don't take me as a general example—probably I'm just a special case: one of the men who like women, but don't love women—and even hate them if they force me into a pretence of love—or an entangled appearance—"

"But doesn't it make you sad?"

"Why should it? Not a bit! I look at Charlie May—and the rest of the men who have affairs—No, I don't envy them a bit. If fate sent me a woman I wanted, well and good. Since I don't know any woman I want, and never see one—why, I presume I'm cold, and I really *like* some women very much—"

"Do you like me?"

"Very much! And you see there's no question of kissing between us, is there?"

"None at all!" said Connie. "But oughtn't there to be?"

"*Why*, in God's name? I like Clifford. But what would you say if I went and kissed him?"

"But isn't there a difference?"

"Where does it lie, as far as we're concerned? We're all intelligent human beings, and the male and female business is in abeyance. Just in abeyance. How would you like me to start acting up like a continental male at this moment, and parading the sex thing?"

"I should hate it."

"Well then!—I tell you, if I'm really a male thing at all, I never run across the female of my species. And I don't miss her. I just *like* women—who's going to force me into loving, or pretending to love them, working up the sex game?"

"No, I'm not. But isn't something wrong?"

"You may feel it—I don't."

"Yes—I feel something is wrong between men and women. A woman has no glamour for a man any more."

"Has a man for a woman?"

She pondered the other side of the question.

"Not much," she said truthfully.

"Then let's leave it all alone, and just be decent and simple like proper human beings with one another. Be damned to the artificial sex compulsion—I refuse it."

Connie knew he was right, really. Yet it left her feeling so forlorn: so forlorn and stray. Like a chip on a dreary pond, she felt. What was the point, to her or anything.

It was her youth which rebelled. These men seemed so old and cold. Everything seemed old and cold. And Michaelis let one down so. He was no good. The men didn't want one. They just didn't really want a woman—even Michaelis didn't. And the bounders who pretended they did, and started working the sex game, they were worse than ever.

It was just dismal, and one had to put up with it. It was quite true, men had no real glamour for a woman: if you could fool yourself into thinking they had, even as she had fooled herself over Michaelis, that was the best you could do. Meanwhile you just lived on, and there was nothing to it. She understood perfectly well why people had cocktail parties and jazzed and Charlestoned till they were ready to drop. You had to take it out some way or other—your youth—or it ate you up. But what a ghastly thing, this youth! You felt as old as Methuselah, and yet the thing fizzed somehow, and didn't let you be comfortable. A mean sort of life!—and no prospect! She almost wished she had gone off with Mick, and made her life one long cocktail party and jazz evening. Anyhow that was better than just mooning yourself into the grave.

On one of her bad days she went out alone to walk in the wood, ponderously, heeding nothing, not even noticing where she was. The report of a gun not far off startled and angered her.

Then as she went, she heard voices, and recoiled. People! She didn't want people. But her quick ear caught another sound, and she roused. It was a child sobbing. At once she attended. Someone was ill-treating a child.

She strode surging down the wet drive, her sullen resentment uppermost. She felt just prepared to make a scene.

Turning the corner, she saw two figures in the drive beyond her: the keeper, and a little girl in a purple coat and moleskin cap, crying.

"Ah, shut it up, tha false little bitch!" came the man's angry voice: and the child sobbed louder.

Constance strode nearer, with blazing eyes. The man turned and looked at her, saluting coolly. But he was pale with anger.

"What's the matter? Why is she crying?" demanded Constance, a little breathlessly, peremptorily.

A faint smile, like a sneer, came on the man's face.

"Nay, yo' mun ax 'er," he replied callously, in broad vernacular.

Connie felt as if he had hit her in the face, and she changed colour. Then she gathered her defiance, and looked at him, her dark blue eyes blazing rather vaguely.

"I asked *you*!" she panted.

He gave a queer little bow, lifting his hat.

"You did, your ladyship—" he said; then, with a return to the vernacular: "but I canna tell yer."

And he became a soldier, inscrutable, only pale with annoyance.

Connie turned to the child—a ruddy, black-haired thing of nine or ten.

"What is it, dear? Tell me why you're crying!" she said, with the conventionalised sweetness suitable.

More violent sobs—self-conscious!

Still more sweetness on Connie's part.

"There there, don't you cry! Tell me what they've done to you!"—an intense tenderness of tone. At the same time she felt in the pockets of her knitted jacket, and luckily found a sixpence.

"Don't you cry then!" she said, bending in front of the child. "See! See what I've got for you!"

Sobs, snuffles, and a fist taken from a blubbered face, and a black, shrewd eye cast for a second on the sixpence. Then more sobs, but subduing.

"There! Tell me what's the matter! Tell me!" said Connie, putting the coin into the child's chubby hand, which closed over it.

"It's the—it's the—pussy!"

Shudders of subsiding sobs.

"What pussy then?"

After a silence, a shy fist clenching on sixpence pointing into the bramble brake.

"There!"

Connie looked. And there, sure enough, was a big black cat stretched out grimly, with a bit of blood on it.

"Oh!" she said, in repulsion.

"A poacher, your ladyship," said the man, satirically.

She glanced up at him angrily.

"No wonder the child cried," she said, "if you shot it when she was there. No wonder she cried!"

He looked into Connie's eyes, laconic, contemptuous, not hiding his feelings. And again Connie flushed: she felt she had been making a scene. The man did not respect her.

"What is your name?" she said playfully to the child. "Won't you tell me your name?"

Sniffs! Then, very affectedly, in a piping voice:

"Connie Mellors!"

"Connie Mellors! Well that's a nice name!—And did you come out with your father, and he shot a pussy? But it was a bad pussy!"

The child looked at her with bold dark eyes of scrutiny, sizing her up, and her condolence.

"I wanted to stop with my Gran," said the little girl.

"Did you! But where is your Gran?"

The child lifted an arm, pointing down the drive.

"At th' cottidge."

"At the cottage! And would you like to go back to her?"

Sudden shuddering quivers of reminiscent sobs:

"Yes!"

"Come then! Shall I take you? Shall I take you to your Gran? Then your father can do what he has to do."—She turned to the man. "It is your little girl, isn't it?"

He saluted, and gave a slight movement of the head, in affirmation.

"I suppose I can take her to the cottage?" said Connie to him.

"If your ladyship wishes."

Again he looked into her eyes, with that calm, searching yet detached glance. A man very much alone, and on his own.

"Would you like to come with me to the cottage, to your Gran, dear?"

The child peeped up again.

"Yes!" she simpered.

Connie disliked her—the spoilt, false little female. Nevertheless, she wiped her face and took her hand. The keeper saluted in silence.

"Goodmorning!" said Connie.

It was nearly a mile to the cottage, and Connie elder was well bored by Connie junior by the time the gamekeeper's picturesque little house was in sight. The child was already full to the brim with tricks, as a little monkey: and so self-assured.

At the cottage, the door stood open, and there was a rattling heard inside. Connie lingered, the child slipped her hand and ran indoors.

"Gran! Gran!—"

"Why, are yer back a'ready?"

The grandmother had been blackleading the fireplace—it was

Saturday morning. She came to the door in her sacking apron, a blacklead-brush in her hand, and a smudge of blacklead on her nose. She was a little, rather dry woman.

"Why, whatever!" she said, hastily wiping her arm across her face, as she saw Connie standing outside.

"Goodmorning!" said Connie. "She was crying, so I just brought her home."

The grandmother looked round swiftly at the child.

"Why, wheer was yer dad?"

The child clung to her grandmother's skirts, and simpered.

"He was there!" said Connie. "But he'd shot a poaching cat, and the child was upset."

"Oh, you'd no right t' ave bothered, Lady Chatterley, I'm sure! I'm sure it was very good of you. But you shouldn't 'ave bothered. Why did ever you know!"—and the old woman turned to the child. "Fancy Lady Chatterley takin' all that trouble over you! Why she shouldn't 'ave bothered!"

"It was no bother—just a walk," said Connie, smiling.

"Why I'm sure it was very kind of you, I must say! So she was cryin'! I knew there'd be something, afore they got far. She's frightened of 'im, that's where it is. You see 'e's almost a stranger to 'er—fair a stranger—and I don't think they're two as 'd hit it off very easy. He's got funny ways—"

Connie didn't know what to say.

"Look, Gran!" simpered the child.

The old woman looked down at the sixpence in the little girl's hand.

"An' sixpence an' all! Oh, Lady Chatterley, you shouldn't, you shouldn't! Why, isn't Lady Chatterley *good* to you! My word, you're a lucky girl this morning!"

She pronounced the name, as all the people did, Chat'ley!—"Isn't Lady Chat'ley *good* to you!"—Connie couldn't help looking at the smudge on the old woman's nose, and the latter again vaguely wiped her face with the back of her wrist, but missed the smudge.

Connie was moving away.

"Well thank you *ever* so much, Lady Chat'ley, I'm sure.—Say *thank you*! to Lady Chat'ley!"—this last to the child.

"Thank you!" piped the child.

"There's a dear!" laughed Connie, and she moved away, saying Good-morning, heartily relieved to get away from the contact.—

Curious! she thought,—that that thin proud man should have that little sharp woman for a mother!—

And the old woman, as soon as Connie was gone, rushed to the bit of mirror in the scullery, and looked at her face. Seeing it, she stamped her foot with impatience. "Of *course* she had to catch me in my coarse apron, and a dirty face! Nice idea she'd get of *me*!"

Connie went slowly home to Wragby. "Home!" It was a warm word to use for that great weary warren. But then it was a word that had had its day. It was, somehow, cancelled. All the great words, it seemed to Connie, were cancelled for her generation: love, joy, happiness, home, mother, father, husband, all these great dynamic words were half-dead now, and dying from day to day. Home was a place you lived in, love was a thing you didn't fool yourself about, joy was a word you applied to a good Charleston, happiness was a term of hypocrisy you used out of cant, to bluff other people, a father was an individual who enjoyed his own existence, a husband was a man you lived with and kept going, in spirits. As for sex, the last of the great words, it was just a cocktail term for an excitement that bucked you up for a while, then left you more raggy than ever. Frayed! It was as if the very material you were made of was cheap stuff, and was fraying out to nothing.

All that really remained was a stubborn stoicism: and in that there was a certain pleasure. In the very experience of the nothingness of life, phase after phase, *étape* after *étape*, there was a certain grisly satisfaction. So that's *that*!—Always this was the last utterance: home, love, marriage, Michaelis: So that's *that*!—And when one died, the last words to life would be: So that's *that*!—

Money? Perhaps one couldn't say the same there. Money one always wanted. Money, success—the bitch-goddess, as Tommy Dukes persisted in calling it, after Henry James—that was a permanent necessity. You couldn't spend your last sou, and say finally: So that's *that*!—No, if you lived even another ten minutes, you wanted a few more sous for something or other. Just to keep the business mechanically going, you needed money. You had to have it. Money you *have* to have. You needn't really have anything else. So that's *that*!—

Since, of course, it's not your own fault you are alive. Once you are alive, then money is a necessity—and the only absolute necessity. All the rest you can get along without, at a pinch. But not money. Emphatically that's *that*!—

She thought of Michaelis, and the money she might have had with him. And even that she didn't want. She preferred the lesser amount which she helped Clifford to make by his writing. That she actually helped to make. "Clifford and I together, we make twelve hundred a year out of writing"—so she put it to herself. Make money! Make it! Out of nowhere! Wring it out of the thin air! The last feat to be humanly proud of! The rest all my-eye-Betty-Martin.

So she plodded home to Clifford, to join forces with him again, to make another story, out of nothingness: and a story meant money. Clifford seemed to care very much whether his stories were considered first-class literature or not. Strictly, she didn't care. Nothing in it! said her father. Twelve hundred pounds, last year! was the retort simple and final.

If you were young, you just set your teeth and bit on, and held on, till the money began to flow from the invisible. It was a question of power. It was a question of will. A subtle, subtle, powerful emanation of will out of yourself brought back to you the mysterious nothingness of money: a word on a bit of paper. It was a sort of magic. Certainly it was triumph. The bitch-goddess! Well, if one had to prostitute oneself, let it be to a bitch-goddess! One could always despise her even whilst one prostituted oneself to her. Which was good!

Clifford, of course, had still many childish taboos and fetishes. He wanted to be thought "really good." Which was all cock-a-whoopy nonsense. What was really good was what actually caught on. It was no good being really good, and getting left with it. It seemed as if most of the "really good" men just missed the bus. After all, you only lived one life: and if you missed the bus, you just were left on the pavement, along with the rest of the failures.

Connie was contemplating a winter in London, with Clifford, next winter. He and she had caught the bus all right, so they might as well ride on top for a bit, and show it.

The worst of it was, Clifford tended to become vague, absent, and to fall into fits of vacant depression. It was the wound to his psyche coming out. But it made Connie want to scream. Oh God, if the mechanism of the consciousness itself was going to go wrong, then what *was* one to do! Hang it all, one did one's bit! Must one be let down *absolutely*.

Sometimes she wept bitterly, but even as she wept she was saying to herself: Silly fool, wetting hankies! As if that would get you anywhere!

Since Michaelis, she had made up her mind she wanted nothing. That seemed the simplest solution of the otherwise insoluble. She wanted nothing more than what she'd got. Only, she wanted to get ahead with what she'd got. Clifford, the stories, Wragby, the Lady-Chatterley business, money, and fame, such as it was—she wanted to go ahead with it all. Love, sex, all that sort of stuff, just water-ices. Lick it up and forget it. If you don't hang on to it in your mind, it's nothing. Sex especially—nothing. Make up your mind to it, and you've solved the problem. Sex—a cocktail—they both lasted about as long, had the same effect, and amounted to about the same thing.

But a child—a baby! That was still one of the sensations. She would venture very gingerly on that experiment. There was the man to consider. And it was curious, there wasn't a man in the world whose children you wanted. Mick's children! Repulsive thought! As leave have a child to a rabbit. Tommy Dukes—he was very nice, but somehow, you couldn't associate him with a baby, another generation. He ended in himself. And out of all the rest of Clifford's pretty wide acquaintance, there was not a man who did not rouse her contempt, when she thought of having a child by him. There were several who would have been quite possible as lovers—even Mick. But to let them breed a child on you! Ugh! humiliation and abomination.

So that was *that*!

Nevertheless, Connie had the child at the back of her mind. Wait! Wait! She could sift the generations of men through her sieve, and see if she couldn't find one that would do.—"Go ye into the streets and by-ways of Jerusalem, and see if ye can find *a man*."—It had been impossible to find a man in the Jerusalem of the prophet—though there were thousands of male humans. But *a man*! C'est une autre chose!

She had an idea that he would have to be a foreigner: not an Englishman, still less a Scotchman, less still an Irishman. A real foreigner.

But wait! Wait! Next winter she would get Clifford to London: the following winter she would get him abroad, to the south of France, Italy—. Wait! She was in no hurry about the child. That was her own private affair, and the one point on which, in her queer, female way, she was serious to the bottom of her soul. She was not going to risk any chance comer. Not she. One might take a lover almost at any moment. But a man who should beget a child on one!—Wait! Wait! It's a very different matter.—"Go ye into the streets and by-ways of Jerusalem—."—It was not a question of love. It was a question of *a man*. Why, one might even rather hate him, personally. Yet if he was the man, what would one's personal hate matter! This business concerned another part of oneself.

It had rained as usual, and the paths were too sodden for Clifford's chair. But Connie would go out. She went out alone every day now, mostly in the wood, where she was really alone. She saw nobody there—

This day, however, Clifford wanted to send a message to the keeper, and as the boy was laid up with influenza—somebody always seemed to have influenza at Wragby—Connie said she would call at the cottage.

The air was soft and dead, as if all the world were slowly dying. Grey and clammy, and silent even of the shuffling of the collieries, for the pits were working short time, today they were stopped altogether. The end of all things!

In the wood, all was utterly inert and motionless. Only great drops fell from the bare boughs, with a hollow little crash. For the rest, among the old trees was depth within depth of grey hopeless inertia, silence, nothingness.

Constance walked dimly on. From the old wood came an ancient melancholy, somehow soothing to her, better than the harsh insentience of the outer world. She liked the *inwardness* of the remnant of forest, the unspeaking reticence of the old trees. They seemed a very power of silence, and yet, a vital presence. They too were waiting: obstinately, stoically waiting, and given a potency of silence. Perhaps they were only waiting for the end: to be cut down, cleared away—the end of the forest; for them, the end of all things. But perhaps their strong and aristocratic silence, the silence of strong trees, meant something else.

As she came out of the wood on the north side, the keeper's cottage, a rather dark, brown-stone cottage with gables and a handsome chimney, looked uninhabited, it was so silent and alone. But a thread of smoke rose from the chimney—and the little, railed-in garden in front of the house was dug and kept very tidy. The door was shut.

Now she was here, she felt a little shy of the man with his curious, clear-seeing eyes. She did not like bringing him orders. She felt like going away again. She knocked softly. No-one came. She knocked again—but still not loudly. There was no answer. She peeped through the window, and saw the rather dark little room, with its almost sinister privacy, not wanting to be invaded.

She stood and listened. And it seemed to her she heard sounds from the back of the cottage. Having failed to make herself heard, her mettle was roused. She would not be defeated.

So she went round the side of the house. At the back of the cottage, the land rose rather steeply, so the back yard was sunken and enclosed in a low stone wall. She turned the corner of the house, and stopped. In the little yard two paces beyond her, the man was washing himself, utterly unaware. He was naked to the hips, his velveteen breeches slipping down over his slender loins. And his white, slender back was curved over a big bowl of soapy water, in which he ducked his head, shaking his head with a queer, quick little motion, lifting his slender white arms and pressing the soapy water from his ears: quick, subtle as a weasel playing with water, and utterly alone.

Connie backed away round the corner of the house, and hurried away to the wood. In spite of herself, she had had a shock. After all, merely a man washing himself! Commonplace enough, heaven knows.

Yet, in some curious way, it was a visionary experience: it had hit her in the middle of her body. She saw the clumsy breeches slipping away over the pure, delicate white loins, the bones showing a little, and the sense of aloneness, of a creature purely alone, overwhelmed her. Perfect, white solitary nudity of a creature that lives alone, and inwardly alone. And beyond that, a certain beauty of a pure creature. Not the stuff of beauty, not even the body of beauty, but a certain lambency, the warm white flame of a single life revealing itself in contours that one might touch: a body!

Connie had received the shock of vision in her womb, and she knew it. It lay inside her. But with her mind, she was inclined to ridicule. A man washing himself in a back yard! No doubt with evil-smelling yellow soap!—She was rather annoyed. Why should she be made to stumble on these vulgar privacies!

So she walked away from herself. But after a while, she sat down on a stump. She was too confused to think. But in the coil of her confusion, she was determined to deliver her message to the fellow.

She would not be balked. She must give him time to dress himself, but not time to go out. He was probably preparing to go out somewhere.

So she sauntered slowly back, listening. As she came near, the cottage looked just the same. A dog barked—and she knocked at the door, her heart beating in spite of her.

She heard the man coming lightly downstairs. He opened the door with curious quickness, and startled her. He looked uneasy himself. But instantly a laugh came on his face.

"Lady Chatterley!" he said. "Will you come in?"

His manner was so perfectly easy and good, she stepped over the threshold into the rather dreary little room.

"I only called with a message from Sir Clifford," she said, in her soft, rather breathless voice.

The man was looking at her with those blue, all-seeing eyes of his, which made her turn her face aside a little. He thought her comely, almost beautiful, in her shyness. And he took command of the situation himself, at once.

"Would you care to sit down?" he asked, presuming she would not. The door stood open.

"No thanks! Sir Clifford wondered if you would——" and she delivered her message, looking unconsciously into his eyes again.

And now his eyes looked warm and kind, particularly for a woman: wonderfully warm and kind, and at ease.

"Very good, your ladyship! I will see to it at once."

Taking an order, his whole self had changed, glazed over with a certain hardness and distance.

Connie hesitated. She ought to go. But she looked round the clean, tidy, rather dreary little living-room with a certain dismay.

"Do you live here quite alone?" she asked.

"Quite alone, your ladyship."

"But your mother——?"

"She lives in her own cottage in the village."

"With the child?" asked Connie.

"With the child!"

And his plain, rather worn face took on an indefinable look of derision. It was a face that changed all the time, baffling.

"No," he said, seeing Connie stand at a loss. "My mother comes and cleans up for me on Saturdays: I do the rest myself."

Again Connie looked at him. His eyes were smiling again, a little mockingly, but warm and blue and somehow, kind. She wondered at him. He was in trousers and flannel shirt, with a grey tie, his hair soft and damp, his face rather pale and worn-looking. When the eyes ceased to laugh, they looked as if they had suffered a great deal, still without losing their warmth. But a pallor of isolation came over him—she was not really there for him. And she felt a curious difference about him, a vividness; and yet, not far from death itself.

She wanted to say so many things, and she said nothing. Only she looked up at him again and remarked:

"I hope I didn't disturb you!"

The faint smile of mockery narrowed his eyes.

"Only combing my hair, if you don't mind. I'm sorry I hadn't a coat on! But then I had no idea who was knocking. Nobody knocks, here. And the unexpected sounds ominous."

He went in front of her down the garden path, to hold the gate. In his shirt, without the clumsy velveteen coat, she saw again how slender he was, thin, stooping a little. Yet, as she passed him, there was something young and bright in his soft, fair hair and his quick eyes. He would be a man about thirty-seven or eight.

She plodded on into the wood, knowing he was looking after her. He upset her so much, in spite of herself.

And he, as he went indoors, was thinking: "She's nice: she's real! She's nicer than she knows."

She wondered very much about him: he seemed *so* unlike a gamekeeper, so unlike a working-man anyhow; although he had something in common with the local people. But also, something very uncommon.

"The gamekeeper Mellors is a curious kind of person," she said to Clifford. "He might almost be a gentleman."

"Might he?" said Clifford. "I hadn't noticed."

"But isn't there something special about him?" Connie insisted.

"I think he's quite a nice fellow, but I know very little about him. He only came out of the army last year—less than a year ago. From India, I rather think. He may have picked up certain tricks out there—perhaps he was some officer's servant, and improved on his position. Some of the men were like that. But it does them no good—they have to fall back into their old place when they get home again."

Connie gazed at Clifford contemplatively. She saw in him the peculiar tight rebuff against anyone of the lower classes who might be really climbing up, which she knew was characteristic of his breed.

"But don't you think there is something special about him?" she asked.

"Frankly, no! Nothing I had noticed."

He looked at her curiously—uneasily, half-suspiciously. And she felt he wasn't telling her the *real* truth—he wasn't telling himself the real truth, that was it. He disliked any suggestion of a really exceptional human being. People must be more or less at a level—or below it.

Connie felt again the tightness, niggardliness of the men of her generation. They were so tight, so scared of life!

CHAPTER VII.

When Connie went up to her bedroom she did what she had not done for a long time: took off all her clothes and looked at herself naked in the huge mirror. She did not know what she was looking for, or at, very definitely. Yet she moved the lamp till it shone full on her.

And she thought as she had thought so often: what a frail, easily-hurt, rather pathetic thing a naked human body is: somehow a little unfinished, incomplete!

She was supposed to have a good figure, but now she was out of fashion: a little too female, not enough like an adolescent boy. She was not very tall—a bit Scottish and short: but she had a certain fluent, down-slipping grace that might have been beauty. Her skin was faintly tawny, her limbs had a certain stillness, her body should have had a full, downward-slipping richness. But it lacked something.

Instead of ripening its firm, down-running curves, her body was flattening and going a little harsh. It was as if it had not had enough sun and warmth. It was a little greyish and sapless. Disappointed of its real womanhood, it had not succeeded in becoming boyish and unsubstantial and transparent. Instead, it had gone opaque.

Her breasts were rather small, and dropping pear-shaped. But they were unripe, a little bitter, without meaning hanging there. And her belly had lost the fresh round gleam it had had when she was young, in the days of her German boy, who loved her really physically. Then it was young and expectant, with a real look of its own. Now it was going slack and a little flat, thinner—but with a slack thinness. Her thighs, too, that used to look so quick and glimpsey, in their odd female roundness, somehow they too were going flat, slack, meaningless.

Her body was going meaningless, going dull and opaque, so much insignificant substance. It made her feel immensely depressed, and hopeless. What hope was there? She was old, old at twenty-seven, with no gleam and sparkle in the flesh. Old through neglect and denial: yes, denial. Fashionable women kept their bodies bright, like delicate porcelain, by external attention. There was nothing inside the porcelain.—But she was not even as bright as that. The mental life! Suddenly she hated it with a rushing fury, the swindle!

She looked in the other mirror's reflection at her back, her waist, her loins. She was getting thinner, but to her it was not becoming. The crumple of her waist at the back, as she bent back to look, was a little weary: and it used to be so gay-looking. And the longish slope of her haunches and her buttocks had lost its gleam and its sense of richness. Gone! Only the German boy had loved it, and he was ten years dead, very nearly. How time went by! And she was only twenty-seven. Ten years dead, that healthy boy with his fresh, clumsy sensuality that she had then been so scornful of! Where would she find it now? It was gone out of men. They had their pathetic, two-seconds spasms, like Michaelis. But no healthy, human sensuality that warms the blood and freshens the whole being.

Still she thought the most beautiful part of her was the long-sloping fall of the haunches, from the socket of the back, and the slumberous round stillness of the buttocks. Like hillocks of sand, the Arabs say, soft and downward-slipping with a long slope. Here the life still lingered, hoping.—But here too she was thinner, and going unripe, astringent.

But the front of her body made her miserable. It was already beginning to slacken with a slack sort of thinness, almost withered, going old before it had ever really lived. She thought of the child she might somehow bear. Was she fit, anyhow?

She slipped into her nightdress and went to bed, where she sobbed bitterly. And in her bitterness burned a cold indignation against Clifford and his writings and his talk: against all the men of his sort, who defrauded a woman even out of her own body. Unjust! Unjust! The sense of deep physical injustice burned through her very soul.

But in the morning, all the same, she was up at seven, and going downstairs to Clifford. She had to help him in all the intimate things, for he had no man, and refused a woman-servant. The house-keeper's husband, who had known him as a boy, helped him and did any heavy lifting. But Connie did the personal things. And she did them willingly. It was a demand on her, but she had wanted to do what she could.

So she hardly ever went away from Wragby, and never for more than a day or two: when Mrs Betts, the housekeeper, attended to Clifford. Clifford, as was inevitable, in the course of time took all the service for granted. It was natural he should.

And yet, deep inside herself, a sense of injustice, of being defrauded, began to burn in Connie. The physical sense of injustice is a dangerous feeling, once it is awakened. It must have outlet, or it eats away the one in whom it is aroused.

Poor Clifford, he was not to blame. His was the greater misfortune. It was all part of the general catastrophe.

And yet, was he not in a way to blame? This lack of warmth, this lack of the simpler, warm physical contact—was he not to blame for that? He was never really warm, but never. Kind, thoughtful, considerate, in a well-bred, cold sort of way! But never warm as a man can be warm to a woman: as even Connie's father could be warm to her, with the warmth of a man who did himself well, and intended to, but who still could comfort a woman with a bit of his masculine glow—

But Clifford was not like that. His whole race was not like that. They were all inwardly hard and separate, and warmth to them was just bad taste. You had to get on without it, and hold your own. Which was all very well, if you were of the same class and race. Then you could keep yourself cold and be very estimable, and hold your own and enjoy the satisfaction of holding it. But if you were of another class and another race, it wouldn't do; there was no fun merely holding your own and feeling you belonged to the ruling class. What was the point, when even the smartest aristocrats had really nothing positive of their own to hold, and their rule was really a farce, not rule at all! What was the point? It was all cold nonsense.

A sense of rebellion smouldered in Connie. What was the good of it all! What was the good of her sacrifice, her devoting her life to Clifford? What was she serving, after all? A cold spirit of vanity, that had no warm human contacts, and that was as corrupt as any low-born Jew in craving for the prostitution with the bitch-goddess, Success. Even Clifford's cool and contactless assurance that he belonged to the ruling class didn't prevent his tongue from lolling out of his mouth as he panted after the bitch-goddess. After all, Michaelis was really more dignified in the matter, and far, far more successful. After all, if you really looked closely at Clifford panting after the bitch-goddess, he was a buffoon. And a buffoon is more humiliating than a bounder.

In a choice of men, Michaelis really had far more use for her than Clifford had. He had even more need of her. Any good nurse can attend to crippled legs! And as for the heroic effort, Michaelis was a heroic rat, and Clifford was very much of a poodle showing off.

There were people staying in the house, among them Clifford's Aunt Eva, Lady Bennerley. She was a thin woman of sixty, with a red nose, a widow, and still something of a *grande dame*. She belonged to one of the best families, and had the character to carry it off. Connie liked her, she was so perfectly simple and frank, as far as she intended to be frank, and superficially kind. Inside herself, she was a past-mistress in holding her own and holding other people a little lower. She was not at all a snob—far too sure of herself. She was perfect in the social athletic sport of coolly holding her own and making people defer to her.

She was kind to Connie, and tried to worm into her woman's soul with the sharp gimlet of her well-born woman's observations.

"You're quite wonderful, in my opinion," she said to Connie. "You've done wonders with Clifford. I never saw any budding genius myself, and there he is, all the rage."—Aunt Eva was quite complacently proud of Clifford's success. Another feather in the family cap! She didn't care a straw about his books: but why should she?

"Oh, I don't think it's my doing," said Connie.

"It must be! Can't be anybody else's. And it seems to me you don't get enough out of it."

"How?"

"Look at the way you are shut up here. I said to Clifford: if that child rebels one day, you'll have yourself to thank—"

"But Clifford never denies me anything," said Connie.

"Look here, my dear child—" and Lady Bennerley laid her thin hand on Connie's arm—"a woman has to live her life, or live to repent not having lived it. Believe me!"—And she took another sip of brandy, which maybe was her form of repentance.

"But I *do* live my life, don't I?"

"Not in my idea! Clifford should bring you to London and let you go about. His sort of friends are all right for him—but what are they for you? If I were you I should think it wasn't good enough.

You'll let your youth slip by, and you'll spend your old age—and your middle age too—repenting it."

Her ladyship lapsed into contemplative silence, soothed by the brandy.

But Connie was not keen on going to London and being steered into the smart world by Lady Bennerley. She didn't feel really smart: it wasn't interesting. And she did feel the peculiar withering coldness under it all. Like the soil of Labrador, which has gay little flowers on its surface, and a foot down, is frozen.

Tommy Dukes was at Wragby: and another man, Harry Winterslow, and Jack Strangeways with his wife Olive. The talk was much more desultory than when only the cronies were there—and everybody was a bit bored, for the weather was bad, and there was only billiards, and the pianola to dance to.

Olive was reading a book about the future, when babies would be bred in bottles and women would be "immunised."

"Jolly good thing too!" she said. "Then a woman can live her own life."

Strangeways wanted children, and she didn't.

"How'd you like to be *immunised*?" Winterslow asked her, with an ugly smile.

"I hope I am—naturally," she said. "Anyhow the future's going to have more sense, and a woman needn't be dragged down by her *functions*—"

"Perhaps she'll float off into space altogether," said Dukes.

"I do think sufficient civilisation ought to eliminate a lot of the physical disabilities," said Clifford. "All the love business, for example, it might just as well go. I suppose it would, if we could breed babies in bottles."

"No!" cried Olive. "That might leave all the more room for fun."

"I suppose," said Lady Bennerley contemplatively, "if the love business went, something else would take its place. Morphia, perhaps. A little morphine in all the air. It would be wonderfully refreshing for everybody."

"The government releasing ether into the air on Saturdays, for a cheerful week-end!" said Jack.—"Sounds all right. But where should we be by Wednesday?"

"So long as you can forget your body, you are happy," said Lady Bennerley. "And the moment you begin to be aware of your body, you are wretched. So if civilisation is any good, it has to help us to forget our bodies, and then time passes happily, without our knowing it."

"Help us to get rid of our bodies altogether," said Winterslow.— "It's quite time man began to improve on his *own* nature, especially the physical side of it."

"Imagine if we floated like tobacco-smoke!" said Connie.

"It won't happen," said Dukes. "Our old show will come flop: our civilisation is going to fall. It's going down the bottomless pit, down the chasm. And believe me, the only bridge across the chasm will be the phallus!"

"Oh do! *do* be impossible, General!" cried Olive.

"*I* believe our civilisation is going to collapse," said Aunt Eva.

"And what will come after it?" asked Clifford.

"I haven't the faintest idea. But something, I suppose," said the elderly lady.

"Connie says people like wisps of smoke, and Olive says immunised women and babies in bottles, and Dukes says the phallus is the bridge to what comes next. I wonder what it will really be—" said Clifford.

"Oh, don't bother! Let's get on with today," said Olive. "Only hurry up with the breeding-bottle, and let us poor women off."

"There might even be real men, in the next phase," said Tommy. "Real intelligent wholesome men, and wholesome nice women! wouldn't that be a change? An enormous change from *us! We're* not men—and the women aren't women. We're only cerebrating make-shifts, mechanical and intellectual experiments.—There may even come a civilisation of genuine men and women, instead of our little lot of clever-jacks all at the intelligence-age of seven. It would be even more amazing than wisps of smoke or babies in bottles."

"Oh, when people begin to talk about real women, I give up," said Olive.

"Certainly nothing but the spirit in us is worth having," said Winterslow.

"Spirits!" said Jack, drinking his whiskey and soda.

"Think so?—Give me the resurrection of the body!" said Dukes. "But it'll come, in time—when we've shoved the cerebral stone away a bit, the money and the rest. Then we'll get a democracy of touch, instead of a democracy of pocket."

Something echoed inside Connie. "Give me the resurrection of the body! the democracy of touch!" She didn't at all know what the latter meant, but it comforted her, as meaningless things may do.

Anyhow everything was terribly silly, and she was exasperatedly bored by it all, by Clifford, by Aunt Eva, by Olive and Jack and Winterslow, and even by Dukes. Talk, talk, talk! What hell it was, the continual rattle of it!

Then when all the people went, it was no better. She continued plodding on, but exasperation and irritation had got hold of her lower body, she couldn't escape. The days seemed to grind by with curious painfulness, yet nothing happened. Only she was getting thinner. Even the housekeeper said it, and asked her about herself. Even Tommy Dukes insisted she was not well. But she said she was all right. Only she began to be afraid of the ghastly white tombstones, that peculiarly loathsome whiteness of Carrara marble, detestable as false teeth, which stuck up on the hillside under Tevershall Church, and which she saw with such grim plainness from the park. The bristling of the hideous false teeth of tombstones on the hill affected her with a grisly kind of horror. She felt the time not far off when she would be buried there, added to the ghastly host under there, under the tombstones and the monuments, in these filthy Midlands.

She needed help, and she knew it. So she wrote a little *cri de cœur* to her sister Hilda. "I'm not well lately, and I don't know what's the matter with me."

Down posted Hilda from Scotland, where she had taken up her abode. She came in March, alone, driving herself in a nimble two-seater. Up the drive she came, tooting up the incline, then sweeping round the oval of grass where the two great, wild beech-trees stood, on the flat in front of the house.

Connie had run out to the steps. Hilda pulled up her car, got out, and kissed her sister.

"But Connie!" she said. "Whatever is the matter!"

"Nothing!" said Connie, rather shamefacedly.

But she knew how she suffered in contrast to Hilda. Both sisters had the same rather golden, glowing skin and soft brown hair and naturally strong, warm physique. But now, Connie was thin and earthy-looking, with a thin yellowish neck that stuck out of her jumper.

"But you're ill, child!" said Hilda, in the soft, rather breathless voice that both sisters had alike. Hilda was nearly, but not quite, two years older than Connie.

"No, not ill. Perhaps I'm bored," said Connie a little pathetically.

The light of battle glowed in Hilda's face: she was a woman, soft and still as she seemed, of the old amazon sort, not made to fit with men.

"This wretched place!" she said softly, looking at poor old lumbering Wragby with real hate. She looked soft and warm, herself, as a ripe pear: and she was an amazon of the real old breed.

She went quietly in to Clifford. He thought how handsome she looked: but also, he shrank from her. His wife's family did not have his sort of manners and his sort of etiquette. He considered them rather outsiders: but once they got inside, they made him jump through the hoop.

He sat square and well-groomed in his chair, his hair sleek, blond, his face fresh, his blue eyes pale and a little prominent, his expression inscrutable but well-bred—Hilda thought it sulky and stupid—and he waited. He had an air of aplomb, but Hilda didn't care what he had an air of. She was up in arms, and if he'd been Pope or Emperor it would have been just the same.

"Connie's looking awfully unwell," she said in her soft voice, fixing him with her beautiful, glowering grey eyes. She looked so maidenly: so did Connie. But he well knew the stone of Scottish obstinacy underneath.

"She's a little thinner," he said.

"Haven't you done anything about it?"

"Do you think it necessary?" he asked, in his suavest English stiffness: for the two things often go together.

Hilda only glowered at him without replying. Repartee was not her forte: nor Connie's. So she glowered, and he was much more uncomfortable than if she had said things.

"I'll take her to a doctor," said Hilda at length. "Can you suggest a good one round here?"

"I'm afraid I can't."

"Then I'll take her to London, where we have a doctor we trust."

Though boiling with rage, Clifford said nothing.

"I suppose I may as well stay the night," said Hilda, pulling off her gloves, "and I'll drive her to town tomorrow."

Clifford was yellow at the gills with anger, and at evening the whites of his eyes were a little yellowed too. He ran to liver. But Hilda was consistently modest and maidenly.

"You must have a nurse, or somebody, to look after you personally. You should really have a manservant," said Hilda, as they sat with apparent calmness at coffee after dinner. She spoke in her soft, seemingly gentle way, but Clifford felt she was hitting him on the head with a bludgeon.

"You think so?" he said coldly.

"I'm sure! It's necessary. Either that, or father and I must take Connie away for some months. This can't go on."

"What can't go on?"

"Haven't you looked at the child?" asked Hilda gazing at him full stare.

He looked rather like a huge boiled cray-fish at the moment: or so she thought.

"Connie and I will discuss it," he said.

"I've already discussed it with her," said Hilda.

Clifford had been long enough in the hands of nurses. He hated them, because they left him no real privacy. And a manservant!—he couldn't stand a man hanging round him. Almost better *any* woman. But why not Connie?

The two sisters drove off in the morning, Connie looking like an Easter lamb, rather small beside Hilda, who held the wheel. Sir Malcolm was away, but the Kensington house was open.

The doctor examined Connie carefully, and asked her all about her life. "I see your photograph, and Sir Clifford's, in the illustrated papers sometimes. Almost notorieties, aren't you? That's how the quiet little girls grow up. Though you're only a quiet little girl even now, in spite of the illustrated papers.—No no, there's nothing organically wrong. But it won't do, it won't do! Tell Sir Clifford he's got to bring you to town, or take you abroad, and amuse you. You've got to be amused, you have! Your vitality is much too low: no reserves, no reserves. The nerves of the heart a bit queer already: oh yes! Nothing but nerves; I'd put you right in a month, at Cannes or Biarritz. But it mustn't go on: *mustn't*, I tell you: or I won't be answerable for consequences. You're spending your life without renewing it. You've got to be amused, properly healthily amused. You're spending your vitality without making any. Can't go on, you know. Depression! Avoid depression!"

Hilda set her jaw, and that meant something.

Michaelis heard they were in town, and came running with roses.

"Why whatever's wrong!" he cried. "You're a shadow of yourself. Why I never saw such a change! Why ever didn't you let me know!———Come to Nice with me! Come down to Sicily! Go on, come to Sicily with me, it's lovely there just now. You want sun! You want life! Why you're wasting away! Come away with me! Come to Africa! Oh hang Sir Clifford! Chuck him and come along with me. I'll marry you the minute he divorces you. Come along, and try a life! God's love, that place Wragby would kill anybody. Beastly place, foul place, kill anybody. Come away with me, into the sun! It's the sun you want, of course, and a bit of normal life——"

But Connie's heart simply stood still at the thought of abandoning Clifford there and then. She couldn't do it. No—no! She just couldn't. She had to go back to Wragby.

Michaelis was disgusted. Hilda didn't like Michaelis, but she *almost* preferred him to Clifford. Back went the sisters to the Midlands.

Hilda talked to Clifford—who still had yellow eyeballs when they got back. He too, in his way, was overwrought. But he had to listen to all Hilda said, all the doctor had said: not what Michaelis had said, of course. And he sat mum through the ultimatum.

"Here is the address of a good manservant who served an invalid patient of the doctor's till he died last month. He is really a good man: and fairly sure to come."

"But I'm not an invalid, and I will *not* have a manservant," said Clifford, poor devil.

"And here are the addresses of two women: I saw one of them: she would do very well, a woman of about fifty, quiet, strong, kind, and in her way, cultured——"

Clifford only sulked, and would not answer.

"Very well, Clifford. If we don't settle something by tomorrow, I shall telegraph to father, and we shall take Connie away."

"Will Connie go?" asked Clifford.

"She doesn't want to. But she knows she must. Mother died of cancer, brought on by fretting. We're not running any risks."

So next day, Clifford suggested Mrs Bolton, Tevershall parish nurse. Apparently Mrs Betts had suggested her: Mrs Bolton was just retiring from her parish duties, to take up private nursing jobs. Clifford had a queer dread of delivering himself into the hands of a stranger. But Mrs Bolton had once nursed him through scarlet fever, so he knew her.

The two sisters at once called on Mrs Bolton, in a newish house in a row in Tevershall, quite select for Tevershall. They found a rather good-looking woman of forty-odd, in a nurse's uniform with a white collar and apron, just making herself tea in a crowded, small sitting room.

Mrs Bolton was most attentive and polite, seemed quite nice, spoke with a bit of a broad slur, like, but in heavily correct English, and, from having bossed the sick colliers for a good many years, having a very good opinion of herself and a fair amount of assurance. In short, in her tiny way, one of the governing class in the village, very much respected.

"Yes, Lady Chatterley's not looking at *all* well! Why she used to be that bonny, didn't she now! But she's been failing all winter! Oh, it's hard, it is! poor Sir Clifford! Eh, that war, it's a lot to answer for."

And Mrs Bolton would come to Wragby at once if Dr Shardlow would let her off. She had another fortnight's parish nursing to do, by rights. "But they might get a substitute, you know."

Hilda posted off to Dr Shardlow. And on the following Sunday, Mrs Bolton drove up in Leiver's cab to Wragby, with two trunks. Hilda had talks with her. Mrs Bolton was ready at any moment to talk. And she seemed so young! the way the passion would flush in her rather pale cheek. She was forty-seven.

Her husband Ted Bolton had been killed in the pit twenty-two years ago: twenty-two years last Christmas: just at Christmas time: leaving her with two children, one a baby in arms.—Oh, the baby was married now, Edith, to a young man in Boots Cash Chemist in Sheffield. The other one was a school-teacher in Chesterfield, she came home week-ends, when she wasn't asked out somewhere. Young folks enjoyed themselves nowadays—not like when she, Ivy Bolton, was young.

Ted Bolton was twenty-eight when he was killed in an explosion down pit. The butty in front shouted to them all to lie down quick, they were four of them, and they all lay down in time and were safe, only Ted, and it killed him. Then at the enquiry on the masters' side they said Bolton had been frightened and trying to run away, and not obeying orders, so it was like his own fault, really. So the compensation was only three hundred pounds, and they made out as if it was more of a gift than a legal compensation, because it was really the man's own fault. And they wouldn't let her have the money down: she wanted to start a little shop. But they said she'd no doubt squander it, perhaps in drink!! So she had to draw it thirty shillings a week. Yes, she had to go every Monday morning down to the offices and stand there a couple of hours waiting for her turn. Yes, for almost four years she went every Monday. And what could she do, with two little children on her hands! But Ted's mother was very good to her. When the baby could toddle, she'd keep both the children for the day, while she, Ivy Bolton, went to Sheffield and attended classes in ambulance, special ambulance, and then the fourth year she even took a nursing course, and got qualified. She was determined to be independent and keep her children. So she was assistant at Uthwaite hospital, just a little place, for a while. But when the Company—the Tevershall Colliery Company, really Sir Geoffrey—saw that she could get on by herself, they were very good to her, gave her the parish nursing, and stood by her, she would say that for them. And she'd done it ever since, till now it was getting a bit much for her, she needed something a bit lighter, there was *such* a lot of traipsing round, when you were district nurse.

"Yes, the Company's been very good to *me*, I always say it. But I should never forget what they said about Ted, for he was as steady and fearless a chap as ever set foot on the cage, and it was as good as branding him a coward. But there, he was dead and could say nothing, to none of 'em!"

It was a queer mixture of feelings the woman showed as she talked. She liked the colliers, whom she had nursed for so long: but she felt very superior to them. She felt almost upper class. At the same time, a resentment against the owning class smouldered in her. The masters! In a question of the masters and the men, she was always for the men. But when there was no question of contest, she was pining to be superior, to be one of the upper classes. The upper classes fascinated her, appealing to her peculiar English passion for superiority. She was thrilled to come to Wragby. She was thrilled to talk to Lady Chatterley—my word, different from the common colliers' wives! She said in so many words.

And one could see a grudge against the Chatterleys peep out in her: the grudge against the masters.

"Why yes, of course it would wear Lady Chatterley out! It's a mercy she had a sister to come and help her. Men don't think. High and low alike, they take what a woman does for them for granted. Oh, I've told the colliers off about it, many a time. But it's very hard, you know, for Sir Clifford, crippled like that. They was always a haughty family, stand-offish in a way—as they've a right to be. But then to be brought down like that!—And it's very hard on Lady Chatterley, perhaps harder on her. What she misses! I only had Ted three years, but my word, while I had him I had a husband I could never forget. He was one in a thousand, and jolly as the day. Who'd ever have thought he'd get killed! I don't believe it to this day—somehow I've never believed it—though I washed him with my own hands. But he was never dead for me, he never was. I never took it in—"

This was a new voice in Wragby, very new for Connie to hear. It roused a new ear in her.

For the first week or so Mrs Bolton, however, was very quiet at Wragby. Her assured, bossy manner left her, and she was nervous. With Clifford she was shy, almost frightened, and silent. He liked that, and soon recovered his self-possession, letting her do things for him without ever noticing her.

"She's a useful nonentity!" he said.

Connie opened her eyes in wonder, but did not contradict him. So different are impressions on two different people!

And he soon became rather superb, somewhat lordly with the nurse. She had rather expected it, and he played up without knowing. So susceptible we are to what is expected of us. The colliers had been so like children, talking to her and telling her what hurt them, when she bandaged them or nursed them. They had always made her feel so grand and almost superhuman, in her administrations. Now Clifford made her feel small and like a servant, and she accepted it without a word, adjusting herself to the upper classes.

She came very mute, with her long, handsome face and downcast eyes, to administer to him. And she said very humbly: "Shall I do this, now, Sir Clifford? Shall I do that?"

"No, leave it for a time. I'll have it done later."

"Very well, Sir Clifford."

"Come in again in half an hour."

"Very well, Sir Clifford."

"And just take those old papers out, will you?"

"Very well, Sir Clifford."

She went softly: and in half an hour, she knocked softly again. She was bullied, but she didn't mind. She was experiencing the upper classes. She neither resented nor disliked Clifford. He was just part of a phenomenon, the phenomenon of the high-class folks, so far unknown to her, but now to be known. She felt more at home with Lady Chatterley—and after all, it's the mistress of the house matters most.

Mrs Bolton helped Clifford to bed at night, and slept across the passage from his room, and came if he rang for her in the night. She also helped him in the morning, and soon valeted him completely, even shaving him, in her soft, tentative woman's way. She was very good and competent. And she soon knew how to have him in her power. He wasn't so very different from the colliers after all, when you lathered his chin and softly rubbed the bristles. The stand-offishness and the lack of frankness didn't bother her. She was having a new experience.

Clifford, however, inside himself never quite forgave Connie for giving up her personal care of him to a strange hired woman. It killed, he said to himself, the real flower of the intimacy between him and her. But Connie didn't mind that. The fine flower of their intimacy was to her rather like an orchid, a bulb stuck parasitic on her tree of life, and producing, to her eyes, a rather shabby flower.

Now she had more time to herself. She could softly play the piano, up in her own room, and sing: "Touch not the nettle— — —for the bonds of love are ill to loose." She had not realised till lately how ill to loose they were, these bonds of love. But thank heaven she had loosened them. She was so glad to be alone, not always to have to talk to him. When he was alone, he tap-tap-tapped on a typewriter, to infinity. But when he was not "working," and she was there, he talked, always talked, infinite small analysis of people and motives and results, characters and personalities—till now she had had enough. For years she had loved it—till she had had enough, and then, suddenly, it was too much. She was thankful to be alone.

It was as if thousands and thousands of little roots and threads of consciousness in him and her had grown together into a tangled mass, till they could crowd no more, and the plant was dying. Now quietly, subtly, she was untangling the tangle of his consciousness and hers, breaking the threads quietly, one by one, with patience and impatience, to get clear. But the bonds of such love are more ill to loose even than most bonds. Though the coming of Mrs Bolton had been a great help.

But he still wanted the old intimate evenings of talk with Connie: talk, or reading aloud. But now she could fix that Mrs Bolton should come at ten to disturb them. At ten o'clock Connie could go upstairs and be alone. Clifford was in good hands with Mrs Bolton.

Mrs Bolton ate with Mrs Betts in the housekeeper's room—since they were all agreeable. And it was curious how much closer the servants' quarters seemed to have come: right up to the doors of Clifford's study, when before they were so remote. For Mrs Betts would sometimes sit in Mrs Bolton's room, and Connie heard their lowered voices, and felt, somehow, the strong, other vibration of the working people almost invading the sitting-rooms, when she and Clifford were alone. So changed was Wragby, merely by Mrs Bolton's coming.

And Connie felt herself released, in another world. She felt she breathed differently. But still she was afraid, how many of her roots, perhaps mortal ones, were tangled with Clifford's. Yet still, she breathed freer. A new phase was going to begin, in her life.

CHAPTER VIII

Mrs Bolton also kept a cherishing eye on Connie, feeling she must extend to her her female and professional protection. She was always urging her ladyship to walk out, to drive to Uthwaite, to be in the air. For Connie had got into the habit of sitting still by the fire, pretending to read, or to sew feebly, and hardly going out at all.

It was a blowy day soon after Hilda had gone, that Mrs Bolton said: "Now why don't you go for a walk through the wood and look at the daffs behind the keeper's cottage? They're the prettiest sight you'd see in a day's march. And you could put some in your room. Wild daffs are always so cheerful looking, aren't they!"

Connie took it in good part: even daffs for daffodils. Wild daffodils! After all, one should not stew in one's own juice. The spring came back. "Seasons return, but not to me returns Spring——"

And the keeper—his thin white body like a lonely pistil of an invisible flower! She had forgotten him, in her unspeakable depression. But now something roused. "Pale beyond porch and portal"—the thing to do was to pass the porches and the portals.

She was stronger—she could walk better. And in the wood the wind would not be so tiring as it was across the park, flattening against her. She wanted to forget, to forget the world and all the dreadful carrion-bodied people. "Ye must be born again!—I believe in the resurrection of the body!—Except a grain of wheat fall into the earth and die, it shall by no means bring forth.—When the crocus cometh forth I too will emerge and see the sun!" In the wind of March, endless phrases swept through her consciousness.

Little gusts of sunshine blew, strangely bright, and lit up the celandines by the wood's edge, under the hazel-rods. They spangled out bright and yellow. And the wood was still, stiller, but yet gusty and with crossing sun. The first windflowers were out, and even the wood seemed pale with the pallor of endless little anemones sprinkling the shaken floor. "The world has grown pale with thy breath." But it was the breath of Persephone, this time. She was out

85

of hell, on a cold morning. Cold breaths of wind came, and overhead there was an anger of entangled wind caught among the twigs. It too was caught and trying to tear itself free, the wind, like Absalom. How cold the anemones looked, bobbing their naked white shoulders over crinoline skirts of green. But they stood it. A few first bleached little primroses too by the path, and yellow buds undoing themselves.

The roaring and swaying was overhead, only cold currents came down below. Connie was strangely excited in the wood, and the colour flew in her cheeks and burned blue in her eyes. She walked ploddingly, picking a few primroses and the first violets, that smelled sweet and cold, sweet and cold. And she drifted on without knowing where she was.

Till she came to the clearing on the far end of the wood, and saw the green-stained stone cottage looking almost rosy, like the flesh underneath a mushroom, its stone warmed in a burst of sun. And there was a sparkle of yellow jasmine by the door: the closed door. But no sound: no smoke from the chimney: no dog barking.

She went quietly round to the back, where the bank rose up. She had an excuse: to see the daffodils.

And they were there, the short-stemmed flowers, rustling and fluttering and shivering so bright and alive, but with nowhere to hide their faces, as they turned them away from the wind.

They shook their bright, sunny little rags in bouts of distress. But perhaps they liked it, really. Perhaps they really liked the tossing.

Constance sat down with her back to a young pine-tree, that swayed against her with curious life, elastic and powerful rising up. The erect alive thing, with its top in the sun! And she watched the daffodils go sunny in a burst of sun, that was warm on her hands and lap. Even she caught the faint tarry scent of the flowers. And then, being so still and alone, she seemed to get into the current of her proper destiny. She had been fastened by a rope, and jagging and snarring like a boat at its moorings. Now she was loose and adrift.

The sunshine gave way to chill. The daffodils were in shadow, dipping silent. So they would dip through the day and the long cold night. So strong in their frailty!

She rose, a little stiff, took a few daffodils and went down. She hated breaking the flowers. But she wanted just one or two to go with her. She would have to go back to Wragby and its walls. And now she hated it, especially its thick walls. Walls! Always walls! Yet one needed them, in this wind.

When she got home, Clifford asked her:

"Where did you go?"

"Right across the wood! Look, aren't the little daffodils adorable! To think they should come out of the earth!"

"Just as much out of the air and sunshine," he said.

"But modelled in the earth," she retorted, with a prompt contradiction that surprised her a little.

The next afternoon she went to the wood again. She followed the broad riding that swerved round and up through the larches to a spring called John's Well. It was cold on this hillside, and not a flower in the darkness of larches. But the icy little spring softly pressed upwards from its little well-bed of pure reddish white pebbles. How icy and clear it was! brilliant! The new keeper had no doubt put in fresh pebbles. She heard the faint tinkle of water, as the tiny overflow trickled over and downhill. Even above the hissing boom of the larch wood, that spread its bristling, leafless, wolfish darkness on the down-slope, she heard the tinkle as of tiny water-bells.

This place was a little sinister, cold, damp. Yet the well must have been a drinking-place for hundreds of years. Now no more. Its tiny cleared space was lush and cold and dismal.

She rose, and went slowly towards home. As she went, she heard a faint tapping away on the right, and stood to listen. Was it hammering, or a woodpecker? It was surely hammering.

She walked on, listening. And then she noticed a narrow track between young fir-trees, a track that seemed to lead nowhere. But she felt it had been used. She turned down it adventurously, between the thick young firs, which gave way soon to the old oak-wood. She followed the track, and the hammering grew nearer, in the silence of the windy wood. For trees make a silence even in their noise of wind.

She saw a secret little clearing, and a secret little hut made of rustic poles. And she had never been here before! She realised it was the quiet place where the young pheasants were reared. The keeper, in his shirt-sleeves, was kneeling hammering. The dog trotted forward with a short sharp bark. The keeper lifted his face suddenly, and saw her. He had a startled look in his eyes.

He straightened himself and saluted, watching her in silence as she came forward with weakening limbs. He resented the intrusion: he cherished his solitude as his only and last freedom in life.

"I wondered what the hammering was," she said, feeling weak and breathless, and a little afraid of him, as he looked so straight at her.

"Ah'm gettin' th' coops ready for th' young bods," he said, in broad vernacular.

She did not know what to say, and she felt weak.

"I should like to sit down a bit," she said.

"Come an' sit 'ere i' th' ut," he said, going in front of her to the hut, pushing aside some timber and stuff, and drawing out a rustic chair made of hazel sticks.

"Am Ah ter light y' a little fire?" he asked, with the curious naïveté of the dialect.

"Oh, don't bother!" she said.

But he looked at her hands: they were rather blue. So he quickly took some larch-twigs to the little brick fire-place in the corner, and in a moment the yellow flame was running up the chimney. He made a place by the brick hearth.

"Sit 'ere then a bit, an' warm yer," he said.

She obeyed him. He had that curious kind of protective authority she obeyed at once. So she sat and warmed her hands at the blaze, and dropped little logs on the fire, while outside he was hammering again. She did not really want to sit poked in a corner by the fire. She would rather have watched from the door. But she was being looked after, so she had to submit.

The hut was quite cosy, panelled with unvarnished deal, having a little rustic table and a stool, besides her chair, and a carpenter's bench, then a big box, tools, new boards, nails, and many things hung from pegs: axe, hatchet, traps, leather things, things in sacks, his coat. It had no window, the light came in through the open door. It was a jumble. But also, it was a sort of little sanctuary.

She listened to the tapping of the man's hammer. It was not so happy. He was oppressed. Here was a trespass on his privacy, and a dangerous one! A woman! He had reached the point where all he wanted on earth was to be alone. And yet he was powerless to preserve his privacy. He was a hired man, and these people were his masters.

Especially he did not want to come into contact with a woman again. He feared it: and he had a big wound from old contacts. He felt, if he could not be alone, and if he could not be left alone, he would die. His recoil away from the outer world was complete. His last refuge was this wood. To hide himself there!

Connie grew warm by the fire, which she had made too big: then she grew hot. She went and sat on the stool in the doorway, watching the man at work. He seemed not to notice her: but he knew. Yet he worked on, as if absorbedly, and his brown dog sat on her tail near him, and surveyed the untrustworthy world.

Slender, quiet and quick, the man finished the coop he was making, turned it over, tried the sliding door, then set it aside. Then he rose, went for an old coop, and took it to the chopping-log where he was working. Crouching, he tried the bars. Some broke in his hands. He began to draw the nails. Then he turned the coop over, and deliberated. And he gave absolutely no sign of awareness of the woman's presence.

So Connie watched him fixedly. And the same solitary aloneness she had seen in him naked, she now saw in him clothed: solitary, and intent, like an animal that works alone, but also brooding, like a soul that recoils away, away from all human contact. Silently, patiently, he was recoiling away from her even now. It was the stillness, and the timeless sort of patience, in a man impatient and passionate, that touched Connie's womb. She saw it in his bent head, the quick, quiet hands, the crouching of his slender, sensitive loins: something patient and withdrawn. She felt his experience had been deeper, and wider than her own: much deeper and wider, and perhaps more deadly. And this relieved her of herself. She felt almost irresponsible.

So she sat in the doorway of the hut in a dream, utterly unaware of time and of particular circumstances. She was so drifted away that he glanced up at her quickly, and saw the utterly still, waiting look on her face. To him it was a look of waiting. And a little, thin tongue of fire suddenly flickered in his loins, at the root of his back, and he groaned in spirit. He dreaded with a repulsion almost of death, any further close human contact. He wished above all things she would go away and leave him to his own privacy. He dreaded her will, her female will, and her modern, female insistency. And above all, he dreaded her cool, upper-class impudence of having her own way. For after all he was only a hired man. He hated her presence there.

Connie came to herself with sudden uneasiness. She rose. The afternoon was passing to evening. Yet she could not go away. She went over to the man. He stood up at attention, his worn face stiff and blank, his eyes watching her.

"It is so nice here, so restful," she said. "I have never been here before."

"No?"

"I think I shall come and sit here sometimes."

"Yes!"

"Do you lock the hut when you're not here?"

"Yes, your ladyship."

"Do you think I could have a key too? So that I could sit sometimes! Are there two keys?"

"Not as Ah know on, the' isna."

He had lapsed into the vernacular. Connie hesitated. He was putting up an opposition. Was it his hut, after all?

"Couldn't we get another key?" she said, in her soft voice, that underneath had the ring of a woman determined to get her way.

"Another!" he said, glancing at her with a flash of anger touched with derision.

"Yes! A duplicate," she said, flushing.

"'Appen Sir Clifford 'ud know," he said, putting her off.

"Yes!" she said. "He might have another. Otherwise we could have one made from the one you have. It would only take a day or so, I suppose. You could spare your key for so long."

"Ah canna tell yer, ma lady! Ah know nob'dy as ma'es keys round 'ere."

Connie suddenly flushed with anger.

"Very well!" she said. "I'll see to it."

"All right, your ladyship."

Their eyes met. His had a cold, ugly look of dislike and contempt, and indifference to what would happen. Hers were hot with rebuff.

But her heart sank. She saw how utterly he disliked her, when she went against him. And she saw in him a sort of desperation.

"Good-afternoon!"

"Afternoon, my lady!"—He saluted, and turned abruptly away. She had wakened the sleeping dogs of old, voracious anger in him, anger against the self-willed female. And he was powerless, powerless! He knew it!

And she was angry against the self-willed male. A servant too! She walked sullenly home.

She found Mrs Bolton under the great beech-tree on the knoll, looking for her.

"I just wondered if you'd be coming, my lady," the woman said brightly.

"Am I late?" said Connie.

"Oh—! Only Sir Clifford was waiting for his tea."

"Why didn't *you* make it then?"

"Oh, I don't think it's hardly my place. I don't think Sir Clifford would like it at all, my lady."

"I don't see why not," said Connie.

She went indoors, to Clifford's study, where the old brass kettle was simmering on the tray.

"Am I late, Clifford!" she said, putting down her few flowers and taking up the tea-caddy, as she stood before the tray in her hat and scarf. "I'm sorry! Why didn't you let Mrs Bolton make the tea?"

"I didn't think of it," he said ironically. "I don't quite see her presiding at the tea-table."

"Oh, there's nothing sacrosanct about a silver tea-pot," said Connie.

He glanced up at her curiously.

"What did you do all afternoon?" he said.

"Walked—and sat in a sheltered place. Do you know, there are still berries on the big holly-tree."

She took off her scarf, but not her hat, and sat down to make tea. The toast would certainly be leathery. She put the tea-cosy over the tea-pot, and rose to get a little glass for her violets. The poor flowers hung over, limp on their stalks.

"They'll revive again!" she said, putting them before him in their glass, for him to smell.

"Sweeter than the lids of Juno's eyes," he quoted.

"I don't see a bit of connection, with the actual violets," she said. "The Elizabethans are rather upholstered."

She poured him his tea.

"Do you think there is a second key to that little hut not far from John's Well, where the pheasants are reared?" she said.

"There may be. Why?"

"I happened to find it today—and I'd never seen it before. I think it's a darling place. I could sit there sometimes, couldn't I?"

"Was Mellors there?"

"Yes! That's how I found it: his hammering. He didn't seem to like my intruding at all. In fact he was almost rude when I asked about a second key."

"What did he say?"

"Oh nothing: just his manner! And he said he knew nothing about keys."

"There may be one, in father's study. Betts knows them all: they're all there. I'll get him to look."

"Oh do!" she said.

"So Mellors was almost rude!"

"Oh, nothing, really! But I don't think he wanted me to have the freedom of the castle, quite."

"I don't suppose he did."

"Still, I don't see why he should mind. It's not his home, after all! It's not his private abode. I don't see why I shouldn't sit there, if I want to."

"Quite!" said Clifford. "He thinks too much of himself, that man."

"Do you think he does?"

"Oh decidedly! He thinks he's something exceptional. You know he had a wife he didn't get on with, so he joined up in 1915, and was sent out to India, I believe. Anyhow he was blacksmith to the cavalry in Egypt for a time; always was connected with horses, a clever fellow that way. Then some Indian colonel took a fancy to him, and made him a lieutenant. Yes, they gave him a commission. I believe he went back to India with his colonel, and up to the north-west frontier. He was ill; he has a pension. He didn't come out of the army till last year, I believe.—And then, naturally, it isn't easy for a man like that to get back to his own level. He's bound to flounder. But he does his duty all right, as far as I'm concerned. Only I'm not having any of the Lieutenant Mellors touch."

"How could they make him an officer, when he speaks broad Derbyshire?"

"He doesn't—except by fits and starts. He can speak perfectly well—for him. I suppose he has an idea, if he's come down to the ranks again he'd better speak as the ranks speak."

"Why didn't you tell me about him before?"

"Oh—I've no patience with these romances. They're the ruin of all order. It's a thousand pities they ever happened."

Connie was inclined to agree. What was the good of discontented people who fitted in nowhere!

In the spell of fine weather Clifford too decided to go to the wood. The wind was cold, but not so tiresome, and the sunshine was like life itself, warm and full.

"It's amazing," said Connie, "how different one feels when there's a really fresh, fine day. Usually one feels the very air is half dead. People are killing the very air."

Lady Chatterley's Lover

"Do you think people are doing it?" he asked.

"I do! The steam of so much discontent and boredom and anger out of all the people just kills the vitality in the air. I'm sure of it."

"Perhaps some condition of the atmosphere lowers the vitality of the people," he said.

"No! It is man that poisons the universe," she asserted.

"Fouls his own nest!" remarked Clifford.

The chair puffed on. In the hazel copse catkins were hanging pale gold, and in sunny places the wood-anemones were wide open as if exclaiming with the joy of life, just as good as in past days, when people could exclaim along with them. They had a faint scent of apple-blossom. Connie gathered a few for Clifford.

He took them and looked at them curiously.

"'Thou still unravished bride of quietness,'" he quoted.—"It seems to fit flowers so much better than Greek vases."

"Ravished is such a horrid word!" she said. "It's only people who ravish things."

"Oh I don't know—snails and things," he said.

"Even snails only eat them. And bees don't ravish."

She was angry with him, turning everything into words. Violets were Juno's eyelids and windflowers were unravished brides. How she hated words, always coming between her and life! They did the ravishing, if anything did: ready-made words and phrases sucking all the life-sap out of living things.

The walk with Clifford was not quite a success. Between him and Connie there was a tension that each pretended not to notice, but there it was. Suddenly, with all the force of her female instinct, she was silently shoving him off. She wanted to be clear of him, and especially of his consciousness, his words, his obsession with himself—his endless treadmill obsession with himself and his own words.

The weather came rainy again. But after a day or two she went out in the rain. And she went to the wood. And once there, she went towards the hut. It was raining, but not so cold. And the wood felt so silent and remote, inaccessible in the dusk of rain.

She came to the clearing. No one there! The hut was locked. But she sat on the log doorstep, under the rustic porch, and snuggled into her own warmth. So she sat looking at the rain, listening to the many noiseless noises of it, and to the strange soughings of wind in upper branches, when there seemed no wind. Old oak trees stood around, grey powerful trunks rain-blackened, round and vital, throwing off reckless limbs. The ground was fairly free of undergrowth, the windflowers sprinkled, there was a bush or two, elder or guelder-rose, and a purplish tangle of bramble—the old russet of bracken almost vanished under green anemone ruffs. Perhaps this was one of the unravished places. Unravished! The whole world was ravished.

Some things can't be ravished. You can't ravish a tin of sardines. And so many women are like that: and men. But the earth—!

The rain was abating. It was hardly making darkness among the oaks any more. Connie wanted to go. Yet she sat on. But she was getting cold. Yet the overwhelming inertia of her inner resentment kept her there as if paralysed.

Ravished! How ravished one could be without ever being touched! Ravished by dead words become obscene, and dead ideas become obsessions.

A wet brown dog came running, and did not bark, lifting a wet feather of a tail. The man followed—in a wet black oilskin jacket like a chauffeur, and a face flushed a little. She felt him recoil in his quick walk, when he saw her. She stood up, in the handbreadth of dryness under the rustic porch. He saluted without speaking, coming slowly near. She began to withdraw.

"I'm just going," she said.

"Was yer waitin' ter get in?" he asked, looking at the hut, not at her.

"No! I only sat a few minutes in the shelter," she said, with quiet dignity.

He looked at her. She looked cold.

"Sir Clifford 'adn't got no other key then?" he asked.

"No! But it doesn't matter. I can sit perfectly dry under the porch. Good-afternoon!"

She hated the excess of vernacular in his speech.

He watched her closely, as she was moving away. Then he hitched up his jacket and put his hand in his breeches pocket, taking out the key of the hut.

"'Appen yer'd better 'ave this key, an' Ah mun fend for t' bods some other road."

She looked at him.

"What do you mean?" she said.

"I mean as 'appen Ah can find anuther pleece as'll du for rearin'

94

th' pheasants. If yo' want ter be 'ere, yo' ll non want me messin' abaht a' t' time."

She looked at him, getting his meaning through the fog of the dialect.

"Why don't you speak ordinary English?" she said coldly.

"Me!—I thowt it *wor*' ordinary."

She was silent for a few moments, in anger.

"So if yer want t' key, yer'd better ta'e it. Or 'appen Ah'd better gi'e 't yer termorrer, an' clear all t' stuff aht fust. Would that du for yer?"

She became more angry.

"I didn't want your key," she said. "I don't want you to clear anything out at all. I don't in the least want to turn you out of your hut, thank you! I only wanted to be able to sit here sometimes—like today. But I can sit perfectly well under the porch. So please say no more about it."

He looked at her again, with his wicked blue eyes.

"Why," he began, in the broad, slow dialect, "your ladyship's as welcome as Christmas ter th' ut an' th' key an' iverythink as is. On'y this time o' th' year the 's bods ter set, an' Ah've got ter be potterin' abaht a good bit seein' after 'em an' a'! Winter time I ned 'ardly come nigh t' pleece. But what wi' spring, an' Sir Clifford wantin' ter start t' pheasants———An' your ladyship 'ud not want *me* tinkerin' around an' about when she was here, a' t' time—"

She listened with a dim kind of amazement.

"Why should I mind your being here?" she asked.

He looked at her curiously.

"T' nuisance on me!" he said, briefly, but significantly. And she flushed.

"Very well!" she said finally. "I won't trouble you. But I don't think I should have minded at all sitting and seeing you look after the birds. I should have liked it. But since you think it interferes with you, I won't disturb you, don't be afraid. You are Sir Clifford's keeper, not mine."

The phrase sounded queer—she didn't know why. But she let it pass.

"Nay, your ladyship. It's your ladyship's own 'ut. It's as your ladyship likes an' pleases, every time. You can turn me off at a wik's notice. It wor on'y—"

"Only what?" she said, baffled.

He pushed back his hat, in an odd, comic way.

"On'y as 'appen yo'd like th' pleece ter yersen, when yer did come, an' not me messin' abaht."

"But why?" she said, angry. "Aren't you a civilised human being? Do you think I ought to be afraid of you? Why should I take any notice of you, and your being here or not? Why is it important?"

He looked at her, all his face glimmering with wicked laughter.

"It's not, your ladyship. Not in the very least," he said.

"Well why then——?" she asked.

"Shall I get your ladyship another key then?"

"No thank you! I don't want it."

"Ah'll get it anyhow. We'd best 'ave two keys ter th' place."

"And I consider you are insolent," said Connie, her colour up, panting a little.

"Nay nay!" he said quickly. "Dunna yer say that! Nay nay, I niver meant nothink! Ah on'y thought as if yo' come 'ere, Ah sh' 'ave ter clear out. An' it 'ud mean a lot o' work, settin' up somewhere else. But if your ladyship isn't goin' ter take no notice o' me, then——it's Sir Clifford's 'ut, an' everythink is as your ladyship likes: everythink is as your ladyship likes an' pleases, barrin' you take no notice o' me, doin' th' bits o' jobs as Ah've got ter do."

Connie went away completely bewildered. She was not sure whether she had been insulted and mortally offended or not. Perhaps the man really only meant what he said: that he thought she would expect him to keep away. As if she would dream of it! And as if he could possibly be so important, he and his stupid presence.

She went home in a confusion, not knowing what she thought or felt.

CHAPTER IX.

Connie was surprised at her own feeling of aversion from Clifford. What is more, she felt she had always really disliked him. Not hate: there was no passion in it. But a profound physical dislike. Almost it seemed to her she had married him because she disliked him, in a secret, physical sort of way. But of course, she had married him really because in a mental way he attracted her and excited her. He had seemed, in some way, her master, beyond her.

Now the mental excitement had worn itself out and collapsed, and she was aware only of the physical aversion. It rose up in her from her depths: and she realised how it had been eating her life away.

She felt weak and utterly forlorn. She wished some help would come from outside. But in the whole world there was no help. Society was terrible because it was insane.

Civilised society is insane. Money and so-called love are its two great manias; money a long way first. The individual asserts himself in his disconnected insanity in these two modes: money and love. Look at Michaelis! His life and activity were just insanity. His love was a sort of insanity. His very plays were a sort of insanity.

And Clifford the same. All that talk! All that writing! All that wild struggling to shove himself forwards! It was just insanity. And it was getting worse, really maniacal.

Connie felt washed-out with fear. But at least, Clifford was shifting his grip from her on to Mrs Bolton. He did not know it. Like many insane people, his insanity might be measured by the things he was *not* aware of: the great desert tracts in his consciousness.

Mrs Bolton was admirable in many ways. But she had that queer, unconscious sort of bossiness, endless assertion of her own will, which is one of the signs of insanity in modern woman. She *thought* she was utterly subservient and living for others. Clifford fascinated her because he always, or so often, just calmly frustrated her will, as if by a finer instinct. He had a finer, subtler will of self-assertion than herself. This was his charm for her.

Perhaps that had been his charm, too, for Connie.

"It's a lovely day today!" Mrs Bolton would say, in her caressive, persuasive voice. "I should think you'd enjoy a little run in your chair today, the sun's just lovely."

"Yes?—Will you give me that book—there, that yellow one. And I think I'll have those hyacinths taken out."

"Why they're *so* beautiful!"—she pronounced it with the 'y' sound: be-yutiful!—"And the scent is simply gorgeous."

"The scent is what I object to," he said. "It's a little funereal."

"Do you think so!" she exclaimed in surprise, just a little offended, but impressed. And she carried the hyacinths out of the room, impressed by his higher fastidiousness.

"Shall I shave you this morning, or would you rather do it yourself?"—Always the same soft, caressive, subservient, yet managing voice.

"I don't know. Do you mind waiting a while. I'll ring when I'm ready."

"Very good, Sir Clifford!" she replied, so soft and submissive, with-drawing quietly. But every rebuff stored up new energy of will in her.

When he rang, after a time, she would appear at once. And then he would say:

"I think I'd rather you shaved me this morning."

Her heart gave a little thrill, and she replied with extra softness: "Very good, Sir Clifford!"

She was very deft, with a soft, lingering touch, a little slow. At first he had resented the infinitely soft touch of her fingers on his face. But now he liked it, with a growing voluptuousness. He let her shave him nearly every day: her face near his, her eyes so very concen-trated, watching that she did it right. And gradually her finger-tips knew his cheeks and lips, his jaw and chin and throat, perfectly. He was well-fed and well-liking, his face and throat were handsome enough, and he was a gentleman.

She too was handsome, pale, her face rather long and absolutely still, her eyes bright, but revealing nothing. Gradually, with infinite softness, almost with love, she was getting him by the throat, and he was yielding to her.

She now did almost everything for him, and he felt more at home with her, less ashamed of accepting her menial offices, than with Connie. She liked handling him. She loved having his body in her charge, absolutely, to the last menial offices. She said to Connie one day: "All men are babies, when you come to the bottom of them.

Why, I've handled some of the toughest customers as ever went
down Tevershall pit. But let anything ail them, so that you have to do
for them, and they're babies, just big babies. Oh, there's not much
difference in men!"

At first Mrs Bolton had thought there really was something
different in a gentleman, a *real* gentleman, like Sir Clifford. So
Clifford had got a good start of her. But gradually, as she came to the
bottom of him, to use her own term, she found he was like the rest, a
baby grown to man's proportions: but a baby with a queer temper
and a fine manner and money and power in its control, and all sorts
of odd knowledge that she had never dreamed of, with which he
could still bully her.

Connie was sometimes tempted to say to him: "For God's sake,
don't sink so horribly into the hands of that woman!" But she found
she didn't care for him enough to say it, in the long run.

It was still their habit to spend the evening together, till ten
o'clock. Then they would talk, or read together, or go over his
manuscript. But the thrill had gone out of it. She was bored by his
manuscripts. She still dutifully typed them out for him. But in time
Mrs Bolton would do even that.

For Connie herself had suggested to Mrs Bolton that she should
learn to use a typewriter. And Mrs Bolton, always ready, had begun
at once, and practised assiduously. So now Clifford would sometimes dictate a letter to her, and she would take it down rather slowly,
but correctly. And he was very patient spelling for her the difficult
words, or the occasional phrases in French. She was so thrilled, it
was almost a pleasure to instruct her.

Now Connie would sometimes plead a headache, as an excuse for
going up to her room after dinner.

"Perhaps Mrs Bolton will play piquet with you," she said to
Clifford.

"Oh, I shall be perfectly all right. You go to your room and rest,
darling."

But no sooner had she gone, than he rang for Mrs Bolton, and
asked her to take a hand at piquet or bezique, or even chess. He had
taught her all these games. And Connie found it curiously objection-
able to see Mrs Bolton, flushed and tremulous like a young girl,
touching her queen or her knight with uncertain fingers, then
drawing away again. And Clifford, faintly smiling with a half-teasing
superiority, saying to her:

"You must say *j'adoube!*"

She looked up at him with bright, startled eyes, then murmured shyly, obediently:

"J'adoube!"

Yes, he was educating her. And he enjoyed it, it gave him a sense of power. And she was thrilled. She was coming bit by bit into possession of all that the gentry knew, all that made them upper class: apart from the money. That thrilled her. And at the same time, she was making him want to have her there with him. It was a subtle deep flattery to him, her genuine thrill.

To Connie, Clifford seemed to be coming out in his true colours: a little vulgar, a little common, and uninspired; rather fat. Ivy Bolton's tricks and humble bossiness were also only too transparent. But Connie did wonder at the genuine thrill which the woman got out of Clifford. To say she was in love with him would be putting it wrongly. She was thrilled by her contact with this man of the upper class, this titled gentleman, this author who could write books and poems, and whose photograph appeared in the illustrated papers. She was thrilled to a weird passion. And his "educating" her roused in her a passion of excitement and response much deeper than any love affair could have done. In truth, the very fact that there could *be* no love affair left her free to thrill to her very marrow with his other passion, the peculiar passion of *knowing*, knowing as he knew.

There was no mistake that the woman was in some way in love with him: whatever force we like to give to the word love. She looked so handsome, and so young, and her grey eyes were sometimes marvellous. At the same time, there was a lurking sort of satisfaction about her, even of triumph, which Connie hated. Secret triumph, and private satisfaction! Ugh, that private satisfaction! How Connie hated it!

But no wonder Clifford was caught by the woman! She absolutely adored him, in her persistent fashion, and put herself absolutely at his service, for him to use as he liked. No wonder he was flattered!

Connie heard long conversations going on between the two. Or rather, it was mostly Mrs Bolton talking. She had unloosed to him the stream of her gossip about Tevershall village. It was more than gossip. It was Mrs Gaskell and George Eliot and Miss Mitford all rolled in one, with a great deal more, that these women left out. Once started, Mrs Bolton was better than any book, about the lives of the people. She knew them all so intimately, and had such a peculiar, flamey zest in all their affairs, it was wonderful, if just a *trifle* humiliating, to listen to her. At first she had not ventured to "talk Tevershall," as she called it, to Clifford. But once started, it went. Clifford was listening for "material," and he found it in plenty. Connie realised that his so-called "genius" was just this: a peculiar talent for perspicuous personal gossip, clever and apparently detached. Mrs Bolton, of course, was very warm when she "talked Tevershall." Carried away, in fact. And it was marvellous, the things that happened and that she knew about. She would have run to dozens of volumes.

Connie was fascinated, listening to her. But afterwards, always a little ashamed. She ought not to listen with this queer rabid curiosity. After all, one may hear the most private affairs of other people, but only in a spirit of respect for the struggling, battered thing which any human soul is, and in a spirit of fine, discriminative sympathy. For even satire is a form of sympathy. It is the way our sympathy flows and recoils that really determines our lives. And here lies the vast importance of the novel, properly handled. It can inform and lead into new places the flow of our sympathetic consciousness, and it can lead our sympathy away in recoil from things gone dead. Therefore the novel, properly handled, can reveal the most secret places of life: for it is in the *passional* secret places of life, above all, that the tide of sensitive awareness needs to ebb and flow, cleansing and freshening.

But the novel, like gossip, can also excite spurious sympathies and recoils, mechanical and deadening to the psyche. The novel can glorify the most corrupt feelings, so long as they are *conventionally* "pure." Then the novel, like gossip, becomes at last vicious, and, like gossip, all the more vicious because it is always ostensibly on the side of the angels. Mrs Bolton's gossip was always on the side of the angels. "And he was such a *bad* fellow, and she was such a *nice* woman——" whereas, as Connie could see even from Mrs Bolton's gossip, the woman had been merely a mealy-mouthed sort, and the man angrily honest. But angry honesty made a "bad man" of him, and mealy-mouthedness made a "nice woman" of her, in the vicious, conventional channeling of sympathy by Mrs Bolton.

For this reason, the gossip was humiliating. And for the same reason, most novels, especially popular ones, are humiliating too. The public responds now only to an appeal to its vices.

Nevertheless, one got a new vision of Tevershall village from Mrs Bolton's talk. A terrible, seething welter of ugly life it seemed: not at all the flat drabness it looked from outside. Clifford of course knew by sight most of the people mentioned, Connie knew only one or two. But it sounded really more like a central African jungle than an English village.

"I suppose you heard as Miss Allsop was married last week! Would you ever! Miss Allsop, old James's daughter, the boot-and-shoe Allsop. You know they built a house up at Pye Croft. The old man died last year from a fall: eighty-three, he was, an' nimble as a lad. An' then he slipped on Bestwood Hill, on a slide as the lads 'ad made last winter, an' broke his thigh, and that finished him, poor old man, it did seem a shame. Well he left all his money to Tattie: didn't leave the boys a penny. And Tattie, I know, is five years—yes, she's fifty-three last autumn. And you know they were such chapel people, my word! She taught Sunday School for thirty years, till her father died. And then she started carrying on with a fellow from Kinbrook, I don't know if you know him, an oldish fellow with a red nose, rather dandified, Willcock, as works in Hanson's woodyard. Well he's sixty-five if he's a day, yet you'd have thought they were a pair of young turtle-doves, to see them, arm in arm, and kissing at the gate: yes, an' she sitting on his knee right in the bay window on Pye Croft road, for anybody to see. And he's got sons over forty: only lost his wife two years ago. If old James Allsop hasn't risen from his grave, it's because there is no rising: for he kept her that strict! Now they're married and gone to live down at Kinbrook, and they say she goes round in a dressing-gown from morning to night, a veritable sight. I'm sure it's awful, the way the old ones go on! Why they're a *lot* worse than the young, and a sight more disgusting. I lay it down to the pictures, myself. But you can't keep them away. I was always saying: Go to a good instructive film, but do for goodness sake keep away from these melodramas and love films. Anyhow keep the children away!—But there you are, the grown-ups are worse than th' children: and the old ones beat the band. Talk about morality! nobody cares a thing. Folks does as they like, and much better off they are for it, I must say. But they're having to draw their horns in nowadays, now th' pits are working so bad, and they haven't got the money. And the grumbling they do, it's awful, especially the women. The men are so good and patient! What can they do, poor chaps! But the women, oh, they do carry on! They go and show off, giving contributions for a wedding-present for Princess Mary, and then when they see all the grand things that's been given, they simply

rave:—'who's she, any better than anybody else! Why doesn't Swan
and Edgars give me *one* fur coat, instead of giving her six. I wish I'd
kept my ten shillings! What's she going to give *me*, I should like to
know? Here I can't get a new spring coat, my dad's working that bad,
and she gets van-loads. It's time it was stopped. I'm about fed up. It's
time as poor folks had some money to spend, rich ones 'as 'ad it long
enough. I want a new spring coat, I do; an' wheer am I going to get
it?—' —I say to them, be thankful you're well fed and well clothed,
without all the new finery you want!—And they fly back at me: 'Why
isn't Princess Mary thankful to go about in her old rags, then, an'
have nothing! Folks like *her* get van-loads, an' I can't have a new
spring coat. It's a damned shame. Princess! bloomin' rot about
Princess! It's munney as matters, an' cos she's got lots, they give her
more! Nobody's givin' me any, an' I've as much right as anybody
else. Don't talk to me about education. It's munney as matters. I want
a new spring coat, I do, an' I shan't get it, cos there's no munney—'
That's all they care about, clothes. They think nothing of giving
seven and eight guineas for a winter coat—colliers' daughters, mind
you—and two guineas for a child's summer hat. And then they go to
the Primitive Chapel in their two-guinea hat, girls as would have
been proud of a three-and-sixpenny one in my day. I heard that at
the Primitive Methodist anniversary this year, when they have a
built-up platform for the Sunday School children, like a grand stand
going almost up to th' ceiling, I heard Miss Thompson, who has the
first class of girls in the Sunday School, say there'd be over a
thousand pounds in new Sunday clothes sitting on that platform!
And times are what they are! But you can't stop them. They're mad
for clothes. And boys the same. The lads spend every penny on
themselves, clothes, smoking, drinking in the Miner's Welfare,
jaunting off to Sheffield two or three times a week. Why it's another
world. And they fear nothing, and they respect nothing, the young
don't. The older men are that patient and good, really, they let the
women take everything. And this is what it leads to. The women are
positive demons. But the lads aren't like their dads. They're
sacrificing nothing, they aren't: they're all for self. If you tell them
they ought to be putting a bit by, for a home, they say: That'll keep,
that will. I'm goin' t' enjoy mysen while I can. Owt else'll keep!—Oh,
they're rough an' selfish, if you like. Everything falls on the older
men, an' it's a bad lookout all round.—"

Clifford began to get a new idea of his own village. The place had always frightened him, but he had thought it more or less stable. Now—?

"Is there much socialism, bolshevism, among the people?" he asked.

"Oh!" said Mrs Bolton. "You hear a few loud-mouthed ones. But they're mostly women who've got into debt. The men take no notice. I don't believe you'll ever turn our Tevershall men into reds. They're too decent for that. But the young ones blether sometimes. Not that they care for it really. They only want a bit of money in their pocket, to spend at the Welfare, or go gadding to Sheffield. That's all they care. When they've got no money, they'll listen to the reds spouting. But nobody believes in it, really."

"So you think there's no danger?"

"Oh no! Not if trade was good, there wouldn't be. But if things were bad for a long spell, the young ones might go funny. I tell you, they're a selfish, spoilt lot. But I don't see how they'd ever do anything. They aren't ever serious about anything, except showing off on motor-bikes and dancing at the Palais-de-danse in Sheffield. You can't *make* them serious. The serious ones dress up in evening clothes and go off to the Pally to show off before a lot of girls and dance these new Charlestons and what not. I'm sure sometimes the bus'll be full of young fellows in evening suits, collier lads, off to the Pally: let alone those that have gone with their girls in motors or on motor-bikes. They don't give a serious thought to a thing—save Doncaster races, and the Derby: for they all of them bet on every race. And football! But even football's not what it was, not by a long chalk. It's too much like hard work, they say. No, they'd rather be off on motor-bikes to Sheffield or Nottingham, Saturday afternoons."

"But what do they do when they get there?"

"Oh, hang round—and have tea in some fine tea-place like the Mikado—and go to the Pally or the Pictures or the Empire, with some girl. The girls are as free as the lads. They do just what they like."

"And what do they do when they haven't the money for these things?"

"They seem to get it, somehow. And they begin talking nasty then. But I don't see how you're going to get bolshevism, when all the lads want is just money to enjoy themselves, and the girls the same, with fine clothes: and they don't care about another thing. They haven't the brains to be socialists. They haven't enough seriousness to take anything really serious, and they never will have."

Connie thought, how extremely like all the rest of the classes the lower classes sounded. Just the same thing over again, Tevershall or Mayfair or Kensington. There was only one class nowadays: money-boys. The moneyboy and the moneygirl, the only difference was how much you'd got, and how much you wanted.

Under Mrs Bolton's influence, Clifford began to take a new interest in the mines. He began to feel he belonged. A new sort of self-assertion came into him. After all, he was the real boss in Tevershall, he was really the pits. It was a new sense of power, something he had till now shrunk from with dread.

Tevershall pits were running thin. There were only two collieries: Tevershall itself, and New London. Tevershall had once been a famous mine, and had made famous money. But its best days were over. New London was never very rich, and in ordinary times just got along decently. But now times were bad, and it was pits like New London that got left.

"There's a lot of Tevershall men left and gone to Stacks Gate and Whiteover," said Mrs Bolton. "You've not seen the new works at Stacks Gate, opened after the war, have you Sir Clifford? Oh, you must go one day, they're something quite new: great big chemical works at the pit-head, doesn't look a bit like a colliery. They say they get more money out of the chemical by-products than out of the coal—I forget what it is. And the grand new houses for the men, fair mansions! Of course it's brought a lot of riff-raff from all over the country. But a lot of Tevershall men got on there, and doin' well, a lot better than our own men. They say Tevershall's done, finished: only a question of a few more years, and it'll have to shut down. And New London 'll go first. My word, won't it be funny, when there's no Tevershall pit working. It's bad enough during a strike, but my word, if it closes down for good, it'll be like the end of the world. Even when I was a girl it was the best pit in the country, and a man counted himself lucky if he could get on here. Oh, there's been some money made in Tevershall. And now the men say it's a sinking ship, and it's time they all got out. Doesn't it sound awful! But of course there's a lot as'll never go till they have to. They don't like these newfangled mines, such a depth, and all machinery to work them. Some of them simply dreads those iron men, as they call them, those machines for hewing the coal, where men always did it before. And they say it's wasteful as well. But what goes in waste is saved in wages, and a lot more. It seems soon there'll be no use for men on the face of the earth, it'll be all machines. But they say that's what folks said when they had to give up the old stocking-frames. I can remember one or two. But my word, the more machines, the more people, that's what it looks like! They say you can't get the same chemicals out of Tevershall coal as you can out of Stacks Gate, and that's funny, they're not three miles apart. But they say so. But everybody says it's a shame something can't be started, to keep the men going a bit better, and employ the girls. All the girls traipsing off to Sheffield every day! My word, it would be something to talk about if Tevershall collieries took a new lease of life, after everybody saying they're finished, and a sinking ship, and the men ought to leave them like rats leave a sinking ship. But folks talk so much. Of course there was a boom during the war, when Sir Geoffrey made a trust of himself and got the money safe forever, somehow. So they say! But they say even the masters and the owners don't get much out of it now. You can hardly believe it, can you! Why I always thought the pits would go on forever and ever. Who'd have thought, when I was a girl! But New England's shut down, so is Colwick Wood: yes, it's fair haunting to go through that coppy and see Colwick Wood standing there deserted among the trees, and bushes growing up all over the pit-head, and the lines red rusty. My word, you feel you see ghosts! It's like death itself, a dead colliery. Why whatever we should do if Tevershall shut down——! it doesn't bear thinking of. Always that throng it's been, except at strikes, and even then the fan-wheels didn't stand, except when they fetched the ponies up. I'm sure it's a funny world, you don't know where you are from year to year, you really don't."

It was Mrs Bolton's talk that really put a new fight into Clifford. His income, as she pointed out to him, was secure, from his father's trust, even though it was not large. The pits did not really concern him. It was the other world he wanted to capture, the world of literature and fame; the popular world, not the working world.

Now he realised the distinction between popular success and working success: the populace of pleasure and the populace of work. He, as a private individual, had been catering with his stories for the populace of pleasure. And he had caught on. But beneath the populace of pleasure lay the populace of work, grim, grimey, and rather terrible. They too had to have their providers. And it was a much grimmer business, providing for the populace of work, than for the populace of pleasure. While he was doing his stories, and "getting on" in the world, Tevershall was going to the wall.

He realised now that the bitch-goddess of success had two main appetites: one for flattery, adulation, stroking and tickling such as writers and artists gave her; but the other a grimmer appetite for meat and bones. And the meat and bones for the bitch-goddess were provided by the men who made money in industry.

Yes, there were two great groups of dogs wrangling for the bitch-goddess: the group of the flatterers, those who offered her amusement, stories, films, plays: and the other, much less showy, much more savage breed, those who gave her meat, the real substance of money. The well-groomed showy dogs of amusement wrangled and snarled among themselves for the favours of the bitch-goddess. But it was nothing to the silent fight-to-the-death that went on among the indispensables, the bone-bringers.

But under Mrs Bolton's influence, Clifford was tempted to enter this other fight, to capture the bitch-goddess by brute means of industrial production. Somehow, he got his pecker up. In one way, Mrs Bolton made a man of him, as Connie never did. Connie kept him apart, and made him sensitive and conscious of himself and his own states. Mrs Bolton made him aware only of outside things. Inwardly he began to go soft as pulp. But outwardly he began to be effective.

He even roused himself to go to the mines once more: and when he was there, he went down in a tub, and in a tub he was hauled out into the workings. Things he had learned before the war, and seemed utterly to have forgotten, now came back to him. He sat there, crippled, in a tub, with the underground manager showing him the seam with a powerful torch. And he said little. But his mind began to work.

He began to read again his technical works on the coal-mining industry, he studied the government reports, and he read with care the latest things on mining and the chemistry of coal and of shale which were written in German. Of course the most valuable discoveries were kept secret as far as possible. But once you started a sort of research in the field of coal-mining, a study of methods and means, a study of by-products and the chemical possibilities of coal, it was astounding, the ingenuity and the almost uncanny cleverness of the modern technical mind, as if really the devil himself had lent fiends' wits to the technical scientists of industry. It was far more interesting than art, than literature, poor emotional, half-witted stuff, was this technical science of industry. In this field, men were like gods, or demons, inspired to discoveries, and fighting to carry them out. In this activity, men were beyond any mental age calculable. But Clifford knew that when it did come to the emotional and human life, these self-same men were of a mental age of about thirteen, feeble boys. The discrepancy was enormous and appalling.

But let that be. Let man slide down to general idiocy in the emotional and "human" mind, Clifford did not care. Let all that go hang. He was interested in the technicalities of modern coal-mining, and in pulling Tevershall out of the hole.

He went down the pit day after day, he studied, he put the general manager, and the overhead manager, and the underground manager, and the engineers through a mill they had never dreamed of. Power! He felt a new sense of power flowing through him: power over all these men, over the hundreds and hundreds of colliers. He was finding out: and he was getting things into his grip.

And he seemed verily to be re-born. *Now* life came into him! He had been gradually dying, with Connie, in the isolated private life of the artist and the conscious being. Now let all that go. Let it sleep. He simply felt life rush into him out of the coal, out of the pit. The very stale air of the colliery was better than oxygen to him. It gave him a sense of power, power. He was doing something: and he was *going* to do something. He was going to win, to win: not as he had won with his stories, mere publicity, amid a whole yapping of envy and malice. But a man's victory, over the coal, over the very dirt of Tevershall pit.

At first he thought the solution lay in electricity: convert the coal into electric power, there at the pit-head, and sell the power. Then a new idea came. The Germans invented a new locomotive engine with a self-feeder, that did not need a fireman. And it was to be fed with a new fuel, that burnt in small quantities at a great heat, under peculiar conditions.

The idea of a new concentrated fuel that burnt with a hard slowness at a fierce heat was what first attracted Clifford. There must be some sort of external stimulus to the burning of such fuel, not merely air supply. He began to experiment, and got a clever young fellow who had proved brilliant in chemistry, to help him.

And he felt triumphant. He had at last got out of himself. He had fulfilled his life-long secret yearning: to get out of himself. Art had not done it for him. Art had only made it worse. But now, now he had done it.

He was not aware how much Mrs Bolton was behind him. He did not know how much he depended on her. But for all that, it was evident that when he was with her his voice dropped to an easy rhythm of intimacy, almost a trifle vulgar.

With Connie, he was a little stiff. He felt he owed her everything, everything, and he showed her the utmost respect and consideration, so long as she gave him mere outward respect. But it was obvious he had a secret dread of her. The new Achilles in him had a heel, and in this heel the woman, the woman like Connie his wife, could lame him fatally. He went in a certain half-subservient dread of her, and was extremely nice to her. But his voice was a little tense when he spoke to her, and he began to be silent whenever she was present.

Only when he was alone with Mrs Bolton did he really feel a lord and a master, and his voice ran on with her almost as easily and garrulously as her own could run. And he let her shave him or sponge all his body as if he were a child, really as if he were a child.

CHAPTER X

Connie was a good deal alone now, fewer people came to Wragby. Clifford no longer wanted them. He had turned against even the cronies. He was queer. He preferred the radio, which he had installed at some expense, with a good deal of success at last. He could sometimes get Madrid, or Frankfurt, even there in the uneasy Midlands.

And he would sit alone for hours listening to the loud-speaker bellowing forth. It amazed and stunned Connie. But there he would sit, with a blank, entranced expression on his face, like a person losing his mind, and listen, or seem to listen, to the unspeakable thing.

Was he really listening? Or was it a sort of soporific he took, while something else worked on underneath in him? Connie did not know. She fled up to her room: or out of doors, to the wood. A kind of terror filled her sometimes: a terror of the incipient insanity of the whole civilised species.

But now that Clifford was drifting off to this other weirdness of industrial activity, becoming almost suddenly changed into a creature with a hard, efficient shell of an exterior and a pulpy interior, one of the amazing crabs and lobsters of the modern industrial and financial world, invertebrates of the crustacean order, with shells of steel, like machines, and inner bodies of soft pulp, Connie herself was really completely stranded.

She was not even free, for Clifford must have her there. He seemed to have a nervous terror that she would leave him. The curious pulpy part of him, the emotional and humanly-individual part, depended on her with terror, like a child, almost like an idiot. She must be there, there at Wragby, as Lady Chatterley, his wife. Otherwise he would be lost like an idiot on a moor.

This amazing dependence Connie realised with a sort of horror. She heard him with his pit-managers, with the members of his board, with young scientists, and she was amazed at his shrewd insight into things, his power, his uncanny material power over what are called practical men. He had become a practical man himself, and an amazingly astute and powerful one: a master. Connie attributed it to Mrs Bolton's influence upon him, just at a crisis in his life.

But this astute and powerful practical man was almost an idiot when left alone to his own emotional life. He worshipped Connie. She was his wife, a higher being, and he worshipped her with a queer craven idolatry, like a savage: a worship based on enormous fear, and even hate, of the powers of the idol, the dread idol. All he wanted was for Connie to swear, to swear not to leave him, not to give him away.

"Clifford!" she said to him—but this was after she had the key to the hut—"Would you really like me to have a child one day?"

He looked at her with a furtive apprehension in his rather prominent pale eyes.

"I shouldn't mind, if it made no difference between us," he said.

"No difference to what?" she asked.

"To you and me: to our love for one another! If it's going to affect that, then I'm all against it.—Why I might even one day have a child of my own!"

She looked at him in amazement.

"I mean it might come back to me, one of these days."

She still stared in amazement, and he was uncomfortable.

"So you wouldn't like it if I had a child?" she said.

"I tell you," he replied quickly, like a cornered dog. "I'm quite willing, provided it doesn't touch your love for me. If it would touch that, I'm dead against it."

Connie could only be silent, in cold fear and contempt. Such talk was really the gabbling of an idiot. He no longer knew what he was talking about.

"Oh, it wouldn't make any difference to my feeling for you," she said, with a certain sarcasm.

"There!" he said. "That's the point! In that case I don't mind in the least. I mean it would be awfully nice to have a child running about the house, and feel one was building up a future for it. I should have something to strive for then. And I should know it was your child, shouldn't I, dear! and it would seem just the same as my own. Because it's you who count, in these matters. You know that, don't you dear? I don't enter. I'm a cypher. You are the great I-am! as far as life goes. You know that, don't you? I mean as far as I'm concerned. I mean but for you, I'm absolutely nothing. I live for your sake, and your future. I'm nothing to myself—"

Connie heard it all with deepening dismay and repulsion. It was one of the ghastly half-truths that poison human existence. What man in his senses would say such things to a woman? But men aren't in their senses. What man with a spark of honour would put this ghastly burden of all life-responsibility upon a woman, and leave her there, in the void?

Moreover, in half an hour's time Connie heard Clifford talking to Mrs Bolton, in a hot, impulsive voice, revealing himself in a sort of passionless passion to the woman, as if she were half mistress, half foster-mother to him. And Mrs Bolton was carefully dressing him in evening clothes, for there were important business guests in the house.

Connie really sometimes felt she would die, at this time. She felt she was being crushed to death by weird lies, and by an amazing cruelty of idiocy. Clifford's strange business efficiency in a way over-awed her, and his declaration of private worship put her into a panic. There was nothing between them. She never even touched him nowadays, and he never touched her. He never even took her hand and held it kindly. No! And because they were so utterly utterly out of touch, he tortured her with his declarations of idolatry. It was the cruelty of utter impotence. And she felt her reason would give way, or she would die.

She fled as much as possible to the wood. One afternoon as she sat brooding, watching the water bubbling coldly in John's Well, the keeper had strode up to her.

"I got you a key made, my Lady!" he said, saluting. And he offered her the key.

"Thank you so much!" she said, startled.

"The hut's not very tidy, if you don't mind," he said. "I cleared it what I could."

"But I didn't want you to trouble!" she said.

"Oh, it wasn't any trouble. I'm setting the hens in about a week: but they won't be scared o' you. I s'll have to see to them morning and night, but I shan't bother you any more than I can help."

"But you wouldn't bother me," she pleaded. "I'd rather not go to the hut at all, if I'm going to be in the way."

He looked at her with his keen blue eyes. He seemed kindly, but distant. But at least he was sane, sane and wholesome, if even he looked thin and ill. A cough troubled him.

"You have a cough!" she said.

"Nothing—a cold! The last pneumonia left me with a cough—but it's nothing."

He kept distant from her, and would not come any nearer.

She went fairly often to the hut, in the morning or in the afternoon: but he was never there. No doubt he avoided her on purpose. He wanted to keep his own privacy.

He had made the hut tidy, put the little table and chair near the fire-place, left a little pile of kindling and small logs, and put the tools and traps away as far as possible, effacing himself. Outside, by the clearing, he had built a low little roof of boughs and straw, a shelter for the birds, and under it stood the five coops. And one day, when she came, she found two brown hens sitting alert and fierce in the coops, sitting on pheasants' eggs, and fluffed out so proud and deep in all the heat of the pondering female blood. This almost broke Connie's heart. She herself was so forlorn and unused, not a female at all, just a mere thing of terrors.

Then all the five coops were occupied by hens, three brown and a grey and a black. All alike they clustered themselves down on the eggs in the soft nestling ponderosity of the female urge, the female nature, fluffing out their feathers. And with brilliant eyes they watched Connie, as she crouched before them, and they gave sharp clucks of anger and alarm, but chiefly of female anger at being approached.

Connie found corn in the corn-bin in the hut. She offered it to the hens in her hand. They would not eat it. Only one hen pecked at her hand with a fierce little jab, so Connie was frightened. But she was pining to give them something: the brooding mothers who neither fed themselves nor drank. She brought water in a little tin, and was delighted when one of the hens drank.

Now she came every day to the hens: they were the only things in the world that warmed her heart. Clifford's protestations made her go cold from head to foot. Mrs Bolton's voice made her go cold: and the sound of the business men who came. An occasional letter from Michaelis affected her with the same sense of chill. She felt she would surely die, if it lasted much longer.

Yet it was spring, and the bluebells were coming in the wood, and the leaf-buds on the hazels were opening like a spatter of green rain. How terrible it was that it should be spring, and everything cold-hearted, cold-hearted. Only the hens, fluffed so wonderfully on the eggs, were warm: their warm, hot, brooding female bodies! Connie felt herself living on the brink of fainting all the time.

Then one day, a lovely sunny day with great tufts of primroses under the hazels, and many violets dotting the path, she came in the afternoon to the coops and there was one tiny, tiny perky chicken tinily prancing round in front of a coop, and the mother-hen clucking in terror. The slim little chick was greyish-brown with dark markings, and it was the most alive little spark of a creature in seven kingdoms, at that moment. Connie crouched to watch in a sort of ecstasy. Life! Life! Pure, sparky, fearless new life! New life! So tiny, and so utterly without fear! Even when it scampered a little scramblingly into the coop again, and disappeared under the hen's feathers, in answer to the mother-hen's wild alarm-cries, it was not really frightened, it took it as a game, the game of living. For in a moment a tiny sharp head was poking through the gold-brown feathers of the hen, and eyeing the cosmos.

Connie was fascinated. And at the same time, never had she felt so acutely the agony of her own female forlornness. It was becoming unbearable.

She had only one desire now, to go to the clearing in the wood. The rest was a kind of painful dream. But sometimes she was kept all day at Wragby, by her duties as hostess. And then she felt as if she too were going blank, just blank and insane.

One evening, guests or no guests, she escaped after tea. It was late, and she fled across the park like one who fears to be called back. The sun was setting rosy as she entered the wood, but she pressed on among the flowers. The light would last long overhead.

She arrived at the clearing flushed and semi-conscious. The keeper was there, in his shirt-sleeves, just closing up the coops for the night, so the little occupants would be safe. But still one little trio was pattering about on tiny feet, alert drab mites, under the straw shelter, refusing to be called in by the anxious mother.

"I had to come and see the chickens!" she said, panting, glancing shyly at the keeper, almost unaware even of him. "Are there any more?"

"Thirty-six so far!" he said. "Not bad!"

He too took a curious pleasure in watching the young things come out.

Connie crouched in front of the last coop. The three chicks had run in. But still their cheeky heads came poking sharply through the yellow feathers, then withdrawing, then only one beady little head eyeing forth from the vast mother-body.

"I'd love to touch them!" she said, putting her fingers gingerly through the bars of the coop. But the mother-hen pecked at her hand fiercely, and Connie drew back startled and frightened.

"How she pecks at me! She hates me!" she said, in a wondering voice. "But I wouldn't hurt them!"

The man standing above her laughed, and crouched down beside her, knees apart, and put his hand with quiet confidence slowly into the coop. The old hen pecked at him, but not so savagely. And slowly, softly, with sure gentle fingers, he felt among the old bird's feathers and drew out a faintly-peeping chick in his closed hand.

"There!" he said, holding out his hand to her.

She took the little drab thing between her hands, and there it stood, on its impossible little stalks of legs, its atom of balancing life trembling through its almost weightless feet into Connie's hands. But it lifted its handsome, clean-shaped little head boldly, and looked sharply round, and gave a little 'peep!'

"So adorable! So cheeky!" she said softly.

The keeper, squatting beside her, was also watching with an amused face the bold little bird in her hands. Suddenly he saw a tear fall on to her wrist.

And he stood up, and stood away, moving to the other coop. For suddenly he was aware of the old flame shooting and leaping up in his loins, that he had hoped was quiescent forever. He fought against it, turning his back to her. But it leapt, and leapt downwards, circling in his knees.

He turned again to look at her. She was kneeling and holding her two hands slowly forward, blindly, so that the chicken should run in to the mother-hen again. And there was something so mute and forlorn in her, compassion flamed in his bowels for her.

Without knowing, he came quickly towards her and crouched beside her again, taking the chick from her hands, because she was afraid of the hen, and putting it back in the coop. At the back of his loins the fire suddenly darted stronger.

He glanced apprehensively at her. Her face was averted, and she was crying blindly, in all the anguish of her generation's forlornness. His heart melted suddenly, like a drop of fire, and he put out his hand and laid his fingers on her knee.

"You shouldn't cry!" he said softly.

But then she put her hands over her face, and felt that really her heart was broken, and nothing mattered any more.

He laid his hand on her shoulder, and softly, gently it began to travel down the curve of her back, blindly, with a blind stroking motion, to the curve of her crouching loins. And there his hand softly, softly stroked the curve of her flank, in the blind instinctive caress.

She had found her scrap of handkerchief and was blindly trying to dry her face.

"Shall you come to th' hut?" he said, in a quiet, neutral voice.

And closing his hand softly on her upper arm, he drew her up and led her slowly to the hut, not letting go of her till she was inside. Then he cleared aside the chair and table, and took a brown soldier's blanket from the tool chest, spreading it slowly. She glanced at his face, as she stood motionless.

His face was pale and without expression, like that of a man submitting to fate.

"You lie there!" he said softly: and he shut the door, so that it was dark, quite dark.

With a queer obedience, she lay down on the blanket. Then she felt the soft, groping, helplessly desirous hand touching her body, feeling for her face. The hand stroked her face softly, softly, with infinite soothing and assurance, and at last there was the soft touch of a kiss on her cheek.

She lay quite still, in a sort of sleep, in a sort of dream. Then she quivered as she felt his hand groping softly, yet with queer thwarted clumsiness, among her clothing. Yet the hand knew, too, how to unclothe her where it wanted. He drew down the thin silk sheath, slowly, carefully, right down and over her feet. Then with a quiver of exquisite pleasure he touched her warm soft body, and touched her navel for a moment in a kiss. And he had to come in to her at once, to enter the peace on earth of her soft, quiescent body. It was the moment of pure peace for him, the entry into the body of the woman.

She lay still, in a kind of sleep, always in a kind of sleep. The activity, the orgasm was his, all his: she could strive for herself no more. Even the tightness of his arms round her, even the intense movement of his body, and the springing of his seed in her, was a kind of sleep, from which she did not begin to rouse till he had finished and lay softly panting against her breast.

Then she wondered, just dimly wondered, why? Why was this necessary? Why had it lifted a great cloud from her, and given her peace? Was it real? Was it real?

Her tormented modern woman's brain still had no rest. Was it real?—And she knew, if she gave herself to the man, it was real. But if she kept herself for herself, it was nothing. She was old: millions of years old, she felt. And at last, she could bear the burden of herself no more. She was to be had for the taking. To be had for the taking.

The man lay in a mysterious stillness. What was he feeling? What was he thinking? She did not know. He was a strange man to her, she did not know him. She must only wait, for she did not dare to break his mysterious stillness. He lay there with his arms round her, his body on hers, his wet body touching hers: so close. And completely unknown. Yet not unpeaceful. His very stillness was peaceful.

She knew that, when at last he roused and drew away from her. It was like an abandonment. He drew her dress in the darkness down over her knees, and stood a few moments, apparently adjusting his own clothing. Then he quietly opened the door and went out.

She saw a very brilliant little moon shining above the after-glow over the oaks. Quickly she got up and arranged herself: she was tidy. Then she went to the door of the hut.

All the lower wood was in shadow, almost darkness. Yet the sky overhead was crystal. But it shed hardly any light. He came through the lower shadow towards her, his face lifted like a pale blotch.

"Shall we go, then?" he said.

"Where?"

"I'll go with you to the gate."

He arranged things his own way. He locked the door of the hut and came after her.

"You aren't sorry, are you?" he asked, as he went at her side.

"Me? No! Are you?" she said.

"For that! no!" he said. Then after a while he added: "But there's the rest of things."

"What rest of things?" she said.

"Sir Clifford. Other folks! All the complications."

"Why complications?" she said, disappointed.

"It's always so. For you as well as for me. There's always complications." He walked on steadily in the dark.

"And are you sorry?" she said.

"In a way!" he replied, looking up at the sky. "I thought I'd done with it all. Now I've begun again."

"Begun what?"

"Life."

"Life!" she re-echoed, with a queer thrill.

"It's life," he said. "There's no keeping clear. And if you do keep clear, you might almost as well die. So if I've got to be broken open again, I have—"

She did not quite see it that way, but still—.

"It's just love," she said cheerfully.

"Whatever that may be!" he replied.

They went on through the darkening wood in silence, till they were almost at the gate.

"But you don't hate me, do you?" she said, wistfully.

"Nay nay!" he replied. And suddenly he held her fast against his breast again, with the old connecting passion. "Nay, for me it was good, it was good. Was it for you?"

"Yes, for me too," she answered, a little untruthfully, for she had not been conscious of much.

He kissed her softly, softly, with the kisses of warmth.

"If only there weren't so many other people in the world!" he said lugubriously.

She laughed. They were at the gate to the park. He opened for her.

"I won't come any further," he said.

"No!" and she held out her hand, as if to shake hands. But he took it in both his.

"Shall I come again?" she asked wistfully.

"Yes! Yes!"

She left him, and went across the park.

He stood back and watched her going into the dark, against the pallor of the horizon. Almost with bitterness he watched her go. She had connected him up again, when he had wanted to be alone. She had cost him that bitter privacy of a man who at last wants only to be alone.

He turned into the dark of the wood. All was still, the moon had set. But he was aware of the noises of the night, the engines at Stacks Gate, the traffic on the main road. Slowly he climbed the denuded knoll. And from the top he could see the country, bright rows of lights at Stacks Gate, smaller lights at Tevershall pit, the yellow lights of Tevershall, and lights everywhere, here and there, on the dark country, with the distant blush of furnaces, faint and rosy, since the night was clear, the rosiness of the outpouring of whitehot metal. Sharp, wicked electric lights at Stacks Gate! An undefinable quick of evil in them! And all the unease, the ever-shifting dread of the industrial night in the Midlands! He could hear the winding-engines at Stacks Gate turning down the seven-o'clock miners. The pit worked three shifts.

He went down again, into the darkness and seclusion of the wood. But he knew that the seclusion of the wood was illusory. The industrial noises broke the solitude, the sharp lights, though unseen, mocked it. A man could no longer be private and withdrawn. The world allows no hermits. And now he had taken the woman, and brought on himself a new cycle of pain and doom. For he knew by experience what it meant.

It was not woman's fault, nor even love's fault, nor the fault of sex. The fault lay there, out there, in those evil electric lights and diabolical rattlings of engines. There, in the world of the mechanical greedy, greedy mechanism and mechanised greed, sparkling with lights and gushing hot metal and roaring with traffic, there lay the vast evil thing, ready to destroy whatever did not conform. Soon it would destroy the wood, and the bluebells would spring no more. All vulnerable things must perish under the rolling and running of iron.

He thought with infinite tenderness of the woman. Poor forlorn thing, she was nicer than she knew, and oh, so much too nice for the tough lot she was in contact with! Poor thing, she too had some of the vulnerability of the wild hyacinths, she wasn't all tough rubber-goods-and-platinum, like the modern girl. And they would do her in! As sure as life, they would do her in, as they do in all naturally tender life. Tender! Somewhere she was tender, tender with a tenderness of the growing hyacinths, something that has gone out of the celluloid women of today. But he would protect her with his heart for a little while. For a little while, before the insentient iron world and the Mammon of mechanised greed did them both in, her as well as him.

He went home with his gun and his dog, to the dark cottage, lit the lamp, started the fire, and ate his supper of bread and cheese, young onions and beer. He was alone, in a silence he loved. His room was clean and tidy, but rather stark. Yet the fire was bright, the hearth white, the petroleum lamp hung bright over the table, with its white oil-cloth. He tried to read a book about India, but tonight he could not read. He sat by the fire in his shirt-sleeves, not smoking, but with a mug of beer in reach. And he thought about Connie.

To tell the truth, he was sorry for what had happened, perhaps most for her sake. He had a sense of foreboding. No sense of wrong or sin: he was troubled by no conscience in that respect. He knew that conscience was chiefly fear of society: or fear of oneself. He was not afraid of himself. But he was quite consciously afraid of society, which he knew by instinct to be a malevolent, partly-insane beast.

The woman! If she could be there with him, and there were nobody else in the world! The desire rose again, his penis began to stir like a live bird. At the same time an oppression, a dread of exposing himself and her to that outside Thing that sparkled viciously in the electric lights, weighed down his shoulders. She, poor young thing, was just a young female creature to him: but a young female creature whom he had gone in to, and whom he desired again.

Stretching with the curious yawn of desire, for he had been alone and apart from man or woman for four years, he rose and took his coat again, and his gun, lowered the lamp and went out into the starry night, with the dog. Driven by desire, and by dread of the malevolent Thing outside, he made his round in the wood, slowly, softly. He loved the darkness and folded himself into it. It fitted the turgidity of his desire which, in spite of all, was like a riches: the stirring restlessness of his penis, the stirring fire in his loins! Oh, if only there were other men to be with, to fight that sparkling-electric Thing outside there, to preserve the tenderness of life, the tenderness of women, and the natural riches of desire. If only there were men to fight side by side with! But the men were all outside there, glorying in the Thing, triumphing or being trodden down in the rush of mechanised greed or of greedy mechanism.

Constance, for her part, had hurried across the park, home, almost without thinking. As yet she had no afterthought. She would be in time for dinner.

She was annoyed to find the doors fastened, however, so that she had to ring. Mrs Bolton opened.

"Why there you are, your ladyship! I was beginning to wonder if you'd gone lost!" she said a little roguishly. "Sir Clifford hasn't asked for you, though: he's got Mr Linley in with him, talking over something. It looks as if he'd stay to dinner, doesn't it, my lady?"

"It does rather," said Connie.

"Shall I put dinner back a quarter of an hour? That would give you time to dress in comfort."

"Perhaps you'd better."

Mr Linley was the general manager of the collieries, an elderly man from the north, with not quite enough punch to suit Clifford: not up to post-war conditions, nor post-war colliers either, with their "ca' canny" creed. But Connie liked Mr Linley, though she was glad to be spared the toadying of his wife.

Linley stayed to dinner, and Connie was the hostess men liked so much, so modest, yet so attentive and aware, with big, wide blue eyes and a soft repose that sufficiently hid what she was really thinking. Connie had played this woman so much, it was almost second nature to her: but still, decidedly second. Yet it was curious how everything disappeared from her consciousness while she played it.

She waited patiently till she could go upstairs and think her own thoughts. She was always waiting, it seemed to be her *forte*.

Once in her room, however, she felt still vague and confused. She didn't know what to think. What sort of a man was he, really? Did he really like her? Not much, she felt. Yet he was kind. There was something, a sort of warm, naïve kindness, curious and sudden, that almost opened her womb to him. But she felt he might be kind like that to any woman. Though even so, it was curiously soothing, comforting. And he was a passionate man, wholesome and passionate. But perhaps he wasn't quite individual enough: he might be the same with any woman as he had been with her. It wasn't really personal. She was only really a female to him.

But perhaps that was better. And after all, he was kind to the female in her, which no man had ever been. Men were very kind to the *person* she was, but rather cruel to the female, despising her or ignoring her altogether. Men were awfully kind to Constance Reid or to Lady Chatterley: but not to her womb they weren't kind. And he took no notice of Constance or of Lady Chatterley: he just softly stroked her loins or her breasts.

She went to the wood next day. It was a grey, still afternoon, with the dark-green dog's-mercury spreading under the hazel copse, and all the trees making a silent effort to open their buds. Today she could almost feel it in her own body, the huge heave of the sap in the massive trees, upwards, up, up to the bud-tips, there to push into little flamey oak-leaves, bronze as blood. It was like a tide running turgid upward, and spreading on the sky.

She came to the clearing, but he was not there. She had only half expected him. The pheasant chicks were running lightly abroad, light as insects, from the coops where the yellow hens clucked anxiously. Connie sat and watched them, and waited. She only waited. Even the chicks she hardly saw. She waited.

The time passed with dream-like slowness, and he did not come. She had only half expected him. He never came in the afternoon. She must go home to tea. But she had to force herself to leave.

As she went home, a fine drizzle of rain fell.

"Is it raining again?" said Clifford, seeing her shake her hat.

"Just drizzle."

She poured tea in silence, absorbed in a sort of obstinacy. She did want to see the keeper today, to see if it were really real. If it were really real!

"Shall I read a little to you afterwards," said Clifford.

She looked at him. Had he sensed something.

"The spring makes me feel queer—I thought I might rest a little," she said.

"Just as you like. Not feeling really unwell, are you?"

"No! Only rather tired—with the spring. Will you have Mrs Bolton to play something with you?"

"No! I think I'll listen in."

She heard the curious satisfaction in his voice. She went upstairs to her bedroom. There, she heard the loud-speaker begin to bellow, in an idiotically velveteen-genteel sort of voice, something about a series of street-cries, the very cream of genteel affectation imitating old criers. She pulled on her old violet-coloured mackintosh, and slipped out of the house at the side door.

The drizzle of rain was like a veil over the world, mysterious, hushed, not cold. She got very warm as she hurried across the park. She had to open her light water-proof.

The wood was silent, still and secret in the evening drizzle of rain, full of the mystery of eggs and half-open buds, half-unsheathed flowers. In the dimness of it all trees glistened naked and dark, as if they had unclothed themselves, and the green things on earth seemed to burn with greenness.

There was still no-one at the clearing. The chicks had nearly all gone under the mother-hens, only one or two last adventurous ones still dibbed about in the dryness under the straw roof-shelter. And they were doubtful of themselves.

So! He still had not been. He was staying away on purpose. Or perhaps something was wrong. Perhaps she should go to the cottage and see.

But she was born to wait. She opened the hut with her key. It was all tidy, the corn put in the bin, the blankets folded on the shelf, the straw neat in a corner: a new bundle of straw. The hurricane-lamp hung on a nail. The table and chair had been put back, where she had lain.

She sat down on a stool in the doorway. How still everything was! The fine rain blew very softly, filmily, but the wind made no noise. Nothing made any sound. The trees stood like powerful beings, dim, twilit, silent and alive. How alive everything was!

Night was drawing near again: she would have to go. He was avoiding her.

But suddenly he came striding into the clearing, in his black oilskin jacket like a chauffeur, shining with wet. He glanced quickly at the hut, half-saluted, then veered aside and went on to the coops. There he crouched in silence, looking carefully at everything, then carefully shutting the hens and chicks up safe against the night.

At last he came slowly towards her. She still sat on her stool. He stood before her under the porch.

"You come then," he said, using the intonation of the dialect.

"Yes!" she said, looking up at him. "You're late!"

"Ay!" he replied, looking away into the wood.

She rose slowly, drawing aside her stool.

"Did you want to come in?" she asked.

He looked down at her shrewdly.

"Won't folks be thinkin' somethink, you comin' here every night?" he said.

"Why?"—She looked up at him, at a loss. "I said I'd come. Nobody knows."

"They soon will, though," he replied. "An' what then?"

She was at a loss for an answer.

"Why should they know?" she said.

"Folks always does," he said fatally.

Her lip quivered a little.

"Well I can't help it," she faltered.

"Nay!" he said. "You can help it by not comin'.—If yer want to," he added, in a lower tone.

"But I don't want to," she murmured.

He looked away into the wood, and was silent.

"But what when folks finds out?" he asked at last. "Think about it! Think how lowered you'll feel, one of your husband's servants!"

She looked up at his averted face.

"Is it—" she stammered, "is it that you don't want me?"

"Think!" he said. "Think what if folks finds out—Sir Clifford an' a'—an' everybody talkin'—"

"Well, I can go away."

"Where to?"

"Anywhere! I've got money of my own. My mother left me twenty thousand pounds in trust—and I know Clifford can't touch it. I can go away."

"But 'appen you don't want to go away."

"Yes! Yes! I don't care what happens to me."

"Ay, you think that! But you'll care! You'll have to care, everybody has. You've got to remember. Your Ladyship carrying on with a gamekeeper! It's not as if I was a gentleman. Yes, you'd care. You'd care!"

"I shouldn't. What do I care about my ladyship. I hate it really. I feel people are jeering every time they say it. And they are! they are! Even you jeer when you say it."

"Me!"

For the first time he looked straight at her, and into her eyes.

"I don't jeer at you," he said.

As he looked into her eyes she saw his own eyes go dark, quite dark, the pupil dilating.

"Don't you care about a' th' risk?" he asked, in a husky voice. "You should care! Don't care when it's too late!—"

There was a curious warning pleading in his voice.

"But I've nothing to lose!" she said fretfully. "If you knew what it is, you'd think I'd be glad to lose it.—But are you afraid for yourself?"

"Ay!" he said briefly. "I am! I'm afraid. I'm afraid. I'm afraid o' things."

"What things?" she asked.

He gave a curious backward jerk of his head, indicating the outer world.

"Things! Everybody! The lot of 'em."

Then he bent down and suddenly kissed her unhappy face.

"Nay, I don't care!" he said. "Let's have it, an' damn the rest. But if you was to feel sorry you'd ever done it——"

"Don't put me off!" she pleaded.

He put his fingers to her cheek, and kissed her again suddenly.

"Let me come in then," he said softly. "An' take off your mackintosh."

He hung up his gun, slipped out of his wet leather jacket, and reached for the blankets.

"I brought another blanket," he said, "so we can put one over us if we like."

"I can't stay long," she said. "Dinner is half-past seven."

He looked at her swiftly—then at his watch.

"All right!" he said.

He shut the door, and lit a tiny light in the hanging hurricane-lamp.

"One time we'll have a long time," he said.

He put the blankets down carefully, one folded for her head. Then he sat down a moment on the stool, and drew her to him, holding her close with one arm, feeling for her body with his free hand. She heard the catch of his intaken breath as he found her. Under her frail petticoat she was naked.

"Eh! what it is to touch thee!" he said, as his fingers caressed the delicate, warm, secret skin of her waist and hips. He put his face down and rubbed his cheek against her belly and against her thighs, again and again. And again she wondered a little over the sort of rapture it was to him. She did not understand the beauty he found in her, through touch upon her living secret body, almost the ecstasy of beauty. For passion alone is awake to it. And when passion is dead, or absent, then the magnificent throb of beauty is incomprehensible and even a little despicable: live, warm beauty of contact, so much deeper than the beauty of vision. She felt the glide of his cheek on her thighs and belly and buttocks, and the close brushing of his moustache and his soft thick hair, and her knees began to quiver. Far down in her she felt a new stirring, a new nakedness emerging. And she was half afraid. Half she wished he would not caress her so. He was encompassing her somehow. Yet she was waiting, waiting.

And when he came in to her, with an intensification of relief and consummation that was pure peace to him, still she was waiting. She felt herself a little left out. And she knew, partly it was her own fault. She willed herself into this separateness. Now perhaps she was condemned to it. She lay still, feeling his motion within her, his deep-sunk intentness, the sudden quiver of him at the springing of his seed, then the slow-subsiding thrust. That thrust of the buttocks, surely it was a little ridiculous! If you were a woman, and apart in all the business, surely that thrusting of the man's buttocks was supremely ridiculous. Surely the man was intensely ridiculous in this posture and this act!

But she lay still, without recoil. Even, when he had finished, she did not rouse herself to get a grip on her own satisfaction, as she had done with Michaelis. She lay still, and the tears slowly filled and ran from her eyes.

He lay still, too. But he held her close, and tried to cover her poor naked legs with his legs, to keep them warm. He lay on her with a close, undoubting warmth.

"Are ter cold?" he asked, in a soft, small voice, as if she were close, so close. Whereas she was left out, distant.

"No! But I must go," she said gently.

He sighed, held her closer, then relaxed to rest again. He had not guessed her tears. He thought she was there with him.

"I must go," she repeated.

He lifted himself, kneeled beside her a moment, kissed the inner side of her thighs, then drew down her skirts, buttoning his own clothes unthinking, not even turning aside, in the faint, faint light from the lantern.

"Tha mun come ter th' cottage one time," he said, looking down at her with a warm, sure, easy face.

But she lay there inert, and was gazing up at him thinking: Stranger! Stranger! She even resented him a little.

He put on his coat, and looked for his hat, which had fallen. Then he slung on his gun.

"Come then!" he said, looking down at her with those warm, peaceful sort of eyes.

She rose slowly. She didn't want to go. She also rather resented staying. He helped her with her thin waterproof, and saw she was tidy.

Then he opened the door. The outside was quite dark. The faithful dog under the porch stood up with pleasure, seeing him. The drizzle of rain drifted greyly past, upon the darkness. It was quite dark.

"Ah mun ta'e th' lantern!" he said. "The'll be nob'dy!"

He walked just before her in the narrow path, swinging the hurricane-lamp low, revealing the wet grass, the black shiny tree-roots like snakes, the wan flowers. For the rest, all was grey rain-mist and complete darkness.

"Tha mun come ter th' cottage one time," he said, as they came into the broad riding, and he walked abreast. "Shall ter? We might as well be hung for a sheep as for a lamb."

It puzzled her, his queer, persistent wanting her, when there was nothing between them, when he never *really* spoke to her. And in spite of herself, she resented the dialect. His "tha mun come" seemed not addressed to her, but some common woman.

She recognised the fox-glove leaves of the riding, and knew more or less where they were.

"It's quarter past seven," he said. "You'll do it."

He had changed his voice, seemed to feel her distance.

As they turned the last bend in the riding, towards the hazel-walls and the gate, he blew out the light.

"We s'll see from here," he said, taking her gently by the arm.

But it was difficult. The earth under their feet was a mystery. But he felt his way by tread: he was used to it.

At the gate he gave her his electric torch.

"It's a bit lighter i' th' park," he said. "But take it, for fear you get off th' path."

It was true, there seemed a ghost-glimmer of greyness in the open space of the park.

He suddenly drew her to him, and whipped his hand under her skirts again, feeling her warm body with his wet, chill hand.

"I could die for the touch of a woman like thee," he said in his throat. "If tha could stop another minute——"

She felt the sudden force of his wanting her again.

"No! I must run," she said, a little wildly.

"Ay!" he replied, suddenly changed, letting her go.

She turned away. And on the instant she turned back to him, saying:

"Kiss me!"

He bent over her indistinguishable face, and kissed her—on the left eye. She held her mouth, and he softly kissed it, but at once drew away. He hated mouth-kisses.

"I'll come tomorrow," she said, drawing away. "If I can," she added.

"Ay! Not so late," he replied out of the darkness. Already she could not see him at all.

"Goodnight!" she said.

"Goodnight, your Ladyship," came his voice.

She stopped, and looked back into the wet dark. She could just see the bulk of him.

"Why did you say that?" she said.

"Nay!" he replied. "Goodnight then! Run!"

She plunged on in the dark-grey, tangible night.

She found the side door open, and slipped into her room unseen. As she closed the door, the gong sounded. But she would take her bath all the same. She must take her bath.

"But I won't be late any more," she said to herself. "It's too annoying."

The next day she did not go to the wood. She went instead with Clifford to Uthwaite. He would occasionally go out now in the car, and had got a strong young man as chauffeur, who could help him out of the car, if need be.

And he particularly wanted to see his godfather, Leslie Winter, who lived at Shipley Hall, not far from Uthwaite. Winter was an elderly gentleman now—wealthy, one of the wealthy coal-owners who had had their hey-day in King Edward's time. King Edward had stayed more than once at Shipley, for the shooting. It was a handsome old stucco hall, very elegantly appointed, for Winter was a bachelor and prided himself on his style. But the place was beset by collieries.

Leslie Winter was attached to Clifford, but personally did not entertain a great respect for him, because of the photographs in illustrated papers, and the literature. The old man was a buck of the King Edward school, who thought life was life, and the scribbling fellows were something else.

Towards Connie the squire was always rather gallant. He thought her an attractive demure maiden, and rather wasted on Clifford, and it was a thousand pities she stood no chance of bringing forth an heir to Wragby. He himself had no heir.

Connie wondered what he would say if he knew that Clifford's gamekeeper had been having intercourse with her, and saying to her: Tha mun come ter th' cottage one time! He would detest and despise her, for he had come almost to hate the shoving forward of the working classes. A man of her own class he would not mind.

128

But Connie was gifted from nature with this appearance of demure, submissive maidenliness, and perhaps it was part of her nature. Winter called her: dear child! and gave her a rather lovely miniature of an eighteenth-century lady. He always gave her something, much against her will.

But Connie was pre-occupied with her affair with the keeper. After all, Mr Winter, who was really a gentleman and a man of the world, treated her as a person and a discriminating individual. He did not lump her together with all the rest of female womanhood in his "thee" and "tha."

She did not go to the wood that day, nor the next, nor the day following. She did not go so long as she felt, or imagined she felt, the man waiting for her, wanting her.

But the fourth day she was terribly unsettled and uneasy. She still refused to go to the wood, and open her thighs once more to the man. She thought of all the things she might do—drive to Sheffield, pay visits. And the thought of all these things was repellant.

So at last she decided to take a walk *not* towards the wood, but in the opposite direction. She would go to Marehay, through the little iron gate in the other side of the park fence.

It was a quiet grey day of spring, almost warm. She walked on unheeding, absorbed in thoughts she was not even conscious of. She was not really aware of anything outside her, until she was startled by the loud barking of the dog at Marehay Farm. Marehay Farm! its pastures ran up to Wragby park fence, so they were neighbours. But it was some time since Connie had called.

"Bell!" she said to the big white bull-terrier. "Bell! Have you forgotten me? Don't you know me?"

She was afraid of dogs. And Bell stood back and bellowed. And she wanted to pass through the farm-yard on to the warren path.

Mrs Flint appeared. She was a woman of Constance's own age: had been a school-teacher: had rather a charming way with her, but Connie suspected her of being a false little thing.

"Why it's Lady Chatterley! Why!"—and Mrs Flint's eyes glowed again, and she flushed like a young girl. "Bell! Bell! why, barking at Lady Chatterley—! Bell! Be quiet!"—She darted forward and slashed at the dog with a white cloth she held in her hand; then came forward to Connie.

"She used to know me," said Connie, shaking hands. The Flints were Chatterley tenants.

"Of course she knows your Ladyship! She's just showing off," said Mrs Flint, glowing and looking up with a sort of flushed confusion. "But it's so long since she's seen you. I do hope you are better?"

"Yes, thanks, I'm all right."

"We've hardly seen you all winter.—Will you come in and look at baby?"

"Well!" Connie hesitated. "Just for a minute."

Mrs Flint flew wildly in, to tidy up, and Connie came slowly after, hesitating in the rather dark kitchen, where the kettle was boiling by the fire. Back came Mrs Flint.

"I do hope you'll excuse me," she said. "Will you come in here?"

They went into the living-room, where a baby was sitting on the rag hearth-rug, and the table was roughly set for tea. A young servant-girl backed down the passage, shy and awkward.

The baby was a perky little thing of about a year, with red hair like its father, and cheeky pale-blue eyes. It was a girl, and not to be daunted. It sat among cushions, and was surrounded with rag dolls and other toys, in modern excess.

"Why what a dear she is!" said Connie. "And how she's grown! A big girl! A big girl!"

She had given it a shawl when it was born, and celluloid ducks for Christmas.

"There, Josephine! Who's *that* come to see you? Who's this, Josephine! Lady Chatterley! You know Lady Chatterley, don't you?"

The queer, pert little mite gazed cheekily at Connie. Ladyships were still all the same to her.

"Come! Will you come to me?" said Connie to the baby.

The baby didn't care, one way or another. So Connie picked her up and held her in her lap. How warm and lovely it was, to hold a child in one's lap! And the soft little arms, the unconscious, cheeky little legs.

"I was just having a rough cup of tea all by myself. Luke's gone to market, so I can have it when I like. Would you care for a cup, Lady Chatterley? I don't suppose it's what you're used to, but—if you *would*—"

Connie would; though she didn't want to be reminded of what she was used to. There was a great re-laying of the table, and the best cups brought, and the best tea-pot.

"If only you wouldn't take any trouble!" said Connie.

But if Mrs Flint took no trouble, where was the fun! So Connie

played with the child, and was amused by its little female dauntless-
ness, and got a deep voluptuous pleasure out of its soft young
warmth. Young life! And so fearless! So fearless, because so
defenceless! All the older people, so narrow with fear!

She had a cup of tea, which was rather strong, and very good
bread and butter, and bottled damsons. Mrs Flint flushed and
glowed and bridled with excitement, as if Connie were some gallant
knight. And they had a real female chat, and both of them enjoyed it.

"It's a poor little tea, though," said Mrs Flint.

"It's much nicer than at home," said Connie truthfully.

"Oh—h!" said Mrs Flint, not believing, of course.

But at last Connie rose.

"I *must* go!" she said. "My husband has no idea where I am. He'll
be wondering all kinds of things."

"He'll never think you're here!" laughed Mrs Flint excitedly.
"He'll be sending the crier round!"

"Goodbye Josephine!" said Connie, kissing the baby and ruffling
its red, wispy hair.

Mrs Flint insisted on opening the locked and barred front door.
Connie emerged in the farm's little front garden, shut in by a privet
hedge. There were two rows of auriculas by the path, very velvety
and rich.

"Lovely auriculas!" said Connie.

"Recklesses, as Luke calls them!" laughed Mrs Flint. "Have
some!"

And eagerly she picked the velvet and primrose flowers.

"Enough! Enough!" said Connie.

They came to the little garden gate.

"Which way were you going?" asked Mrs Flint.

"By the warren."

"Let me see!—Oh yes, the cows are in the gin close. But they're
not up yet.—But the gate's locked, you'll have to climb."

"I can climb," said Connie.

"Perhaps I can just go down the close with you."

They went down the poor, rabbit-bitten pasture. Birds were
whistling in wild evening triumph in the wood. A man was calling up
the last cows, which trailed slowly over the path-worn pasture.

"They're late, milking, tonight," said Mrs Flint severely. "They
know Luke won't be back till after dark."

They came to the fence, beyond which the young fir-wood bristled dense. There was a little gate, but it was locked. In the grass on the inside stood a bottle, empty.

"There's the keeper's empty bottle, for his milk," explained Mrs Flint. "We bring it as far as here for him, and he fetches it then himself."

"When?" said Connie.

"Oh, any time he's around. Often in the morning.—Well, goodbye Lady Chatterley! And *do* come again! It was so lovely having you."

Connie climbed the fence into the narrow path between the dense, bristling young firs. Mrs Flint went running back across the pasture, uphill: in a sunbonnet, because she was really a school-teacher.

Constance didn't like this dense new part of the wood. It seemed gruesome, and choking. She hurried on, with her head down, thinking of the Flints' baby. It was a dear little thing—but it would be a bit bow-legged, like its father—it showed already. But perhaps it would grow out of it. How warm and fulfilling, somehow, to have a baby. And how Mrs Flint had showed it off: she had something, anyhow, that Connie hadn't got and apparently couldn't have. Yes, Mrs Flint had flaunted her motherhood. And Connie had been just a bit, just a little bit jealous. She couldn't help it.

She started out of her muse, and gave a little cry of fear. A man was there.

It was the keeper, he stood in the path like Balaam's ass, barring her way.

"How's this?" he said in surprise.

"How did you come?" she panted.

"How did *you*? Have you been to the hut?"

"No! No! I went to Marehay."

He looked at her curiously, searchingly, and she hung her head a little guiltily.

"And were you going to the hut now?" he asked, rather sternly.

"No! I mustn't! I stayed at Marehay. No-one knows where I am. I'm late. I've got to run—"

"Giving me the slip, like?" he said, with a faint, ironic smile.

"No! No! Not that! Only—!"

"Why what else!" he said. And he stepped up to her, and put his arm round her. She felt the front of his body terribly near to her, and alive.

"Oh, not now! Not now!" she cried, trying to push him away.

"Why not? It's only six o'clock. You've got half-an-hour. Nay nay! I want you."

He held her fast, and she felt his urgency. Her old instinct was to fight for her freedom. But something else in her was strange and inert and heavy. His body was urgent against her, and she hadn't the heart any more to fight.

He looked round.

"Come—come here! through here!" he said, looking penetratingly into the dense fir-trees, that were young and not more than half-grown.

He looked back at her. She saw his eyes tense and brilliant, fierce, not loving. But her will had left her. A strange weight was on her limbs. She was giving way. She was giving up.

He led her through the wall of prickly trees, that were difficult to come through, to a place where was a little space and a pile of dead boughs. He threw one or two dry ones down, put his coat and waistcoat over them, and she had to lie down there, under the boughs of the tree, like an animal, while he waited, standing there in his shirt and breeches, watching her with haunted eyes. But still he was provident—he made her lie properly, properly. Yet he broke the band of her underclothes, for she did not help him, only lay inert.

He too had bared the front part of his body, and she felt his naked flesh against her as he came in to her. For a moment he was still, inside her, turgid there and quivering. Then as he began to move in the sudden helpless orgasm, there awoke in her new strange thrills rippling inside her, rippling, rippling, like a flapping overlapping of soft flames, soft as feathers, running to points of brilliance, exquisite, exquisite, and melting her all molten inside. It was like bells, rippling up and up to a culmination. She lay unconscious of the wild little cries she uttered at the last. But it was over too soon, too soon!

And now she could no longer force her own conclusion, with her own activity. This was different, different, she could do nothing. She could no longer harden and grip for her own satisfaction upon him. She could only wait, wait, and moan in spirit as she felt him inside her withdrawing, withdrawing and contracting, coming to the terrible moment when he would slip out of her, and be gone; whilst all her womb was open and soft and softly clamouring like a sea-anemone under the tides, clamouring for him to come in again and make a fulfilment for her.

She clung to him unconscious in passion, and he never quite

slipped from her. And she felt the soft bud of him within her stirring and in strange rhythms flushing up into her, with a strange, rhythmic growing motion, swelling and swelling till it filled all her cleaving consciousness. And then began again the unspeakable motion that was not really motion, but pure deepening whirlpools of sensation, swirling deeper and deeper through all her tissue and consciousness, till she was one perfect concentric fluid of feeling. And she lay there crying in unconscious, inarticulate cries, the voice out of the uttermost night, the life-exclamation. And the man heard it beneath him with a kind of awe, as his life sprang out into her. And as it subsided he subsided too, and lay utterly still, unknowing, while her grip on him slowly relaxed, and she lay inert.

And they lay, and knew nothing, not even of each other, both lost.

Till at last he began to rouse, and become aware of his defenceless nakedness. And she was aware that his body was loosening its clasp on her, he was coming apart. But in her breast she felt she could not bear him to leave her uncovered. He must cover her now for ever.

But he drew away at last, and kissed her, and covered her over, then began to cover himself. She lay looking up through the boughs of the tree, unable as yet to move. He stood and fastened up his breeches, looking round. All was dense and silent, save for the awed dog, that lay with its paws against its nose.

He sat down again on the brushwood, and took Connie's hand in silence. She turned and looked at him.

"We came-off together, that time," he said.

She did not answer.

"It's good when it's like that. Most folks lives their lives through, and they never know it," he said, speaking rather dreamily.

She looked into his brooding face.

"Do they!" she said. "Are you glad?"

He looked back into her eyes.

"Glad!" he said. "Ay! But niver mind!"—He did not want her to talk.

And he bent over her and kissed her, and she felt, so he must kiss her for ever.

At last she sat up.

"Don't people often come-off together?" she asked, with naïve curiosity.

"A good many of 'em, never. You can see by the raw look of them."—He spoke unwillingly, regretting he had begun.

"Have you come-off like that with other women?"

He looked at her, amused.

"I don't know," he said. "I don't know."

And she knew he would never tell her anything he didn't want to tell her. She watched his face, and the passion for him moved in her bowels. She resisted it as far as she could, for it was the loss of herself to herself.

He put on his waistcoat and his coat, and pushed a way through to the path again. The last level rays of the sun touched the wood.

"I won't come with you," he said. "Better not."

She looked at him wistfully, before she turned. His dog was waiting so anxiously for him to go. And he seemed to have nothing whatever to say: nothing left.

Connie went slowly home, realising the depth of the other thing in her. Another self was alive in her, burning molten and soft and sensitive in her womb and bowels. And with this self, she adored him, she adored him till her knees were weak as she walked. In her womb and bowels she was flowing and alive now, and vulnerable, and helpless in adoration of him as the most naïve woman.

"It feels like a child!" she said to herself. "It feels like a child in me."

So it did. As if her womb, that had always been shut, had opened and filled with a new life, almost a burden, yet lovely.

"If I had a child!" she thought to herself. "If I had him inside me, in a child!"

And her limbs turned molten at the thought. And she realised the immense difference between having a child to oneself, and having a child to a man whom one's bowels yearned towards. The former seemed, in a sense, ordinary. But to have a child to a man whom one adored in one's bowels and one's womb! it made her feel she was very different from her old self, and as if she was sinking deep, deep to the centre of all womanhood, and the sleep of creation.

It was not the passion that was new to her. It was the yearning adoration. She knew she had always feared it. For it left her helpless. She feared it still. For if she adored him too much, then she would lose herself, become effaced. And she did not want to be effaced. A slave, like a savage woman. She must not become a slave.

She feared her adoration. Yet she would not at once fight against it. She knew she could fight it. She had a devil of self-will in her breast that could have fought the full, soft, heavy adoration of her womb and bowels, and crushed it. She could, even now. Or she thought so. And she could then take up her passion with her own will.

Ah yes, to be passionate like a bacchante, like a bacchanal, fleeing wild through the woods. To call on Iacchos, the bright phallos that had no independent personality behind it, but was pure god-servant to the woman! The man, the individual, let him not dare intrude. He was but a temple-servant, the bearer and keeper of the bright phallos, her own.

So, in the flux of new awakening, the old hard passion flamed in her for a time, and the man dwindled to a contemptible object, the mere phallos-bearer, to be torn to pieces when his service was performed. She felt the force of the Bacchae in her limbs and her body: the woman gleaming and rapid, beating down the male.

But while she felt this, her heart was heavy. She did not want it. It was known and barren, birthless. The adoration was her treasure. It was so fathomless, so soft, so deep, so unknown. No no! she would give up her own hard, bright female power. She was weary of it, stiffened with it. She would sink in the new bath of life, in the depths of her womb and her bowels, that sang the voiceless song of adoration. It was early yet, to begin to fear the man.

"I walked over by Marehay, and I had tea with Mrs Flint," she said to Clifford. "I wanted to see the baby. It's so adorable, with hair like red cobwebs! Such a dear! Mr Flint had gone to market, so she and I and the baby had tea together. Did you wonder where I was?"

"Well, I wondered. But I guessed you had dropped in somewhere to tea," said Clifford jealously.

With a sort of second sight, he sensed something new in her, something to him quite incomprehensible. But he ascribed it to the baby. He thought that all that ailed Connie was that she did not have a baby: automatically bring one forth, so to speak.

"I saw you go across the park to the iron gate, my Lady," said Mrs Bolton. "So *I* thought perhaps you'd called at the rectory."

"I nearly did. Then I turned towards Marehay instead."

The eyes of the two women met: Mrs Bolton's grey and bright and searching, Connie's blue and veiled, and strangely beautiful. Mrs Bolton was almost sure she had a lover. Yet how could it be? *Who* could it be? Where was there a man?

"Oh, it's so good for you if you'll go out and see a bit of company sometimes," said Mrs Bolton. "I was saying to Sir Clifford, it would do her ladyship a world of good if she'd go out among people more."

"Yes, I'm glad I went.—And such a quaint, dear, cheeky baby, Clifford!" said Connie. "It's got hair just like spider-webs, and bright orange! and the oddest, cheekiest pale-blue china eyes! Of course it's a girl, or it wouldn't be so bold; bolder than any little Sir Frances Drake."

"You're right, my Lady: a regular little Flint! They were always a forward sandy-headed family," said Mrs Bolton.

"But wouldn't you like to see it, Clifford? I've asked them to tea, for you to see it."

"Who?" he asked, looking at Connie in great uneasiness.

"Mrs Flint and the baby—next Monday."

"You can have them to tea up in your room," he said.

"Why, don't you want to see the baby?" she cried.

"Oh, I'll see it. But I don't want to sit through a tea-time with them."

"Oh!" said Connie, looking at him with wide veiled eyes. She did not really see him. He was somebody else.

"You can have a nice cosy tea up in your room, my Lady, and Mrs Flint will be more comfortable than if Sir Clifford was there," said Mrs Bolton.

She was sure Connie had a lover. And something in her soul exulted. But who was he, who was he? Perhaps Mrs Flint would provide a clue.

Connie would not take her bath this evening. The sense of his flesh touching her, the very stickiness upon her, was dear to her, and in a sense, holy.

Clifford was very uneasy. He would not let her go after dinner. And she had wanted so much to be alone! She looked at him, but was curiously submissive.

"Shall we play a game?—or shall I read to you?—or what shall it be?" he asked uneasily.

"You read to me," said Connie.

"What shall I read? verse or prose? or drama?"

"Read Racine," she said.

It had been one of his stunts, in the past, to read Racine in the real French grand manner. But he was rusty now, and a little self-conscious. He really preferred the loud-speaker.

But Connie was sewing, sewing a little silk frock of primrose silk, cut out of one of her dresses, for Mrs Flint's baby. Between coming home and dinner, she had cut it out. And she sat in the soft, quiescent rapture of herself, sewing, while the noise of the reading went on. Inside herself she could feel the humming of passion, like the after-humming of deep bells.

Clifford said something to her about the Racine. She caught the sense after the words had gone.

"Yes! Yes!" she said, looking up at him. "It *is* splendid."

Again he was frightened at the deep blue blaze of her eyes, and at her soft stillness, sitting there. She had never been so utterly soft and still. She fascinated him helplessly, as if some perfume about her intoxicated him. So he went on helplessly with his reading, and the throaty sound of the French was like the wind in the chimneys to her. Of the Racine she heard not one syllable.

She was gone in her own soft rapture, like a forest soughing with the dim, glad moan of spring, moving into bud. She could feel in the same world with her the man, the nameless man, moving on beautiful feet, beautiful in the phallic mystery. And in herself, in all her veins, she felt him and his child, him and his child. His child was in all her veins, like a twilight.

> "For hands she hath none, nor eyes, nor feet, nor golden
> Treasure of hair—"

She was like a forest, like the dark interlacing of the oakwood, humming inaudibly with myriad unfolding buds. Meanwhile the birds of desire were asleep in the vast interlaced intricacy of her body.

But Clifford's voice went on, clapping and gurgling with unusual sounds. How extraordinary it was! How extraordinary he was, bent there over the book, queer and rapacious and civilised, with broad shoulders and no real legs! What a strange creature, with the sharp, cold, inflexible will of some bird, and no warmth, no warmth at all! One of those creatures of the afterwards, that have no soul, but an extra-alert will, cold will. She shuddered a little, afraid of him. But then, the soft warm flame of life was stronger than he, and the real things were hidden from him.

The reading finished. She was startled. She looked up, and was more startled still to see Clifford watching her with pale, uncanny eyes, like hate.

"Thank you *so* much! You do read Racine beautifully!" she said softly.

"Almost as beautifully as you listen to him," he said cruelly.

"What are you making?" he asked.

"I'm making a child's dress, for Mrs Flint's baby."

He turned away. A child! a child! that was all her obsession.

"After all," he said, in a declamatory voice, "one gets all one wants out of Racine. Emotions that are ordered and given shape are more important than disorderly emotions."

She watched him with wide, vague, veiled eyes.

"Yes, I'm sure they are," she said.

"The modern world has only vulgarised emotion by letting it loose. What we need is classic control."

"Yes!" she said slowly, thinking of him listening with vacant face to the emotional idiocy of the radio. "People pretend to have emotions, and they really feel nothing. I suppose that is being romantic."

"Exactly!" he said.

As a matter of fact, he was tired. This evening had tired him. He would rather have been with his technical books, or his pit-manager, or listening-in to the radio.

Mrs Bolton came in with two glasses of malted milk: for Clifford, to make him sleep, and for Connie, to fatten her again. It was a regular night-cap she had introduced.

Connie was glad to go, when she had drunk her glass: and thankful she needn't help Clifford to bed. She took his glass and put it on the tray, then took the tray, to leave it outside.

"Good-night Clifford! *Do* sleep well!—The Racine gets into one like a dream.—Good-night!"

She had drifted to the door. She was going without kissing him good-night. He watched her with sharp, cold eyes. So! She did not even kiss him good-night, after he had spent an evening reading to her. Such depths of callousness in her! Even if the kiss was but a formality, it was on such formalities that life depends. She was a bolshevik, really. Her instincts were bolshevistic! He gazed coldly and angrily at the door whence she had gone. Anger!

And again the dread of the night came on him. He was a net-work of nerves, and when he was not braced up to work, and so full of energy: or when he was not listening-in, and so utterly neuter: then he was haunted by anxiety and a sense of dangerous, impending void. He was afraid. And Connie could keep the fear off him, if she would. But it was obvious she wouldn't, she wouldn't. She was callous, cold, and callous to all that he did for her. He gave up his life for her, and she was callous to him. She only wanted her own way. "The lady loves her will." Now it was a baby she was obsessed by. Just so that it should be her own, all her own, and not his!

Clifford was so healthy, considering. He looked so well and ruddy, in the face, his shoulders were broad and strong, his chest deep, he had put on flesh. And yet, at the same time, he was afraid of death. A terrible hollow seemed to menace him somewhere, somehow, a void, and into this void his energy would collapse. Energyless, he felt at times he was dead, really dead.

So his rather prominent, pale eyes had a queer look, furtive, and yet a little cruel, so cold: and at the same time, almost impudent. It was a very odd look, this look of impudence: as if he were triumphing over life in spite of life. "Who knoweth the mysteries of the will— —for it can triumph even against the angels—"

But his dread was the nights when he could not sleep. Then it was awful indeed, when annihilation pressed in on him on every side. Then it was ghastly, to exist without having any life: lifeless, in the night, to exist.

But now he could ring for Mrs Bolton. And she would always come. That was a great comfort. She would come in her dressing-gown, with her hair in a plait down her back, curiously, girlish and dim, though the brown plait was streaked with grey. And she would make him coffee or camomile tea, and she would play chess or piquet with him. She had a woman's queer faculty of playing even chess well enough, when she was three parts asleep, well enough to make her worth beating. So, in the silent intimacy of the night, they sat, or she sat and he lay in the bed, with the reading-lamp shedding its solitary light on them, she almost gone in sleep, he almost gone in a sort of fear, and they played, played together—then they had a cup of coffee and a biscuit together—hardly speaking, in the silence of night—but being a reassurance to one another.

And this night she was wondering who Lady Chatterley's lover was. And she was thinking of her own Ted, so long dead, yet for her never quite dead. And when she thought of him, her old, old grudge against the world rose up, but especially against the masters—that they had killed him. They had not really killed him. Yet, to her, emotionally, they had. And somewhere deep in herself, because of it, she was a nihilist, and really anarchic.

In her half-sleep, thoughts of her Ted and thoughts of Lady

Chatterley's unknown lover commingled, and then she felt she shared with the other woman a great grudge against Sir Clifford and all he stood for. At the same time, she was playing piquet with him, and they were gambling sixpences. And it was a source of satisfaction to be playing piquet with a baronet, and even losing sixpences to him.

When they played cards, they always gambled. It made him forget himself. And he usually won. Tonight too he was winning. So he would not go to sleep till the first dawn appeared. Luckily it began to appear at half-past four or thereabouts.

Connie was in bed, and fast asleep all this time. But the keeper, too, could not rest. He had closed the coops and made his round of the wood, then gone home and eaten supper. But he did not go to bed. Instead he sat by the fire and thought.

He thought of his boyhood in Tevershall, and of his five or six years of married life. He thought of his wife, and always bitterly. She had seemed so brutal. But he had not seen her now since 1915, in the spring when he joined up. Yet there she was, not three miles away, and more brutal than ever. He hoped never to see her again while he lived.

He thought of his life abroad, as a soldier: India, Egypt, then India again: the blind, thoughtless life with the horses: the colonel who had loved him and whom he had loved: the several years that he had been an officer, a lieutenant with a very fair chance of being a captain. Then the death of the colonel from pneumonia, and his own narrow escape from death: his damaged health: his deep restlessness: his leaving the army and coming back to England to be a working man again.

He was temporising with life. He had thought he would be safe, at least for a time, in this wood. There was no shooting as yet: he had to rear the pheasants. He would have no guns to serve. He would be alone, and apart from life, which was all he wanted. He had to have some sort of a background. And this was his native place. There was even his mother, though she had never meant very much to him. And so he could go on in life, existing from day to day, without connection and without hope. For he did not know what to do with himself.

He did not know what to do with himself. Since he had been an officer for some years, and had mixed among the other officers and civil servants, with their wives and families, he had lost all ambition to "get on." There was a toughness, a curious rubber-necked toughness and unlivingness about the middle and upper classes, as he had known them, which just left him feeling cold and different from them.

So, he had come back to his own class. To find there, what he had forgotten during his absence of years, a pettiness and a vulgarity of manner extremely distasteful. He admitted now at last, how important manner was. He admitted, also, how important it was even *to pretend* not to care about the halfpence and the small things of life. But among the common people there was no pretense. A penny more or less on the bacon was worse than a change in the Gospel. He could not stand it.

And again, there was the wage-squabble. Having lived among the owning classes, he knew the utter futility of expecting any solution of the wage-squabble. There was no solution, short of death. The only thing was not to care, not to care about the wages.

Yet, if you were poor and wretched, you *had* to care. Anyhow, it was becoming the only thing they did care about. The *care* about money was like a great cancer, eating away the individuals of all classes. He refused to *care* about money.

And what then? What did life offer apart from the care of money? Nothing.

Yet he could live alone, in the wan satisfaction of being alone: and raise pheasants to be shot ultimately by fat men after breakfast. It was futility, futility to the nth power.

But why care, why bother! And he had not cared nor bothered till now, when this woman had come into his life. He was nearly ten years older than she. And he was a thousand years older in experience, starting from the bottom. The connection between them was growing closer. He could see the day when it would clinch up, and they would have to make a life together. "For the bonds of love are ill to loose!"

And what then? What then? Must he start again, with nothing to start on? Must he entangle this woman? Must he have the horrible broil with her lame husband?—and also, some sort of horrible broil with his own brutal wife, who hated him? Misery! lots of misery! And he was no longer young and merely buoyant. Neither was he the insouciant sort. Every bitterness and every ugliness would hurt him: and the woman!

But even if they got clear of Sir Clifford and of his own wife, even if they got clear, what were they going to do? What was he, himself, going to do? What was he going to do with his life? For he must do something. He couldn't be a mere hanger-on, on her money and his own very small pension.

It was the insoluble. He could only think of going to America, to try a new air. He disbelieved in the dollar utterly. But perhaps, perhaps there was something else.

He could not rest nor even go to bed. After sitting in a stupor of bitter thoughts until midnight, he got suddenly from his chair and reached for his coat and gun.

"Come on, lass," he said to the dog. "We're best outside."

It was a starry night, but moonless. He went on a slow, scrupulous, soft-stepping and stealthy round. The only thing he had to contend with was the colliers setting snares for rabbits, particularly the Stacks Gate colliers, on the Marehay side. But it was breeding season, and even colliers respected it a little. Nevertheless the stealthy beating of the round in search of poachers soothed his nerves and took his mind off his thoughts.

But when he had done his slow cautious beating of his bounds—it was nearly a five-mile walk—he was tired. He went to the top of the knoll and looked out. There was no sound save the noise, the faint shuffling noise from Stacks Gate colliery, that never ceased working: and there were hardly any lights, save the brilliant electric rows at the works. The world lay darkly and fumily sleeping. It was half-past two. But even in its sleep it was an uneasy, cruel world, stirring with the noise of a train or some great lorry on the road, and flashing with some rosy lightning-flash from the furnaces. It was a world of iron and coal, the cruelty of iron and the smoke of coal, and the endless, endless greed that drove it all. Only greed, greed stirring in its sleep.

It was cold, and he was coughing. A fine cold draught blew over the knoll. He thought of the woman. Now he would have given all he had or ever might have to hold her warm in his arms, both of them wrapped in one blanket, and sleep. All hopes of eternity and all gain from the past he would have given to have her there, to be wrapped warm with him in one blanket, and sleep, only sleep. It seemed the sleep with the woman in his arms was the only necessity.

He went to the hut, and wrapped himself in the blankets and lay on the floor to sleep. But he could not, he was cold. And besides, he felt cruelly his own unfinished nature. He felt his own unfinished condition of aloneness cruelly. He wanted her, to touch her, to hold her fast against him in one moment of completeness and sleep.

He got up again and went out, towards the park gates this time:

then slowly along the path towards the house. It was nearly four o'clock, still clear, and cold, but no sign of dawn. He was so used to the dark, he could see well.

Slowly, slowly the great house drew him, as a magnet. He wanted to be near her. It was not desire, not that. It was the cruel sense of unfinished aloneness, that needed a silent woman folded in his arms. Perhaps he could find her. Perhaps he could even call her out to him: or find some way in to her. For the need was imperious.

He slowly, silently climbed the incline to the hall. Then he came round the great trees at the top of the knoll, on to the drive, which made a grand sweep round a lozenge of grass in front of the entrance. He could already see the two magnificent beeches which stood in this big level lozenge in front of the house, detaching themselves darkly on the dark air.

There was the house, low and long and obscure, with one light burning downstairs, in Sir Clifford's room. He knew it was Sir Clifford's room. But which room she was in, the woman who held the other end of the frail thread which drew him so mercilessly, that he did not know.

He went a little nearer, gun in hand, and stood motionless on the drive, watching the house. Perhaps even now he could find her, come at her in some way. The house was not impregnable: he was as clever as burglars are. Why not come to her.

He stood motionless, waiting, while the dawn faintly and imperceptibly paled behind him. He saw the light in the house go out. But he did not see Mrs Bolton come to the window and draw back the old curtains of dark-blue silk, and stand herself in the dark room, looking out on the half-dark of the approaching day, looking for the longed-for dawn, waiting, waiting for Clifford to be really re-assured that it was daybreak. For when he was sure of daybreak, he would sleep almost at once.

She stood blind with sleep at the window, waiting. And as she stood, she started, and almost cried out. For there was a man out there on the drive, a black figure in the twilight. She woke up greyly, and watched, but without making a sound to disturb Sir Clifford.

The daylight began to rustle in to the world, and the dark figure seemed to go smaller and more defined. She made out the gun and gaiters and baggy jacket—it would be Oliver Mellors, the keeper. Yes, for there was the dog nosing around like a shadow, and waiting for him!

What did the man want? Did he want to rouse the house? What was he standing there for, transfixed, looking up at the house like a love-sick male dog outside the house where the bitch is!

Goodness! The knowledge went through Mrs Bolton like a shot. He was Lady Chatterley's lover! He! He!

To think of it! Why, she, Ivy Bolton, had once been a tiny bit in love with him herself, when he was a lad of sixteen and she a woman of twenty-six. It was when she was studying, and he had helped her a lot with the anatomy and things she had had to learn. He'd been a clever boy, had a scholarship for Sheffield Grammar School, and learned French and things: and then after all had become an overhead blacksmith shoeing horses, because he was fond of horses, he said: but really, because he was frightened to go out and face the world, only he'd never admit it.

But he'd been a nice lad, a nice lad, had helped her a lot, so clever at making things clear to you. He was quite as clever as Sir Clifford: and always one for the women. More with women than men, they said.

Till he'd gone and married that Bertha Coutts, as if to spite himself. Some people do marry to spite themselves, because they're disappointed of something. And no wonder it had been a failure.— For years he was gone, all the time of the war: and a lieutenant and all: quite the gentleman, really, quite the gentleman!—Then to come back to Tevershall and go as a gamekeeper!—Really, some people can't take their chances when they've got them! And talking broad Derbyshire again like the worst, when she, Ivy Bolton, knew he spoke like any gentleman, *really*.

Well well! So her ladyship had fallen for him! Well—her ladyship wasn't the first: there was something about him. But fancy! a Tevershall lad born and bred, and she her-ladyship in Wragby Hall! My word, that was a slap back at the high-and-mighty Chatterleys!

But he, the keeper, as the day grew, had realised: it's no good! It's no good trying to get rid of your own aloneness. You've got to stick to it—all your life. Only at times, at times, the gap will be filled in. At times! But you have to wait for the times. Accept your own aloneness and stick to it, all your life. And then accept the times when the gap is filled in, when they come. But they've got to come. You can't force them.

With a sudden snap, the bleeding desire that had drawn him after her broke. He had broken it, because it must be so. There must be a coming together on both sides. And if she wasn't coming to him, he wouldn't track her down. He mustn't. He must go away, till she came.

He turned slowly, ponderingly, accepting again the isolation. He knew it was better so. She must come to him: it was no use his trailing after her. No use!

Mrs Bolton saw him disappear, saw his dog run after him.

"Well well!" she said. "He's the one man I never thought of; and the one man I might have thought of. He was nice to me when he was a lad, after I lost Ted. Well well! Whatever would *he* say if he knew!"

And she glanced triumphantly at the already-sleeping Clifford, as she stepped softly from the room.

CHAPTER XI.

Connie was sorting out one of the Wragby lumber rooms. There were several: the house was a warren, and the family never sold anything. Sir Geoffrey's father had liked pictures and Sir Geoffrey's mother had liked cinquecento furniture. Sir Geoffrey himself had liked old oak carved chests, vestry chests. So it went on through the generations. Clifford collected very modern pictures—at very moderate prices.

So in the lumber room there were bad Sir Edwin Landseer's and pathetic William Henry Hunt birds' nests: and other academy stuff, enough to frighten the daughter of an R. A. She determined to look through it one day, and clear it all. And the grotesque furniture interested her.

Wrapped up carefully to preserve it from damage and dry-rot was the old family cradle, of rose-wood. She had to unwrap it, to look at it. It had a certain charm: she looked at it a long time.

"It's a thousand pities it won't be called for," sighed Mrs Bolton, who was helping. "Though cradles like that are out of date nowadays."

"It might be called for. I might have a child," said Connie casually, as if saying she might have a new hat.

"You mean—if anything happened to Sir Clifford?" stammered Mrs Bolton.

"No! I mean as things are. It's only muscular paralysis with Sir Clifford—it doesn't affect *him*," said Connie, lying as naturally as breathing.

Clifford had put the idea into her head. He had said: "Of course *I* may have a child yet. I'm not really mutilated at all. The potency may easily come back, if even the muscles of the hips and legs are paralysed. And then the seed may be transferred."

He really felt, when he had his periods of energy and worked so hard at the question of the mines, as if his sexual potency were returning. Connie had looked at him in terror. But she was quite quick-witted enough to use his suggestion for her own preservation. For she would have a child if she could: but not his.

Mrs Bolton was for a moment breathless, flabbergasted. Then she didn't believe it: she saw in it a ruse. Yet doctors could do such things nowadays. They might sort of graft seed——

"Well my Lady, I only hope and pray you may. It would be lovely for you: and for everybody. My word, a child in Wragby, what a difference it would make!"

"Wouldn't it!" said Connie.

And she chose three R. A. pictures of sixty years ago, to send to the Duchess of Shortlands for that lady's next charitable bazaar. She was called "the bazaar duchess": and she always asked all the county to send things for her to sell. She would be delighted with three framed R. A.'s. She might even call, on the strength of them. How furious Clifford was when she called!

But oh my dear! Mrs Bolton was thinking to herself.—Is it Oliver Mellors' child you're preparing us for? Oh my dear, that *would* be a Tevershall baby in the Wragby cradle, my word! Wouldn't shame it, neither!

Among other monstrosities in this lumber room was a largeish black japanned box, excellently and ingeniously made some sixty or seventy years ago, and fitted with every imaginable object. On top was a con-centrated toilet set: brushes, bottles, mirrors, combs, boxes, even three beautiful little razors in safety sheaths, shaving-bowl and all. Underneath came a sort of escritoire outfit: blotters, pens, ink-bottles, paper, envelopes, memorandum books: and then a perfect sewing outfit, with three different-sized scissors, thimbles, needles, silks and cottons, darning egg, all of the very best quality and perfectly finished. Then there was a little medicine store, with bottles labelled Lauda-num, Tincture of Myrrh, Ess. Cloves and so on: but empty. Every-thing was perfectly new. And the whole thing when shut up was as big as a small, but fat week-end bag. And inside, it fitted together like a puzzle. The bottles could not possibly have spilled: there wasn't room.

The thing was wonderfully made and contrived, excellent crafts-manship of the best Victorian order. But somehow it was monstrous. Some Chatterley must even have felt it, for the thing had never been used. It had a peculiar soullessness.

Yet Mrs Bolton was thrilled.

"Look what beautiful brushes, so expensive, even the shaving brush! *Look* at the lovely fine tooth-brushes, three perfect ones! No, and those scissors! They're the best that money could buy. Oh, I call it *lovely*!"

"Do you?" said Connie. "Then you have it."

"Oh no, my Lady!"

"Of course! It will only lie here till Doomsday. If you won't have it, I'll send it to the Duchess as well as the pictures—and she doesn't deserve so much. Do have it!"

"Oh your Ladyship! Why I shall never be able to thank you—"

"You needn't try," laughed Connie.

And Mrs Bolton sailed down with the huge and very black box in her arms, flushing bright pink in her excitement.

Mr Betts drove her in the trap to her house in the village, with the box. And she *had* to have a few friends in, to show it: the schoolmistress, the chemist's wife, Mrs Weedon the under-cashier's wife. They thought it marvellous. And then started the whisper of Lady Chatterley's child.

"Wonders'll never cease!" said Mrs Weedon.

But Mrs Bolton was *convinced*, if it did come, it would be Sir Clifford's child. So there—!

Not long after, the rector said gently to Clifford:

"And may we really hope for an heir to Wragby? Ah, that would be the hand of God in mercy, indeed!"

"Well! we may *hope*," said Clifford, with a faint irony, and at the same time, a certain conviction. He had begun to believe it really possible it might even be *his* child.

Then one afternoon came Leslie Winter, Squire Winter, as everybody called him: lean, immaculate, and seventy: and every inch a gentleman, as Mrs Bolton said to Mrs Betts. Every millimetre indeed! And, with his old-fashioned, rather haw-haw! manner of speaking, he seemed more out of date than bag wigs. Time, in her flight, drops these fine old feathers.

They discussed the collieries. Clifford's idea was, that his coal, even the poor sort, could be made into hard concentrated fuel that would burn at great heat if fed with certain damp, acidulated air at a fairly strong pressure. It had long been observed, that in a particular strong, wet wind the pit-bank burned very vivid, gave off hardly any fumes, and left a fine powder of ash, instead of the slow pink gravel.

"But where will you find the proper engines for burning your fuel?" asked Winter.

"I'll make them myself. And I'll use my fuel myself. And I'll sell electric power. I'm certain I could do it."

"If you can do it, then splendid, splendid, my dear boy. Haw!

Splendid! If I can be of any help, I shall be delighted. I'm afraid I am a little out of date, and my collieries are like me. But who knows, when I am gone, there may be men like you. Splendid! It will employ all the men again, and you won't have to sell your coal, or fail to sell it. A splendid idea, and I hope it will be a success. If I had sons of my own, no doubt they would have up-to-date ideas for Shipley: no doubt!—By the way, dear boy, is there any foundation to the rumour that we may entertain hopes of an heir to Wragby?"

"Is there a rumour?" asked Clifford.

"Well, my dear boy, Marshall from Fillingwood asked *me*—that's all I can say about a rumour. Of course I wouldn't repeat it for the world, if there were no foundation."

"Well, Sir," said Clifford uneasily, but with strange bright eyes. "There is a hope. There is a hope."

Winter came across the room and wrung Clifford's hand.

"My dear boy, my dear lad, can you believe what it means to me, to hear that!—And to hear you are working in the hopes of a son: and that you may again employ every man at Tevershall.—Ah, my boy!—to keep up the level of the race, and to have work waiting for any man who cares to work!—"

The old man was really moved.

Next day Connie was arranging tall yellow tulips in a glass vase.

"Connie," said Clifford, "did you know there was a rumour that you are going to supply Wragby with a son and heir?"

Connie felt dim with terror, yet she stood quite still, touching the flowers.

"No!" she said. "Is it a joke? or malice?"

He paused before he answered:

"Neither, I hope. I hope it may be a prophecy."

Connie went on with her flowers.

"I had a letter from father this morning," she said. "He wants to know if I am aware he has accepted Sir Alexander Cooper's invitation for me for July and August, to the Villa Esmeralda in Venice."

"July *and* August?" said Clifford.

"Oh, I wouldn't stay all that time.—Are you sure you wouldn't come?"

"I won't travel abroad," said Clifford promptly.

She took her flowers to the window.

"Do you mind if I go?" she said. "You know it was promised, for this summer."

"For how long would you go?"

"Perhaps three weeks."

There was silence for a time.

"Well!" said Clifford slowly, and a little gloomily. "I suppose I could stand it for three weeks: if I were absolutely sure you'd want to come back."

"I should want to come back," she said, with quiet simplicity, heavy with conviction. She was thinking of the other man.

Clifford felt her conviction, and somehow he believed her, he believed it was for him. He felt immensely relieved, joyful at once.

"In that case," he said, "I think it would be all right—don't you?"

"I think so," she said.

"You'd enjoy the change?"

She looked up at him with strange blue eyes.

"I should like to see Venice again," she said, "and to bathe from one of the shingle islands across the lagoon. But you know I loathe the Lido! And I don't fancy I shall like Sir Alexander Cooper and Lady Cooper. But if Hilda is there—and we have a gondola of our own: yes, it will be rather lovely. I *do* wish you'd come."

She said it sincerely. She would so love to make him happy, in these ways.

"Ah, but think of me, though, at the Gare du Nord: at Calais quay!"

"But why not! I see other men carried in litter-chairs, who have been wounded in the war. Besides, we'd motor all the way."

"We should need to take two men."

"Oh no! With Field, there would always be another man there."

But Clifford shook his head.

"Not this year, dear! Not this year! Next year probably I'll try."

She went away gloomily. Next year! What would next year bring? She herself did not really want to go to Venice: not now, now there was the other man. But she was going as a sort of discipline: and also because, if she had a child, Clifford could think she had had a lover in Venice.

It was already May, and in June they were supposed to start. Always these arrangements! always one's life arranged for one! Wheels that worked one and drove one, and over which one had no real control!

It was May, but cold and wet again. A cold wet May, good for corn and hay! Much the corn and hay matter nowadays! Connie had to go in to Uthwaite, which was their little town, where the Chatterleys were still *the* Chatterleys. She went alone, Field driving her.

In spite of May and a new greenness, the country was dismal. It was rather chilly, and there was smoke on the rain, and a certain sense of exhaust vapour in the air. One just had to live from one's resistance. No wonder these people were ugly and tough.

The car ploughed uphill through the long squalid straggle of Tevershall, the blackened brick dwellings, the black slate roofs glistening their sharp edges, the mud black with coal-dust, the pavements wet and black. It was as if dismalness had soaked through and through everything. The utter negation of natural beauty, the utter negation of the gladness of life, the utter absence of the instinct for shapely beauty which every bird and beast has, the utter death of the human intuitive faculty was appalling. The stacks of soap in the grocers' shops, the rhubarb and lemons in the greengrocers', the awful hats in the milliners', all went by ugly, ugly, ugly, followed by the plaster-and-gilt horror of the cinema with its wet picture-announcements, "A Woman's Love!" and the new big Primitive chapel, primitive enough in its stark brick and big panes of greenish and raspberry glass in the windows. The Wesleyan chapel, higher up, was of blackened brick and stood behind iron railings and blackened shrubs. The Congregational chapel, which thought itself superior, was built of rusticated sandstone and had a steeple, but not a very high one. Just beyond were the new school buildings, expensive pink brick, and gravelled play-ground inside iron railings, all very imposing, and mixing the suggestion of a chapel and a prison. Standard Five girls were having a singing lesson, just finishing the la—me—doh—la exercises and beginning a "sweet children's song." Anything more unlike song, spontaneous song, would be impossible to imagine: a strange, bawling yell that followed the outlines of a tune. It was not like savages: savages have subtle rhythms. It was not like animals: animals *mean* something when they yell. It was like nothing on earth, and it was called singing. Connie sat and listened with her heart in her boots, as Field was filling petrol. What could possibly become of such a people, a people in whom the living intuitive faculty was dead as nails, and only queer mechanical yells and uncanny will-power remained?

A coal-cart was coming downhill, clanking in the rain. Field started upwards, past the big but weary-looking drapers and clothing shops, the post-office, into the little market-place of forlorn space, where Sam Black was peering out of the door of the "Sun," that called itself an inn, not a pub, and where the commercial travellers stayed, and was bowing to Lady Chatterley's car.

The church was away on the left, among black trees. The car slid on downhill, past the Miners Arms. It had already passed the Wellington, the Nelson, the Three Tunns and the Sun, now it passed the Miners Arms, then the Mechanics Hall, then the new and almost gaudy Miners Welfare—and so, past a few new "villas," out into the blackened road between dark hedges and dark-green fields, towards Stacks Gate.

Tevershall! That was Tevershall! Merrie England! Shakespeare's England! No, but the England of today, as Connie had realised since she had come to live in it. It was producing a new race of mankind, over-conscious in the money and social and political side, on the spontaneous intuitive side dead, but dead. Half-corpses, all of them: but with a terrible insistent consciousness in the other half. There was something uncanny and underground about it all. It was an under-world. And quite incalculable. How shall we understand the reactions in half-corpses? When Connie saw the great lorries full of steel-workers from Sheffield, weird distorted smallish beings like men, off for an excursion to Matlock, her bowels fainted, and she thought: Ah God, what has man done to man? What have the leaders of men been doing to their fellow men? They have reduced them to less than humanness, and now there can be no fellowship any more! It is just a nightmare.

She felt again in a wave of terror the grey, gritty hopelessness of it all. With such creatures for the industrial masses, and the upper classes as she knew them, there was no hope, no hope any more. Yet she was wanting a baby, and an heir to Wragby! An heir to Wragby! She shuddered with dread.

Yet Mellors had come out of all this.—Yes, but he was as apart from it as she was. Even in him, there was no fellowship left. It was dead. The fellowship was dead. There was only apartness, and hopelessness, as far as all this was concerned. And this was England, the vast bulk of England: as Connie knew, since she had motored from the centre of it.

The car was rising towards Stacks Gate. The rain was holding off, and in the air came a queer pellucid gleam of May. The country rolled away in long undulations, south towards the Peak, east towards Mansfield and Nottingham. Connie was travelling south.

As she rose on to the high country, she could see on her left, on a height above the rolling land the shadowy, powerful bulk of Warsop Castle, dark-grey, with below it the reddish plastering of miners' dwellings, newish, and below those, the plumes of dark smoke and white steam from the great colliery which put so many thousands of pounds per annum into the pockets of the Duke and the other shareholders. The powerful old castle was a ruin, yet still it hung its bulk on the low sky-line, over the black plumes and the white that waved on the damp air below.

A turn, and they ran on the high level to Stacks Gate. Stacks Gate, as seen from the high-road, was just a huge and gorgeous new hotel, the Coningsby Arms, standing red and white and gilt in barbarous isolation off the road. But if you looked, you saw on the left rows of handsome "modern" dwellings, set down like a game of dominoes, with spaces and gardens, a queer game of dominoes that some weird "masters" were playing on the surprised earth. And beyond these blocks of dwellings, at the back, rose all the astonishing and frightening overhead erections of a really modern mine, chemical works and long galleries, enormous, and of shapes not before known to man. The head-stocks and pit-bank of the mine itself were insignificant among the huge new installations. And in front of this, the game of dominoes stood forever in a sort of surprise, waiting to be played.

This was Stacks Gate, new on the face of the earth, since the war. But as a matter of fact, though even Connie did not know it, downhill half-a-mile below the "hotel" was old Stacks Gate, with a little old colliery and blackish old brick dwellings, and a chapel or two and a shop or two and a little pub or two.

But that didn't count any more. The vast plumes of smoke and vapour rose from the new works up above, and was now Stacks Gate: no chapels, no pubs, even no shops. Only the great "works," which are the modern Olympia with temples to all the gods; then the model dwellings: then the hotel. The hotel in actuality was nothing but a miners' pub, though it looked first-classy.

Even since Connie's arrival at Wragby this new place had arisen on the face of the earth, and the model dwellings had filled with riff-raff drifting in from anywhere, to poach Clifford's rabbits among other occupations.

The car ran on, along the uplands, seeing the rolling county spread out. The county! It had once been a proud and lordly county.

In front, looming again and hanging on the brow of the sky-line, was the huge and splendid bulk of Chadwick Hall, more window than wall, one of the most famous Elizabethan houses. Noble it stood alone above a great park, but out of date, passed over. It was still kept up, but as a show place. "Look how our ancestors lorded it!"

That was the past. The present lay below. God alone knows where the future lies. The car was already turning, between little old blackened miners' cottages, to descend to Uthwaite. And Uthwaite, on a damp day, was sending up a whole array of smoke plumes and steam, to whatever gods there be. Uthwaite down in the valley, with all the steel threads of the railways to Sheffield drawn through it, and the coal-mines and the steel-works sending up smoke and glare from long tubes, and the pathetic little cork-screw spire of the church, that is going to tumble down, still pricking the fumes, always affected Connie strangely. It was an old market-town, centre of the dales. One of the chief inns was the Chatterley Arms. There, in Uthwaite, Wragby was known as Wragby, as if it were a whole place, not just a house, as it was to outsiders: Wragby Hall, near Tevershall. Wragby, a "seat."

The miners' cottages, blackened, stood flush on the pavement, with that intimacy and smallness of colliers' dwellings over a hundred years old. They lined all the way. The road had become a street, and as you sank, you forgot instantly the open, rolling country where the castles and big houses still dominated, but like ghosts. Now you were just above the tangle of naked railway-lines, and foundries and other "works" rose about you, so big you were only aware of walls. And iron clanked with a huge reverberating clank, and huge lorries shook the earth, and whistles screamed.

Yet again, once you had got right down and into the twisted and crooked heart of the town, behind the church, you were in the world of two centuries ago, in the crooked streets where the Chatterley Arms stood, and the old pharmacy, streets which used to lead out to the wild open world of the castles and stately, couchant houses.

But at the corner a policeman held up his hand as three lorries laden with iron rolled past, shaking the poor old church. And not till the lorries were past could he salute her ladyship.

So it was. Upon the old, crooked burgess streets hordes of oldish, blackened miners' dwellings crowded, lining the roads out. And immediately after these came the newer, pinker rows of rather larger houses, plastering the valley: the homes of more modern workmen.

And beyond again, in the wide, rolling region of the castles, smoke waved against steam, and patch after patch of raw reddish brick showed the newer mining settlements, sometimes in the hollows, sometimes gruesomely ugly along the skyline of the slopes. And between, in between, were the tattered remnants of the old coaching and cottage England, even the England of Robin Hood, where the miners prowled with the dismalness of suppressed sporting instincts, when they were not at work.

England my England! But which is *my* England? The stately homes of England make good photographs, and create the illusion of a connection with the Elizabethans. The handsome old halls are there, from the days of Good Queen Anne and Tom Jones. But smuts fall blacker and blacker on the drab stucco, that has long ceased to be golden. And one by one, like the stately homes, they are abandoned. Now they are being pulled down. As for the cottages of England, there they are—great plasterings of brick dwellings on the hopeless countryside.

Now they are pulling down the stately homes, the Georgian halls are going. Fritchley, a perfect old Georgian mansion, was even now, as Connie passed in the car, being demolished. It was in perfect repair: till the war, the Weatherbys had lived in style there. But now it was too big, too expensive, and the country had become too uncongenial. The gentry were departing to pleasanter places, where they could spend their money without having to see how it was made.

This is history. One England blots out another. The mines had made the halls wealthy. Now they were blotting them out, as they had already blotted out the cottages. The industrial England blots out the agricultural England. One meaning blots out another. The new England blots out the old England. And the continuity is not organic, but mechanical.

Connie, belonging to the leisured classes, had clung to the remnants of the old England. It had taken her years to realise that it was really blotted out by this terrifying, new and gruesome England, and that the blotting out would go on till it was complete. Fritchley was gone, Eastwood was gone, Shipley was going: Squire Winter's beloved Shipley.

Connie called for a moment at Shipley. The park gates, at the back, opened just near the level crossing of the colliery railway; the Shipley colliery itself stood just beyond the trees. The gates stood open, because through the park was a right-of-way that the colliers used. They hung around the park.

The car passed the ornamental ponds, in which the colliers threw their newspapers, and took the private drive to the house. It stood above, aside, a very pleasant stucco building from the middle of the eighteenth century. It had a beautiful alley of yew trees, that had approached an older house, and the hall stood serenely spread out, winking its Georgian panes as if cheerfully. Behind, there were really beautiful gardens.

Connie liked the interior much better than Wragby. It was much lighter, more alive, shapen and elegant. The rooms were panelled with creamy-painted panelling, the ceilings were touched with gilt, and everything was kept in exquisite order, all the appointments were perfect, regardless of expense. Even the corridors managed to be ample and lovely, softly curved and full of life.

But Leslie Winter was alone. He had adored his house. But his park was bordered by three of his own collieries. He had been a generous man in his ideas. He had almost welcomed the colliers in his park. Had the mines not made him rich! So, when he saw the gangs of unshapely men lounging by his ornamental waters—not on the *private* part of the park, no, he drew the line there—he would say: "The miners are perhaps not so ornamental as deer, but they are far more profitable."

But that was in the golden—monetarily—latter half of Queen Victoria's reign. Miners were then "good working men."

Winter had made this speech, half apologetic, to his guest, the then Prince of Wales. And the Prince had replied, in his rather guttural English:

"You are quite right. If there were coal under Sandringham, I would open a mine on the lawns, and think it first-rate landscape gardening. Oh, I am quite willing to exchange roe-deer for colliers, at the price. Your men are good men too, I hear."

But then, the Prince had perhaps an exaggerated idea of the beauty of money, and the blessings of industrialism.

However, the Prince had been a King, and the King had died, and now there was another King, whose chief function seemed to be, to open soup-kitchens.

And the good working men were somehow hemming Shipley in. New mining villages crowded on the park, and the Squire felt somehow that the population was alien. He used to feel, in a good-natured but quite grand way, lord of his own domain and of his own colliers. Now, by a subtle pervasion of the new spirit, he had somehow been pushed out. It was *he* who did not belong any more. There was no mistaking it. The mines, the industry had a will of its own, and this will was against the gentleman-owner. All the colliers took part in the will, and it was hard to live up against it. It either shoved you out of the place, or out of life altogether.

Squire Winter, a soldier, had stood it out. But he no longer cared to walk in the park after dinner. He almost hid, indoors. Once he had walked, bareheaded, and in his patent-leather shoes and purple silk socks, with Connie down to the gate, talking to her in his well-bred rather haw-haw fashion. But when it came to passing the little gangs of colliers who stood and stared without either salute or anything else, Connie felt how the lean, well-bred old man winced, winced as an elegant antelope stag in a cage winces from the vulgar stare. The colliers were not *personally* hostile: not at all. But their spirit was cold, and shoving him out. And deep down, there was a profound grudge. They "worked for him." And in their ugliness, they resented his elegant, well-groomed, well-bred existence. "Who's he—!" It was the *difference* they resented.

And somewhere, in his secret English heart, being a good deal of a soldier, he believed they were right to resent the difference. He felt himself a little in the wrong, for having all the advantages. Nevertheless, he represented a system, and he would not be shoved out.

Except by death. Which came on him soon after Connie's call, suddenly. And he remembered Clifford handsomely in his will.

The heirs at once gave out the order for the demolishing of Shipley. It cost too much to keep up. No-one would live there. So it was broken up. The avenue of yews was cut down. The park was denuded of its timber, and divided into lots. It was near enough to Uthwaite. In the strange bald desert of this still-one-more no-man's-land, new little streets of semi-detacheds were run up, very desirable! The Shipley Hall Estate!

Within a year of Connie's last call, it had happened. There stood Shipley Hall Estate, an array of red-brick semi-detached "villas" in new streets. No-one would have dreamed that the stucco hall had stood there twelve months before.

But this is a later stage of King Edward's landscape-gardening, the sort that has an ornamental coal-mine on the lawn.

One England blots out another. The England of the Squire

Winters and the Wragby Halls was gone, dead. The blotting out was only not yet complete.

What would come after? Connie could not imagine. She could only see the new brick streets spreading into the fields, the new erections rising at the collieries, the new girls in their silk stockings, the new collier lads lounging into the Pally or the Welfare. The younger generation were utterly unconscious of the old England. There was a gap in the continuity of consciousness, almost American: but industrial, really. What next?

Connie always felt there was no next. She wanted to hide her head in the sand: or at least, in [the] bosom of a living man.

The world was so complicated and weird and gruesome! The common people were so many, and really, so terrible. So she thought as she was going home, and saw the colliers trailing from the pits, grey-black, distorted, one shoulder higher than the other, slurring their heavy ironshod boots. Underground grey faces, whites of eyes rolling, necks cringing from the pit roof, shoulders out of shape. Men! Men! Alas, in some ways patient and good men. In other ways, non-existent. Something that men *should* have was bred and killed out of them. Yet they were men. They begot children. One might bear a child to them. Terrible, terrible thought! They were good and kindly. But they were only half, only the grey half of a human being. As yet, they were "good." But even that was the goodness of their halfness. Supposing the dead in them ever rose up! But no, it was too terrible to think of. Connie was absolutely afraid of the industrial masses. They seemed so *weird* to her. A life with utterly no beauty in it, no intuition, always "in the pit."

Children from such men! Oh God Oh God!

Yet Mellors had come from such a father. Not quite. Forty years had made a difference, an appalling difference in manhood. The iron and the coal had eaten deep into the bodies and souls of the men.

Incarnate ugliness, and yet alive! What would become of them all? Perhaps with the passing of the coal they would disappear again, off the face of the earth. They had appeared out of nowhere in their thousands, when the coal had called for them. Perhaps they were only weird fauna of the coal-seams. Creatures of another reality, they were elementals, serving the element of coal, as the metal-workers were elementals, serving the element of iron. Men not men, but animas of coal and iron and clay. Fauna of the elements, carbon, iron, silicon: elementals. They had perhaps some of the weird inhuman beauty of minerals, the lustre of coal, the weight and blueness and resistance of iron, the transparency of glass. Elemental creatures, weird and distorted, of the mineral world! They belonged to the coal, the iron, the clay, as fish belong to the sea and worms to dead wood. The anima of mineral disintegration!

Connie was glad to be home, to bury her head in the sand. She was glad even to babble to Clifford. For her fear of the mining and iron Midlands affected her with a queer feeling that went all over her, like influenza.

"Of course I had to have tea in Miss Bentley's shop," she said.

"Really! Winter would have given you tea."

"Oh yes! But I daren't disappoint Miss Bentley."

Miss Bentley was a sallow old maid with a rather large nose and romantic disposition, who served tea with a careful intensity worthy of a sacrament.

"Did she ask after me?" said Clifford.

"Of course!—*May* I ask your Ladyship how Sir Clifford is!—I believe she ranks you even higher than Nurse Cavell!"

"And I suppose you said I was blooming."

"Yes! And she looked as rapt as if I had said the heavens had opened to you. I said if she ever came to Tevershall she was to come and see you."

"Me! Whatever for! See *me*!"

"Why yes, Clifford. You can't be so adored without making some slight return. Saint George of Cappadocia was nothing to you, in her eyes."

"And do you think she'll come?"

"Oh, she blushed! and looked quite beautiful, for a moment, poor thing! Why don't men marry the women who would really adore them?"

"The women start adoring too late.—But did she say she'd come?"

"Oh—!" Connie imitated the breathless Miss Bentley—"your Ladyship, if ever I should dare to presume—!"

"Dare to presume! how absurd! But I hope to God she won't turn up.—And how was her tea?"

"Oh—Liptons—and *very* strong! But Clifford, do you realise you are the *Roman de la rose* of Miss Bentley and lots like her?"

"I'm not flattered, even then."

"They treasure up every one of your pictures in the illustrated papers—and probably pray for you every night. It's rather wonderful."

She went upstairs to change.

That evening he said to her:

"You do think, don't you, that there is something eternal in marriage?"

She looked at him.

"But Clifford, you make eternity sound like a lid—or a long long chain that trailed after one, no matter how far one went."

He looked at her, annoyed.

"What I mean," he said, "is, that if you go to Venice, you won't go in the hopes of some love affair that you can take *au grand sérieux*, will you?"

"A love affair in Venice *au grand sérieux*? no, I assure you! No, I'd never take a love affair in Venice more than *au très petit sérieux*."

She spoke with a queer kind of contempt. He knitted his brows, looking at her.

Coming downstairs in the morning, she found the keeper's dog Flossie sitting in the corridor outside Clifford's room, and whimpering very faintly.

"Why Flossie!" she said softly. "What are you doing here?"

And she quietly opened Clifford's door. Clifford was sitting up in bed, with the bed-table and type-writer pushed aside, and the keeper was standing attention at the foot of the bed. Flossie ran in. With a faint gesture of head and eyes, Mellors ordered her to the door again, and she slunk out.

"Oh Good-morning Clifford!" she said. "I didn't know you were busy." Then she looked at the keeper, saying Good-morning! to him. He murmured his reply, looking at her as if vaguely. But she felt a whiff of passion touch her, from his mere presence.

"Did I interrupt you, Clifford? I'm sorry."

"No, it's nothing of any importance."

She slipped out of the room again, and up to the blue boudoir on the first floor. She sat in the window, and saw him go down the drive, with his curious silent motion, effaced. He had a natural sort of quiet distinction, an aloof pride, and also, a certain look of frailty. A hireling! One of Clifford's hirelings! "The fault, dear Brutus, is not in our stars, but in ourselves, that we are underlings."

Was he an underling? Was he? What did he think of *her*?

It was a sunny day, and Connie was working in the garden, and Mrs Bolton was helping her. For some reason, the two women had drawn together, in one of the unaccountable flows and ebbs of sympathy that exist between people. They were pegging down carnations, and putting in small plants for the summer. It was work they both liked. Connie especially felt a delight in putting the soft roots of young plants into a soft black puddle, and cradling them down. On this spring morning she felt a quiver in her womb, too, as if the sunshine had touched it and made it happy.

"It is many years since you lost your husband?" she said to Mrs Bolton, as she took up another little plant and laid it in its hole.

"Twenty-three!" said Mrs Bolton, as she carefully separated the young columbines into single plants. "Twenty-three years since they brought him home."

Connie's heart gave a lurch, at the terrible finality of it. "Brought him home!"

"Why did he get killed, do you think?" she asked. "He was happy with you."

It was a woman's question to a woman. Mrs Bolton put aside a strand of hair from her face, with the back of her hand.

"I don't know, my Lady! He sort of wouldn't give in to things: he wouldn't really go with the rest. And then he hated ducking his head, for anything on earth. A sort of obstinacy, that *gets* itself killed. You see he didn't really care. I lay it down to the pit. He ought never to have been down pit. But his dad made him go down, as a lad; and then, when you're over twenty, it's not very easy to come out."

"Did he say he hated it?"

"Oh no! Never! He never said he hated anything. He just made a funny face. He was one of those who wouldn't take care: like some of the first lads as went off so blithe to the war and got killed right away. He wasn't really wezzle-brained. But he wouldn't care. I used to say to him: You care for nought nor nobody!—But he did! The way he sat when my first baby was born, motionless, and the sort of fatal eyes he looked at me with, when it was over! I had a bad time—but I had to comfort *him*. 'It's all right, lad, it's all right!' I said to him. And he gave me a look, and that funny sort of smile. He never said anything. But I don't believe he ever had any right pleasure with me at nights after—he'd never really let himself go. I used to say to him: Oh, let thysen go, lad!—I'd talk broad to him sometimes.—And he said nothing. But he wouldn't let himself go—or he couldn't. He didn't want me to have any more children. I *always* blamed his mother, for letting him in th' room. He'd no right t' ave been there. Men makes so much more of things than they should, once they start brooding."

"Did he mind so much?" said Connie in wonder.

"Yes—he sort of couldn't take it for natural—all that pain. And it spoilt his pleasure in his bit of married love. I said to him: If I don't care, why should you? It's my look-out!—But all he'd ever say was: It's not right!"

"Perhaps he was too sensitive," said Connie.

"That's it! When you come to know men, that's how they are: too sensitive, in the wrong place. And I believe, unbeknown to himself, he hated the pit: just hated it. He looked so quiet when he was dead, as if he'd got free. He was such a nice-looking lad. It just broke my heart to see him, so still and pure looking, as if he'd *wanted* to die. Oh, it broke my heart, that did. But it was the pit—"

She wept a few bitter tears, and Connie wept more. It was a warm spring day, with a perfume of earth and of yellow flowers, many things rising to bud, and the garden still with the very sap of sunshine.

"It must have been terrible for you!" said Connie.

"Oh, my Lady! I never realised at first. I could only say: Oh my lad, what did you want to leave me for!—That was all my cry.—But somehow, I felt he'd come back—"

"But he *didn't* want to leave you," said Connie.

"Oh no, my Lady! That was only my silly cry. And I kept expecting him back. Especially at nights. I kept waking up thinking: Why, he's not in bed with me!—It was as if my *feelings* wouldn't believe he'd gone. I just felt he'd *have* to come back and lie against me, so I could feel him with me. That was all I wanted, to feel him there with me, warm. And it took me a thousand shocks before I knew he wouldn't come back—it took me years."

"The touch of him," said Connie.

"That's it, my Lady! the touch of him! I've never got over it to this day, and never shall. And if there's a heaven above, he'll be there, and will lie up against me so I can sleep."

Connie glanced at the handsome, brooding face in fear. Another passionate one, out of Tevershall! The touch of him! For the bonds of love are ill to loose!

"It's terrible, once you've got a man into your blood!" she said.

"Oh my Lady!—And that's what makes you feel so bitter. You feel folks *wanted* him killed. You feel the pit fair *wanted* to kill him. Oh, I felt, if it 'adn't been for th' pit, an' them as runs the pit, there'd have been no leaving me. But they all *want* to separate a woman and a man, if they're together—"

"If they're physically together," said Connie.

"That's right my Lady! There's a lot of hard-hearted folks in the world. And every morning when he got up and went to th' pit, I felt it was wrong, wrong. But what else could he do? What can a man do?"

A queer hate flared in the woman.

"But can a touch last so long?" Connie asked suddenly. "That you could feel him so long!"

"Oh my Lady, what else is there to last? Children grows away from you. But the man—! Well! But even *that* they'd like to kill in you, the very thought of the touch of him. Even that! Even your own children! Ah well! We might have drifted apart, who knows. But the *feeling's* something different.—It's 'appen better never to care.—But there, when I look at women who's never really been warmed through by a man—well, they seem to me poor dool-owls after all, no matter how they may dress up and gad. No, I'll abide by my own. I've not much respect for people—"

CHAPTER XII

Connie went to the wood directly after lunch. It was really a lovely day, the first dandelions making suns, the first daisies so white. The hazel-thicket was a lace-work of half-open leaves, and the last dusty perpendicular of the catkins. Yellow celandines now were in crowds, flat open, pressed back in urgency and the yellow glitter of themselves. It was the yellow, the triumphant powerful yellow of early summer. And primroses were broad and full of pale abandon, thick-clustered primroses no longer shy. The lush dark green of hyacinths was a sea, with buds rising like pale corn, while in the riding the forget-me-nots were fluffing up, and columbines were unfolding their ink-purple ruches, and there were bits of blue bird's-egg shell under a bush. Everywhere the bud-knots and the leap of life!

The keeper was not at the hut. Everything was serene, brown chickens running lustily. Connie walked on towards the cottage, because she wanted to find him.

The cottage stood in the sun, off the wood's edge. In its little garden the double daffodils rose in tufts near the wide-open door, and red double daisies made a border to the path. There was the bark of a dog, and Flossie appeared in the doorway.

The wide-open door! so he was at home. And the sunlight falling on the red brick floor! As she went up the path she saw him through the window, sitting at table in his shirt-sleeves, eating. The dog wuffed softly, slowly wagging her tail.

He rose and came to the door, wiping his mouth with a red handkerchief, still chewing.

"May I come in?" she said.

"Come in!"

The sun shone into the bare room, which still smelled of a mutton chop done in a dutch oven before the fire—because the dutch oven still stood on the fender, with the black potato-saucepan on a piece of paper, beside it on the white hearth. The fire was red, rather low, the bar dropped, the kettle singing.

On the table was his plate, with potatoes and the remains of the chop: also bread in a basket, salt, and a blue mug with beer. The table-cloth was white oil-cloth. He stood in the shade.

"You are very late," she said. "Do go on eating!"

She sat down in a wooden chair in the sunlight by the door.

"I had to go to Uthwaite," he said, sitting down at table, but not eating.

"Do eat!" she said.

But he did not touch the food.

"Shall y' ave something?" he asked her. "Shall y' ave a cup o' tea?—t' kettle's on t' boil?"—He half rose again from his chair.

"If you'll let me make it myself," she said, rising.

He seemed sad, and she felt she was bothering him.

"Well!—Tea-pot's in there—" he pointed to a little drab corner-cupboard—"an' cups! An' tea's on t' mantel ower yer 'ead."

She got the black tea-pot, and the tin of tea from the mantel-shelf. She rinsed the tea-pot with hot water, and stood a moment wondering where to empty it.

"Throw it out," he said, aware of her. "It's clean."

She went to the door and threw the drop of water down the path. How lovely it was here, so still, so really wood-land. The oaks were putting out ochre-yellow leaves; in the garden the red daisies were like red plush buttons. She glanced at the big hollow sandstone slab of the threshold, now crossed by so few feet.

"But it's lovely here!" she said. "Such a beautiful stillness, everything alive and still."

He was eating again, rather slowly and unwillingly, and she could feel he was discouraged. She made the tea in silence, and set the tea-pot on the hob, as she knew the people did. He pushed his plate aside and went to the back place. She heard a latch click, then he came back with cheese on a plate, and butter.

She set the two cups on the table: there were only two.

"Will you have a cup of tea?" she said.

"If you like. Sugar's in th' cupboard—an' there's a little cream-jug. Milk's in a jug i' th' pantry."

"Shall I take your plate away?" she asked him.

He looked up at her with a faint ironical smile.

"Why—if you like," he said, slowly eating bread and cheese.

She went to the back, into the pent-house scullery where the pump was. On the left was a door, no doubt the pantry door. She unlatched it, and almost smiled at the place he called a pantry: a long, narrow, whitewashed slip of a cupboard. But it managed to contain a little barrel of beer, as well as a few dishes and bits of food. She took a little milk from the yellow jug.

"How do you get your milk?" she asked him when she came back to the table.

"Flints! They leave me a bottle at th' warren-end. You know, when I met you!"

But he was discouraged.

She poured out the tea, poising the cream-jug.

"No milk," he said.

Then he seemed to hear a noise, and looked keenly through the doorway.

"'Appen we'd better shut," he said.

"It seems a pity!" she replied. "Nobody will come, will they?"

"Not unless it's one time in a thousand. But you never know."

"And even then it's no matter," she said. "It's only a cup of tea. Where are the spoons?"

He reached over, and pulled open the table drawer. Connie sat at table in the sunshine of the doorway.

"Flossie!" he said to the dog, who was lying on a little mat at the stair-foot. "Go an' hark! *hark!*"

He lifted his finger, and his "hark!" was very vivid. The dog trotted out to reconnoitre.

"Are you sad today?" she asked him.

He turned his blue eyes quickly, and gazed direct on her.

"Sad! No! Bored! I had to go getting summonses for two poachers I caught—and—oh well, I don't like people—"

He spoke cold, good English, and there was anger in his voice.

"Do you hate being a gamekeeper?" she asked.

"Being a gamekeeper? No—so long as I'm left alone. But when I have to go messing around at the police-station and various other places, and waiting for a lot of fools to attend to me—oh well, I get mad—" And he smiled with a certain faint humour.

"Couldn't you be really independent?" she said.

"Me? I suppose I could, if you mean manage to exist on my pension. I could! But I've got to work, or I should die. That is, I've got to have something that keeps me occupied. And I'm not in a good enough temper to work for myself. It's got to be a sort of job for somebody else, or I should throw it up in a month, out of bad temper. So altogether, I'm very well off here—especially lately—"

He laughed at her again, with mocking humour.

"But why are you in a bad temper?" she said. "Do you mean you are *always* in a bad temper?"

"Pretty well," he said, laughing. "I don't quite digest my bile."

"But what bile?" she asked.

"Bile!" he said. "Don't you know what that is?"

She was silent, and disappointed. He was taking no notice of her.

"I'm going away for a while next month," she said.

"You are! Where to?"

"Venice."

"Venice! With Sir Clifford? For how long?"

"For a month or so," she replied. "Clifford won't go."

"He'll stay here?" he asked.

"Yes! He's ashamed to travel, as he is."

"Ay, poor devil!" he said with sympathy.

There was a pause.

"You won't forget me, when I'm gone, will you?" she asked.

Again he lifted his eyes and looked full at her.

"Forget!" he said. "You know nobody forgets. It's not a question of memory."

She wanted to say: "What then?" but she didn't. Instead she said, in a mute kind of voice:

"I told Clifford I might have a child."

Now he really looked at her, intense and searching.

"You did!" he said at last. "And what did he say?"

"Oh, he wouldn't mind. He'd be glad, really; so long as it *seemed* to be his." She dared not look up at him.

He was silent a long time. Then he gazed again on her face.

"No mention of *me*, of course?" he said.

"No! No mention of you," she said.

"No! He'd hardly swallow me as a substitute breeder.—Then where are you supposed to be getting the child?"

"I might have a love-affair in Venice," she said.

"You might," he replied slowly. "So that's why you're going?"

"Not to *have* the love-affair," she said, looking up at him pleading.

"Just the appearance of one," he said.

There was silence. He sat staring out of the window with a faint grin, half mockery, half bitterness, on his face. She hated his grin.

"You've not taken any precautions against having a child, then?" he asked her suddenly. "Because I haven't."

"No!" she said faintly. "I should hate that."

He looked at her—then again, with the peculiar subtle grin, out of the window. There was a tense silence.

At last he turned to her, and said satirically:

"That was why you wanted me, then?—to get a child?"

She hung her head.

"No! Not really!" she said.

"What then, *really*?" he asked rather bitingly.

She looked up at him reproachfully.

"I don't know," she said slowly.

He broke into a laugh.

"Then I'm damned if I do," he said.

There was a long pause of silence, a cold silence.

"Well," he said at last. "It's as your Ladyship likes. If you get the baby, Sir Clifford's welcome to it. I shan't have lost anything. On the contrary, I've had a very nice experience: very nice indeed!" And he stretched in a half-suppressed sort of yawn. "If you've made use of me," he said, "it's not the first time I've been made use of: and I don't suppose it's ever been as pleasant as this time: though of course, one can't feel tremendously dignified about it."—He stretched again, curiously, his muscles quivering and his jaw oddly set.

"But I didn't make use of you," she said, pleading.

"At your Ladyship's service," he replied.

"No!" she said. "I liked your body."

"Did you?" he replied, and he laughed. "Well then we're quits, because I liked yours."

He looked at her with queer, darkened eyes.

"Would you like to go upstairs now?" he asked her, in a strangled sort of voice.

"No, not now! Not here!" she said heavily. Though if he had used any power over her, she would have gone, for she had no strength against him.

He turned his face away again, and seemed to forget her.

"I want to touch you like you touch me," she said. "I've never really touched your body."

He looked at her, and grinned again.

"Now?" he said.

"No! No! Not here! At the hut! Would you mind?"

"How do I touch you?" he asked.

"When you feel me."

He looked at her, and met her heavy, anxious eyes.

"And do you like it, when I feel you?" he asked, laughing at her still.

"Yes! Do you?" she said.

"Oh me!" Then he changed his tone. "Yes!" he said. "You know without asking."

Which was true.

She rose, and picked up her hat.

"I must go," she said.

"Will you go?" he replied politely.

She wanted him to touch her, to say something to her. But he said nothing, only waited politely.

"Thank you for the tea," she said.

"I haven't thanked your Ladyship for doing me the honours of my tea-pot," he said.

She went down the path, and he stood in the doorway faintly grinning. Flossie came running, with her tail lifted. And Connie had to plod dumbly across into the wood, knowing he was standing there watching her with that incomprehensible grin on his face.

She walked home very much downcast and annoyed. She didn't at all like his having said he had been made use of: because, in a sense, it was true. But he oughtn't to have said it. Therefore, again she was divided between two feelings: resentment against him, and a desire to make it up with him.

She passed a very uneasy and irritated tea-time, and at once went up to her room. And when she was there, it was no good. She could neither sit nor stand. She would have to do something about it. She would have to go back to the hut. If he was not there, well and good.

She slipped out of the side door, and took her way direct and a little sullen. When she came to the clearing she was terribly uneasy. But there he was, again in his shirt-sleeves, stooping letting the hens out of the coops, among the chicks that were now growing a little gawky, but were much more trim than hen-chickens.

She went straight across to him.

"You see I've come!" she said.

"Ay, I see it!" he said, straightening his back and looking at her with a faint amusement.

"Do you let the hens out now?" she asked.

"Yes—they've sat themselves to skin an' bone," he said. "An' now they're not all that anxious to come out an' feed. There's no self in a sitting hen: she's all in the eggs or the chicks."

The poor mother-hens: such blind devotion! even to eggs not their own! Connie looked at them in compassion. A helpless silence fell between the man and the woman.

"Shall we go in th' ut?" he asked.

"Do you want me?" she asked, glancing at him in a sort of mistrust.

"Ay, if you want to come."

She was silent.

"Come then!" he said.

And she went with him to the hut. It was quite dark when he had shut the door, so he made a small light in the lantern, as before.

"Have you left your underthings off?" he asked her.

"Yes!"

"Ay, well—then I'll take my things off as well."

He spread the blankets, putting one at the side for a coverlet. She took off her hat and shook her hair. He sat down, undoing his shoes and gaiters, and taking off his cord breeches.

"Lie down then!" he said when he stood in his shirt. She obeyed in silence, and he lay beside her and pulled the blanket over them both.

"There!" he said.

And he lifted her dress right back, till he came even to her breasts. He kissed them softly, taking the nipples in his lips in tiny caresses.

"Eh, but tha 'rt nice, tha 'rt nice!" he said, suddenly rubbing his face with a snuggling movement against her warm belly.

And she put her arms round him, under his shirt. But she was afraid, afraid of his thin, smooth naked body, that seemed so powerful, afraid of the violent muscles. She shrank, afraid.

And when he said, with a sort of little sigh: "Ay, tha 'rt nice!" something in her quivered, and something in her spirit stiffened in resistance: stiffened from the terribly physical intimacy, and from the peculiar haste of his possession. And this time the sharp ecstasy of her own passion did not overcome her, she lay with her hands inert on his striving body, and do what she might, her spirit seemed to look on from the top of her head, and the butting of his haunches seemed ridiculous to her, and the sort of anxiety of his penis to come to its little evacuating crisis seemed farcical. Yes, this was love, this ridiculous bouncing of the buttocks, and the wilting of the poor, insignificant, moist little penis. This was the divine love! After all, the moderns were right when they felt contempt for the perform-ance: for it was a performance. It was quite true, as some poets said, that the God who created man must have had a sinister sense of humour, creating him a reasonable being, yet forcing him to take this ridiculous posture and driving him with blind craving for this humiliating performance. Even a Maupassant found it a humiliating anti-climax. Men despised the intercourse act, and yet did it.

Cold and derisive her queer female mind stood apart. And, though she lay perfectly still, her instinct was to heave her loins and throw the man out, escape his ugly grip and the butting over-riding of his absurd haunches. His body was a foolish, impudent, imperfect thing, a little disgusting in its unfinished clumsiness. For surely a complete evolution would eliminate this performance, this "function."

And yet, when he had finished, soon over, and lay very, very still, receding into a silence and a strange motionless distance far, farther than the horizon of her awareness, her heart began to weep. She could feel him ebbing away, ebbing away, leaving her there like a stone on a shore. He was withdrawing. His spirit was leaving her. He knew.

And in real grief, tormented by her own double consciousness and reaction, she began to weep. He took no notice: or did not even know. The storm of weeping swelled and shook her: and shook him.

"Ay!" he said. "It was no good that time. You wasn't there."

So he knew! Her sobs became violent.

"But what's amiss!" he said. "It's once in a while that way."

"I—I can't love you!" she sobbed, suddenly feeling her heart breaking.

"Canna ter! Well dunna thee fret! There's no law says as tha's got to. Ta'e 't for what it is."

He still lay with his hand on her breast. But she had drawn both her hands from him.

His words were small comfort. She sobbed aloud.

"Nay nay!" he said. "Ta'e th' thick wi' th' thin. This wor a bit o' thin, for once."

She wept bitterly, sobbing:

"But I want to love you—and I *can't*. It only seems horrid."

He laughed a little, half bitter, half amused.

"It isna horrid," he said, "even if tha thinks it is. An' tha canna ma'e it horrid. Dunna fret thysèn about luvin' me! Tha 'lt niver force thysèn to 't. There's sure to be a bad nut in a basketful. Tha mun ta'e th' rough wi' t' smooth."

He took his hand away from her breast and lay still, not touching her. And now she was untouched. She took an almost perverse satisfaction in it. She hated the dialect: the *thee* and the *tha* and the *thysèn*. He could get up if he liked: and stand there above her buttoning down those absurd corduroy breeches, straight in front of her. After all, Michaelis had had the decency to turn away. This man was so assured in himself, he didn't know what a clown other people found him: a half-bred fellow.

Yet, as he was drawing away, to rise silently and leave her, she clung to him in terror.

"Don't! Don't go! Don't leave me! Don't be cross with me! Hold me! Hold me fast!" she whispered in blind frenzy, not even knowing what she said, and clinging to him with uncanny force. It was from herself she wanted to be saved, from her own inward anger and resistance. Yet how powerful was that inward resistance that possessed her!

He took her in his arms again and drew her to him, and suddenly she became small in his arms, small and nestling. It was gone, the resistance was gone, and she began to melt in a marvellous peace. And as she melted small and wonderful in his arms, she became infinitely desirable to him, all his blood-vessels seemed to scald with intense yet tender desire, for her, for her softness, for the penetrating beauty of her in his arms, passing into his blood. And softly, with that marvellous swoon-like caress of his hand in pure soft desire, softly he stroked the silky slope of her loins, down, down between her soft, warm buttocks, coming nearer and nearer to the very quick of her. And she felt him like a flame of desire, yet tender, and she felt herself melting in the flame. She let herself go. She felt his penis risen against her with silent amazing force and assertion, and she let herself go to him. She yielded with a quiver that was like death, she went all open to him. And oh, if he were not tender to her now, how cruel, for she was all open to him and helpless!

She quivered again at the potent inexorable entry inside her, so strange and terrible. It might come with the thrust of a sword in her softly-opened body, and that would be death. She clung in a sudden anguish of terror. But it came with a strange slow thrust of peace, the dark thrust of peace and a ponderous, primordial tenderness, such as made the world in the beginning. And her terror subsided in her breast, her breast dared to be gone in peace, she held nothing. She dared to let go everything, all herself, and be gone in the flood.

And it seemed she was like the sea, nothing but dark waves rising and heaving, heaving with a great swell, so that slowly her whole darkness was in motion, and she was ocean rolling its dark, dumb mass. Oh, and far down inside her the deeps parted and rolled asunder, in long, far-travelling billows, and ever, at the quick of her, the depths parted and rolled asunder, from the centre of soft plunging, as the plunger went deeper and deeper, touching lower, and she was deeper and deeper and deeper disclosed, and heavier the billows of her rolled away to some shore, uncovering her, and closer and closer plunged the palpable unknown, and further and further rolled the waves of herself away from herself, leaving her, till suddenly, in a soft, shuddering convulsion, the quick of all her plasm was touched, she knew herself touched, the consummation was upon her, and she was gone. She was gone, she was not, and she was born: a woman.

Ah, too lovely, too lovely! In the ebbing she realised all the loveliness. Now all her body clung with tender love to the unknown man, and blindly to the wilting penis, as it so tenderly, frailly, unknowingly withdrew, after the fierce thrust of its potency. As it drew out and left her body, the secret, sensitive thing, she gave an unconscious cry of pure loss, and she tried to put it back. It had been so perfect! And she loved it so!

And only now she became aware of the small, bud-like reticence and tenderness of the penis, and a little cry of wonder and poignancy escaped her again, her woman's heart crying out over the tender frailty of that which had been the power.

"It was so lovely!" she moaned. "It was so lovely!" But he said nothing, only softly kissed her, lying still above her. And she moaned with a sort of bliss, as a sacrifice, and a new-born thing.

And now in her heart the queer wonder of him was awakened. A man! the strange potency of manhood upon her! Her hands strayed over him, still a little afraid. Afraid of that strange, hostile, slightly repulsive thing that he had been to her, a man. And now she touched him, and it was the sons of god with the daughters of men. How beautiful he felt, how pure in tissue! How lovely, how lovely, strong, and yet pure and delicate, such stillness of the sensitive body! Such utter stillness of potency and delicate flesh! How beautiful, how beautiful. Her hands came timorously down his back, to the soft, smallish globes of the buttocks. Beauty! what beauty! a sudden little flame of new awareness went through her. How was it possible, this beauty here, where she had previously only been repelled? The unspeakable beauty to the touch, of the warm, living buttocks! The life within life, the sheer warm, potent loveliness. And the strange weight of the balls between his legs! What a mystery! What a strange heavy weight of mystery, that could lie soft and heavy in one's hand! The roots, root of all that is lovely, the primeval root of all full beauty.

She clung to him with a hiss of wonder that was also awe, terror. He held her close, but he said nothing. He would never say anything. She crept nearer to him, nearer, only to be near to the sensual wonder of him. And out of his utter, incomprehensible stillness, she felt again the slow, momentous, surging rise of the phallus again, the other power. And her heart melted out with a kind of awe.

And this time his being within her was all soft and iridescent, purely soft and iridescent, such as no consciousness could seize. Her whole self quivered unconscious and alive, like plasm. She could not know what it was. She could not remember what it had been. Only that it had been more lovely than anything ever could be. Only that. And afterwards she was utterly still, utterly unknowing, she was not aware for how long. And he was still with her, in an unfathomable silence along with her. And of this, they would never speak.

When awareness of the outside began to come back, she clung to his breast, murmuring: "My love! my love!" And he held her silently. And she curled on his breast, perfect.

But his silence was fathomless. His hands held her like flowers, so still and strange. "Where are you?" she whispered to him. "Where are you? Speak to me! Say something to me!"

He kissed her softly, murmuring: "Ay, my lass!"

But she did not know what he meant, she did not know where he was. In his silence he seemed lost to her.

"You love me, don't you?" she murmured.

"Ay, tha knows!" he said.

"But tell me!" she pleaded.

"Ay! Ay! 'asn't ter felt it?" he said dimly, but softly and surely. And she clung close to him, closer. He was so much more peaceful in love than she was, and she wanted him to reassure her.

"You do love me!" she whispered, assertive. And his hands stroked her softly, as if she were a flower, without the quiver of desire, but with delicate nearness. And still there haunted her a restless necessity to get a grip on love.

"Say you'll always love me!" she pleaded.

"Ay!" he said, abstractedly. And she felt her questions driving him away from her.

"Mustn't we get up?" he said at last.

"No!" she said.

But she could feel his consciousness straying, listening to the noises outside.

"It'll be nearly dark!" he said. And she heard the pressure of circumstance in his voice. She kissed him, with a woman's grief at yielding up her hour.

He rose, and turned up the lantern, then began to pull on his clothes, quickly disappearing inside them. Then he stood there, above her, fastening his breeches and looking down at her with dark, wide eyes, his face a little flushed and his hair ruffled, curiously warm and still and beautiful in the dim light of the lantern, so beautiful, she would never tell him how beautiful. It made her want to cling fast to him, to hold him, for there was a warm, half-sleepy remoteness in his beauty that made her want to cry out and clutch him, to have him. She would never have him. So she lay on the blanket with curved, soft naked haunches, and he had no idea what she was thinking, but to him too she was beautiful, the soft, marvellous thing he could go into, beyond everything.

"I love thee that I can go into thee," he said.

"Do you like me?" she said, her heart beating.

"It heals it all up, that I can go into thee. I love thee that tha opened to me. I love thee that I came into thee like that."

He bent down and kissed her soft flank, rubbed his cheek against it, then covered it up.

"And will you never leave me?" she said.

"Dunna ask them things," he said.

"But you do believe I love you?" she said.

"Tha loved me just now, wider than iver tha thout tha would. But who knows what'll 'appen, once tha starts thinkin' about it!"

"No, don't say those things!—And you don't really think that I wanted to make use of you, do you?"

"How?"

"To have a child—?"

"Now anybody can 'ave any childt i' th' world," he said, and he sat down fastening on his leggings.

"Ah no!" she cried. "You don't mean it."

"Eh well!" he said, looking at her under his brows. "This wor t' best."

She lay still. He softly opened the door. The sky was dark blue, with crystalline, turquoise rim. He went out, to shut up the hens, speaking softly to his dog. And she lay and wondered at the wonder of life, and of being.

When he came back, she was still lying there, glowing like a gipsy. He sat on the stool by her.

"Tha mun come one naight ter th' cottage, afore tha goos—sholl ter?" he asked, lifting his eyebrows as he looked at her, his hands dangling between his knees.

"Sholl ter?" she echoed, teasing.

He smiled.

"Ay, sholl ter?" he repeated.

"Ay!" she said, imitating the dialect sound.

"Yi!" he said.

"Yi!" she repeated.

"An' slaip wi' me," he said. "It needs that. When sholt come?"

"When sholl I?" she said.

"Nay," he said, "tha canna do 't.—When sholt come then?"

"'Appen Sunday," she said.

"'Appen a' Sunday! Ay!"

"Ay!" she said.

He laughed at her quickly.

"Nay, tha canna," he protested.

"Why canna I?" she said.

He laughed. Her attempts at the dialect were so ludicrous, somehow.

"Coom then, tha mun goo!" he said.

"Mun I?" she said.

"Maun Ah!" he corrected.

"Why should I say *maun* when you said *mun*," she protested. "You're not playing fair."

"Arena Ah!" he said, leaning forward and softly stroking her face. "Tha 'rt good cunt, though, aren't ter? Best bit o' cunt left on earth. When ter likes! When tha 'rt willin'!"

"What is cunt?" she said.

"An' doesn't ter know? Cunt! It's thee down theer; an' what I get when I'm i'side thee—an' what tha gets when I'm i'side thee—it's a' as it is—all on't!"

"All on't!" she teased. "Cunt! It's like fuck then."

"Nay nay! Fuck's only what you do. Animals fuck. But cunt's a lot more than that. It's thee, dost see: an' tha 'rt a lot besides an animal, aren't ter?—even ter fuck! Cunt! Eh, that's the beauty o' thee, lass!"

She got up and kissed him between the eyes, that looked at her so dark and soft and unspeakably warm, so unbearably beautiful.

"Is it!" she said. "And do you care for me?"

He kissed her without answering.

"Tha mun goo—let me dust thee," he said.

His hand passed over the curves of her body, firmly, without desire, but with soft, intimate knowledge.

As she ran home in the twilight, the world seemed a dream; the trees in the park seemed bulging and surging at anchor on a tide, and the heave of the slope to the house was alive.

CHAPTER XIII.

On Sunday Clifford wanted to go into the wood. It was a lovely morning, the pear-blossom and plum had suddenly appeared in the world, in a wonder of white here and there.

It was cruel for Clifford, while the world bloomed, to have to be helped from chair to bath-chair. But he had forgotten, and even seemed to have a certain conceit of himself in his lameness. Connie still suffered, having to lift his inert legs into place. Mrs Bolton did it now, or Field.

She waited for him at the top of the drive, at the edge of the screen of beeches. His chair came puffing along with a sort of valetudinarian slow importance. As he joined his wife, he said:

"Sir Clifford on his foaming steed!"

"Snorting, at least!" she laughed.

He stopped and looked round at the façade of the long, low old brown house.

"Wragby doesn't wink an eyelid!" he said. "But then, why should it! I ride upon the achievement of the mind of man, and that beats a horse."

"I suppose it does. And the souls in Plato riding up to heaven in a two-horse chariot would go in a Ford car now," she said.

"Or a Rolls-Royce: Plato was an aristocrat!"

"Quite! No more black horse to thrash and maltreat. Plato never thought we'd go one better than his black steed and his white steed, and have no steeds at all, only an engine!"

"Only an engine—and gas!" said Clifford. "I hope I can have some repairs done to the old place next year. I think I shall have about a thousand to spare for that: but work costs so much!"

"Oh good!" said Connie. "If only there aren't more strikes!"

"What would be the use of their striking again! Merely ruin the industry, what's left of it: and surely the owls are beginning to see it!"

"Perhaps they don't mind ruining the industry," said Connie.

"Ah, don't talk like a woman! The industry fills their bellies, even if it can't keep their pockets quite so flush," he said, using turns of speech that oddly had a twang of Mrs Bolton.

"But didn't you say the other day you were a conservative-anarchist?" she asked innocently.

"And did you understand what I meant?" he retorted. "All I meant is, people can be what they like and feel what they like and do what they like, strictly privately, so long as they keep the *form* of life intact, and the apparatus."

Connie walked on in silence a few paces. Then she said, obstinately:

"It sounds like saying an egg may go as addled as it likes, so long as it keeps its shell whole. But addled eggs do break of themselves."

"I don't think people are eggs," he said. "Not even angels' eggs, my dear little evangelist."

He was in rather high feather this bright morning. The larks were trilling away over the park, the distant pit in the hollow was fuming silent steam. It was almost like old days, before the war. Connie didn't really want to argue. But then she didn't really want to go to the wood with Clifford either. So she walked beside his chair in a certain obstinacy of spirit.

"No," he said. "There will be no more strikes, if the thing is properly managed."

"Why not?"

"Because strikes will be made as good as impossible."

"But will the men let you?" she asked.

"We shan't ask them. We shall do it while they aren't looking: for their own good, to save the industry."

"For your own good too," she said.

"Naturally! For the good of everybody. But for their good even more than mine. I can live without the pits. They can't. They'll starve if there are no pits. I've got other provision."

They looked up the shallow valley at the mine, and beyond it, at the black-lidded houses of Tevershall crawling like some serpent up the hill. From the old brown church the bells were ringing: Sunday, Sunday, Sunday!

"But will the men let you dictate terms?" she said.

"My dear, they'll have to: if one does it gently."

"But mightn't there be a mutual understanding?"

"Absolutely: when they realise that the industry comes before the individual."

"But must you own the industry?" she said.

"I don't. But to the extent I do own it, yes, most decidedly. The ownership of property has now become a religious question: as it has been since Jesus and St. Francis. The point is *not*, take all thou hast and give to the poor, but use all thou hast to encourage the industry and give work to the poor. It's the only way to feed all the mouths and clothe all the bodies. Giving away all we have to the poor spells starvation for the poor just as much as for us. And universal starvation is no high aim. Even general poverty is no lovely thing. Poverty is ugly."

"But the disparity?"

"That is fate. Why is the star Jupiter bigger than the star Neptune? You can't start altering the make-up of things!"

"But when this envy and jealousy and discontent has once started—" she began.

"Do your best to stop it. Somebody's *got* to be boss of the show."

"But who is boss of the show?" she asked.

"The men who own and run the industries!"

There was a long silence.

"It seems to me they're a bad boss," she said.

"Then you suggest what they should do."

"They don't take their boss-ship seriously enough," she said.

"They take it far more seriously than you take your ladyship," he said.

"That's thrust upon me. I don't really want it," she blurted out. He stopped the chair and looked at her.

"Who's shirking their responsibility now!" he said. "Who is trying to get away *now* from the responsibility of their own boss-ship, as you call it?"

"But I don't want any boss-ship," she protested.

"Ah! But that is funk. You've got it: fated to it. And you should live up to it. Who has given the colliers all they have that's worth having: all their political liberty, and their education, such as it is, their sanitation, their health-conditions, their books, their music, everything. Who has given it them? Have colliers given it to colliers? No! All the Wragbys and Shipleys in England have given their part, and must go on giving. There's your responsibility."

Connie listened, and flushed very red.

"I'd like to give something," she said. "But I'm not allowed. Everything is to be sold and paid for now; and all the things you mention now, Wragby and Shipley *sell* them to the people, at a good profit. Everything is sold. You don't give one heart-beat of real sympathy. And besides, who has taken away from the people their natural life and manhood, and given them this industrial horror? Who has done that?"

"And what must I do?" he asked, green. "Ask them to come and pillage me?"

"Why is Tevershall so ugly, so hideous? Why are their lives so hopeless?"

"They built their own Tevershall—that's part of their display of freedom. They built themselves their pretty Tevershall, and they live their own pretty lives. I can't live their lives for them. Every beetle must live its own life."

"But you make them work for you. They live the life of your coal-mine."

"Not at all. Every beetle finds its own food. Not one man is forced to work for me."

"Their lives are industrialised and hopeless, and so are ours," she cried.

"I don't think they are. That's just a romantic figure of speech, a relic of the swooning and die-away romanticism. You don't look at all a hopeless figure standing there, Connie my dear."

Which was true. For her dark blue eyes were flashing, her colour was hot in her cheek, she looked full of a rebellious passion far from the dejection of hopelessness. She noticed, in the tussocky places of the grass, cottony young cowslips standing up still bleared in their down. And she wondered with rage, why it was she felt Clifford was so *wrong*, yet she couldn't say it to him, she couldn't say exactly *where* he was wrong.

"No wonder the men hate you," she said.

"They don't!" he replied. "And don't fall into error: in your sense of the word, they are *not* men. They are animals you don't understand, and never could. Don't thrust your illusions on other people. The masses were always the same, and will always be the same. Nero's slaves were extremely little different from our colliers or the Ford motor-car workmen. I mean Nero's mine slaves and his field slaves. It is the masses: they are the unchangeable. An individual may emerge from the masses. But the emergence doesn't alter the mass. The masses are unalterable. It is one of the most momentous facts of social science. Panem et circenses! Only today education is one of the bad substitutes for a circus. What is wrong today, is that we've made a profound hash of the circuses part of the programme, and poisoned our masses with a little education."

When Clifford became really roused in his feelings about the common people, Connie was frightened. There was something devastatingly true in what he said. But it was a truth that killed. Seeing her pale and silent, Clifford started the chair again, and no more was said till he halted again at the wood gate, while she opened.

"And what we need to take up now," he said, "is whips, not swords. The masses have been ruled since time began, and till time ends, ruled they will have to be. It is sheer hypocrisy and farce to say they can rule themselves."

"But can you rule them?" she asked.

"I? Oh yes! Neither my mind nor my will is crippled, and I don't rule with my legs. I can do my share of ruling: absolutely, my share. And give me a son, and he will be able to rule his portion after me."

"But he wouldn't be your own son, of your own ruling class—or perhaps not—" she stammered.

"I don't care who his father may be, so long as he is a healthy man not below normal intelligence. Give me the child of any healthy, normally intelligent man, and I will make a perfectly competent Chatterley of him. It is not who begets us, that matters, but where fate places us. Place any child among the ruling classes, and he will grow up, to his own extent, a ruler. Put kings' and dukes' children among the masses, and they'll be little plebeians, mass products. It is the overwhelming pressure of environment."

"Then the common people aren't a race—and the aristocrats aren't blood—" she said.

"No my child! All that is romantic illusion. Aristocracy is a function, a part of fate. And the masses are a functioning of another part of fate. The individual hardly matters. It is a question of which function you are brought up to and adapted to. It is not the individuals that make an aristocracy: it is the functioning of the aristocratic whole. And it is the functioning of the whole mass that makes the common man what he is."

"Then there is no common humanity between us all!"

"Just as you like. We all need to fill our bellies. But when it comes to expressive or executive functioning, I believe there is a gulf and an absolute one, between the ruling and the serving classes. The two functions are opposed. And the function determines the individual."

Connie looked at him with dazed eyes.

"Won't you come on?" she said.

And he started his chair. He had said his say. Now he lapsed into his peculiar and rather vacant apathy, that Connie found so trying. In the wood, anyhow, she was determined not to argue.

In front of them ran the open cleft of the riding, between the hazel walls and the gay grey trees. The chair puffed slowly on, slowly surging into the forget-me-nots that rose up in the drive like milk-froth, beyond the hazel shadows. Clifford steered the middle course, where feet passing had kept a channel through the flowers. But Connie, walking behind, had watched the wheels jolt over the wood-ruff and the bugle, and squash the little yellow cups of the creeping-jenny. Now they made a wake through the forget-me-nots.

All the flowers were there, the first bluebells in blue pools, like standing water.

"You are quite right about its being beautiful," said Clifford. "It is so amazingly. What is *quite* so lovely as an English spring!"

Connie thought it sounded as if even the spring bloomed by act of Parliament. An English spring! Why not an Irish one, or Jewish!

The chair moved slowly ahead, past tufts of sturdy bluebells that stood up like wheat, and over grey burdock leaves. When they came to the open place where the trees had been felled, the light flooded in rather stark. And the bluebells made sheets of bright blue colour, here and there, sheering off into lilac and purple. And between, the bracken was lifting its brown curled heads, like legions of young snakes with a new secret to whisper to Eve.

Clifford kept the chair going till he came to the brow of the hill. Connie followed slowly behind. The oak-buds were opening soft and brown. Everything came tenderly out of the old hardness. Even the snaggy craggy oak-trees put out the softest young leaves, spreading thin, brown little wings like young bats-wings in the light. Why had men never any newness in them, any freshness to come forth with? Stale men!

Clifford stopped the chair at the top of the rise and looked down. The bluebells washed blue like flood-water over the broad riding, and lit up the downhill with a warm blueness.

"It's a very fine colour in itself," said Clifford, "but useless for making a painting."

"Quite!" said Connie, completely uninterested.

"Shall I venture as far as the spring?" said Clifford.

"Will the chair get up again?" she said.

"We'll try. Nothing venture, nothing win!"

And the chair began to advance slowly, joltingly down the beautiful broad riding washed over with blue encroaching hyacinths. Oh last of all ships, through the hyacinthine shallows! oh pinnace on the last wild waters, sailing in the last voyage of our civilisation! Whither, oh weird wheeled ship, your slow course steering—!! Quiet and complacent, Clifford sat at the wheel of adventure: in his old black hat and tweed jacket, motionless and cautious. Oh captain, my Captain, our splendid trip is done! Not yet though! Downhill, in the wake, came Constance in her grey dress, watching the chair jolt downwards.

They passed the narrow track to the hut. Thank heaven it was not wide enough for the chair: hardly wide enough for one person. The chair reached the bottom of the slope, and swerved round, to disappear. And Connie heard a low whistle behind her. She glanced sharply round: the keeper was striding downhill towards her, his dog keeping behind him.

"Is Sir Clifford going to the cottage?" he asked, looking into her eyes.

"No, only to the well."

"Ah! Good! Then I can keep out of sight. But I shall see you tonight. I shall wait for you at the park gate—about ten."

He looked again direct into her eyes.

"Yes," she faltered.

They heard the Papp! Papp! of Clifford's horn, tooting for Connie. She "coo-eeed!" in reply. The keeper's face flickered with a little grimace, and with his hand he softly brushed her breast upwards, from underneath. She looked at him, frightened, and started running down the hill, calling Coo-ee! again to Clifford. The man above watched her—then turned, grinning faintly, back into his path.

She found Clifford slowly mounting to the spring, which was half-way up the slope of the dark larch-wood. He was there by the time she caught him up.

"She did that all right," he said, referring to the chair.

Connie looked at the great grey leaves of burdock that grew out ghostly from the edge of the larch-wood. The people call it Robin Hood's Rhubarb. How silent and gloomy it seemed by the well! Yet the water bubbled so bright, wonderful! and there were bits of eyebright, and strong blue bugle. And there, under the bank, the yellow earth was moving. A mole! It emerged, rowing its pink hands, and waving its blind gimlet of a face, with the tiny pink nose-tip uplifted.

"It seems to see with the end of its nose," said Connie.

"Better than with its eyes!" he said. "Will you drink?"

"Will you?"

She took an enamel mug from a twig on a tree, and stooped to fill it for him. He drank in sips. Then she stooped again, and drank a little herself.

"So icy!" she said, gasping.

"Good, isn't it! Did you wish?"

"Did you?"

"Yes, I wished. But I won't tell."

She was aware of the rapping of a wood-pecker—then of the wind, soft and eerie through the larches. She looked up. White clouds were crossing the blue.

"Clouds!" she said.

"White lambs only," he replied.

A shadow crossed the little clearing. The mole had swum out on to the soft yellow earth.

"Unpleasant little beast—we ought to kill him," said Clifford.

"Look! He's like a parson in a pulpit," said she.

She gathered some sprigs of woodruff and brought them to him.

"New-mown-hay!" he said. "Doesn't it smell like the romantic ladies of the last century, who had their heads screwed on the right way after all?"

She was looking at the white clouds.

"I wonder if it will rain," she said.

"Rain! Why? Do you want it to?"

They started on the return journey, Clifford jolting cautiously downhill. They came to the dark bottom of the hollow, turned to the right, and after a hundred yards, swerved up the foot of the long slope, where bluebells stood in the light.

"Now old girl!" said Clifford, putting the chair to it.

It was a steep and jolty climb. The chair pugged slowly, in a struggling, unwilling fashion. Still, she nosed her way up unevenly, till she came to where the hyacinths were all around her, then she balked, struggled, jerked a little way out of the flowers, then stopped.

"We'd better sound the horn and see if the keeper will come," said

Connie. "He could push her a bit. For that matter, I will push. It helps."

"We'll let her breathe," said Clifford. "Do you mind putting a scotch under the wheel?"

Connie found a stone, and they waited. After a while Clifford started his motor again, then set the chair in motion. It struggled and faltered like a sick thing, with curious noises.

"Let me push!" said Connie, coming up behind.

"No! Don't push!" he said angrily. "What's the good of the damned thing, if it has to be pushed! Put the stone under!"

There was another pause, then another start; but more ineffectual than before.

"You *must* let me push," she said. "Or sound the horn for the keeper."

"Wait!"

She waited; and he had another try, doing more harm than good.

"Sound the horn then, if you won't let me push," she said.

"Hell! Be quiet a moment!"

She was quiet a moment: he made shattering efforts with the little motor.

"You'll only break the thing down altogether, Clifford," she remonstrated; "besides wasting your nervous energy."

"If I could only get out and look at the damned thing!" he said, exasperated. And he sounded the horn stridently. "Perhaps Mellors can see what's wrong."

They waited, among the mashed flowers, under a sky softly curdling with cloud. In the silence a wood-pigeon began to coo, roo-hoohoo! roo-hoohoo! Clifford shut her up with a blast on the horn.

The keeper appeared directly, striding enquiringly round the corner. He saluted.

"Do you know anything about motors?" asked Clifford sharply.

"I'm afraid I don't. Has she gone wrong?"

"Apparently!" snapped Clifford.

The man crouched solicitously by the wheel, and peered at the little engine.

"I'm afraid I know nothing at all about these mechanical things, Sir Clifford," he said calmly. "If she has enough petrol and oil—"

"Just look carefully and see if you can see anything broken," snapped Clifford.

The man laid his gun against a tree, took off his coat and threw it beside it. The brown dog sat guard. Then he sat down on his heels and peered under the chair, poking with his finger at the greasy little engine, and resenting the grease-marks on his clean Sunday shirt.

"Doesn't seem anything broken," he said. And he stood up, pushing back his hat from his forehead, rubbing his brow and apparently studying.

"Have you looked at the rods underneath?" asked Clifford. "See if they are all right!"

The man lay flat on his stomach on the floor, his neck pressed back, wriggling under the engine and poking with his finger. Connie thought what a pathetic sort of thing a man was, feeble and small-looking, when he was lying on his belly on the big earth.

"Seems all right as far as I can see," came his muffled voice.

"I don't suppose you can do anything," said Clifford.

"Seems as if I can't!"—And he scrambled up and sat on his heels again, collier fashion. "There's certainly nothing obviously broken."

"Look out! I'll start her again."

Clifford started his engine, then put her in gear. She would not move.

"Run her a bit hard, like," suggested the keeper.

Clifford resented the interference: but he made his engine buzz like a blue-bottle. Then she coughed and snarled, and seemed to go better.

"Sounds as if she'd come clear," said Mellors.

But Clifford had already jerked her into gear. She gave a sick lurch, and ebbed weakly forwards.

"If I give her a push, she'll do it," said the keeper, going behind.

"Keep off!" snapped Clifford. "She'll do it by herself."

"But Clifford!" put in Connie from the bank. "You know it's too much for her. Why are you so obstinate!"

Clifford was pale with anger. He jabbed at his levers. The chair gave a sort of scurry, reeled on a few more yards, and came to her end amid a particularly promising patch of bluebells.

"She's done!" said the keeper. "Not power enough."

"She's been up here before," said Clifford coldly.

"She won't do it this time," said the keeper.

Clifford did not reply. He began doing things with his engine, running her fast and slow, as if to get some sort of tune out of her.

The wood re-echoed with weird noises. Then he put her in gear with a jerk, having jerked off his brake.

"You'll rip her inside out," murmured the keeper.

The chair charged in a sick lurch sideways at the ditch.

"Clifford!" cried Connie, rushing forward.

But the keeper had got the chair by the rail. Clifford, however, putting on all his pressure, managed to steer in to the riding, and with a strange noise the chair was fighting the hill. Mellors pushed steadily behind, and up she went, as if to retrieve herself.

"You see she's doing it!" said Clifford, victorious, glancing over his shoulder. Then he saw the keeper's face.

"Are you pushing her?"

"She won't do it without."

"Leave her alone. I asked you not."

"She won't do it."

"*Let her try*!" snarled Clifford, with all his emphasis.

The keeper stood back: then turned to fetch his coat and gun. The chair seemed to strangle immediately. She stood inert. Clifford, seated a prisoner, was white with vexation. He jerked at the levers with his hand—his feet were no good. He got queer noises out of her. In savage impatience he moved little handles and got more noises out of her. But she would not budge. No, she would not budge. He stopped the engine and sat rigid with anger.

Constance sat on the bank and looked at the wrecked and trampled bluebells. "Nothing quite so lovely as an English spring." "I can do my share of ruling." "What we need to take up now is whips, not swords." "The ruling classes!"

The keeper strode up with his coat and gun, Flossie cautiously at his heels. Clifford asked the man to do something or other to the engine. Connie, who understood nothing at all of the technicalities of motors, and who had had experience of break-downs, sat patiently on the bank as if she were a cypher. The keeper lay on his stomach again. The ruling classes and the serving classes!

He got to his feet, and said patiently:

"Try her again, then."

He spoke in a quiet voice, almost as if to a child.

Clifford tried her, and Mellors stepped quickly behind and began to push. She was going, the engine doing about half the work, the man the rest.

Clifford glanced round, yellow with anger.

"Will you get off there!"

The keeper dropped his hold at once, and Clifford added: "How shall I know what she's doing—!"

The man put his gun down and began to pull on his coat: he'd done. The chair began slowly to run backwards.

"Clifford, your brake!" cried Connie.

She, Mellors, and Clifford moved at once, Connie and the keeper jostling lightly. The chair stood. There was a moment of dead silence.

"It's obvious I'm at everybody's mercy!" said Clifford. He was yellow with anger. No-one answered. Mellors was slinging his gun over his shoulder, his face queer and expressionless, save for an abstracted look of patience. The dog Flossie, standing on guard almost between her master's legs, moved uneasily, eyeing the chair with great suspicion and dislike, and very much perplexed between the three human beings. The *tableau vivant* remained set among the squashed bluebells, nobody proffering a word.

"I expect she'll have to be pushed," said Clifford at last, with an affectation of *sang froid*.

No answer. Mellors' abstracted face looked as if he had heard nothing. Connie glanced anxiously at him. Clifford too glanced round.

"Do you mind pushing her home, Mellors!" he said in a cool, superior tone. "I hope I have said nothing to offend you," he added, in a tone of dislike.

"Nothing at all, Sir Clifford! Do you want me to push that chair?"

"If you please."

The man stepped up to it: but this time he was without effect. The brake was jammed. They poked and pulled, and the keeper took off his gun and his coat once more. And now Clifford said never a word. At last the keeper heaved the back of the chair off the ground, and with an instantaneous push of his foot, tried to loosen the wheels. He failed, the chair sank. Clifford was clutching the sides. The man gasped with the weight.

"Don't do it!" cried Connie to him.

"If you'll pull the wheel that way—so!"—he said to her, showing her how.

"No! You mustn't lift it! You'll strain yourself," she said, flushed now with anger.

But he looked into her eyes and nodded. And she had to go and take hold of the wheel, ready. He heaved and she tugged, and the chair reeled.

"For God's sake!" cried Clifford in terror.

But it was all right, and the brake was off. The keeper put a stone under the wheel, and went to sit on the bank, his heart beating and his face white with the effort, semi-conscious. Connie looked at him, and almost cried with anger. There was a pause and a dead silence. She saw his hands trembling on his thighs.

"Have you hurt yourself?" she asked, going to him.

"No-no!" he turned away almost angrily.

There was dead silence. The back of Clifford's fair head did not move. Even the dog stood motionless. The sky had clouded over.

At last he sighed, and blew his nose on his red handkerchief.

"That pneumonia took a lot out of me," he said.

No-one answered. Connie calculated the amount of strength it must have taken to heave up that chair and the bulky Clifford: too much, far too much! The man must have extraordinary strength, really. If it hadn't killed him.

He rose, and again picked up his coat, slinging it through the handle of the chair.

"Are you ready then, Sir Clifford?"

"When you are!"

He stooped and took out the scotch, then put his weight against the chair. He was paler than Connie had ever seen him: and more absent. Clifford was a heavy man: and the hill was steep. Connie stepped to the keeper's side.

"I'm going to push too!" she said.

And she began to shove with a woman's turbulent energy of anger. The chair went faster. Clifford looked round.

"Is that necessary?" he said.

"Very! Do you want to kill the man! If you'd let the motor work while it would—"

But she did not finish. She was already panting. She slackened off a little, for it was surprisingly hard work.

"Ay, slower!" said the man at her side, with a faint smile of the eyes.

"Are you sure you've not hurt yourself?" she said fiercely.

He shook his head. She looked at his smallish short, alive hand, browned by the weather. It was the hand that caressed her. She had never even looked at it before. It seemed so still, like him, with a curious inward stillness that made her want to clutch it, as if she could not reach it. All her soul suddenly swept towards him: he was so silent, and out of reach! And he felt his limbs revive. Shoving with his left hand, he laid his right on her round white wrist, softly enfolding her wrist, with caress. And the flamy sort of strength went down his back and his loins, reviving him. And she, panting, bent suddenly and kissed his hand. Meanwhile the back of Clifford's head was held sleek and motionless, just in front of them.

At the top of the hill they rested, and Connie was glad to let go. She had had fugitive dreams of a friendship between these two men: one her husband, the other the father of her child. Now she saw the screaming absurdity of her dreams. The two males were as hostile as fire and water. They mutually exterminated one another. And she realised for the first time, what a queer subtle thing hate is. For the first time, she had consciously and definitely hated Clifford, with vivid hate: as if he ought to be obliterated from the face of the earth. And it was strange, how free and full of life it made her feel, to hate him and to admit it fully to herself.—"Now I've hated him, I shall never be able to go on living with him," came the thought into her mind.

On the level, the keeper could push the chair alone. Clifford made a little conversation with her, to show his complete composure: about Aunt Eva, who was at Dieppe, and about Sir Malcolm, who had written to ask would Connie drive with him in his small car, to Venice, or would she and Hilda go by train.

"I'd much rather go by train," said Connie. "I don't like long motor drives, especially when there's dust. But I shall see what Hilda wants."

"She will want to drive her own car, and take you with her," he said.

"Probably!—I must help up here. You've no idea how heavy this chair is."

She went to the back of the chair, and plodded side by side with the keeper, shoving up the pink path. She did not care who saw.

"Why not let me wait, and fetch Field. He is strong enough for the job," said Clifford.

"It's so near," she panted.

But both she and Mellors wiped the sweat from their faces when they came to the top. It was curious, but this bit of work together had brought them much closer than they had been before.

"Thanks so much, Mellors," said Clifford, when they were at the house door. "I must get a different sort of motor, that's all.—Won't you go to the kitchen and have a meal?—it must be about time."

"Thank you, Sir Clifford. I was going to my mother for dinner today—Sunday."

"As you like."

Mellors slung into his coat, looked at Connie, saluted, and was gone. Connie, furious, went upstairs.

At lunch she could not contain her feeling.

"Why are you so abominably inconsiderate, Clifford?" she said to him.

"Of whom?"

"Of the keeper! If that is what you call the ruling classes, I'm sorry for you."

"Why?"

"A man who's been ill, and isn't strong! My word, if I were the serving classes, I'd let you wait for service. I'd let you whistle."

"I quite believe it."

"If *he'd* been sitting in a chair with paralysed legs, and behaved as you behaved, what would you have done for *him*?"

"My dear evangelist, this confusing of persons and personalities is in bad taste."

"And your nasty, sterile want of common sympathy is in the worst taste imaginable. *Noblesse oblige*! You and your ruling class!"

"And to what should it oblige me? To have a lot of unnecessary emotions about my gamekeeper? I refuse. I leave it all to my evangelist."

"As if he weren't a man as much as you are, my word!"

"My gamekeeper to boot, and I pay him two pounds a week, and give him a house."

"Pay him! What do you think you pay for, with two pounds a week and a house?"

"His services."

"Bah! I would tell you to keep your two pounds a week and your house."

"Probably he would like to: but can't afford the luxury!"

"You, and *rule*!" she said. "You don't rule, don't flatter yourself. You have only got more than your share of the money, and make people work for you for two pounds a week, or threaten them with starvation. Rule! What do you give forth of rule? Why you're dried up! You only bully with your money, like any Jew or any Schieber!"

"You are very elegant in your speech, Lady Chatterley!"

"I assure you, you were very elegant altogether out there in the wood. I was utterly ashamed of you. Why my father is ten times the human being you are: you *gentleman*!"

He reached and rang the bell for Mrs Bolton. But he was yellow at the gills.

She went up to her room, furious, saying to herself: "Him and buying people! Well he doesn't buy me, and therefore there's no need for me to stay with him. Dead fish of a gentleman, with his celluloid soul! And how they take one in, with their manners and their mock wistfulness and gentleness. They've got about as much feeling as celluloid has."

She made her plans for the night, and determined to get Clifford off her mind. She didn't want to hate him. She didn't want to be mixed up very intimately with him in any sort of feeling. She wanted him not to know anything at all about herself: and especially, not to know anything about her feeling for the keeper. This squabble of her attitude to the servants was an old one. He found her too familiar, she found him stupidly insentient, tough and india-rubbery where other people were concerned.

She went downstairs calmly, with her old demure bearing, at dinner-time. He was still yellow at the gills: in for one of his liver bouts, when he was really very queer.—He was reading a French book.

"Have you ever read Proust?" he asked her.

"I've tried—but he bores me."

"He's really very extraordinary."

"Possibly! But he bores me: all that sophistication! He doesn't have feelings, he only has streams of words about feelings. I'm tired of self-important mentalities."

"Would you prefer self-important animalities?"

"Perhaps! But one might possibly get something that wasn't self-important."

"Well, I like Proust's subtlety and his well-bred anarchy."

"It makes you very dead, really."

"There speaks my evangelical little wife."

They were at it again, at it again! But she couldn't help fighting him. He seemed to sit there like a skeleton, sending out a skeleton's cold grisly *will* against her. Almost she could feel the skeleton clutching her and pressing her to its cage of ribs. He too was really up in arms: and she was a little afraid of him.

She went upstairs as soon as possible, and went to bed quite early. But at half-past nine she got up, and went outside to listen. There was no sound. She slipped on a dressing-gown and went downstairs. Clifford and Mrs Bolton were playing cards, gambling. They would probably go on until midnight.

Connie returned to her room, threw her pyjamas on the tossed bed, put on a thin night-dress and over that a woolen day-dress, put on rubber tennis-shoes, and then a light coat, and she was ready. If she met anybody, she was just going out for a few minutes. And in the morning, when she came in again, she would just have been for a little walk in the dew, as she fairly often did before breakfast. For the rest, the only danger was that someone should go into her room during the night. But that was most unlikely: not one chance in a hundred.

Betts had not yet locked up. He fastened up the house at ten o'clock, and unfastened it again at seven in the morning. She slipped out silently and unseen. There was a half-moon shining, enough to make a little light in the world, not enough to show her up in her dark-grey coat. She walked quickly across the park, not really in the thrill of the assignation, but with a certain anger and rebellion burning in her heart. It was not the right sort of heart to take to a love-meeting. But à la guerre comme à la guerre!

CHAPTER XIV.

When she got near the park-gate, she heard the click of the latch. He was there, then, in the darkness of the wood, and had seen her!

"You are good and early," he said out of the dark. "Was everything all right!"

"Perfectly easy."

He shut the gate quietly after her, and made a spot of light on the dark drive, showing the pallid flowers still standing there open in the night. They went on apart, in silence.

"Are you sure you didn't hurt yourself this morning with that chair?" she asked.

"No no!"

"When you had that pneumonia, what did it do to you?"

"Oh—nothing! It left my heart not so strong—and the lungs not so elastic. But it always does that."

"And you ought not to make violent physical efforts?"

"Not often."

She plodded on in an angry silence.

"Did you hate Clifford?" she said at last.

"Hate him, no! I've met too many like him, to upset myself hating him. I know beforehand I don't care for his sort, and I let it go at that."

"What is his sort?"

"Nay, you know better than I do. The sort of youngish gentleman a bit like a lady, and no balls."

"What balls?"

"Balls! A man's balls!"

She pondered this.

"But—is it a question of that?" she said, a little annoyed.

"You say a man's got no brain, when he's a fool: and no heart, when he's mean; and no stomach, when he's a funker. And when he's got none of that spunky wild bit of a man in him, you say he's got no balls. When he's sort of tame."

She pondered this.

"And is Clifford tame?" she asked.

"Tame, and nasty with it: like most such fellows, when you come up against 'em."

"And do you think you're not tame?"

"Maybe not quite—quite!"

At length she saw in the distance a yellow light. She stood still.

"There is a light," she said.

"I always leave a light in the house," he said.

She went on again at his side, but not touching him, wondering why she was going with him at all.

He unlocked, and they went in, he bolting the door behind them. As if it were a prison, she thought! The kettle was singing by the red fire, there were cups on the table.

She sat in the wooden arm-chair by the fire. It was warm after the chill outside.

"I'll take off my shoes, they are wet," she said.

She sat with her stockinged feet on the bright steel fender. He went to the pantry, bringing food: bread and butter and pressed tongue. She was warm: she took off her coat. He hung it on the door.

"Shall you have cocoa or tea or coffee to drink?" he asked.

"I don't think I want anything," she said, looking at the table. "But you eat."

"Nay, I don't care about it. I'll just feed the dog."

He tramped with a quiet inevitability over the brick floor, putting food for the dog in a brown bowl. The spaniel looked up at him anxiously.

"Ay, this is thy supper—tha nedna look as if tha wouldna get it!" he said.

He set the bowl on the stairfoot mat, and sat himself on a chair by the wall, to take off his leggings and boots. The dog, instead of eating, came to him again, and sat looking up at him, troubled. He slowly unbuckled his leggings. The dog edged a little nearer.

"What's amiss wi' thee then? Art upset because there's somebody else here? Tha 'rt a female, tha art! Go an' eat thy supper."

He put his hand on her head, and the bitch leaned her head sideways against him. He slowly, softly pulled her long silky ear.

"There!" he said. "There! Go an' eat thy supper! Go!"

He tilted his chin towards the pot on the mat, and the dog meekly went, and fell to eating.

"Do you like dogs?" Connie asked him.

"No, not really. They're too tame and clinging."

He had taken off his leggings and was unlacing his heavy boots. Connie had turned from the fire. How bare the little room was! Yet over his head on the wall hung a hideous enlarged photograph of a young married couple, apparently him and a bold-faced young woman, no doubt his wife.

"Is that you?" Connie asked him.

He twisted and looked at the enlargement above his head.

"Ay! Taken just afore we was married—when I was twenty-one." He looked at it impassively.

"Do you like it?" Connie asked him.

"Like it? No! I never liked the thing. But she fixed it all up to have it done, like—"

He returned to pulling off his boots.

"If you don't like it, why do you keep it hanging there? Perhaps your wife would like to have it," she said.

He looked up at her with a sudden grin.

"She carted off ivrything as was worth taking from th' ouse," he said. "But she left *that*."

"Then why do you keep it? for sentimental reasons?"

"Nay, I niver look at it. I hardly knowed it wor theer. It's bin theer sin' we come to this place—"

"Why don't you burn it?" she said.

He twisted round again and looked at the enlarged photograph. It was framed in a brown-and-gilt frame, hideous. It showed a clean-shaven, alert, very young-looking young man in a rather high collar, and a somewhat plump, bold young woman with hair fluffed out and crimped, and wearing a dark satin blouse.

"It wouldn't be a bad idea, would it?" he said.

He had pulled off his boots, and put on a pair of slippers. He stood up on the chair, and lifted down the photograph. It left a big pale place on the greenish wall-paper.

"No use dusting it now," he said, setting the thing against the wall.

He went to the scullery, and returned with hammer and pincers. Sitting where he had sat before, he started to tear off the back-paper from the big frame, and to pull out the sprigs that held the back-board in position, working with the immediate quiet absorption that was characteristic of him.

He soon had the nails out: then he pulled out the backboards, then the enlargement itself in its solid white mount. He looked at the photograph with amusement.

"Shows me for what I was, a young curate, and her for what she was, a bully," he said. "The prig and the bully!"

"Let me look!" said Connie.

He did look indeed very clean-shaven and very clean altogether, one of the clean young men of twenty years ago. But even in the photograph his eyes were alert and dauntless. And the woman was not altogether a bully, though her jowl was heavy. There was a touch of appeal in her.

"One should never keep these things," said Connie.

"That one shouldn't! One should never have them made!"

He broke the cardboard photograph and mount over his knee, and when it was small enough, put it on the fire.

"It'll spoil the fire though," he said.

The glass and the backboards he carefully took upstairs. The frame he knocked asunder with a few blows of the hammer, making the stucco fly. Then he took the pieces into the scullery.

"We'll burn that tomorrow," he said. "There's too much plaster-moulding on it."

Having cleared away, he sat down.

"Did you love your wife?" she asked him.

"Love?" he said. "Did you love Sir Clifford?"

But she was not going to be put off.

"But you cared for her?" she insisted.

"Cared?" he grinned.

"Perhaps you care for her now," she said.

"Me!" His eyes widened. "Ah no, I can't think of her," he said quietly.

"Why?"

But he shook his head.

"Then why don't you get a divorce? She'll come back to you one day," said Connie.

He looked up at her sharply.

"She wouldn't come within a mile of me. She hates me a lot worse than I hate her."

"You'll see she'll come back to you."

"That she never shall. That's done! It would make me sick to see her."

"You will see her. And you're not even legally separated, are you?"

"No."

"Ah well then—she'll come back, and you'll have to take her in."

He gazed at Connie fixedly. Then he gave the queer toss of his head.

"You may be right. I was a fool ever to come back here. But I felt stranded, and had to go somewhere. A man's a poor bit of a wastrel, blown about. But you're right—I'll get a divorce and get clear. I hate those things like death—officials and courts and judges. But I've got to go through with it. I'll get a divorce."

And she saw his jaw set. Inwardly she exulted.

"I think I will have a cup of weak tea," she said.

He rose to make it. But his face was set.

As they sat at table she asked him:

"Why did you marry her? She was commoner than you. Mrs Bolton told me about her. She could never understand why you married her."

He looked at her fixedly.

"I'll tell you," he said. "The first girl I had, I began with when I was sixteen. She was a schoolmaster's daughter over at Ollerton—pretty, beautiful really. I was a supposed-to-be clever sort of young fellow from Sheffield Grammar School, with a bit of French and German, very much up aloft. She was the romantic sort that hated commonness. She egged me on to poetry and reading: in a way, she made a man of me. I read and I thought like a house on fire, for her. And I was a clerk in Butterley Offices, thin, white-faced fellow fuming with all the things I read. And about *everything* I talked to her: but everything. We talked ourselves into Persepolis and Timbuctoo. We were the most literary-cultured couple in ten counties. I held forth with rapture to her, positively with rapture. I simply went up in smoke. And she adored me.—The serpent in the grass was sex. She somehow didn't have any—at least, not where it's supposed to be. I got thinner and crazier. Then I said we'd got to be lovers. I talked her into it, as usual. So she let me. I was excited, and she never wanted it. She just didn't want it. She adored me, she loved me to talk to her and kiss her: in that way, she had a passion for me. But the other, she just didn't want. And there are lots of women like her. And it was just the other that I *did* want. So there we split. I was cruel, and left her.—Then I took on with another girl, a teacher, who had made a scandal by carrying on with a married man and driving him nearly out of his mind. She was a soft, white-skinned, soft sort of woman, older than me, and played the fiddle. And she was a demon. She loved everything about love, except the sex. Clinging, caressing, creeping into you in every way: but if you forced her to the sex itself, she just ground her teeth and sent out hate. I forced her to it: and she could simply numb me with hate because of it. So I was balked again. I loathed all that. I wanted a woman who wanted me, and wanted *it*.—Then came Bertha Coutts. They'd lived next door to us when I was a little lad, so I knew 'em alright. And they were common. Well, Bertha went away to some place or other in Birmingham, she said, as a lady's companion; everybody else said, as a waitress or something in an hotel. Anyhow just when I was more than fed up with that other girl, when I was twenty-one, back comes Bertha, with airs and graces and smart clothes and a sort of bloom on her: a sort of sensual bloom that you'd see sometimes on a woman, or on a trolly. Well I was in a state of murder. I chucked up my job at Butterley because I thought I was a weed, clerking there: and I got on as overhead blacksmith at Tevershall: shoeing horses mostly. It had been my Dad's job, and I'd always been with him. It was a job I liked: handling horses: and it came natural to me. So I stopped talking 'fine,' as they call it—talking pure English—and went back to talking broad. I still read books, at home: but I blacksmithed and had a pony-trap of my own, and was My Lord Duckfoot. My Dad left me three hundred pounds when he died.—So I took on with Bertha, and I was glad she was common. I wanted her to be common. I wanted to be common myself.—Well, I married her, and she wasn't bad. Those other 'pure' women had nearly taken all the balls out of me, but she was all right that way. She wanted me, and made no bones about it. And I was as pleased as punch. That was what I wanted: a woman who *wanted* me to fuck her. So I fucked her like a good un. And I think she despised me a bit, for being so pleased about it, and bringing her her breakfast in bed sometimes. She sort of let things go, didn't get me a proper dinner when I came home from work, and if I said anything, flew out at me. And I flew back, hammer and tongues. She flung a cup at me and I took her by the scruff of the neck and squeezed the life out of her. That sort of thing! But she treated me with insolence. And she got so's she'd never have me when I wanted her: never. Always put me off, brutal as you like. And then when she'd put me right off, and I didn't want her, she'd come all lovey-dovey, and get me. And I always went. But when I had her, she'd never come-off when I did. Never! She'd just wait. If I kept back for half an hour, she'd keep back longer. And when I'd come and really finished, then she'd start on her own account, and I had to stop inside her till she brought herself off, wriggling and shouting. And when I'd gone little as anything, she'd clutch clutch clutch with herself down there, an' then she'd come-off, fair in ecstasy. An' then she'd say: That was lovely!—Gradually I got sick of it: and she got worse. She sort of got harder and harder to bring off, and she'd sort of tear at me down there, as if it was a beak tearing at me. By God, you think a woman's soft down there, like a fig. But I tell you the old rampers have beaks between their legs, and they tear at you with it till you're sick. Self! self! self! all self! tearing and shouting! They talk about men's sensual selfishness, but I doubt if it can ever touch a woman's blind beakishness, once she's gone that way. Like an old trull! And she couldn't help it. I told her about it, I told her how I hated it. And she'd even try. She'd try to lie still and let *me* work the business. She'd try. But it was no good. She got no feeling off it, from my working. She had to work the thing herself, grind her own coffee. And it came back on her like a raving necessity, she had to let herself go, and tear, tear, tear, as if she had no sensation in her except in the top of her beak, the very outside top tip, that rubbed and tore. That's how old whores used to be, so men used to say. It was a low kind of self-will in her, a raving sort of self-will: like in a woman who drinks. Well in the end I couldn't stand it. We slept apart. She herself had started it, in her bouts when she wanted to be clear of me, when she said I bossed her. She had started having a room for herself. But the time came when I wouldn't have her coming to my room. I wouldn't! I hated it. And she hated me. My God, how she hated me before that child was born! I often think she conceived it out of hate. Anyhow, after the child was born I left her alone. And then came the war, and I joined up. And I didn't come back till I knew she was with that fellow at Stacks Gate."

He broke off, pale in the face.

"And what is the man at Stacks Gate like?" asked Connie.

"A big baby sort of fellow, very low-mouthed. She bullies him, and they both drink."

"My word, if she came back!"

"My God, yes! I should just go—disappear again."

There was a silence. The pasteboard in the fire had turned to grey ash.

"So when you did get a woman who wanted you," said Connie, "you got a bit too much of a good thing."

"Ay! Seems so! Yet even then I'd rather have her than the never-never ones: the white love of my youth, and that other poison-smelling lily, and the rest."

"What about the rest?" said Connie.

"The rest? There is no rest. Only to my experience the mass of women are like this: most of them want a man, but don't want the sex, but they put up with it, as part of the bargain. The more old-fashioned sort just lie there like nothing and let you go ahead. They don't mind afterwards: then they like you. But the actual thing itself is nothing to them, a bit distasteful. And most men like it that way. I hate it. But the sly sort of women who are like that pretend they're not. They pretend they're passionate and have thrills. But it's all cockaloopy. They make it up.—Then there's the ones that love everything, every kind of feeling and cuddling and going off, every kind except the natural one. They always make you go off when you're *not* in the only place you should be, when you go off.— Then there's the hard sort, that are the devil to bring off at all, and bring themselves off, like my wife. They want to be the active party.— Then there's the sort that's just dead inside: but dead: and they know it. Then there's the sort that puts you out before you really 'come,' and go on writhing their loins till they bring themselves off against your thighs. But they're mostly the Lesbian sort. It's astonishing how Lesbian women are, consciously or unconsciously. Seems to me they're nearly all Lesbian—"

"And do you mind?" asked Connie.

"I could kill them. When I'm with a woman who's really Lesbian, I fairly howl in my soul, wanting to kill her."

"And what do you do?"

"Just get away as fast as I can."

"But do you think Lesbian women any worse than homosexual men?"

"*I* do! Because I've suffered more from them. In the abstract, I've no idea. When I get with a Lesbian woman, whether she knows she's one or not, I see red. No no! But I wanted to have nothing to do with any woman any more. I wanted to keep to myself: keep my privacy and my decency—"

He looked pale, and his brows were sombre.

"And were you sorry when I came along?" she asked.

"I was sorry—and I was glad."

"And what are you now?"

"I'm sorry, from the outside: all the complications and the ugliness and recrimination that's bound to come, sooner or later. That's when my blood sinks, and I'm low. But when my blood comes up, I'm glad. I'm even triumphant. I was really getting bitter. I thought there was no real sex left: never a woman who'd really 'come' naturally with a man: except black women—and somehow—well, we're white men: and they're a bit like mud."

"And now, are you glad of me?" she asked.

"Yes! When I can forget the rest. When I can't forget the rest, I want to get under the table and die."

"Why under the table?"

"Why?" he laughed. "Hide, I suppose. Baby!"

"You do seem to have had awful experiences of women," she said.

"You see, I couldn't fool myself. That's where most men manage. They take an attitude, and accept a lie. I could never fool myself. I knew what I wanted with a woman—and I could never say I'd got it when I hadn't."

"But have you got it now?"

"Looks as if I might have."

"Then why are you so pale and gloomy?"

"Bellyful of remembering: and perhaps afraid of myself."

She sat in silence. It was growing late.

"And you do think it's important—a man and a woman?" she asked him.

"For me it is. For me it's the core to my life: if I have a right relation with a woman."

"And if you didn't get it?"

"Then I'd have to do without."

Again she pondered, before she asked:

"And do you think you've always been right, with women?"

"God, no! I let my wife get to what she was: my fault a good deal. I spoilt her. And I'm very mistrustful. You'll have to expect it. It takes a lot to make me trust anybody, inwardly. So perhaps I'm a fraud too. I mistrust. And tenderness is not to be mistaken."

She looked at him.

"You don't mistrust with your body, when your blood comes up," she said. "You don't mistrust then, do you?"

"No alas! That's how I've got into all the trouble. And that's why my mind mistrusts so thoroughly."

"Let your mind mistrust. What does it matter!"

The dog sighed with discomfort on the mat. The ash-clogged fire sank.

"We *are* a couple of battered warriors," said Connie.

"Are you battered too?" he laughed. "And here we are returning to the fray!"

"Yes! I feel really frightened."

"Ay!"

He got up, and put her shoes to dry, and wiped his own and set them near the fire. In the morning he would grease them. He poked the ash of pasteboard as much as possible out of the fire. "Even burnt, it's filthy," he said. Then he brought sticks and put them on the hob for the morning. Then he went out awhile with the dog.

When he came back, Connie said:

"I want to go out too, for a minute."

She went alone into the darkness. There were stars overhead. She could smell flowers on the night air. And she could feel her wet shoes getting wetter again. But she felt like going away, right away from him and everybody.

It was chilly. She shuddered, and returned to the house. He was sitting in front of the low fire.

"Ugh! Cold!" she shuddered.

He put the sticks on the fire, and fetched more, till they had a good crackling chimneyful of blaze. The rippling running yellow flame made them both happy, warmed their faces and their souls.

"Never mind!" she said, taking his hand as he sat silent and remote. "One does one's best."

"Ay!"—He sighed, with a twist of a smile.

She slipped over to him, and into his arms, as he sat there before the fire.

"Forget then!" she whispered. "Forget!"

He held her close, in the running warmth of the fire. The flame itself was like a forgetting. And her soft, warm, ripe weight! Slowly his blood turned, and began to ebb back into strength and reckless vigour again.

"And perhaps the women *really* wanted to be there and to love you properly, only perhaps they couldn't. Perhaps it wasn't all their fault," she said.

"I know it. Do you think I don't know what a broken-backed snake that's been trodden on I was myself!"

She clung to him suddenly. She had not wanted to start all this again. Yet some perversity had made her.

"But you're not now," she said. "You're not that now: a broken-backed snake that's been trodden on!"

"I don't know what I am. There's black days ahead."

"No!" she protested, clinging to him. "Why? Why?"

"There's black days coming—for us all and for everybody," he repeated with a prophetic gloom.

"No! You're not to say it!"

He was silent. But she could feel the black void of despair inside him. That was the death of all desire, the death of all love: this despair that was like the dark cave inside the men, in which their spirit was lost.

"And you talk so coldly about sex," she said. "You talk as if you had only wanted your own pleasure and satisfaction."

She was protesting nervously against him.

"Nay!" he said. "I wanted to have my pleasure and satisfaction of a woman, and I never got it: because I could never get my pleasure and satisfaction of *her* unless she got hers of me at the same time. And it never happened. It takes two."

"But you never believed in your women. You don't even believe really in me," she said.

"I don't know what believing in a woman means."

"That's it, you see!"

She still was curled on his lap. But his spirit was grey and absent, he was not there for her. And everything she said drove him further.

"But what *do* you believe in?" she insisted.

"I don't know."

"Nothing—like all the men I've ever known," she said.

They were both silent. Then he roused himself and said:

"Yes, I do believe in something. I believe in being warm-hearted. I believe especially in being warm-hearted in love, in fucking with a warm heart. I believe if men could fuck with warm hearts, and the women take it warm-heartedly, everything would come all right. It's all this cold-hearted fucking that is death and idiocy."

"But you don't fuck me cold-heartedly," she protested.

"I don't want to fuck you at all. My heart's as cold as cold potatoes just now."

"Oh—!" she said, kissing him mockingly. "Let's have them *sauté*."

He laughed, and sat erect.

"It's a fact!" he said. "Anything for a bit of warm-heartedness. But the women don't like it. Even you don't really like it. You like good, sharp, piercing cold-hearted fucking, and then pretending it's all sugar. Where's your tenderness for me? You're as suspicious of me as a cat is of a dog. I tell you it takes two even to be tender and warm-hearted. You love fucking all right: but you want it to be called something grand and mysterious, just to flatter your own self-importance. Your own self-importance is more to you, fifty times more, than any man, or being together with a man."

"But that's what I'd say of you. Your own self-importance is everything to you."

"Ay! Very well then!" he said, moving as if he wanted to rise. "Let's keep apart then. I'd rather die than do any more cold-hearted fucking."

She slid away from him, and he stood up.

"And do you think *I* want it?" she said.

"I hope you don't," he replied. "But anyhow, you go to bed—an' I'll sleep down here."

She looked at him. He was pale, his brows were sullen, he was as distant in recoil as the cold pole. Men were all alike.

"I can't go home till morning—" she said.

"No! Go to bed. It's a quarter to one."

"I certainly won't," she said.

He went across and picked up his boots.

"Then I'll go out!" he said.

He began to put on his boots. She stared at him.

"Wait!" she faltered. "Wait! What's come between us?"

He was bent over, lacing his boot, and did not reply. The moments passed. A dimness came over her, like a swoon. All her consciousness died, and she stood there wide-eyed, looking at him from the unknown, knowing nothing any more.

He looked up, because of the silence, and saw her wide-eyed and lost. And as if a wind tossed him he got up and hobbled over to her, one shoe off and one shoe on, and took her in his arms, pressing her against his body, which somehow felt hurt right through. And there he held her, and there she remained.

Till his hands reached blindly down and felt for her, and felt under her clothing to where she was smooth and warm.

"Ma lass!" he murmured. "Ma little lass! Dunna let's fight! Dunna let's niver fight! I love thee an' th' touch on thee. Dunna let's talk! Dunna argue wi' me! Dunna! Dunna! Dunna! Let's be together."

She lifted her face and looked at him.

"Don't be upset," she said steadily. "It's no good being upset. Do you really want to be together with me?"

She looked with wide, steady eyes into his face. He stopped, and went suddenly still, turning his face aside. All his body went perfectly still, but did not withdraw. Then he lifted his head and looked into her eyes, with his odd faint smile, his emotion subsided.

"Ay!" he said. "Let's be together! Let's be together on oath."

"But really?" she said, her eyes filling with tears.

"Ay really! Heart an' belly an' cock—"

He still smiled faintly down on her, with the flicker of irony in his eyes, and a touch of bitterness.

She was silently weeping, and he lay with her and went into her there on the hearthrug, and so they gained a measure of equanimity. And then they went quickly to bed, for it was growing chill, and they had tired each other out. And she nestled up to him, feeling small and enfolded, and they both went to sleep at once, fast in one sleep. And so they lay and never moved, till the sun rose over the wood and day was beginning.

Then he woke up and looked at the light. The curtains were drawn. He listened to the loud wild calling of blackbirds and thrushes in the wood. It would be a brilliant morning, about half-past five, his hour for rising. He had slept so fast! It was such a new day! The woman was still curled asleep and tender. His hand moved on her, and she opened her blue, wondering eyes, smiling unconsciously into his face.

"Are you awake?" she said to him.

He was looking into her eyes. He smiled, and kissed her. And suddenly she roused and sat up.

"Fancy that I am here!" she said.

She looked round the whitewashed little bedroom with its sloping ceiling and gable window where the white curtains were closed. The room was bare save for a little yellow-painted chest of drawers, and a chair: and the smallish white bed in which she lay with him.

"Fancy that we are here!" she said, looking down at him. He was lying watching her, stroking her breasts with his fingers, under the thin nightdress. When he was warm and smoothed out, he looked young and handsome. His eyes could look so warm. And she was fresh and young like a flower.

"I want to take this off!" he said, gathering the thin batiste nightdress and pulling it over her head. She sat there with bare shoulders and longish breasts faintly golden. He loved making her breasts swing softly, like bells.

"You must take off your pyjamas too," she said.

"Eh nay!"

"Yes! Yes!" she commanded.

And he took off his old cotton pyjama-jacket, and pushed down the trousers. Save for his hands and wrists and face and neck he was white as milk, with fine slender muscular flesh. To Connie he was suddenly piercingly beautiful again, as when she had seen him that afternoon washing himself.

A gold of sunshine touched the closed white curtains. She felt it wanted to come in.

"Oh, do let's draw the curtains! The birds are singing so! Do let the sun in," she said.

He slipped out of bed with his back to her, naked and white and thin, and went to the window, stooping a little, drawing the curtains and looking out for a moment. The back was white and fine, the small buttocks beautiful with an exquisite, delicate manliness, the back of the neck ruddy and delicate and yet strong. There was an inward, not an outward strength in the delicate fine body.

"But you are beautiful!" she said. "So pure and fine! Come!"—She held her arms out.

He was ashamed to turn to her, because of his aroused nakedness. He caught his shirt off the floor, and held it to him, coming to her.

"No!" she said, still holding out her beautiful slim arms from her drooping breasts. "Let me see you!"

He dropped the shirt and stood still, looking towards her. The sun through the low window sent in a beam that lit up his thighs and slim belly, and the erect phallos rising darkish and hot-looking from the little cloud of vivid gold-red hair. She was startled and afraid.

"How strange!" she said slowly. "How strange he stands there! So big! and so dark and cock-sure! Is he like that?"

The man looked down the front of his slender white body, and laughed. Between the slim breasts the hair was dark, almost black. But at the root of the belly, where the phallos rose thick and arching, it was gold-red, vivid in a little cloud.

"So proud!" she murmured, uneasy. "And so lordly! Now I know why men are so overbearing! But he's lovely, *really*. Like another being! A bit terrifying! But lovely really! And he comes to *me*!—" She caught her lower lip between her teeth, in fear and excitement.

The man looked down in silence at the tense phallos, that did not change.—"Ay!" he said at last, in a little voice. "Ay ma lad! tha'rt theer right enough. Yi, tha mun rear thy head! Theer on thy own, eh? an' ta'es no count o' nob'dy! Tha ma'es nowt o' me, John Thomas. Art boss? of me? Eh well, tha'rt more cocky than me, an' tha says less. John Thomas! Dost want *her*? Dost want my lady Jane? Tha's dipped me in again, tha hast. Ay, an' tha comes up smilin'.— Ax 'er then! Ax lady Jane! Say: Lift up your heads o' ye gates, that the king of glory may come in. Ay, th' cheek on thee! Cunt, that's what tha'rt after. Tell lady Jane tha wants cunt. John Thomas, an' th' cunt o' lady Jane!—"

"Oh, don't tease him!" said Connie, crawling on her knees on the bed towards him and putting her arms round his white slender loins, and drawing him to her so that her hanging, swinging breasts touched the tip of the stirring, erect phallos, and caught the drop of moisture. She held the man fast.

"Lie down!" he said. "Lie down! Let me come!"

He was in a hurry now.

And afterwards, when they had been quite still, the woman had to uncover the man again, to look at the mystery of the phallos.

"And now he's tiny, and soft like a little bud of life!" she said, taking the soft small penis in her hand. "Isn't he somehow lovely! so on his own, so strange! And *so* innocent! And he comes so far into me! You must *never* insult him, you know. He's mine too. He's not only yours. He's mine! And so lovely and innocent!" And she held the penis soft in her hand.

He laughed.

"Blest be the tie that binds our hearts in kindred love," he said.

"Of course!" she said. "Even when he's soft and little, I feel my heart simply tied to him. And how lovely your hair is here! quite quite different!"

"That's John Thomas' hair, not mine!" he said.

"John Thomas! John Thomas!" and she quickly kissed the soft penis, that was beginning to stir again.

"Ay!" said the man, stretching his body almost painfully. "He's got his root in my soul, has that gentleman! An' sometimes I don' know what ter do wi' him. Ay, he's got a will of his own, an' it's hard to suit him. Yet I wouldn't have him killed."

"No wonder men have always been afraid of him!" she said. "He's rather terrible."

The quiver was going through the man's body, as the stream of consciousness again changed its direction, turning downwards. And he was helpless, as the penis in slow soft undulations filled and surged and rose up, and grew hard, standing there hard and overweening, in its curious towering fashion. The woman too trembled a little as she watched.

"There! Take him then! He's thine," said the man.

And she quivered, and her own mind melted out. Sharp soft waves of unspeakable pleasure washed over her as he entered her, and started the curious molten thrilling that spread and spread till she was carried away with the last blind flush of extremity.

He heard the distant hooters of Stacks Gate, for seven o'clock. It was Monday morning. He shivered a little, and with his face between her breasts pressed her soft breasts up over his ears, to deafen him.

She had not even heard the hooters. She lay perfectly still, her soul washed transparent.

"You must get up, mustn't you?" he muttered.

"What time?" came her colourless voice.

"Seven-o'clock blowers a bit sin'."

"I suppose I must."

She was resenting, as she always did, the compulsion from outside.

He sat up and looked blankly out of the window.

"You do love me, don't you?" she asked calmly.

He looked down at her.

"Tha knows what tha knows. What dost ax for!" he said, a little fretfully.

"I want you to keep me—not to let me go," she said.

His eyes seemed full of a warm, soft darkness that could not think. "When? Now?"

"Now in your heart. Then I want to come and live with you always—soon."

He sat naked on the bed, with his head dropped, unable to think.

"Don't you want it?" she asked.

"Ay!" he said.

Then with the same eyes darkened with another flame of consciousness, almost like sleep, he looked at her.

"Dunna ax me nowt now," he said. "Let me be. I like thee. I luv thee when tha lies theer. A woman's a lovely thing when 'er 's deep ter fuck, and cunt's good. Ah luv thee, thy legs, an' th' shape on thee, an' th' womanness on thee. Ah luv th' womanness on thee. Ah luv thee wi' my ba's, an' wi' my heart. But dunna ax me nowt. Dunna ma'e me say nowt. Let me stop as I am while I can. Tha can ax me ivrythink after. Now let me be, let me be!"

And softly, he laid his hand on her mound of Venus, on the soft brown maidenhair, and himself sat still and naked on the bed, his face motionless in physical abstraction, almost like the face of Buddha. Motionless, and in the invisible flame of another consciousness, he sat with his hand on her, and waited for the turn.

After a while, he reached for his shirt and put it on, dressed himself swiftly in silence, looked at her once as she still lay naked and faintly golden like a Gloire de Dijon rose on the bed, and was gone. She heard him downstairs opening the door.

And still she lay musing, musing. It was very hard to go: to go out of his aura. He called from the foot of the stairs: "Half-past seven!" She sighed, and got out of bed. The bare little room! Nothing in it at all but the small chest of drawers and the smallish bed. But the board floor was scrubbed clean. And in a corner by the window gable was a shelf with some books, and some from a circulating library. She looked. There were books about bolshevist Russia, books of travel, a volume about the atom and the electron, another about the composition of the earth's core, and the causes of earthquakes: then a few novels: then three books on India. So! he was a reader after all.

The sun fell on her naked limbs through the gable window. Outside she saw the dog Flossie roaming round. The hazel-brake was misted with green, and dark-green dogs-mercury under. It was a clear clean morning, with birds flying and triumphantly singing. If only she could stay! If only there weren't the other ghastly world of smoke and iron! If only *he* would make her a world.

She came downstairs, down the steep, narrow wooden stairs. Still she would be content with this little house—if only it were in a world of its own.

He was washed and fresh, and the fire was burning.

"Will you eat anything?" he said.

"No! Only lend me a comb."

She followed him into the scullery, and combed her hair before the handbreadth of mirror by the back door. Then she was ready to go.

She stood in the little front garden, looking at the dewy flowers, the grey bed of pinks in bud already.

"I would like to have all the rest of the world disappear," she said, "and live with you here."

"It won't disappear," he said.

They went almost in silence through the lovely dewy wood. But they were together in a world of their own.

It was bitter to her to go on to Wragby.

"I want soon to come and live with you altogether," she said as she left him.

He smiled unanswering.

She got home quietly and unremarked, and went up to her room.

CHAPTER XV.

There was a letter from Hilda on the breakfast-tray.—"Father is going to London this week, and I shall call for you on Thursday week, June 17th. You must be ready so that we can go on at once. I don't want to waste time at Wragby, it's an awful place. I shall probably stay the night at Retford with the Colemans, so I should be with you for lunch, Thursday. Then we could start at tea-time, and sleep perhaps in Grantham. It is no use our spending an evening with Clifford. If he hates your going, it would be no pleasure to him."

So! She was being pushed round on the chess-board again.

Clifford hated her going, but it was only because he didn't feel *safe* in her absence. Her presence, for some reason, made him feel safe, and free to do the things he was occupied with. He was a great deal at the pits, and wrestling in spirit with the almost hopeless problems of getting out his coal in the most economical fashion and then selling it when he'd got it out. He knew he ought to find some way of *using* it, or converting it, so that he needn't sell it, or needn't have the chagrin of failing to sell it. But if he made electric power, could he sell that? or use it? And to convert into oil was as yet too costly and too elaborate. To keep industry alive there must be more industry, and more industry, and more industry, like a madness.

It was a madness, and it required a madman to succeed in it. Well, he was a little mad. Connie thought so. His very intensity and acumen in the affairs of the pits seemed like a manifestation of madness to her, his very inspirations were the inspirations of insanity.

He talked to her of all his serious schemes, and she listened in a kind of wonder, and let him talk. Then the flow ceased, and he turned on the loud speaker, and became a blank, while apparently his schemes coiled on inside him in a kind of dream.

And every night now he played pontoon—that game of the Tommies—with Mrs Bolton, gambling with sixpences. And again, in the gambling, he was gone in a kind of unconsciousness, or blank intoxication, or intoxication of blankness, whatever it was. Connie couldn't bear to see him. But when she had gone to bed, he and Mrs Bolton would gamble on till two and three in the morning, safely, and with strange lust. Mrs Bolton was caught in the lust as much as Clifford: the more so, as she nearly always lost.

She told Connie one day: "I lost twenty-three shillings to Sir Clifford last night."

"And did he take the money from you?" asked Connie aghast.

"Why of course, my lady! Debt of honour!"

Connie expostulated roundly, and was angry with both of them. The upshot was, Sir Clifford raised Mrs Bolton's wages a hundred a year, and she could gamble on that. Meanwhile, it seemed to Connie, Clifford was really going deader.

She told him at length she was leaving on the seventeenth.

"Seventeenth!" he said. "And when will you be back?"

"By the twentieth of July at the latest."

"Yes! The twentieth of July."

Strangely and blankly he looked at her, with the vagueness of a child, but with the queer blank cunning of an old man.

"You won't let me down, now, will you?" he said.

"How?"

"While you're away. I mean, you're sure to come back?"

"I'm as sure as I can be of anything, that I shall come back."

"Yes! Well! Twentieth of July!—"

He looked at her so strangely.

Yet he really wanted her to go. That was so curious. He wanted her to go, positively, to have her little adventures and perhaps come home pregnant, and all that. At the same time, he was afraid of her going, just afraid.

She was quivering, watching her real opportunity for leaving him altogether, waiting till the time, herself, himself should be ripe.

She sat and talked to the keeper of her going abroad.

"And then when I come back," she said, "I can tell Clifford I must leave him. And you and I can go away. They never need even know it is you. We can go to another country, shall we? To Africa or Australia. Shall we?"

She was quite thrilled by her plan.

"You've never been to the colonies, have you?" he asked her.

"No! Have you?"

"I've been in India, and South Africa, and Egypt."

"Why shouldn't we go to South Africa?"

"We might!" he said slowly.

"Or don't you want to?" she asked.

"I don't care. I don't much care what I do."

"Doesn't it make you happy? Why not? We shan't be poor. I have about six hundred a year, I wrote and asked. It's not much, but it's enough, isn't it?"

"It's riches, to me."

"Oh, how lovely it will be!"

"But I ought to get divorced—and so ought you—unless we're going to have complications—"

There was plenty to think about.

Another day she asked him about himself. They were in the hut, and there was a thunderstorm.

"And weren't you happy when you were a lieutenant and an officer and a gentleman?"

"Happy? All right. I liked my Colonel."

"Did you love him?"

"Yes! I loved him."

"And did he love you?"

"Yes! In a way, he loved me."

"Tell me about him."

"What is there to tell? He had risen from the ranks. He loved the army. And he had never married. He was twenty years older than me. He was a very intelligent man: and alone in the army, as such a man is: a passionate man, in his way: and a very clever officer. I lived under his spell, while I was with him. I sort of let him run my life. And I never regret it."

"And did you mind very much when he died?"

"I was as near death myself. But when I came to, I knew another part of me was finished.—But then I'd always known it would end in death. All things do, as far as that goes."

She sat and ruminated. The thunder crashed outside. It was like being in a little ark in the Flood.

"You seem to have such a lot *behind* you," she said.

"Do I? It seems to me I've died once or twice already. Yet here I am, pegging on, and in for more trouble."

She was thinking hard, yet listening to the storm.

"And weren't you happy as an officer and a gentleman, when your Colonel was dead?"

"No! They were a mingy lot." He laughed suddenly. "The

Colonel used to say: Lad, the English middle classes have to chew every mouthful thirty times because their guts are so narrow, a bit as big as a pea would give them a stoppage. They're the mingiest set of ladylike snipe ever invented: full of conceit of themselves, frightened even if their boot-laces aren't correct, rotten as high game, and always in the right. That's what finishes me up. Kow-tow, kow-tow, arse-licking till their tongues are tough: yet they're always in the right. Prigs on top of everything. Prigs! A generation of ladylike prigs with half a ball each.—"

Connie laughed. The rain was rushing down.

"He hated them!"

"No," said he. "He didn't bother. He just disliked them. There's a difference. Because, as he said, the Tommies are getting just as priggish and half-balled and narrow-gutted. It's the fate of mankind, to go that way."

"The common people too—the working people?"

"All the lot. Their spunk's gone dead—motor-cars and cinemas and aeroplanes suck the last bit out of them. I tell you, every generation breeds a more rabbity generation, with indiarubber tubing for guts and tin legs and tin faces. Tin people! It's all a steady sort of bolshevism—just killing off the human thing, and worshipping the mechanical thing. Money, money, money! All the modern lot get their real kick out of killing the old human feeling out of man, making mincemeat of the old Adam and the old Eve. They're all alike. The world is all alike: kill off the human reality, a quid for every foreskin, two quid for every pair of balls. What is cunt but machine-fucking!—It's all alike. Pay 'em money to cut off the world's cock. Pay money, money, money to them as will take the spunk out of mankind, and leave 'em all little twiddling machines."

He sat there in the hut, his face pulled to mocking irony. Yet even then, he had one ear set backwards, listening to the storm over the wood. It made him feel so alone.

"But won't it ever come to an end?" she said.

"Ay, it will. It'll achieve its own salvation. When the last real man is killed, and they're *all* tame: white, black, yellow, all colours of tame ones: then they'll *all* be insane. Because the root of sanity is in the balls.—Then they'll *all* be insane, and they'll make their grand *auto da fé*. You know *auto da fé* means *act of faith*?—Ay—well—they'll make their own grand little act of faith. They'll offer one another up."

217

"You mean kill one another?"

"I do, duckie! If we go on at our present rate then in a hundred years' time there won't be ten thousand people in this island: there may not be ten. They'll have lovingly wiped each other out."—The thunder was rolling further away.

"How nice!" she said.

"Quite nice! To contemplate the extermination of the human species, and the long pause that follows before some other species crops up, it calms you more than anything else.—And if we go on in this way, with everybody, intellectuals, artists, government, industrialists and workers all frantically killing off the last human feeling, the last bit of their intuition, the last healthy instinct—if it goes on in algebraical progression, as it is going now: then ta-tah! to the human species! Good-bye! darling! The serpent swallows itself and leaves a void, considerably messed up, but not hopeless. Very nice! When savage wild dogs bark in Wragby, and savage wild pit-ponies stamp on Tevershall pit-bank! *te deum laudamus!*"

Connie laughed, but not very happily.

"Then you ought to be pleased that they are all bolshevists!" she said. "You ought to be pleased that they hurry on towards the end."

"So I am. I don't stop 'em! Because I couldn't if I would."

"Then why are you so bitter?"

"I'm not! If my cock gives its last crow, I don't mind."

"But if we have a child?" she said.

He dropped his head.

"Why—" he said at last—"it seems to me a wrong and bitter thing to do, to bring a child into this world."

"No! Don't say it! Don't say it!" she pleaded. "I think I'm going to have one. Say you'll be pleased." She laid her hand on his.

"I'm pleased for you to be pleased," he said. "But for me it seems a ghastly treachery to the unborn creature."

"Ah no!" she said, shocked. "Then you *can't* ever really want me! You *can't* want me, if you feel that!"

Again he was silent, his face sullen. Outside there was only the threshing of the rain.

"It's not quite true!" she whispered. "It's not quite true! There's another truth." She felt he was bitter now partly because she was leaving him, deliberately going away to Venice. And this half pleased her.

She pulled open his clothing and uncovered his belly, and

kissed his navel. Then she laid her cheek on his belly, and pushed her arm round his warm, silent loins. They were alone in the Flood.

"Tell me you want a child, in hope!" she murmured, pressing her face against his belly. "Tell me you do!"

"Why!" he said at last: and she felt the curious quivers of changing consciousness and relaxation going through his body. "Why—I've thought sometimes—if one but tried—if one but tried, here among th' colliers even! They workin' bad now, an' not earnin' much. If a man could say to 'em: Dunna think o' nowt but th' money. When it comes ter *wants*, we want but little. Let's not live for money.—"

She softly rubbed her cheek on his belly, and gathered his balls in her hand. The penis stirred softly, with strange life, but did not rise up. The rain beat bruisingly outside.

"Let's live for summat else. Let's not live ter make money, neither for us-selves nor for anybody else. Now we're forced to. We're forced to make a bit for us-selves, an' a fair lot for th' bosses. Let's stop it! Bit by bit, let's stop it. We needn't rant an' rave. Bit by bit, let's drop the whole industrial life, an' go back. The least little bit o' money 'll do. For everybody, me an' you, bosses an' masters, even th' king. The least little bit o' money 'll really do. Just make up your mind to it, an' you've got out o' th' mess." He paused, then went on:

"An' I'd tell 'em: Look! Look at Joe! He moves lovely! Look how he moves, alive and aware. He's beautiful! An' look at Jonah! He's clumsy, he's ugly, because he's niver willin' to rouse himself.—I'd tell 'em: Look! look at yerselves! One shoulder higher than t'other, legs twisted, feet all lumps! What have yer done ter yerselves, wi' the blasted work? Spoilt yerselves an' yer lives. Don't niver work ter spoil yerselves. No need to work that much. Take yer clothes off an' look at yourselves. Yer ought ter be alive an' beautiful, an' yer ugly an' half dead.—So I'd tell 'em. An' I'd get my men to wear different clothes: 'appen close red trousers, bright red, an' little short white jackets. Why, if men had red, fine legs, that alone would change them in a month. They'd begin to be men again, to be men! An' the women could dress as they liked. Because if once the men walked with legs close bright scarlet, and buttocks nice and showing scarlet under a little white jacket: then the women 'ud begin to be women. It's because th' men *aren't* men, that th' women have to be.—An' in time pull down Tevershall and build a few big beautiful buildings, that would hold us all. An' clean the country up again.—An' not have many children, because the world is overcrowded.

"But I wouldn't preach to the men: only strip 'em an' say: Look at yourselves! That's workin' for money!—Hark at yourselves! That's working for money. You've been workin' for money!—Look at Tevershall! It's horrible. That's because it was built while you was working for money.—Look at your girls! They don't care about you, you don't care about them. It's because you've spent your time working and caring for money. You can't talk nor move nor live, you can't properly be with a woman. You're not alive. Look at your-selves!—"

There fell a complete silence. Connie was half listening, and threading in the hair at the root of his belly a few forget-me-nots that she had gathered on the way to the hut. Outside, the world had gone still, and a little icy.

"You've got four kinds of hair," she said to him. "On your chest it's nearly black, and your hair isn't dark on your head: but your moustache is hard and dark red, and your hair here, your love-hair, is like a little bush of bright red-gold mistletoe. It's the loveliest of all!"

He looked down and saw the milky bits of forget-me-nots in the hair on his groin.

"Ay! That's where to put forget-me-nots—in the man-hair, or the maiden-hair.—But don't you care about the future?"

She looked up at him.

"Oh, I do, terribly!" she said.

"Because when I feel the human world is doomed, has doomed itself by its own mingy beastliness—then I feel the colonies aren't far enough. The moon wouldn't be far enough, because even there you could look back and see the earth, dirty, beastly, unsavoury among all the stars: made foul by men. Then I feel I've swallowed gall, and it's eating my inside out, and nowhere's far enough away to get away.—But when I get a turn, I forget it all again. Though it's a shame, what's been done to people these last hundred years: men turned into nothing but labour-insects, and all their manhood taken away, and all their real life. I'd wipe the machines off the face of the earth again, and end the industrial epoch absolutely, like a black mistake. But since I can't, an' nobody can, I'd better hold my peace, an' try an' live my own life: if I've got one to live, which I rather doubt."

The thunder had ceased outside, and the rain, which had abated, suddenly came striking down, with a last blench of lightning and mutter of departing storm. Connie was uneasy. He had talked so long now—and he was really talking to himself, not to her. Despair seemed to come down on him completely, and she was feeling happy, she hated despair. She knew her leaving him, which he had only just realised inside himself, had plunged him back into this mood. And she triumphed a little.

She opened the door and looked at the straight heavy rain, like a steel curtain, and had a sudden desire to rush out into it, to rush away. She got up, and began swiftly pulling off her stockings, then her dress and underclothing, and he held his breath. Her pointed, keen animal breasts tipped and stirred as she moved. She was ivory-coloured in the greenish light. She slipped on her rubber shoes again and ran out with a wild little laugh, holding up her breasts to the heavy rain and spreading her arms, and running blurred in the rain with the eurythmic dance-movements she had learned so long ago in Dresden. It was a strange pallid figure lifting and falling, bending so the rain beat and glistened on the full haunches, swaying up again and coming belly-forward through the rain, then stooping again so that only the full loins and buttocks were offered in a kind of homage towards him, repeating a wild obeisance.

He laughed wryly, and threw off his clothes. It was too much. He jumped out, naked and white, with a little shiver, into the hard, slanting rain. Flossie sprang before him with a frantic little bark. Connie, her hair all wet and sticking to her head, turned her hot face and saw him. Her blue eyes blazed with excitement, as she turned and ran fast, with a strange charging movement, out of the clearing and down the path, the wet boughs whipping her. She ran, and he saw nothing but the round wet head, the wet back leaning forward in flight, the rounded buttocks twinkling: a wonderful cowering female nakedness in flight.

She was nearly at the wide riding when he came up and flung his naked arm round her soft, naked-wet middle. She gave a shriek and straightened herself, and the heap of her soft, chill flesh came up against his body. He pressed it all up against him, madly, the heap of soft chilled female flesh that became quickly warm as flame, in contact. The rain streamed on them till they smoked. He gathered her lovely, heavy posteriors one in each hand and pressed them in towards him in a frenzy, quivering motionless in the rain. Then suddenly he tipped her up and fell with her on the path, in the roaring silence of the rain, and short and sharp, he took her, short and sharp and finished, like an animal.

He got up in an instant, wiping the rain from his eyes.

"Come in," he said, and they started running back to the hut. He ran straight and swift: he didn't like the rain. But she came slower, gathering forget-me-nots and campion and bluebells, running a few steps, and watching him fleeting away from her.

When she came with her flowers, panting to the hut, he had already started a fire, and the twigs were crackling. Her sharp breasts rose and fell, her hair was plastered down with rain, her face was flushed ruddy and her body glistened and trickled. Wide-eyed and breathless, with a small wet head and full, trickling, naïve haunches, she looked another creature.

He took the old sheet and rubbed her down, she standing like a child. Then he rubbed himself, having shut the door of the hut. The fire was blazing up. She ducked her head in the other end of the sheet, and rubbed her wet hair.

"We're drying ourselves together on the same towel, we shall quarrel!" he said.

She looked up for a moment, her hair all odds and ends.

"No!" she said, her eyes wide. "It's not a towel, it's a sheet."

And she went on busily rubbing her head, while he busily rubbed his.

Still panting with their exertions, each wrapped in an army blanket, but the front of the body open to the fire, they sat on a log side by side before the blaze, to get quiet. Connie hated the feel of the blanket against her skin. But now the sheet was all wet.

She dropped her blanket and kneeled on the clay hearth, holding her head to the fire, and shaking her hair, to dry it. He watched the beautiful, curving drop of her haunches. That fascinated him today. How it sloped with a rich down-slope, to the heavy roundness of her buttocks! And in between, folded in the secret warmth, the secret entrances!

He stroked her tail with his hand, long and subtly taking in the curves and the globe-fulness.

"Tha's got such a nice tail on thee," he said, in the throaty, caressive dialect. "Tha's got the nicest arse of anybody. It's the nicest, nicest woman's arse as is! An' ivry bit of it is woman, woman sure as nuts. Tha'rt not one o' them button-arsed lasses as should be lads, are ter! Tha's got a real soft sloping bottom on thee, as a man loves in 'is guts. It's a bottom as could hold the world up, it is."

All the while he spoke he exquisitely stroked the rounded tail, till it seemed as if a slippery sort of fire came from it into his hand. And his finger-tips touched the two secret openings to her body, time after time, with a soft little brush of fire.

"An' if tha shits an' if tha pisses, I'm glad. I don't want a woman as couldna shit nor piss." Connie could not help a sudden snirt of astonished laughter, but he went on unmoved. "Tha'rt real, tha art! Tha'rt real, even a bit of a bitch. Here tha shits an' here tha pisses: an' I lay my hand on 'em both, an' I like thee for it. I like thee for it. Tha's got a proper, woman's arse, proud of itself. It's none ashamed of itself, this isna."

He laid his hand close and firm over her secret places, in a kind of close greeting.

"I like it," he said. "I like it! An' if I only lived ten minutes, an' stroked thy arse an' got to know it, I should reckon I'd lived *one* life, sees ter! Industrial system or not! Here's one o' my lifetimes."

She turned round and climbed into his lap, clinging to him.

"Kiss me!" she whispered.

And she knew the thought of their separation was latent in both their minds, and at last she was sad.

She sat on his thighs, her head against his breast, and her ivory-gleaming legs loosely apart, the fire glowing unequally upon them. Sitting with his head dropped, he looked at the folds of her body in the fire-glow, and at the fleece of soft brown hair that hung down to a point between her open thighs. He reached to the table behind, and took up her bunch of flowers, still so wet that drops of rain fell on to her.

"Flowers stops out of doors all weathers," he said. "They have no houses."

"Not even a hut!" she murmured.

With quiet fingers he threaded a few forget-me-not flowers in the fine brown fleece of the mount of Venus.

"There!" he said. "There's forget-me-nots in the right place!"

She looked down at the milky, odd little flowers among the brown maidenhair at the lower tip of her body.

"Doesn't it look pretty!" she said.

"Pretty as life," he replied.

And he stuck a pink campion-bud among the hair.

"There! That's me where you won't forget me! That's Moses in the bull-rushes."

"You don't mind, do you, that I'm going away?" she asked wistfully, looking up into his face.

But his face was inscrutable, under the heavy brows. He kept it quite blank.

"You do as you wish," he said.

And he spoke in good English.

"But I won't go if you don't wish it," she said, clinging to him.

There was silence. He leaned and put another piece of wood on the fire. The flame glowed on his silent, abstracted face. She waited, but he said nothing.

"Only I thought it would be a good way to begin a break with Clifford. I do want a child. And it would give me a chance to—to—" she resumed.

"To let them think a few lies," he said.

"Yes, that among other things. Do you want them to think the truth?"

"I don't care what they think."

"I do! I don't want them handling me with their unpleasant cold minds: not while I'm still at Wragby. They can think what they like when I'm finally gone."

He was silent.

"But Sir Clifford expects you to come back to him?"

"Oh, I must come back," she said: and there was silence.

"And would you have a child in Wragby?" he asked.

She closed her arm round his neck.

"If you wouldn't take me away, I should have to," she said.

"Take you where to?"

"Anywhere!—away! But right away from Wragby."

"When?"

"Why—when I come back—"

"But what's the good of coming back—doing the thing twice—if you're once gone?" he said.

"Oh, I must come back. I've promised! I've promised so faithfully! Besides, I come back to you, really."

"To your husband's gamekeeper?"

"I don't see that that matters," she said.

"No?" he mused awhile. "And when would you think of going away again, then, finally? when exactly?"

"Oh, I don't know. I'd come back from Venice—and then we'd prepare everything."

"How prepare?"

"Oh—I'd tell Clifford. I'd have to tell him."

"Would you!"

He remained silent. She put her arms fast round his neck.

"Don't make it difficult for me," she pleaded.

"Make what difficult?"

"For me to go to Venice—and arrange things."

A little smile, half a grin, flickered on his face.

"I don't make it difficult," he said. "I only want to find out just what you're after. But you don't really know yourself. You want to take time: get away and look at it. I don't blame you. I think you're wise. You may prefer to stay mistress of Wragby. I don't blame you. I've no Wragbys to offer. In fact, you know what you'll get out of me. No no, I think you're right! I really do! And I'm not keen on coming to live on you, being kept by you. There's that too."

She felt, somehow, as if he were giving her tit for tat.

"But you want me, don't you?" she asked.

"Do you want me?"

"You know I do. *That's* evident."

"Quite! And *when* do you want me?"

"You know we can arrange it all when I come back. Now I'm out of breath with you. I must get calm and clear."

"Quite! Get calm and clear!"

She was a little offended.

"But you trust me, don't you?" she said.

"Oh, absolutely!"

She heard the mockery in his tone.

"Tell me then," she said flatly; "do you think it would be better if I *don't* go to Venice?"

"I'm sure it's better if you *do* go to Venice," he replied, in the cool, slightly mocking voice.

"You know it's next Thursday?" she said.

"Yes!"

She now began to muse. At last she said:

"And we *shall* know better where we are when I come back, shan't we?"

"Oh surely!"

The curious gulf of silence between them!

"I've been to the lawyer about my divorce," he said, a little constrainedly.

She gave a slight shudder.

"Have you!" she said. "And what did he say?"

"He said I ought to have done it before—that may be a difficulty. But since I was in the army—he thinks it'll go through all right.—If only it doesn't bring *her* down on my head!"

"Will she have to know?"

"Yes! She is served with a notice: so is the man she lives with, the co-respondent—"

"Isn't it hateful, all the performances! I suppose I'd have to go through it with Clifford—"

There was a silence.

"And of course," he said, "I have to live an exemplary life for the next six or eight months. So if you go to Venice, there's temptation removed for a week or two, at least."

"Am I temptation!" she said, stroking his face. "I'm so glad I'm temptation to you!—Don't let's think about it! You frighten me when you start thinking: you roll me out flat. Don't let's think about it. We can think so much when we're apart. That's the whole point!—I've been thinking, I *must* come to you for another night before I go. I must come once more to the cottage. Shall I come on Thursday night?"

"Isn't that when your sister will be there?"

"Yes! But she said we'd start at tea-time. So we could start at tea-time. But she could sleep somewhere else, and I could sleep with you."

"But then she'd have to know."

"Oh, I shall tell her. I've more or less told her already. I must talk it all over with Hilda: she's a great help, so sensible."

He was thinking of her plan.

"So you'd start off from Wragby at tea-time, as if you were going to London? Which way were you going?"

"By Nottingham and Grantham."

"And then your sister would drop you somewhere, and you'd walk or drive back here? Sounds very risky, to me."

"Does it?—Well then—well then—Hilda could bring me back. She could sleep at Mansfield, and bring me back here in the evening, and fetch me again in the morning. It's quite easy."

"And the people who see you?"

226

"I'll wear goggles and a veil."

He pondered for some time.

"Well," he said, "you please yourself, as usual."

"But wouldn't it please you?"

"Oh yes! It'd please me all right," he said, a little grimly. "I might as well smite while the iron's hot."

"Do you know what I thought?" she said suddenly. "It suddenly came to me. You are the 'Knight of the Burning Pestle.' "

"Ay! And you? Are you the Lady of the Red-hot Mortar?"

"Yes!" she said. "Yes! You're Sir Pestle and I'm Lady Mortar."

"All right—then I'm knighted. John Thomas is Sir John, to your Lady Jane."

"Yes! John Thomas is knighted! I'm my-lady-maidenhair, and you must have flowers too. Yes!"

She threaded two pink campions in the bush of red-gold hair above his penis.

"There!" she said. "Charming! Charming! Sir John!"

And she pushed a bit of forget-me-not in the dark hair of his breast.

"And you won't forget me *there*, will you?" She kissed him on the breast, and made two bits of forget-me-not lodge one over each nipple, kissing him again.

"Make a calendar of me!" he said. He laughed, and the flowers shook from his breast.

"Wait a bit!" he said.

He rose, and opened the door of the hut. Flossie, lying on the porch, got up and looked at him.

"Ay, it's me!" he said.

The rain had ceased. There was a wet, heavy, perfumed stillness. Evening was approaching.

He went out and down the little path in the opposite direction from the riding. Connie watched his thin, white figure, and it looked to her like a ghost, an apparition moving away from her. When she could see it no more, her heart sank. She stood in the door of the hut, with a blanket round her, looking into the drenched, motionless silence.

But he was coming back, trotting strangely, and carrying flowers. She was a little afraid of him, as if he were not quite human. And when he came near, his eyes looked into hers, but she could not understand the meaning.

He had brought columbines and campions, and new-mown-hay, and oak-tufts and honeysuckle in small bud. He fastened fluffy young oak-sprays round her head, and honeysuckle withes round her breasts, sticking in tufts of bluebells and campion: and in her navel he poised a pink campion flower, and in her maidenhair were forget-me-nots and wood-ruff.

"That's you in all your glory!" he said. "Lady Jane, at her wedding with John Thomas."

And he stuck flowers in the hair of his own body, and wound a bit of creeping-jenny round his penis, and stuck a single bell of a hyacinth in his navel. She watched him with amusement, his odd intentness. And she pushed a campion flower in his moustache, where it stuck, dangling under his nose.

"This is John Thomas marryin' Lady Jane," he said. "An' we mun let Constance an' Oliver go their ways. Maybe—" He spread out his hand with a gesture, and then he sneezed, sneezing away the flowers from his nose and his navel. He sneezed again.

"Maybe what?" she said, waiting for him to go on.

He looked at her a little bewildered.

"Eh?" he said.

"Maybe what? Go on with what you were going to say," she insisted.

"Ay, what *was* I going to say?—"

He had forgotten. And it was one of the disappointments of her life, that he never finished.

A yellow ray of sun shone over the trees.

"Sun!" he said. "And time you went. Time, my lady, time! What's that as flies without wings, your ladyship? Time! Time!"

He reached for his shirt.

"Say goodnight! to John Thomas," he said, looking down at his penis. "He's safe in the arms of creeping-jenny! Not much burning pestle about him just now."

And he put his thin flannel shirt over his head.

"A man's most dangerous moment," he said, when his head had emerged, "is when he's getting into his shirt. Then he puts his head in a bag. That's why I prefer those American shirts, that you put on like a jacket." She still stood watching him. He stepped into his short drawers, and buttoned them round the waist.

"Look at Jane!" he said. "In all her blossoms! Who'll put blossoms on you next year, Jinny? Me, or somebody else? 'Good-bye my bluebell, farewell to you—!' I hate that song, it's early war days." He had sat down, and was pulling on his stockings. She still stood unmoving. He laid his hand on the slope of her buttocks. "Pretty little lady Jane!" he said. "Perhaps in Venice you'll find a man who'll put jasmine in your maidenhair, and a pomegranate flower in your navel. Poor little lady Jane!"

"Don't say those things!" she said. "You only say them to hurt me."

He dropped his head. Then he said, in dialect:

"Ay, maybe I do, maybe I do! Well then, I'll say nowt, an' ha' done wi' t. But tha mun dress thysen, an' go back to thy stately homes of England, how beautiful they stand. Time's up! Time's up for Sir John, an' for little lady Jane! Put thy shimmy on, Lady Chatterley! Tha might be anybody, standin' there be-out even a shimmy, an' a few rags o' flowers. There then, there then, I'll undress thee, tha bob-tailed young throstle—" And he took the leaves from her hair, kissing her damp hair, and the flowers from her breasts, and kissed her breasts, and kissed her navel, and kissed her maidenhair, where he left the flowers threaded. "They mun stop while they will," he said. "So! There tha 'rt bare again, nowt but a bare-arsed lass an' a bit of a lady Jane! Now put thy shimmy on, for tha mun go, or else Lady Chatterley's goin' to be late for dinner, an' where 'ave yer been to my pretty maid!"

She never knew how to answer him when he was in this condition of the vernacular. So she dressed herself and prepared to go a little ignominiously home to Wragby. Or so she felt it: a little ignominiously home.

He would accompany her to the broad riding. His young pheasants were all right under the shelter.

When he and she came out on to the riding, there was Mrs Bolton faltering palely towards them.

"Oh, my Lady, we wondered if anything had happened!"

"No! Nothing has happened."

Mrs Bolton looked into the man's face, that was smooth and new-looking with love. She met his half-laughing, half-mocking eyes. He always laughed at mischance. But he looked at her kindly.

"Evening, Mrs Bolton!—Your Ladyship will be all right now, so I can leave you. Good-night to your Ladyship! Good-night Mrs Bolton!"

He saluted, and turned away.

CHAPTER XVI.

Connie arrived home to an ordeal of cross-questioning. Clifford had been out at tea-time, had come in just before the storm, and where was her ladyship? Nobody knew—only Mrs Bolton suggested she had gone for a walk into the wood. Into the wood, in such a storm!—Clifford for once let himself get into a state of nervous frenzy. He started at every flash of lightning, and blenched at every roll of thunder. He looked at the icy thunder-rain as if it were the end of the world. He got more and more worked up.

Mrs Bolton tried to soothe him.

"She'll be sheltering in the hut till it's over. Don't you worry, her Ladyship is all right."

"I don't like her being in the wood in a storm like this! I don't like her being in the wood at all! She's been gone now more than two hours. When did she go out?"

"A little while before you came in."

"I didn't see her in the park. God knows where she is and what's happened to her."

"Oh, nothing's happened to her. You'll see, she'll be home directly after the rain stops. It's just the rain that's keeping her."

But her ladyship did not come home directly the rain stopped. In fact, time went by, the sun came out for his last yellow glimpse, and still there was no sign of her. The sun was set, it was growing dark, and the first dinner-gong had rung.

"It's no good!" said Clifford in a frenzy. "I'm going to send out Field and Betts to find her."

"Oh don't do that!" cried Mrs Bolton. "They'll think there's suicide or something. Oh don't start a lot of talk going! Let me slip over to the hut and see if she's not there. I'll find her all right."

So, after some persuasion, Clifford allowed her to go.

And so Connie had come upon her in the drive, alone and palely loitering.

"You mustn't mind me coming to look for you, my Lady! But Sir Clifford worked himself up into such a state! He made sure you were struck by lightning, or killed by a falling tree. And he was determined to send Field and Betts to the wood to find the body. So I thought I'd better come, rather than set all the servants agog."

She spoke nervously. She could still see on Connie's face the smoothness and the half-dream of passion, and she could feel the irritation against herself.

"Quite!" said Connie. And she could say no more.

The two women plodded on through the wet world, in silence, while great drops plashed like explosions in the wood. When they came to the park, Connie strode ahead, and Mrs Bolton panted a little. She was getting plumper.

"How foolish of Clifford to make a fuss!" said Connie at length, angrily, really speaking to herself.

"Oh, you know what men are! They like working themselves up. But he'll be all right as soon as he sees your Ladyship."

Connie was very angry that Mrs Bolton knew her secret: for certainly she knew it.

Suddenly Constance stood still on the path.

"It's monstrous that I have to be followed!" she said, her eyes flashing.

"Oh, your Ladyship, don't say that! He'd certainly have sent the two men—and they'd have come straight to the hut. I didn't know where it was, really—"

Connie flushed darker with rage, at the suggestion. Yet, while her passion was on her, she could not lie. She could not even pretend there was nothing between herself and the keeper. She looked at the other woman, who stood so sly, with her head dropped: yet somehow, in her femaleness, an ally.

"Oh well!" she said. "If it is so it is so. I don't mind!"

"Why you're all right, my Lady! You've only been sheltering in the hut. It's all absolutely nothing."

They went on to the house. Connie marched in to Clifford's room, furious with him, furious with his pale, over-wrought face and prominent eyes.

"I must say, I don't think you need send the servants after me!" she burst out.

"My God!" he exploded. "Where have you been, woman? You've been gone hours, hours—and in a storm like this! What the hell do you go to that bloody wood for? What have you been up to? It's hours even since the rain stopped—hours! Do you know what time it is?

You're enough to drive anybody mad. Where have you been? What in the name of hell have you been doing?"

"And what if I don't choose to tell you?"—She pulled her hat from her head and shook her hair.

He looked at her with his eyes bulging, and yellow coming into the whites. It was very bad for him to get in these rages: Mrs Bolton had a weary time with him, for days after. Connie felt a sudden qualm.

"But really!" she said, milder. "Anyone would think I'd been I don't know where! I just sat in the hut during all the storm, and made myself a little fire, and was happy."

She spoke now easily. After all, why work him up any more!—He looked at her suspiciously.

"And look at your hair!" he said. "Look at yourself—!"

"Yes!" she replied calmly. "I ran out in the rain with no clothes on."

He stared at her speechless.

"You must be mad!" he said.

"Why? To like a shower-bath from the rain?"

"And how did you dry yourself?"

"On an old towel—and at the fire."

He still stared at her in a dumbfounded way.

"And supposing anybody came," he said.

"Who should come?"

"Who? Why anybody! And Mellors. Doesn't he come? He must come in the evenings—"

"Yes, he came later, when it had cleared up—to feed the pheasants with corn."

She spoke with amazing nonchalance. Mrs Bolton, who was listening in the next room, heard in sheer admiration. To think a woman could carry it off so naturally!

"And suppose he'd come while you were running about in the rain with nothing on, like a maniac?"

"I suppose he'd have had the fright of his life, and cleared out as fast as he could."

Clifford still stared at her transfixed. What he thought in his under-consciousness he would never know. And he was too much taken aback to form one clear thought in his upper consciousness. He just simply accepted what she said, in a sort of blank. And he admired her. He could not help admiring her. She looked so flushed and handsome and smooth: love-smooth.

"At least," he said, subsiding, "you'll be lucky if you've got off without a severe cold."

"Oh, I haven't got a cold," she replied. She was thinking to herself of the other man's words: Tha's got the nicest woman's arse of anybody!—She wished, she dearly wished she could tell Clifford that this had been said to her, during the famous thunder-storm. However! She bore herself rather like an offended queen, and went upstairs to change.

That evening, Clifford wanted to be nice to her. He was reading one of the latest scientific-religious books: he had a streak of a spurious sort of religion in him, and was ego-centrically concerned with the future of his own ego. It was his habit to make conversation to Connie about some book, since the conversation between them had to be made, almost chemically. They had almost chemically to concoct it in their heads.

"What do you think of this, by the way?" he said, reaching for his book. "You'd have no need to cool your ardent body by running out in the rain, if only we had a few more aeons of evolution behind us. Ah—here it is!—'The universe shows us two aspects: on one side it is physically wasting, on the other it is spiritually ascending—'"

Connie listened, expecting more. But Clifford was waiting. She looked at him in surprise.

"And if it spiritually ascends," she said, "what does it leave down below, in the place where its tail used to be?"

"Ah!" he said. "Take the man for what he means. *Ascending* is the opposite of his *wasting*, I presume."

"Spiritually blown out, so to speak!"

"No but seriously, without joking: do you think there is anything in it?"

She looked at him again.

"Physically wasting?" she said. "I see you getting fatter, and I'm not wasting myself. Do you think the sun is smaller than he used to be? He's not to me. And I suppose the apple Adam offered Eve wasn't really much bigger, if any, than one of our orange pippins. Do you think it was?"

"Well hear how he goes on: 'It is thus slowly passing, with a slowness inconceivable in our measures of time, to new creative conditions, amid which the physical world, as we at present know it, will be represented by a ripple barely to be distinguished from nonentity.'"

233

She listened with a glisten of amusement. All sorts of improper things suggested themselves. But she only said:

"What silly hocus-pocus! As if his little conceited consciousness could know what was happening as slowly as all that! It only means *he's* a physical failure on the earth, so he wants to make the whole universe a physical failure. Priggish little impertinence!"

"Oh but listen! Don't interrupt the great man's solemn words!—'The present type of order in the world has risen from an unimaginable past, and it will find its grave in an unimaginable future. There remains the inexhaustive realm of abstract forms, and creativity, with its shifting character ever determined afresh by its own creatures, and God, upon whose wisdom all forms of order depend.'—There, that's how he winds up!"

Connie sat listening contemptuously.

"He's spiritually blown out," she said. "What a lot of stuff! Unimaginables, and types of order in graves, and realms of abstract forms, and creativity with a shifty character, and God mixed up with forms of order! Why it's idiotic!"

"I must say, it is a little vaguely conglomerate—a mixture of gases, so to speak," said Clifford. "Still, I think there is something in the idea that the universe is physically wasting and spiritually ascending."

"Do you? Then let it ascend, so long as it leaves me safely and solidly physically here below."

"Do you like your physique?" he asked.

"I love it!"—And through her mind went the words: It's the nicest, nicest woman's arse as is!

"But that's really rather extraordinary, because there's no denying it's an encumbrance. But then I suppose a woman doesn't take a supreme pleasure in the life of the mind."

"Supreme pleasure?" she said, looking up at him. "Is that sort of idiocy the supreme pleasure of the life of the mind? No thank you! Give me the body. I believe the life of the body is a greater reality than the life of the mind: when the body is really wakened to life. But so many people, like your famous wind-machine, have only got minds tacked on to their physical corpses."

He looked at her in wonder.

"The life of the body," he said, "is just the life of the animals."

"And that's better than the life of professorial corpses.—But it's not true! The human body is only just coming to real life. With the

Greeks it gave a lovely flicker, then Plato and Aristotle killed it, and Jesus finished it off. But now the body is coming really to life, is really rising from the tomb. And it will be a lovely, lovely life in the lovely universe, the life of the human body."

"My dear, you speak as if you were ushering it all in! True, you are going away on a holiday: but don't please be quite so indecently elated about it.——Believe me, whatever God there is is slowly eliminating the guts and alimentary system from the human being, to evolve a higher, more spiritual being."

"Why should I believe you, Clifford, when I feel that whatever God there is has at last wakened up in my guts, as you call them, and is rippling so happily there, like dawn. Why should I believe you, when I feel so very much the contrary?"

"Oh exactly!——And what has caused this extraordinary change in you? running out stark naked in the rain, and playing Bacchante? desire for sensation, or the anticipation of going to Venice?"

"Both! Do you think it's horrid of me to be so thrilled at going off?" she said.

"Rather horrid to show it so plainly."

"Then I'll hide it."

"Oh, don't trouble! You almost communicate a thrill to me. I almost feel that it is *I* who am going off."

"Well, why don't you come?"

"We've gone over all that. And as a matter of fact, I suppose your greatest thrill comes from being able to say a temporary farewell to all this. Nothing so thrilling, for the moment, as goodbye-to-it-all! But every parting means a meeting elsewhere. And every meeting is a new bondage——"

"I'm not going to enter any new bondages."

"Don't boast, while the gods are listening," he said.

She pulled up short.

"No! I won't boast!" she said.

But she was thrilled, none the less, to be going off: to feel bonds snap. She couldn't help it.

Clifford, who couldn't sleep, gambled all night with Mrs Bolton, till she was too sleepy almost to live.

And the day came round for Hilda to arrive. Connie had arranged with Mellors that if everything promised well for their night together, she would hang a green shawl out of her window. If there were frustration, a red one.

Mrs Bolton helped Connie to pack.

"It will be so good for your Ladyship to have a change."

"I think it will. You don't mind having Sir Clifford on your hands alone for a time, do you?"

"Oh no! I can manage him quite all right. I mean, I can do all he needs me to do. Don't you think he's better than he used to be?"

"Oh much! You do wonders with him."

"Do I though!—But men are all alike: just babies, and you have to flatter them and wheedle them and let them think they're having their own way.—Don't you find it so, my Lady?"

"I'm afraid I haven't much experience."

Connie paused in her occupation.

"Even your husband, did you have to manage him, and wheedle him like a baby?" she asked, looking at the other woman.

Mrs Bolton paused too.

"Well!" she said. "I had to do a good bit of coaxing, with him too. But he always knew what I was after, I must say that. But he generally gave in to me."

"He was never the lord and master thing?"

"No! At least—there'd be a look in his eyes sometimes, and then I knew *I'd* got to give in. But usually he gave in to me. No, he was never lord and master. But neither was I. I knew when I could go no further with him, and then I gave in: though it cost me a good bit, sometimes."

"And what if you had held out against him?"

"Oh, I don't know. I never did. Even when he was in the wrong, if he was fixed, I gave in. You see I never wanted to break what was between us. And if you really set your will against a man, that finishes it. If you care for a man, you have to give in to him once he's really determined; whether you're in the right or not, you have to give in. Else you break something. But I must say, Ted 'ud give in to me sometimes, when I was set on a thing, and in the wrong. So I suppose it cuts both ways."

"And that's how you are with all your patients?" asked Connie.

"Oh, that's different. I don't care at all, in the same way. I know what's good for them, or I try to—and then I just contrive to manage them for their own good. It's not like anybody as you're really fond of. It's quite different. Once you've been really fond of a man, you can be affectionate to almost any man, if he needs you at all. But it's not the same thing. You don't really *care*. I doubt, once you've *really* cared, if you can ever care again."

These words frightened Connie.

"Do you think one can only care once?" she asked.

"Or never. Most women never cares—never begin to. They don't know what it means. Nor men either. But when I see a woman as cares, my heart stands still for her."

"And do you think men easily take offence?"

"Yes! If you wound them on their pride. But aren't women the same? Only our two prides are a bit different."

Connie pondered this. She began again to have some misgiving about her going away. After all, was she not giving her man the go-by, if only for a short time? And he knew it. That's why he was so queer and sarcastic.

Still! the human existence is a good deal controlled by the machine of external circumstance. She was in the power of this machine. She couldn't extricate herself all in five minutes. She didn't even want to.

Hilda arrived in good time on the Thursday morning, in a nimble two-seater car, with her suit-case strapped firmly behind. She looked as demure and maidenly as ever, but she had the same will of her own. She had the very hell of a will of her own, as her husband had found out. But the husband was now divorcing her. Yes—she even made it easy for him to do that, though she had no lover. For the time being, she was "off" men. She was very well content to be quite her own mistress: and mistress of her two children, whom she was going to bring up "properly," whatever that may mean.

Connie was only allowed a suit-case, also. But she had sent on a trunk to her father, who was going by train. No use taking a car to Venice. And Italy much too hot to motor in, in July. He was going comfortably by train. He had just come down from Scotland.

So, like a demure arcadian field-marshall, Hilda arranged the material part of the journey. She and Connie sat in the upstairs room, chatting.

"But Hilda!" said Connie, a little frightened. "I want to stay near here tonight. Not here: near here!"

Hilda fixed her sister with grey, inscrutable eyes. She seemed so calm: and she was so often furious.

"Where, near here?" she asked softly.

"Well—you know I love somebody, don't you—?"

"I gathered there was something."

"Well—he lives near here—and I want to spend this last night with him. I must! I've promised." Connie became insistent.

Hilda bent her Minerva-like head in silence. Then she looked up. "Do you want to tell me who he is?" she said.

"He's our gamekeeper," faltered Connie, and she flushed vividly, like a shamed child.

"Connie!" said Hilda, lifting her nose slightly with disgust: a motion she had from her mother.

"I know: but he's lovely really. He—he—he really understands tenderness," said Connie, trying to apologise for him.

Hilda, like a ruddy, rich-coloured Athena, bowed her head and pondered. She was really violently angry. But she dared not show it, because Connie, taking after her father, would straightway become obstreperous and unmanageable.

It was true, Hilda did not like Clifford: his cool assurance that he was somebody! She thought he made use of Connie shamefully and impudently. She had hoped her sister *would* leave him. But, being solid Scotch middle-class, she loathed any "lowering" of oneself, or the family.

She looked up at last.

"You'll regret it," she said.

"I shan't," cried Connie, flushed red. "He's quite the exception. I *really* love him. He's lovely as a lover."

Hilda still pondered.

"You'll get over him quite soon," she said, "and live to be ashamed of yourself because of him."

"I shan't! I hope I'm going to have a child of his."

"*Connie!*" said Hilda, hard as a hammer-stroke, and pale with anger.

"I shall if I possibly can. I should be fearfully proud if I had a child by him."

It was no use talking to her. Hilda pondered.

"And doesn't Clifford suspect?" she said.

"Oh no! Why should he?"

"I've no doubt you've given him plenty of occasion for suspicion," said Hilda.

"Not at all."

"And tonight's business seems quite gratuitous folly. Where does the man live?"

"In the cottage at the other end of the wood."

"Is he a bachelor?"

"No! His wife left him."

"How old?"

"I don't know. Older than me."

Hilda became more angry at every reply, angry as her mother used to be, in a kind of paroxysm. But still she hid it.

"I would give up tonight's escapade if I were you," she advised calmly.

"I can't! I *must* stay with him tonight, or I can't go to Venice at all. I just can't."

Hilda heard her father over again, and she gave way, out of mere diplomacy. And she consented to drive to Mansfield, both of them, to dinner—to bring Connie back to the lane-end after dark, and to fetch her from the lane-end the next morning: herself sleeping in Mansfield, only half-an-hour away, good going. But she was furious. She stored it up against her sister, this balk in her plans.

Connie flung an emerald-green shawl over her window-sill.

On the strength of her anger, Hilda warmed towards Clifford. After all, he had a mind. And if he had no sex, functionally, all the better: so much the less to quarrel about! Hilda wanted no more of that sex business, where men became nasty, selfish little horrors. Connie really had less to put up with than a great many women, if she did but know it.

And Clifford decided that Hilda, after all, was a decidedly intelligent woman, and would make a man a first-rate help-meet, if he were going in for politics, for example. Yes, she had none of Connie's silliness. Connie was more a child: you had to make excuses for her, because she wasn't altogether dependable—.

There was an early cup of tea in the hall, where doors were open to let in the sun. Everybody seemed to be panting a little.

"Good-bye, Connie girl! Come back to me safely."

"Good-bye, Clifford! Yes, I shan't be long." Connie was almost tender.

"Good-bye, Hilda! You'll keep an eye on her, won't you?"

"I'll even keep two!" said Hilda. "She shan't go very far astray."

"It's a promise!"

"Good-bye, Mrs Bolton! I know you'll look after Sir Clifford nobly."

"I'll do what I can, your Ladyship."

"And write to me if there is any news, and tell me about Sir Clifford, how he is."

"Very good, your Ladyship, I will. And have a good time, and come back and cheer us up."

Everybody waved. The car went off. Connie looked back and saw Clifford sitting at the top of the steps in his house-chair. After all, he was her husband: Wragby was her home: circumstance had done it.

Mrs Chambers held the gate and wished her ladyship a happy holiday. The car slipped out of the dark spinney that masked the park, on to the high-road where the colliers were trailing home. Hilda turned to the Crosshill Road, that was not a main road, but ran to Mansfield. Connie put on goggles. They ran beside the railway, which was in a cutting below them. Then they crossed the cutting on a bridge.

"That's the lane to the cottage!" said Connie.

Hilda glanced at it impatiently.

"It's a frightful pity we can't go straight off!" she said. "We could have been in Pall Mall by nine o'clock."

"I'm sorry for your sake," said Connie, from behind her goggles.

They were soon at Mansfield, that once-romantic, now utterly disheartening colliery town. Hilda stopped at the hotel named in the motor-car book, and took a room. The whole thing was utterly uninteresting, and she was almost too angry to talk. However, Connie *had* to tell her something of the man's history.

"*He*! *He*! What name do you call him by? You only say *he*!" said Hilda.

"I've never called him by any name: nor he me: which is curious, when you come to think of it. Unless we say Lady Jane and John Thomas. But his name is Oliver Mellors."

"And how would you like to be Mrs Oliver Mellors, instead of Lady Chatterley?"

"I'd love it."

There was nothing to be done with Connie. And anyhow, if the man had been a lieutenant in the army in India for four or five years, he must be more or less presentable. Apparently he had character. Hilda began to relent a little.

"But you'll be through with him in a while," she said, "and then you'll be ashamed of having been connected with him. One *can't* mix up with the working people."

"But you're such a socialist! you're always on the side of the working classes."

"I may be on their side in a political crisis, but being on their side makes me know how impossible it is to mix one's life with theirs. Not out of snobbery—but just because the whole rhythm is different."

Hilda had lived among the real political intellectuals, so she was disastrously unanswerable.

The nondescript evening in the hotel dragged out, and at last they had a nondescript dinner. Then Connie slipped a few things into a little silk bag, and combed her hair once more.

"After all, Hilda," she said, "love can be wonderful; when you feel you *live*, and are in the very middle of creation."—It was almost like bragging on her part.

"I suppose every mosquito feels the same," said Hilda.

"Do you think it does? How nice for it!"

The evening was wonderfully clear and long-lingering, even in the dismal town. It would be half-light all night. With a face like a mask, from resentment, Hilda started the car again, and the two sped back on their traces, taking the other road, through Bolsover. Connie wore her goggles and disguising cap, and she sat in silence. Because of Hilda's opposition, she was fiercely on the side of the man, she would stand by him through thick and thin.

They had the head-lights on, by the time they passed Crosshill, and the small lit-up train that chuffed past in the cutting made it seem like real night. Hilda had calculated the turn into the lane at the bridge-end. She slowed up rather suddenly, and swerved off the road, the lights glaring white into the grassy, overgrown lane. Connie looked out. She saw a shadowy figure, and she opened the door.

"Here we are!" she said softly.

But Hilda had switched off the lights, and was absorbed backing, making the turn.

"Nothing on the bridge?" she asked shortly.

"You're all right," said the man's voice.

She backed on to the bridge, reversed, let the car run forwards a few yards along the road, then backed into the lane, under a wych-elm tree, crushing the grass and bracken. Then all the lights went out. Connie stepped down. The man stood under the trees.

"Did you wait long?" Connie asked.

"Not so very," he replied.

They both waited for Hilda to get out. But Hilda shut the door of the car and sat tight.

"This is my sister Hilda. Won't you come and speak to her?—Hilda! This is Mr Mellors."

The keeper lifted his hat, but went no nearer.

"Do walk down to the cottage with us, Hilda," Connie pleaded. "It's not far."

"What about the car?"

"People do leave them in the lanes. You have the key."

Hilda was silent, deliberating. Then she looked backwards down the lane.

"Can I back round that bush?" she said.

"Oh yes!" said the keeper.

She backed slowly round the curve, out of sight of the road, locked the car, and got down. It was night, but luminous dark. The hedges rose high and wild, by the unused lane, and very dark seeming. There was a fresh sweet scent in the air. The keeper went ahead, then came Connie, then Hilda, and in silence. He lit up the difficult places with a flash-light torch, and they went on again, while an owl softly hooted over the oaks, and Flossie padded silently around. Nobody could speak: there was nothing to say.

At length Connie saw the yellow light of the house, and her heart beat fast. She was a little frightened. They trailed on, still in Indian file.

He unlocked the door, and preceded them into the warm, but bare little room. The fire burned low and red in the grate. The table was set with two plates and two glasses, on a proper white table-cloth for once. Hilda shook her hair and looked round the bare, cheerless room. Then she summoned her courage and looked at the man.

He was moderately tall, and thin, and she thought him good-looking. He kept a quiet distance of his own, and seemed absolutely unwilling to speak.

"Do sit down, Hilda," said Connie.

"Do!" he said. "Can I make you tea or anything—or will you drink a glass of beer? It's moderately cool."

"Beer!" said Connie.

"Beer for me, please!" said Hilda, with a mock sort of shyness. He looked at her, and blinked.

He took a blue jug and tramped to the scullery. When he came back with the beer, his face had changed again.

Connie sat down by the door, and Hilda sat in his seat, with the back to the wall, against the window corner.

"That is his chair," said Connie softly. And Hilda rose as if it had burnt her.

"Sit yer still, sit yer still! Ta'e ony cheer as yo'n a mind to, none of us is th' big bear," he said, with complete equanimity.

And he brought Hilda a glass, and poured her beer first from the blue jug.

"As for cigarettes," he said, "I've got none, but 'appen you've got your own. I dunna smoke, mysen.—Shall y' eat summat?"—He turned direct to Connie. "Shall t' eat a smite o' summat, if I bring it thee? Tha can usually do wi' a bite." He spoke the vernacular with a curious calm assurance, as if he were the landlord of the inn.

"What is there?" asked Connie, flushing.

"Boiled ham, cheese, pickled wa'nuts, if yer like.—Nowt much."

"Yes," said Connie. "Won't you, Hilda?"

Hilda looked up at him.

"Why do you speak Yorkshire?" she said softly.

"That! That's non Yorkshire, that's Derby."

He looked back at her with that faint, distant grin.

"Derby, then! Why do you speak Derby? You spoke natural English at first."

"Did Ah though? An' canna Ah change if Ah'n a mind to 't? Nay nay, let me talk Derby if it suits me. If yo'n nowt against it."

"It sounds a little affected," said Hilda.

"Ay, 'appen so! An' up i' Tevershall yo'd sound affected."—He looked again at her, with a queer calculating distance, along his cheek-bones: as if to say: Yi, an' who are you?

He tramped away to the pantry for the food.

The sisters sat in silence. He brought another plate, and knife and fork. Then he said:

"An' if it's the same to you, I s'll ta'e my coat off, like I allers do."

And he took off his coat, and hung it on the peg, then sat down to table in his shirt-sleeves: a shirt of thin, cream-coloured flannel.

"'elp yerselves!" he said. "'elp yerselves! Dunna wait f'r axin!"

He cut the bread, then sat motionless. Hilda felt, as Connie once used to, his power of silence and distance. She saw his smallish, sensitive, loose hand on the table. He was no simple working man, not he: he was acting! acting!

"Still!" she said, as she took a little cheese. "It would be more natural if you spoke to us in normal English, not in vernacular."

He looked at her, feeling her devil of a will.

"Would it?" he said, in the normal English. "Would it? Would anything that was said between you and me be quite natural, unless you said you wished me to hell before your sister ever saw me again: and unless I said something almost as unpleasant back again? Would anything else be natural?"

"Oh yes!" said Hilda. "Just good manners would be quite natural."

"Second nature, so to speak!" he said: then he began to laugh. "Nay," he said. "I'm weary o' manners. Let me be!"

Hilda was frankly baffled, and furiously annoyed. After all, he might show that he realised he was being honoured. Instead of which, with his play-acting and lordly airs, he seemed to think it was he who was conferring the honour. Just impudence! Poor misguided Connie, in the man's clutches!

The three ate in silence. Hilda looked to see what his table-manners were like. She could not help realising that he was instinctively much more delicate and well-bred than herself. She had a certain Scottish clumsiness. And moreover, he had all the quiet, self-contained assurance of the English, no loose edges. It would be very difficult to get the better of him.

But neither would he get the better of her.

"And do you really think," she said, a little more humanly, "it's worth the risk?"

"Is what worth what risk?"

"This escapade with my sister."

He flickered his irritating grin.

"Yo' maun ax 'er!"

Then he looked at Connie.

"Tha comes o' thy own accord, lass, doesn't ter? It's non me as forces thee?"

Connie looked at Hilda.

"I wish you wouldn't cavil, Hilda."

"Naturally I don't want to. But someone has to think about things.—You've got to have some sort of continuity in your life. You can't just go making a mess."

There was a moment's pause.

"Eh, continuity!" he said. "An' what by that? What continuity 'ave

244

yer got i' *your* life? I thought you was gettin' divorced. What continuity's that? Continuity o' yer own stubbornness—I can see that much. An' what good's it goin' to do yer? Yo'll be sick o' yer continuity afore yer a fat sight older. A stubborn woman an' 'er own self-will: ay, they make a fast continuity, they do. Thank Heaven, it isn't me as 'as got th' andlin' of yer!"

"What right have you to speak like that to me?" said Hilda.

"Right! What right ha' yo' ter start harnessin' other folks i' your continuity? Leave folks to their own continuities."

"My dear man, do you think I am concerned with you?" said Hilda softly.

"Ay," he said. "Yo' are. For it's a force-put. Yo' more or less my sister-in-law."

"Still far from it, I assure you."

"Not a' that far, I assure *you*. I've got my own sort o' continuity, back your life! Good as yours, any day. An' if your sister there comes ter me for a bit o' cunt an' tenderness, she knows what she's after. She's been in my bed afore: which you 'aven't, thank the Lord, with your continuity." There was a dead pause, before he added: "—Eh, I don't wear me breeches arse-forrards. An' if I get a windfall, I thank my stars. A man gets a lot of enjoyment out o' that lass theer—which is more than anybody gets out o' th' likes o' you. Which is a pity, for you might 'appen 'a bin a good apple, 'stead of a handsome crab. Women like you needs proper graftin'."

He was looking at her with an odd, flickering smile, faintly sensual and appreciative.

"And men like you," she said, "ought to be segregated: justifying their own vulgarity and selfish lust."

"Ay, ma'am! It's a mercy there's a few men left like me. But you deserve what you get: to be left severely alone."

Hilda had risen and gone to the door. He rose and took his coat from the peg.

"I can find my way quite well alone," she said.

"I doubt you can't," he replied easily.

They tramped in ridiculous file down the lane again, in silence. An owl still hooted. He knew he ought to shoot it.

The car stood untouched, a little dewy. Hilda got in and started the engine. The other two waited.

"All I mean," she said from her entrenchment, "is that I doubt if you'll find it's been worth it—either of you."

"One man's meat is another man's poison," he said, out of the darkness. "But it's meat an' drink to me."

The lights flared out.

"Don't make me wait in the morning, Connie."

"No, I won't. Good night, Hilda!"

The car rose slowly on to the high-road, then slid swiftly away, leaving the night silent.

Connie timidly took his arm, and they went down the lane. He did not speak. At length she drew him to a standstill.

"Kiss me!" she murmured.

"Nay, wait a bit! Let me simmer down," he said.

That amused her. She still kept hold of his arm, and they went quickly down the lane, in silence. She was so glad to be with him, just now. She shivered, knowing that Hilda might have snatched her away. He was inscrutably silent.

When they were in the cottage again, she almost jumped with pleasure, that she should be free of her sister.

"But you were horrid to Hilda," she said to him.

"She should ha' been slapped in time."

"But why?—and she's *so* nice."

He didn't answer, went round doing the evening chores, with a quiet, inevitable sort of motion. He was outwardly angry, but not with her. So Connie felt. He was angry, but at the core of his anger, he liked her. And his anger gave him a peculiar handsomeness, an inwardness and glisten that thrilled her and made her limbs go molten. Still, he took no notice of her.

Till he sat down and began to unlace his boots. Then he looked up at her from under his brows, on which the anger still sat firm.

"Shan't yer go up?" he said. "There's candle!"

He jerked his head slightly to indicate the candle burning on the table. She took it obediently, and he watched the full curve of her hips as she went up the first stairs.

It was a night of sensual passion, in which she was a little startled, and almost unwilling: yet pierced again with piercing thrills of sensuality, different, sharper, more terrible than the thrills of tenderness, but, at the moment, more desirable. Though a little frightened, she let him have his way, and the reckless, shameless sensuality shook her to her foundations, stripped her to the very last, and made a different woman of her. It was not really love. It was not voluptuousness. It was sensuality sharp and searing as fire, burning the soul to tinder.

Burning out the shames, the deepest, oldest shames, in the most secret places. It cost her an effort to let him have his way and his will of her. She had to be a passive, consenting thing, like a slave, a physical slave. Yet the passion licked round her, consuming, and when the sensual flame of it passed through her bowels and breast, she really thought she was dying: yet a poignant, marvellous death.

She had often wondered what Abélard meant, when he said that in their year of love he and Heloïse had passed through all the stages and refinements of passion. The same thing, a thousand years ago: ten thousand years ago! The same on the Greek vases—everywhere! The refinements of passion, the extravagances of sensuality! And necessary, forever necessary, to burn out false shames and smelt out the heaviest ore of the body into purity. With the fire of sheer sensuality.

In this short summer night she learnt so much. She would have thought a woman would have died of shame. Instead of which, the shame died. Shame, which is fear: the deep organic shame, the old, old physical fear which crouches in the bodily roots of us, and can only be chased away by the sensual fire, at last it was roused up and routed by the phallic hunt of the man, and she came to the very heart of the jungle of herself. She felt, now, she had come to the real bed-rock of her nature, and was essentially shameless. She was her sensual self, naked and unashamed. She felt a triumph, almost a vainglory. So! That was how it was! That was life! That was how oneself really was! There was nothing left to disguise or be ashamed of. She shared her ultimate nakedness with a man, another being.

And what a reckless devil the man was! really like a devil! One had to be strong to bear him. But it took some getting at, the core of the physical jungle, the last and deepest recess of organic shame. The phallos alone could explore it. And how he had pressed in on her! And how, in fear, she had hated it! But how she had really wanted it! She knew now. At the bottom of her soul, fundamentally, she had needed this phallic hunting out, she had secretly wanted it, and she had believed she would never get it. Now suddenly there it was, and a man was sharing her last and final nakedness, she was shameless.

What liars poets and everybody were! They made one think one wanted sentiment. When what one supremely wanted was this piercing, consuming, rather awful sensuality. To find a man who dared do it, without shame or sin or final misgiving! If he had been ashamed afterwards, and made one feel ashamed, how awful! What a pity that fine, sensual men are so rare! What a pity most men are so doggy, a bit shameful. Like Clifford! Like Michaelis even! Both sensually a bit doggy and humiliating.—The supreme pleasure of the mind! And what is that to a woman? What is it, really, to the man either! He becomes merely messy and doggy, even in his mind. It needs sheer sensuality even to purify and quicken the mind. Sheer fiery sensuality, not messiness.

Ah God, how rare a thing a man is! They are all dogs that trot and sniff and copulate. To have found a man who was not afraid and not ashamed! She looked at him now, sleeping so like a wild animal asleep, gone, gone in the remoteness of it. She nestled down, not to be away from him.

Till his rousing waked her completely. He was sitting up in bed, looking down at her. She saw her own nakedness in his eyes, immediate knowledge of her. And the fluid, male knowledge of herself seemed to flow to her from his eyes and wrap her voluptuously. Oh, how voluptuous and lovely it was to have limbs and body half-asleep, heavy and suffused with passion!

"Is it time to wake up?" she said.

"Half past six."

She had to be at the lane-end at eight. Always, always, always this compulsion on one!

"But we needn't get up yet," she said.

"I might make the breakfast and bring it up here—should I?"

"Oh yes!"

Flossie whimpered gently below. He got up and threw off his pyjamas, and rubbed himself with a towel. When the human being is courageous and full of life, how beautiful it is! So she thought, as she watched him in silence.

"Draw the curtain, will you?"

The sun was shining already on the tender green leaves of morning, and the wood stood bluey-fresh, in the nearness. She sat up in bed, looking dreamily out through the dormer window, her naked arms pushing her naked breasts together. He was dressing himself. She was half-dreaming of life, a life together with him: just a life.

He was going, fleeing from her dangerous, crouching nakedness.

"Have I lost my nightie altogether?" she said.

He pushed his hand down in the bed, and pulled out the bit of flimsy silk.

"I knowed I felt silk at my ankles," he said.

But the nightdress was slit almost in two.

"Never mind!" she said. "It belongs here, really. I'll leave it."

"Ay, leave it—I can put it atween my legs at night, for company. There's no name nor mark on it, is there?"

"No! It's just a plain old one."

She slipped on the torn thing, and sat dreamily looking out of the window. The window was open, the air of morning drifted in, and the sound of birds. Birds flew continually past. Then she saw Flossie roaming out. It was morning.

Downstairs she heard him making the fire, pumping water, going out at the back door. By and by came the smell of bacon, and at length he came upstairs with a huge black tray that would only just go through the door. He set the tray on the bed, and poured out the tea. Connie squatted in her torn nightdress, and fell on her food hungrily. He sat on the one chair, with his plate on his knees.

"How good it is!" she said. "How nice to have breakfast together."

He ate in silence, his mind on the time that was quickly passing. That made her remember.

"Oh, how I wish I could stay here with you, and Wragby were a million miles away! It's Wragby I'm going away from really. You know that, don't you?"

"Ay!"

"And you promise me we'll live together and have a life together, you and me! You promise me, don't you?"

"Ay! When we can."

"Yes! And we *will*! We *will*, won't we?" She leaned over, making the tea spill, catching his wrist.

"Ay!" he said, tidying up the tea.

"We can't possibly *not* live together now, can we?" she said appealingly.

He looked up at her with his flickering grin.

"No!" he said. "Only you've got to start in twenty-five minutes."

"Have I!" she cried. Suddenly he held up a warning finger, and rose to his feet.

Flossie had given a short bark, then three loud sharp yaps of warning. Silent, he put his plate on the tray, and went downstairs. Constance heard him go down the garden path. A bicycle bell had tinkled outside there.

"Morning, Mr Mellors! Registered letter!"

"Oh ay! Got a pencil?"

"Here y' are!"

There was a pause.

"Canada!" said the stranger's voice.

"Ay! That's a mate o' mine out there in British Columbia. Dunno what he's got to register."

"'Appen sent y' a fortune, like."

"More like wants summat."

Pause.

"Well! Lovely day again!"

"Ay!"

"Morning!"

"Morning!"

After a time he came upstairs again, looking a little angry.

"Postman," he said.

"Very early!" she replied.

"Rural round—he's mostly here by seven, when he does come."

"Did your mate send you a fortune?"

"No! Only some photographs and papers about a place out there in British Columbia."

"Would you go there?"

"I thought perhaps we might."

"Oh yes! I believe it's lovely!"

But he was put out by the postman's coming.

"Them damned bikes, they're on you afore you know where you are. I hope he twigged nothing."

"After all, what could he twig!"

"You must get up now, and get ready. I'm just goin' ter look round outside."

She saw him go reconnoitring into the lane, with dog and gun. She went downstairs and washed, and was ready by the time he came back, with her few things in the little silk bag.

He locked up, and they set off, but through the wood, not down the lane. He was being wary.

"Don't you think one lives for times like last night?" she said to him.

"Ay! But there's th' rest o' times to think on," he replied, rather short.

They plodded on down the overgrown path, he in front, in silence.

"And we *will* live together and make a life together, won't we?" she pleaded.

"Ay!" he replied, striding on without looking round. "When t' time comes! Just now you're off to Venice or somewhere."

She followed him dumbly, with sinking heart. Oh, now she was *wae* to go!

At last he stopped.

"I'll just strike across here," he said, pointing to the right.

But she flung her arms round his neck, and clung to him.

"But you'll keep the tenderness for me, won't you?" she whispered. "I loved last night. But you'll keep the tenderness for me, won't you?"

He kissed her, and held her close for a moment. Then he sighed, and kissed her again.

"I must go an' look if th' car's there."

He strode over the low brambles and bracken, leaving a trail through the fern. For a minute or two he was gone. Then he came striding back.

"Car's not there yet," he said. "But there's th' baker's cart on t' road."

He seemed anxious and troubled.

"Hark!"

They heard a car softly hoot as it came nearer. It slowed up on the bridge.

"There she is! Go!" he said. "I'm not coming. Go! Don't let her stand there."

She plunged with utter mournfulness in his tracks through the fern, and came to a huge holly hedge. He was just behind her.

"Here! Go through there!" he said, pointing to a gap. "I shan't come out."

She looked at him in despair. But he kissed her and made her go. She crept in sheer misery through the holly and through the wooden fence, stumbled down the little ditch and up into the lane, where Hilda was just getting out of the car in vexation.

"Why you're there!" said Hilda. "Where's *he*?"

"He's not coming."

Connie's face was running with tears as she got into the car with her little bag. Hilda snatched up the motoring helmet with the disfiguring goggles.

"Put it on!" she said. And Connie pulled on the disguise, then the long motoring coat, and she sat down, a goggling, inhuman, unrecognisable creature. Hilda started the car with a business-like motion. They heaved out of the lane, and were away down the road. Connie had looked round—but there was no sign of him. Away! away! She sat in bitter tears. The parting had come so suddenly, so unexpectedly. It was like death.

"Thank goodness you'll be away from him for some time!" said Hilda, turning to avoid Crosshill Village.

CHAPTER XVII.

"You see Hilda," said Connie after lunch, when they were nearing London, "you have never known either real tenderness or real sensuality: and if you do know them—with the same person—it—it makes a great difference."

"For mercy's sake, don't brag about your experiences!" said Hilda. "I've never met the man yet who was capable of intimacy with a woman—giving himself up to her. That was what I wanted. I'm not keen on their self-satisfied tenderness, and their sensuality. I'm not content to be any man's little petsy-wetsy, nor his *chair à plaisir* either. I wanted a complete intimacy, and I didn't get it. That's enough for me."

Connie pondered this. Complete intimacy! She supposed that meant revealing everything concerning yourself to the other person, and his revealing everything concerning himself. But that was a bore. All that weary self-consciousness between a man and a woman!—a disease!

"I think you're too conscious of yourself all the time, with everybody," she said to her sister.

"I hope at least I haven't a slave nature," said Hilda.

"But perhaps you have! Perhaps you are a slave to your own idea of yourself."

Hilda drove in silence for some time after this piece of unheard-of insolence from that chit Connie.

"At least I'm not a slave to somebody else's idea of me: and the somebody else a servant of my husband's," she retorted at last, in crude anger.

"You see, it's not so," said Connie calmly.

She had always let herself be dominated by her elder sister. Now, though somewhere inside herself she was weeping, she was free of the dominion of *other women*. Ah! that in itself was a relief, like being given another life: to be free of the strange dominion and obsession of *other women*. How awful they were, women!

She was glad to be with her father, whose favourite she had always been. She and Hilda stayed in a little hotel off Pall Mall, and Sir Malcolm was in his club. But he took his daughters out in the evening, and they liked going with him.

He was still handsome and robust, though just a little afraid of the new world that had sprung up around him. He had got a second wife in Scotland, younger than himself, and richer. But he had as many holidays away from her as possible: just as with his first wife.

Connie sat next to him at the opera. He was moderately stout, and had stout thighs, but they were still strong and well-knit: the thighs of a healthy man who had taken his pleasure in life. His good-humoured selfishness, his dogged sort of independence, his unrepenting sensuality, it seemed to Connie she could see them all in his well-knit straight thighs. Just a man! And now becoming an old man, which is sad. Because in his strong, thick male legs there was none of the alert sensitiveness and power of tenderness which is the very essence of youth, that which never dies, once it is there.

Connie woke up to the existence of legs. They became more important to her than faces, which are no longer very real. How few people had live, alert legs! She looked at the men in the stalls. Great puddingy thighs in black pudding-cloth, or lean wooden sticks in black funeral stuff, or well-shaped young legs without any meaning whatever, either sensuality or tenderness or sensitiveness, just mere leggy ordinariness that pranced around. Not even any sensuality like her father's. They were all daunted, daunted out of existence.

But the women were not daunted. The awful mill-posts of most females! really shocking, really enough to justify murder! Or the poor thin pegs! or the trim neat things in silk stockings, without the slightest look of life! Awful, the millions of meaningless legs prancing meaninglessly around!

She was not happy in London. The people seemed so spectral and blank. They had no alive happiness, no matter how brisk and good-looking they were. It was all barren. And Connie had a woman's blind craving for happiness, to be assured of happiness.

In Paris at any rate she felt a bit of sensuality still. But what a weary, tired, worn-out sensuality, worn-out for lack of tenderness. Oh, Paris was sad, one of the saddest towns: weary of its now-mechanical sensuality, weary of the tension of money, money, money, weary even of resentment and conceit, just weary to death, and still not sufficiently Americanised or Londonised to hide the weariness under a mechanical jig-jig-jig! Ah, these manly he-men, these flâneurs, these oglers, these eaters of good dinners! How weary they were! Weary, worn-out for lack of a little tenderness, given and taken. The efficient, sometimes charming women knew a thing or two about the sensual realities: they had that pull over their jigging English sisters. But they knew even less of tenderness. Dry, with the endless dry tension of will, they too were wearing out. The human world was just getting worn out. Perhaps it would turn purely destructive. A sort of anarchy! Clifford and his conservative anarchy! Perhaps it wouldn't be conservative very much longer. Perhaps it would develop into a very radical anarchy.

Connie found herself shrinking and afraid of the world. Sometimes she was happy for a little while on the Boulevards or in the Bois or the Luxembourg gardens. But already Paris was full of Americans and English, strange Americans in the oddest uniforms, and the usual dreary English that are so hopelessly abroad.

She was glad to drive on. It was suddenly hot weather, so Hilda was going through Switzerland and over the Brenner, then through the Dolomites down to Venice. Hilda loved all the managing and the driving and being mistress of the show. Connie was quite content to keep quiet.

And the trip was really quite nice. Only Connie kept saying to herself: Why don't I really care? Why am I never really thrilled? How awful, that I don't really care about landscape any more! But I don't. It's rather awful. I'm like Saint Bernard, who could sail down the Lake of Lucerne without ever noticing that there were even mountains and green water. I just don't care for landscape any more. Why should one stare at it? Why should one? I refuse to.—

No, she found nothing vital in France or Switzerland or the Tyrol or Italy. She just was carted through it all. And it was all less real than Wragby. Less real than that awful Wragby! She felt she didn't care if she never saw France or Switzerland or Italy again. They'd keep. Wragby was more real.

As for people! people were all alike, with very little differences. They all wanted to get money out of you: or, if they were travellers, they wanted to get enjoyment, perforce, like squeezing blood out of a stone. Poor mountains! poor landscape! it all had to be squeezed and squeezed and squeezed again, to provide a thrill, to provide enjoyment. What did people mean, with this simply *determined* enjoying of themselves?

—No!—said Connie to herself.—I'd rather be at Wragby, where I can go about and be still, and not stare at anything or do any performing of any sort. This tourist performance of enjoying oneself is too hopelessly humiliating: it's such a failure.—

She wanted to go back to Wragby, even to Clifford, even to poor crippled Clifford. He wasn't such a fool as this swarming holidaying lot, anyhow.

But in her inner consciousness she was keeping touch with the other man. She mustn't let her connection with him go: oh, she mustn't let it go, or she was lost, lost utterly in this world of riff-raffy expensive people and joy-hogs. Oh, the joy-hogs! Oh "enjoying oneself"! Another modern form of sickness.

They left the car in Mestre, in garage, and took the regular steamer over to Venice. It was a lovely summer afternoon, the shallow lagoon rippled, the full sunshine made Venice, turning its back to them across the water, look dim.

At the station quay they changed to a gondola, giving the man the address. He was a regular gondolier, in a white-and-blue blouse, not very good-looking, not at all impressive.

"Yes! The Villa Esmeralda! Yes! I know it! I have been the gondolier for a gentleman there. But a fair distance out!"

He seemed a rather childish, impetuous fellow. He rowed with a certain exaggerated impetuosity, through the dark side-canals with the horrible, slimy green walls, the canals that go through the poorer quarters, where the washing hangs high up on ropes, and there is a slight, or strong, odour of sewerage.

But at last he came to one of the open canals with pavement on either side, and looping bridges, that run straight, at right-angles to the Grand Canal. The two women sat under the little awning, the man was perched above, behind them.

"Are the signorine staying long at the Villa Esmeralda?" he asked, rowing easy, and wiping his perspiring face with a white-and-blue handkerchief.

"Some twenty days—we are both married ladies," said Hilda, in her curious hushed voice, that made her Italian sound so foreign.

"Ah! twenty days!" said the man. There was a pause. After which he asked: "Do the signore want a gondola for the twenty days or so that they will stay at the Villa Esmeralda? Or by the day, or by the week?"

Connie and Hilda considered. In Venice, it is always preferable to have one's own gondola, as it is preferable to have one's own car on land.

"What is there at the Villa—what boats?"

"There is a motor-launch, also a gondola. But—" The *but* meant: they won't be your property.—

"How much do you charge?"

It was about thirty shillings a day, or ten pounds a week.

"Is that the regular price?" asked Hilda.

"Less, Signora, less. The regular price—"

The sisters considered.

"Well," said Hilda, "come tomorrow morning, and we will arrange it. What is your name?"

His name was Giovanni, and he wanted to know at what time he should come; and then, for whom should he say he was waiting. Hilda had no card: Connie gave him one of hers. He glanced at it swiftly, with his hot, southern blue eyes—then glanced again.

"Ah!" he said, lighting up. "Milady! Milady, isn't it?"

"Milady Costanza!" said Connie.

He nodded, repeating: "Milady Costanza!" and putting the card carefully away in his blouse.

The Villa Esmeralda was quite a long way out, on the edge of the lagoon looking towards Chioggia. It was not a very old house, and pleasant, with the terraces looking sea-wards, and below, quite a big garden with dark trees, walled in from the lagoon.

Their host was a heavy, rather coarse Scotchman who had made a good fortune in Italy before the war, and had been knighted for his ultra-patriotism during the war. His wife was a thin, pale, sharp kind of person with no fortune of her own, and the misfortune of having to regulate her husband's rather sordid amorous exploits. He was terribly tiresome with the servants. But having had a slight stroke during the winter, he was now more manageable.

The house was pretty full. Besides Sir Malcolm and his two daughters, there were seven more people, a Scotch couple, again with two daughters; a young Italian Contessa, a widow; a young Georgian prince, and a youngish English clergyman who had had pneumonia and was being chaplain to Sir Alexander for his health's sake. The prince was penniless, good-looking, would make an excellent chauffeur, with the necessary impudence, and—basta! The Contessa was a quiet little puss with a game on somewhere. The clergyman was a raw simple fellow from a Bucks vicarage: luckily he had left his wife and two children at home. And the Guthries, the family of four, were good solid Edinburgh middle-class, enjoying everything in a solid fashion, and daring everything while risking nothing.

Connie and Hilda ruled out the prince at once. The Guthries were more or less their own sort, substantial, but boring: and the girls wanted husbands. The chaplain was not a bad fellow, but too deferential. Sir Alexander, after his slight stroke, had a terrible heaviness in his joviality, but he was still thrilled at the presence of so many handsome young women. Lady Cooper was a quiet, catty person who had had a thin time of it, poor thing, and who watched every other woman with a cold watchfulness that had become second nature, and who said cold, nasty little things which showed what an utterly low opinion she had of all human nature. She was also quite venomously overbearing with the servants, Connie found: but in a quiet way. And she skilfully behaved so that Sir Alexander should think that *he* was lord and monarch of the whole caboosh, with his stout, would-be jaunty paunch, and his utterly boring jokes, his humourosity, as Hilda called it.

Sir Malcolm was painting. Yes, he still would do a Venetian lagoon-scape now and then, in contrast to his Scottish landscapes. So in the morning he was rowed off with a huge canvas, to his "site." A little later, Lady Cooper would be rowed off into the heart of the city, with sketching-block and colours. She was an inveterate water-colour painter, and the house was full of rose-coloured palaces, dark canals, soaring bridges, mediaeval façades, and so on. A little later, the Guthries, the prince, the countess, Sir Alexander, and sometimes Mr Lind, the chaplain, would go off to the Lido, where they would bathe, coming home to a late lunch at half-past one.

The house-party, as a house-party, was distinctly boring. But this did not trouble the sisters. They were out all the time. Their father took them to the exhibition, miles and miles of weary paintings. He took them to old cronies of his in the Villa Lucchese, he sat with them on warm evenings in Piazza, having got a table at Florian's: he took them to the theatre, to the Goldoni plays. There were illuminated water-fêtes, there were dances. This was a holiday-place of all holiday-places. The Lido with its acres of sun-pinked or pyjamaed bodies, was like a strand with an endless heap of seals come up for mating. Too many people in piazza, too many limbs and trunks of humanity on the Lido, too many gondolas, too many motor-launches, too many steamers, too many pigeons, too many ices, too many cocktails, too many men-servants wanting tips, too many languages rattling, too much, too much, too much sun, too much smell of Venice, too many cargoes of strawberries, too many silk shawls, too many huge, raw-beef slices of water-melon on stalls: too much enjoyment altogether. Far too much enjoyment!

Connie and Hilda went around in their summery frocks. There were dozens of people they knew, dozens of people knew them. Michaelis turned up like a bad penny. "Hullo! Where you staying? Come an' have an ice or something! Come with me somewhere in my gondola." Even Michaelis *almost* sunburnt: though sun-roasted is more appropriate to the look of the mass of human flesh.

It was pleasant in a way. It was *almost* enjoyment. But anyhow, with all the cocktails, all the lying in warmish water and sun-bathing on hot sand in hot sun, jazzing with your stomach up against some fellow in the warm nights, cooling off with ices, it was a complete narcotic. And that was what they all wanted, a drug: the slow water, a drug; the sun, a drug; jazz, a drug; cigarettes, cocktails, ices, vermouth—To be drugged! Enjoyment! Enjoyment!

Hilda half liked being drugged. She liked looking at all the women, speculating about them. The women were absorbingly interested in the women. How does she look? what man has she captured? what fun is she getting out of it?—The men were like great dogs in white flannel trousers, waiting to be patted, waiting to wallow, waiting to plaster some woman's stomach against their own, in jazz.

Hilda liked jazz, because she could plaster her stomach against the stomach of some so-called man, and let him control her movements from the visceral centre, here and there across the floor, and then she could break loose and ignore "the creature." He had been merely made use of.

Poor Connie was rather unhappy. She wouldn't jazz, because she simply couldn't plaster her stomach against some "creature's" stomach. She hated the conglomerate mass of nearly nude flesh on the Lido: there was hardly enough water to wet them all. She disliked Sir Alexander and Lady Cooper. She didn't want Michaelis or anybody else trailing her.

The happiest times were when she got Hilda to go with her away across the lagoon, far across, to some lonely shingle-bank, where they could bathe quite alone, the gondola remaining on the inner side of the reef.

Then Giovanni got another gondolier to help him, because it was a long way, and he sweated terrifically in the sun. Giovanni was very nice: affectionate, as the Italians are, and quite passionless. The Italians are not passionate: passion has deep reserves. They are easily moved, and often affectionate, but they rarely have any abiding passion of any sort.

So Giovanni. He was already devoted to his ladies, as he had been devoted to cargoes of ladies in the past. He was perfectly ready to prostitute himself to them, if they wanted him. He secretly hoped they would want him: they would give him a handsome present, and it would come in very handy, as he was just going to be married. He told them about his marriage, and they were suitably interested.

He thought this trip to some lonely bank across the lagoon probably meant business: business being *l'amore*, love. So he got a mate to help him—for it *was* a long way: and after all, they were two ladies. Two ladies, two mackerel! Good arithmetic! Beautiful ladies, too! He was justly proud of them. And though it was the Signora who paid him and gave him orders, he rather hoped it would be the young milady who would select him for *l'amore*. She would give more money too.

The mate he brought was called Daniele. He was not a regular gondolier, so he had none of the cadger and prostitute about him. He was a sandola man, a sandola being a big boat that brings in fruit and produce from the islands.

Daniele was beautiful, tall and well-shapen, with a light round head of little, close pale-blond curls, and a good-looking man's face, a little like a lion, and long-distance blue eyes. He was not effusive, loquacious, and bibulous like Giovanni. He was silent, and he rowed with a strength and ease as if he were alone on the waters. The ladies were ladies, remote from him. He did not even look at them. He looked ahead.

He was a real man, a little angry when Giovanni drank too much wine and rowed awkwardly, with effusive shoves of the great oar. He was a man as Mellors was a man, unprostituted. Connie pitied the wife of the easily-overflowing Giovanni. But Daniele's wife would be one of those sweet Venetian women of the people whom one still sees, modest and flowerlike in the back of that labyrinth of a town.

Ah, how sad that man first prostitutes woman, then woman prostitutes man. Giovanni was pining to prostitute himself, dribbling like a dog, wanting to give himself to a woman. And for money!

Connie looked at Venice far off, low and rose-coloured upon the waters. Built of money, blossomed of money, and dead with money. The money-deadness! Money, money, money, prostitution and deadness.

Yet Daniele was still a man, capable of a man's free allegiance. He did not wear the gondolier's blouse: only the knitted blue jersey. He was a little wild, uncouth and proud. So he was hireling to the rather doggy Giovanni, who was hireling again of two women. So it is! When Jesus refused the devil's money, he left the devil like a Jewish banker, master of the whole situation.

Connie would come home from the blazing light of the lagoon, in a kind of stupor, to find letters from home. Clifford wrote regularly. He wrote very good letters: they might all have been printed in a book. And for this reason Connie found them not very interesting.

She lived in the stupor of the light of the lagoon, the lapping saltiness of the water, the space, the emptiness, the nothingness: but health, health, the complete stupor of health. It was gratifying, and she was lulled away in it, not caring for anything. Besides, she was pregnant. She knew now. So the stupor of sunlight and lagoon salt and sea-baths and lying on shingle and finding shells and drifting away, away in a gondola was completed by the pregnancy inside her, another fulness of health, satisfying and stupefying.

She had been at Venice a fortnight, and she was to stay another ten days or a fortnight—the sunshine blazed over any count of time, and the fulness of physical health made forgetfulness complete. She was in a sort of stupor of well-being.

From which a letter of Clifford's roused her.

"We too have had our mild local excitement. It appears the truant wife of Mellors, the keeper, turned up at the cottage, and found herself unwelcome. He packed her off and locked the door. Report has it, however, that when he returned from the wood he found the no longer fair lady firmly established in his bed, *in puris naturalibus*—or one should say, *in impuris naturalibus*. She had broken a window and got in that way. Unable to evict this somewhat man-handled Venus from his couch, he beat a retreat, and retired, it is said, to his mother's house in Tevershall. Meanwhile the Venus of Stacks Gate is established in the cottage, which she claims is her home, and Apollo, apparently, is domiciled in Tevershall.

"I repeat this from hearsay, as Mellors has not come to me personally. I had the particular bit of local garbage from our garbage bird, our ibis, our scavenging turkey-buzzard, Mrs Bolton. I would not have repeated it, had she not exclaimed: Her ladyship will go no more to the wood, if *that woman's* going to be about!

"I like your picture of Sir Malcolm striding into the sea with white hair blowing and pink flesh glowing. I envy you that sun. Here, it rains. But I don't envy Sir Malcolm his inveterate mortal carnality. However, it suits his age. Apparently one grows more carnal and more mortal as one grows older. Only youth has a taste of immortality.—"

This news affected Connie, in her state of semi-stupefied well-being, with vexation amounting almost to exasperation. Now she had got to be bothered by that beast of a woman! Now she must start and fret!

She had no letter from Mellors. They had agreed not to write at all. But now she wanted to hear from him personally. After all, he was the father of the child that was coming. Let him write!

But how hateful! Now everything was messed up. How foul those low people were! How nice it was here, in the sunshine and the indolence, compared to that dismal mess of the English midlands! After all, a clear sky was almost the most important thing in life.

She did not mention the fact of her pregnancy, even to Hilda. She wrote to Mrs Bolton for exact information.

Duncan Forbes, an artist, friend of theirs, had arrived at the Villa Esmeralda, coming north from Rome. Now he made a third in the gondola, and he bathed with them across the lagoon, and was their escort: a quiet, almost taciturn young man, very advanced in his art.

She had a letter from Mrs Bolton: "You will be pleased, I am sure, my Lady, when you see Sir Clifford. He is looking quite blooming, and working very hard, and very hopeful. Of course he is looking forward to seeing you among us again. It is a dull house without my Lady, and we shall all welcome her presence among us once more.

"About Mr Mellors. I don't know how much Sir Clifford told you. It seems his wife came back all of a sudden one afternoon, and he found her sitting on the doorstep when he came in from the wood. She said she was come back to him and wanted to live with him again, as she was his legal wife, and he wasn't going to divorce her. Because it seems Mr Mellors was trying for a divorce. But he wouldn't have anything to do with her, and wouldn't let her in the house, and didn't go in himself, he went back into the wood without ever opening the door.

"But when he came back after dark, he found the house broken into, so he went upstairs to see what she'd done, and he found her in bed without a rag on her. He offered her money, but she said she was his wife and he must take her back—I don't know what sort of scene they had. His mother told me about it, she's terribly upset. Well he told her he'd die rather than ever live with her again, so he took his things and went straight to his mother's on Tevershall hill. He stopped the night, and went to the wood next day through the park, never going near the cottage. It seems he never saw his wife that day. But the day after, she was at her brother Dan's at Beggarlee, swearing and carrying on, saying she was his legal wife, and that he'd been having women at the cottage, because she'd found a scent-bottle in his drawer, and gold-tipped cigarette-ends on the ash-heap, and I don't know what all. Then it seems the postman Fred Kirk says he heard somebody talking in Mr Mellors' bedroom early one morning, and a motor-car had been in the lane. Mr Mellors stayed on with his mother, and went to the wood through the park, and it seems she stayed on at the cottage. Well there was no end of talk. So at last Mr Mellors and Tom Phillips went to the cottage and fetched away most of the furniture and bedding, and unscrewed the handle of the pump, so she was forced to go. But instead of going back to Stacks Gate she went and lodged with that Mrs Swain at Beggarlee, because her brother Dan's wife wouldn't have her. And she kept going to old Mrs Mellors' house, to catch him, and she began swearing he'd got in bed with her in the cottage, and she went to a lawyer to make him pay her an allowance. She's grown heavy, and more common than ever, and as strong as a bull. And she goes about saying the most awful things about him, how he has women at the cottage, and how he behaved to her when they were married, the low, beastly things he did to her, and I don't know what all. I'm sure it's fearful, the mischief a woman can do, once she starts talking. And no matter how low she may be, there'll be some as will believe her, and some of the dirt will stick. I'm sure the way she makes out that Mr Mellors was one of those low, beastly men with women, is simply shocking. And people are only too ready to believe things against anybody, especially things like that. She declares she'll never leave him alone while he lives. Though what I say is, if he was so beastly to her, why is she so anxious to go back to him?—But of course she's coming near her change of life, for she's years older than he is. And these common, violent women always go partly insane when the change of life comes upon them—"

This was a nasty blow to Connie. Here she was, sure as life, coming in for her share of the lowness and dirt. She felt angry with him for not having got clear of a Bertha Coutts: nay, for ever having married her. Perhaps he had a certain hankering after lowness. Connie remembered the last night she had spent with him, and shivered. He had known all that sensuality, even with a Bertha Coutts! It was really rather disgusting. It would be well to be rid of him, clear of him altogether. He was perhaps really common, really low.

She had a revulsion against the whole affair, and almost envied the Guthrie girls their gawky inexperience and crude maidenliness. And she now dreaded the thought that anybody would know about herself and the keeper. How unspeakably humiliating! She was uneasy, afraid, and felt a craving for utter respectability, even the vulgar and deadening respectability of the Guthrie girls. If Clifford knew about her affair—how unspeakably humiliating! She was afraid, terrified of society and its unclean bite. She almost wished she could get rid of the child again, and be quite clear. In short, she fell into a state of funk.

As for the scent-bottle, that was her own folly. She had not been able to refrain from perfuming his one-or-two handkerchieves and his shirts in the drawer—just out of childishness—and she had left a little bottle of Coty's Wood-violet perfume, half-empty, among his things. She wanted him to remember her in the perfume. As for the cigarette-ends, they were Hilda's.

She could not help confiding a little in Duncan Forbes. She didn't say she had been the keeper's lover—she only said she liked him, and told Forbes the history of the man.

"Oh," said Forbes, "you'll see, they'll never rest till they've pulled the man down and done him in. If he has refused to creep up into the middle classes, when he had a chance; and if he's a man who stands up for his own sex, then they'll do him in. It's the one thing they won't let you be, straight and open in your sex. You can be as dirty as you like. In fact the more dirt you do on sex, the better they like it. But if you believe in your own sex, and won't have it done dirt to: they'll down you. It's the one insane taboo left: sex as a natural and vital thing. They won't have it, and they'll kill you before they'll let you have it.—You'll see, they'll hound that man down. And what's he done, after all? If he's made love to his wife all ends on, hasn't he a right to? She ought to be proud of it. But you see, even a low bitch like that turns on him, and uses the hyaena instinct of the mob against sex, to pull him down. You have to snivel and feel sinful or awful about your sex, before you're allowed to have any. Oh, they'll hound the poor devil down——"

Connie had a revulsion in the opposite direction now. What had he done, after all? what had he done to herself, Connie, but give her an exquisite pleasure and a sense of freedom and life? He had released her warm, natural sexual flow. And for that they would hound him down.

No no, it should not be. She saw the image of him, naked white with tanned face and hands, looking down and addressing his erect penis as if it were another being, the odd grin flickering on his face. And she heard his voice again: Tha's got the nicest woman's arse of anybody!—And she felt his hand warmly and softly closing over her tail again, over her secret places, like a benediction. And the warmth ran through her womb, and the little flames flickered in her knees, and she said: Oh no! Oh no! I mustn't go back on it! I must not go back on him. I must stick to him and to what I had of him, through everything. I had no warm, flamy life till he gave it me. And I won't go back on it.

She did a rash thing. She sent a letter to Ivy Bolton, enclosing a note to the keeper, and asking Mrs Bolton to give it him. And she wrote to him: "I am very much distressed to hear of all the trouble your wife is making for you, but don't mind it, it is only a sort of hysteria. It will all blow over as suddenly as it came. But I'm awfully sorry about it, and I do hope you are not minding very much. After all, it isn't worth it. She is only a hysterical woman who wants to hurt you. I shall be home in ten days' time, and I do hope everything will be all right."

A few days later came a letter from Clifford. He was evidently upset.

"I am delighted to hear you are prepared to leave Venice on the sixteenth. But if you are enjoying it, don't hurry home. We miss you, Wragby misses you. But it is essential that you should get your full amount of sunshine, sunshine and pyjamas, as the advertisement of the Lido says. So please do stay on a little longer, if it is cheering you up and preparing you for our sufficiently awful winter. Even today, it rains.

"I am assiduously, admirably looked after by Mrs Bolton. She is a queer specimen. The more I live, the more I realise what strange creatures human beings are. Some of them might just as well have a hundred legs, like a centipede, or six, like a lobster. The human consistency and dignity one has been led to expect from one's fellow-men seem actually non-existent. One doubts if they exist to any startling degree even in oneself.

"The scandal of the keeper continues and gets bigger, like a snowball. Mrs Bolton keeps me informed. She reminds me of a fish which, though dumb, seems to be breathing silent gossip through its gills, while ever it lives. All goes through the sieve of her gills, and nothing surprises her. It is as if the events of other people's lives were the necessary oxygen of her own.

"She is pre-occupied with the Mellors scandal, and if I will let her begin, she takes me down to the depths. Her great indignation, which even then is like the indignation of an actress playing a rôle, is against the wife of Mellors, whom she persists in calling Bertha Coutts. I have been to the depths of the muddy lives of the Bertha Couttses of this world, and when, released from the current of gossip, I slowly rise to the surface again, I look at the daylight in wonder that it ever should be.

"It seems to me absolutely true, that our world, which appears to us the surface of all things, is really the *bottom* of a deep ocean: all our trees are submarine growths, and we are weird, scaly-clad submarine fauna, feeding ourselves on offal, like shrimps. Only occasionally the soul rises gasping through the fathomless fathoms under which we live, far up to the surface of the ether, where there is true air. I am convinced that the air we normally breathe is a kind of water, and men and women are a species of fish.

"But sometimes the soul does come up, shoots like a kittiwake into the light, with ecstasy, after having preyed on the submarine depths. It is our moral destiny, I suppose, to prey upon the ghastly subaqueous life of our fellow-men, in the submarine jungle of mankind. But our immortal destiny is to escape, once we have swallowed our swimmy catch, up again into the bright ether, bursting out from the surface of Old Ocean, into real light. Then one realises one's eternal nature.

"When I hear Mrs Bolton talk, I feel myself plunging down, down, to the depths where the fish of human secrets wriggle and swim. Carnal appetite makes one seize a beakful of prey: then up, up again, out of the dense into the ethereal, from the wet into the dry. To you I can tell the whole process. But with Mrs Bolton I only feel the downward plunge, down, horribly, among the sea-weeds and the pallid monsters of the very bottom.

"I am afraid we are going to lose our gamekeeper. The scandal of the truant wife, instead of dying down, has reverberated to greater and greater dimensions. He is accused of all unspeakable things, and curiously enough, the woman has managed to get the bulk of the colliers' wives behind her, gruesome fish, and the village is putrescent with talk.

"I hear this Bertha Coutts besieges Mellors in his mother's house, having ransacked the cottage and the hut. She seized one day upon her own daughter, as that chip of the female block was returning from school; but the little one, instead of kissing the loving mother hand, bit it firmly, and so received from the other hand a smack in the face which sent her reeling into the gutter: whence she was rescued by an indignant and harassed grandmother.

"The woman has blown off an amazing quantity of poison-gas. She has aired in detail all those incidents of her conjugal life which are usually buried in the deepest grave of matrimonial silence, between married couples. Having chosen to exhume them, after ten years of burial, she has a weird array. I hear these details from Linley and the doctor: the latter being amused. Of course there is really nothing in it. Humanity has always had a strange avidity for unusual sexual postures, and if a man likes to use his wife, as Benvenuto Cellini says, 'in the Italian way,' well, that is a matter of taste. But I had hardly expected our gamekeeper to be up to so many tricks. No doubt Bertha Coutts herself first put him up to them. In any case, it is a matter of their own personal squalor, and nothing to do with anybody else.

"However, everybody listens: as I do myself. A dozen years ago, common decency would have hushed the thing. But common decency no longer exists, and the colliers' wives are all up in arms and unabashed in voice. One would think every child in Tevershall, for the last fifty years, had been an immaculate conception, and every one of our non-conformist females was a shining Joan of Arc. That our estimable gamekeeper should have about him a touch of the great Rabelais seems to make him more monstrous and shocking than a murderer like Crippen. Yet these people in Tevershall are a loose lot, if one is to believe all accounts.

"The trouble is, however, the execrable Bertha Coutts has not confined herself to her own experiences and sufferings. She has discovered, at the top of her voice, that her husband has been 'keeping' women down at the cottage, and has made a few random shots at naming the women. This has brought a few decent names trailing through the mud, and the thing has gone quite considerably too far. An injunction has been taken out against the woman.

"I have had to interview Mellors about the business, as it was impossible to keep the woman away from the wood. He goes about as usual, with his Miller-of-the-Dee air, I care for nobody, no not I, if nobody cares for me! Nevertheless, I shrewdly suspect he feels like a dog with a tin can tied to its tail: though he makes a very good show of pretending the tin can isn't there. But I hear that in the village the women call away their children if he is passing, as if he were the Marquis de Sade in person. He goes on with a certain impudence, but I am afraid the tin can is firmly tied to his tail, and that inwardly he repeats, like Don Rodrigo in the Spanish ballad: 'Ah, now it bites me where I most have sinned!'

"I asked him if he thought he would be able to attend to his duty in the wood, and he said he did not think he had neglected it. I told him it was a nuisance to have the woman trespassing: to which he replied that he had no power to arrest her. Then I hinted at the scandal, and its unpleasant course. 'Ay,' he said. 'Folks should do their own fuckin', then they wouldn't want to listen to a lot of clatfart about another man's.'

"He said it with some bitterness, and no doubt it contains the real germ of truth. The mode of putting it, however, is neither delicate nor respectful. I hinted as much, and then I heard the tin can rattle again. 'It's not for a man i' the shapes you're in, Sir Clifford, to twit me for havin' a cod atween my legs.'

"These things, said indiscriminately to all and sundry, of course do not help him at all, and the rector, and Linley, and Burroughs all think it would be as well if the man left the place.

"I asked him if it was true that he entertained ladies down at the cottage, and all he said was: 'Why what's that to you, Sir Clifford?'—I told him I intended to have decency observed on my estate, to which he replied: 'Then you mun button the mouths o' a' th' women.'—When I pressed him about his manner of life at the cottage, he said: 'Surely you might ma'e a scandal out o' me an' my bitch Flossie. You've missed summat there.'—As a matter of fact, for an example of impertinence he'd be hard to beat.

"I asked him if it would be easy for him to find another job. He said: 'If you're hintin' that you'd like to shunt me out of this job, it'd be easy as wink.' So he made no trouble at all about leaving at the end of next week, and apparently is willing to initiate a young fellow, Joe Chambers, into as many mysteries of the craft as possible. I told him I would give him a month's wages extra, when he left. He said he'd rather I kept my money, as I'd no occasion to ease my conscience. I asked him what he meant, and he said: 'You don't owe me nothing extra, Sir Clifford, so don't pay me nothing extra. If you think you see my shirt hanging out, just tell me.'

"Well, there is the end of it for the time being. The woman has gone away: we don't know where to: but she is liable to arrest if she shows her face in Tevershall. And I hear she is mortally afraid of gaol, because she merits it so well. Mellors will depart on Saturday week, and the place will soon become normal again.

"Meanwhile, my dear Connie, if you would enjoy to stay in Venice or in Switzerland till the beginning of August, I should be glad to think you were out of all this buzz of nastiness, which will have died quite away by the end of the month.

"So, you see, we are deep-sea monsters, and when the lobster walks on mud, he stirs it up for everybody. We must perforce take it philosophically."—

The irritation, and the lack of any sympathy in any direction, of Clifford's letter, had a bad effect on Connie. But she understood it better when she received the following from Mellors: "The cat is out of the bag, along with various other pussies. You have heard that my wife Bertha came back to my unloving arms, and took up her abode in the cottage: where, to speak disrespectfully, she smelled a rat, in the shape of a little bottle of Coty. Other evidence she did not find, at least for some days, when she began to howl about the burnt photograph. She noticed the glass and back-board in the spare bedroom. Unfortunately, on the back-board somebody had scribbled little sketches, and the initials, several times repeated, C. S. R. This, however, afforded no clue until she broke into the hut, and found one of your books, an autobiography of the actress Judith, with your name, Constance Stewart Reid, on the front page. After this, for some days she went round loudly saying that my paramour was no less a person than Lady Chatterley herself. The news came at last to the rector, Mr Burroughs, and to Sir Clifford. They then proceeded to take legal steps against my liege lady, who for her part disappeared, having always had a mortal fear of the police.

"Sir Clifford asked to see me, so I went to him. He talked around things, and seemed annoyed with me. Then he asked if I knew that even her ladyship's name had been mentioned. I said I never listened to scandal, and was surprised to hear this bit from Sir Clifford himself. He said, of course it was a great insult, and I told him there was Queen Mary on a calendar in the scullery, no doubt because Her Majesty formed part of my harem. But he didn't appreciate the sarcasm. He as good as told me I was a disreputable character who walked about with my breeches' buttons undone, and I as good as told him he'd nothing to unbutton anyhow, so he gave me the sack, and I leave on Saturday week, and the place thereof shall know me no more.

"I shall go to London, and my old landlady, Mrs Inger, 17 Coburg Square, will either give me a room or will find one for me.

"Be sure your sins will find you out, especially if you're married and her name's Bertha——"——

There was not a word about herself, or to her. Connie resented this. He might have said some few words of consolation or reassurance. But she knew he was leaving her free, free to go back to Wragby and to Clifford. She resented that too. He need not be so falsely chivalrous. She wished he had said to Clifford: 'Yes, she is my lover and my mistress, and I am proud of it.' But his courage wouldn't carry him so far.

So her name was coupled with his in Tevershall! It was a mess. But that would soon die down.

She was angry, with the complicated and confused anger that made her inert. She did not know what to do nor what to say, so she said and did nothing. She went on at Venice just the same, rowing out in the gondola with Duncan Forbes, bathing, letting the days slip by. Duncan, who had been rather depressingly in love with her ten years ago, was in love with her again. But she said to him: I only want one thing of men, and that is, that they should leave me alone.

So Duncan left her alone: really quite pleased to be able to. All the same, he offered her a soft stream of a queer, inverted sort of love. He wanted to be *with* her.

"Have you ever thought," he said to her one day, "how very little people are connected with one another. Look at Daniele! He is handsome as a son of the sun. But see how alone he looks in his handsomeness. Yet I bet he has a wife and family, and couldn't possibly go away from them."

"Ask him," said Connie.

Duncan did so. Daniele said he was married, and had two children, both male, aged seven and nine. But he betrayed no emotion over the fact.

"Perhaps only people who are capable of real togetherness have that look of being alone in the universe," said Connie. "The others have a certain stickiness, they stick to the mass, like Giovanni."— 'And,' she thought to herself, 'like you, Duncan.'

She had to make up her mind what to do. She would leave Venice on the Saturday that he was leaving Wragby: in six days' time. This would bring her to London on the Monday following, and she would then see him. She wrote to him to the London address, asking him to send her a letter to Hartland's hotel, and to call for her on the Monday evening at seven.

Inside herself, she was curiously and complicatedly angry, and all her responses were numb. She refused to confide even in Hilda, and Hilda, offended by her steady silence, had become rather intimate with a Dutch woman. Connie hated these rather stifling intimacies between women, intimacy into which Hilda always entered ponderously.

Sir Malcolm decided to travel with Connie, and Duncan could come on with Hilda. The old artist always did himself well: he took berths on the Orient Express, in spite of Connie's dislike of *trains de luxe*, the atmosphere of vulgar depravity there is aboard them nowadays. However, it would make the journey to Paris short.

Sir Malcolm was always uneasy going back to his wife. It was habit carried over from the first wife. But there would be a house-party for the grouse, and he wanted to be well ahead. Connie, sunburnt and handsome, sat in silence, forgetting all about landscape.

"A little dull for you, going back to Wragby," said her father, noticing her glumness.

"I'm not sure I shall go back to Wragby," she said, with startling abruptness, looking into his eyes with her big blue eyes. His big blue eyes took on the frightened look of a man whose social conscience is not quite clear.

"You mean you'll stay on in Paris a while?"

"No! I mean never go back to Wragby."

He was bothered by his own little problems, and sincerely hoped he was getting none of hers to shoulder.

"How's that, all at once?" he asked.

"I'm going to have a child."

It was the first time she had uttered the words to any living soul, and it seemed to mark a cleavage in her life.

"How do you know?" said her father.

She smiled.

"How *should* I know!"

"But—but—not Clifford's child, of course?"

"No! Another man's."

She rather enjoyed tormenting him.

"Do I know the man?" asked Sir Malcolm.

"No! You've never seen him."

There was a long pause.

"And what are your plans?"

"I don't know. That's the point."

"No patching it up with Clifford?"

"I suppose Clifford would take it," said Connie. "He told me, after that last time you talked to him, he wouldn't mind if I had a child: so long as I went about it discreetly."

"Only sensible thing he could say, under the circumstances. Then I suppose it'll be all right."

"In what way?" said Connie, looking into her father's eyes. They were big blue eyes rather like her own, but with a certain uneasiness in them, a look sometimes of an uneasy little boy, sometimes a look of sullen selfishness, usually good-humoured and wary.

"You can present Clifford with an heir to all the Chatterleys, and put another baronet in Wragby."

Sir Malcolm's face smiled with a half-sensual smile.

"But I don't think I want to," she said.

"Why not? Feelings entangled with the other man?—Well! If you want the truth from me, my child, it's this. The world goes on. Wragby stands and will go on standing. The world is more or less a fixed thing, and externally, we have to adapt ourselves to it. Privately, in my private opinion, we can please ourselves. Emotions change. You may like one man this year and another next. But Wragby still stands. Stick by Wragby as far as Wragby sticks by you. Then please yourself. But you'll get very little out of making a break. You can make a break if you wish. You have an independent income, the only thing that never lets you down. But you won't get much out of it. Put a little baronet in Wragby. It's an amusing thing to do."

And Sir Malcolm sat back and smiled again. Connie did not answer.

"I hope you had a real man at last," he said to her after a while, sensually alert.

"I did. That's the trouble. There aren't many of them about," she said.

"No, by Gad!" he mused. "There aren't!—Well my dear, to look at you, he was a lucky man. Surely he wouldn't make trouble for you?"

"Oh no! He leaves me my own mistress entirely."

"Quite! Quite! A genuine man would."

Sir Malcolm was pleased. Connie was his favourite daughter, he had always liked the female in her. Not so much of her mother in her as in Hilda. And he had always disliked Clifford. So he was pleased, and very tender with his daughter, as if the unborn child were his child.

He drove with her to Hartland's hotel, and saw her installed: then went round to his club. She had refused his company for the evening.

She found a letter from Mellors. "I won't come round to your hotel, but I'll wait for you outside the Golden Cock in Adam Street at seven—"

There he stood, tall and slender, and so different, in a formal suit of thin dark cloth. He had a natural distinction, but he had not the cut-to-pattern look of her class. Yet, she saw at once, he could go anywhere. He had a native breeding which was really much nicer than the cut-to-pattern class thing.

"Ah, there you are! How well you look!"

"Yes! But not you."

She looked in his face anxiously. It was thin, and the cheek-bones showed. But his eyes smiled at her, and she felt at home with him. There it was: suddenly, the tension of keeping up her appearances fell from her. Something flowed out of him physically, that made her feel inwardly at ease and happy, at home. With a woman's now alert instinct for happiness, she registered it at once. 'I am happy when he's there.'—Not all the sunshine of Venice had given her this inward expansion and warmth.

"Was it horrid for you?" she asked as she sat opposite him at table. He was too thin—she saw it now. His hand lay as she knew it, with that curious loose forgottenness of a sleeping animal. She wanted so much to take it and kiss it. But she did not quite dare.

"People are always horrid," he said.

"And did you mind very much?"

"I minded, as I shall always mind. And I knew I was a fool to mind."

"Did you feel like a dog with a tin can tied to its tail?—Clifford said you felt like that."

He looked at her. It was cruel of her at that moment: for his pride had suffered bitterly.

"I suppose I did," he said.

She never knew the fierce bitterness with which he resented insult.

There was a long pause.

"And did you miss me?" she asked.

"I was glad you were out of it."

Again there was a pause.

"But did people *believe* about you and me?" she asked.

"No! I don't think so for a moment."

"Did Clifford?"

"I should say not. He put it off without thinking about it. But naturally it made him want to see the last of me."

"I'm going to have a child."

The expression died utterly out of his face, out of his whole body. He looked at her with darkened eyes, whose look she could not understand at all: like some dark-flamed spirit looking at her.

"Say you're glad!" she pleaded, groping for his hand. And she saw a certain exultance spring up in him. But it was netted down by things she could not understand.

"It's the future," he said.

"But aren't you glad?" she persisted.

"I have such a terrible mistrust of the future."

"But you needn't be bothered by any responsibility. Clifford would have it as his own—he'd be glad."

She saw him go pale, and recoil under this. He did not answer.

"Shall I go back to Clifford, and put a little baronet into Wragby?" she asked.

He looked at her, pale and very remote. The ugly little grin flickered on to his face.

"You wouldn't have to tell him who the father was."

"Oh!" she said; "he'd take it even then—if I wanted him to."

He thought for a time.

"Ay!" he said at last, to himself. "I suppose he would."

There was silence. A big gulf was between them.

"But you don't want me to go back to Clifford, do you?" she asked him.

"What do you want yourself?" he replied.

"I want to live with you," she said simply.

In spite of himself, little flames ran over his belly as he heard her say it, and he dropped his head. Then he looked up at her again, with those haunted eyes.

"If it's worth it to you," he said. "I've got nothing."

"You've got more than most men. Come, you know it," she said.

"In one way, I know it." He was silent for a time, thinking. Then he resumed: "They used to say I had too much of the woman in me——. But it's not that. I'm not a woman because I don't want to shoot birds: neither because I don't want to make money, or get on. I could have got on in the army, easily—but I didn't like the army. Though I could manage the men all right: they liked me, and they had a bit of a holy fear of me when I got mad. No, it was the stupid, dead-handed higher authority that made the army dead: absolutely fool-dead. I like men, and men like me. But I can't stand the twaddling, bossy impudence of the people who run this world. That's why I can't get on. I hate the impudence of money, and I hate the impudence of class. So in the world as it is, what have I to offer a woman?"

"But why offer anything? It's not a bargain. It's just that we love one another," she said.

"Nay nay! It's more than that. Living is moving, and moving on. My life won't go down the proper gutters, it just won't. So I'm a bit of a waste trickle by myself. And I've no business to take a woman into my life, unless my life does something and gets somewhere, inwardly at least, to keep us both fresh. A man must offer a woman *some* meaning in his life, if it's going to be an isolated life, and if she's a genuine woman.—I can't be just your male concubine."

"Why not?" she said.

"Why, because I can't. And you would soon hate it."

"As if you couldn't trust me," she said.

The grin flickered on his face.

"The money is yours, the position is yours, the decisions will lie with you. I'm not just my lady's fucker, after all."

"What else are you?"

"You may well ask. It no doubt is invisible. Yet I'm something—to myself at least. I can see the point of my own existence—though I can quite understand nobody else's seeing it."

"And will your existence have less point, if you live with me?"

He paused a long time before replying:

"It might."

She too stayed to think about it.

"And what is the point of your existence?"

"I tell you, it's invisible. I don't believe in the world, nor in money, nor in advancement, nor in the future of our civilisation.—If there's got to be a future for humanity, there'll have to be a very big change from what now is."

"And what will the real future have to be like?"

"God knows! I can feel something inside me, all mixed up with a lot of rage. But what it really amounts to, I don't know."

"Shall I tell you?" she said, looking into his face. "Shall I tell you what you have that other men don't have, and that will make the future? Shall I tell you?"

"Tell me then," he replied.

"It's the courage of your own tenderness, that's what it is: like when you put your hand on my tail and say I've got a pretty tail."

The grin came flickering on his face.

"That!" he said.

Then he sat thinking.

"Ay!" he said. "You're right. It's that really. It's that all the way through. I knew it with the men. I had to be in touch with them, physically, and not go back on it. I had to be bodily aware of them—and a bit tender to them—even if I put 'em through hell. It's a question of awareness, as Buddha said. But even he fought shy of the bodily awareness, and that natural physical tenderness, which is the best, even between men; in a proper manly way. Makes 'em really manly, not so monkeyish. Ay! it's tenderness, really; it's really cunt-awareness. Sex is really only touch, the closest of all touch. And it's touch we're afraid of. We're only half-conscious, and half alive. We've got to come alive and aware. Especially the English have got to get into touch with one another, a bit delicate and a bit tender. It's our crying need—"

She looked at him.

"Then why are you afraid of me?" she said.

He looked at her a long time, before he answered.

"It's the money, really, and the position. It's the world in you."

"But isn't there tenderness in me?" she said wistfully.

He looked down at her, with darkened, abstract eyes.

"Ay! It comes an' goes, like in me."

"But can't you trust it—between you and me?" she asked, gazing anxiously at him.

She saw his face all softening down, losing its armour.

"Maybe!" he said.

They were both silent.

"I want you to hold me in your arms," she said. "I want you to tell me you are glad we are having a child."

She looked so lovely and warm and wistful, his bowels stirred towards her.

"I suppose we can go to my room," he said. "Though it's scandalous again."

But she saw the forgetfulness of the world coming over him again, his face taking the soft, pure look of tender passion.

They walked by the remoter streets to Coburg Square, where he had a room at the top of the house, an attic room where he cooked for himself on a gas ring. It was small, but decent and tidy.

She took off her things, and made him do the same. She was lovely in the soft first flush of her pregnancy.

"I ought to leave you alone," he said.

"No!" she said. "Love me! Love me, and say you'll keep me. Say you'll keep me! Say you'll never let me go, to the world nor to anybody."

She crept close against him, clinging fast to his thin, strong naked body, the only home she had ever known.

"Then I'll keep thee," he said. "If tha wants it, then I'll keep thee."

He held her round and fast.

"And say you're glad about the child," she repeated. "Kiss it! Kiss my womb and say you're glad it's there."

But that was more difficult for him.

"I've a dread of puttin' children i' th' world," he said. "I've such a dread o' th' future for 'em."

"But you've put it into me. Be tender to it, and that will be its future already. Kiss it! Kiss it!"

He quivered, because it was true. 'Be tender to it, and that will be its future.'—At that moment he felt a sheer love for the woman. He kissed her belly and her mound of Venus, to kiss down to the womb and the foetus within the womb.

"Oh, you love me! You love me!" she said, in a little cry like one of her blind, inarticulate love-cries. And he went in to her softly, feeling the stream of tenderness flowing in release from his bowels to hers, the bowels of compassion kindled between them.

And he realised as he went in to her that this was the thing he had to do, to come into tender touch, without losing his pride or his dignity or his integrity as a man. After all, if she had money and means, and he had none, he should be too proud and honorable to hold back his tenderness from her on that account. 'I stand for the touch of bodily awareness between human beings,' he said to himself, 'and the touch of tenderness. And she is my mate. And it is a battle against the money, and the machine, and the insentient ideal monkeyishness of the world. And she will stand behind me there. Thank God I've got a woman! Thank God I have got a woman who is with me, and tender and aware of me. Thank God she's not a bully, nor a fool. Thank God she's a tender, aware woman.' And as his seed sprang in her, his soul sprang towards her too, in the creative act that is far more than procreative.

She was quite determined now that there should be no parting between him and her. But the ways and means were still to settle.

"Did you hate Bertha Coutts?" she asked him.

"Don't talk to me about her."

"Yes! You must let me. Because once you liked her. And once you were as intimate with her as you are with me. So you have to tell me. Isn't it rather terrible, when you've been intimate with her, to hate her so? Why is it?"

"I don't know. She sort of kept her will ready against me always, always: her ghastly female will: her freedom! A woman's ghastly freedom, that ends in the most beastly bullying! Oh, she always kept her freedom against me, like vitriol in my face."

"But she's not free of you even now. Does she still love you?"

"No no! If she's not free of me, it's because she's got that mad rage, she *must* try to bully me."

"But she must have loved you."

"No! Well—in specks, she did. She was drawn to me. And I think even that she hated. She loved me in moments. But she always took it back, and started bullying. Her deepest desire was to bully me, and there was no altering her. Her *will* was wrong, from the first."

"But perhaps she felt you didn't really love her, and she wanted to make you."

"My God, it was bloody making."

"But you didn't really love her, did you? You did her that wrong."

"How could I? I began to. I began to love her. But somehow, she always ripped me up. No, don't let's talk of it. It was a doom, that was. And she was a doomed woman. This last time, I'd have shot her like I shoot a stoat, if I'd but been allowed: a raving, doomed thing in the shape of a woman! If only I could have shot her, and ended the whole misery! It ought to be allowed. When a woman gets absolutely possessed by her own will, her own will set against everything, then it's fearful, and she should be shot at last."

"And shouldn't men be shot at last, if they get possessed by their own will?"

"Ay!—the same!—But I must get free of her, or she'll be at me again. I wanted to tell you. I must get a divorce if I possibly can. So we must be careful. We mustn't really be seen together, you and I. I never, *never* could stand it if she came down on me and you."

Connie pondered this.

"Then we can't be together?" she said.

"Not for six months or so. But I think my divorce will go through in September—then till March—"

"But the baby will probably be born at the end of February," she said.

He was silent.

"I could wish the Cliffords and Berthas all dead," he said.

"It's not being very tender to them," she said.

"Tender to them?—Yea, even then the tenderest thing you could do for them, perhaps, would be to give them death. They can't live! They only frustrate life. Their souls are awful inside them. Death ought to be sweet to them. And I ought to be allowed to shoot them."

"But you wouldn't do it," she said.

"I would though! and with less qualms than I shoot a weasel. It anyhow has a prettiness and a loneliness. But they are legion. Oh, I'd shoot them."

"Then perhaps it is just as well you daren't."

"Well—"

Connie had now plenty to think of. It was evident he wanted absolutely to be free of Bertha Coutts. And she felt he was right. The last attack had been too grim.—This meant her living alone, till spring. She would try to get Clifford to divorce her. But how? If Mellors were named, there was an end of *his* divorce. How loathsome! Couldn't one go right away, to the far ends of the earth, and be free from it all?

One could not. The far ends of the earth are not five minutes from Charing Cross, nowadays. While the wireless is active, there are no far ends of the earth. Kings of Dahomey and Lamas of Thibet listen in to London and New York.

Patience! Patience! The world is a vast and ghastly intricacy of mechanism, and one has to be very wary, not to get mangled by it.

Connie confided in her father.

"You see, Father, he was Clifford's gamekeeper: but he was an officer in the army in India. Only he is like Colonel C. E. Florence, who preferred to become a private soldier again."

Sir Malcolm, however, had no sympathy with the unsatisfactory mysticism of the famous C. E. Florence. He saw too much advertisement behind all the humility. It looked just like the sort of conceit the knight most loathed, the conceit of self-abasement.

"Where did your gamekeeper spring from?" asked Sir Malcolm irritably.

"He was a collier's son in Tevershall. But he's absolutely presentable."

The knighted artist became more angry.

"Looks to me like a gold-digger," he said. "And you're a pretty easy gold-mine, apparently."

"No, Father, it's not like that. You'd know if you saw him. He's a man. Clifford always detested him, for not being humble."

"Apparently he had a good instinct, for once."

What Sir Malcolm could not bear, was the scandal of his daughter's having an intrigue with a gamekeeper. He did not mind the intrigue: he minded the scandal.

"I care nothing about the fellow. He's evidently been able to get round you all right. But by Gad, think of all the talk. Think of your step-mother, how she'll take it!"

"I know," said Connie. "Talk is beastly: especially if you live in society. And he wants so much to get his own divorce. I thought we might perhaps say it was another man's child, and not mention Mellors' name at all."

"Another man's! What other man's?"

"Perhaps Duncan Forbes. He has been our friend all his life. And he's a fairly well-known artist. And he's fond of me."

"Well I'm damned! Poor Duncan! And what's he going to get out of it?"

"I don't know. But he might rather like it, even."

"He might, might he? Well he's a funny man, if he does. Why you've never even had an affair with him, have you?"

"No! But he doesn't really want it. He only loves me to be near him—but not to touch him."

"My God, what a generation!"

"He would like me most of all to be a model for him to paint from. Only I never wanted to." ·

"God help him! But he looks down-trodden enough for anything."

"Still, you wouldn't mind so much the talk about him?"

"My God, Connie! All this bloody contriving!"

"I know! It's sickening! But what can I do?"

"Contriving, conniving; conniving, contriving! Makes a man think he's lived too long."

"Come, Father, if you haven't done a good deal of contriving and conniving in your time, you may talk."

"But it was different, I assure you."

"It's *always* different."

Hilda arrived, also furious when she heard of the new developments. And she also simply could not stand the thought of a public scandal about her sister and a gamekeeper. Too, too humiliating!

"Why should we not just disappear, separately, to British Columbia, and have no scandal?" said Connie.

But that was no good. The scandal would come out just the same. And if Connie was going with the man, she'd better be able to marry him. This was Hilda's opinion. Sir Malcolm wasn't so sure. The affair might still blow over.

"But will you see him, Father?"

Poor Sir Malcolm! he was by no means keen on it. And poor Mellors, he was still less keen. Yet the meeting took place: a lunch in a private room at the club, the two men alone, looking one another up and down. Sir Malcolm drank a fair amount of whiskey, Mellors also drank. And they talked all the while about India, on which the younger man was well informed.

This lasted during the meal. Only when coffee was served, and the waiter had gone, Sir Malcolm lit a cigar and said, heartily:

"Well, young man, and what about my daughter?"

The grin flickered on Mellors' face.

"Well, Sir, and what about her?"

"You've got a baby in her all right."

"I have that honour—!" grinned Mellors.

"Honour, by Gad!" Sir Malcolm gave a little squirting laugh, and became Scotch and lewd. "Honour!—How was the going, eh? Good, my boy, what?"

"Good!"

"I'll bet it was! Ha-ha! My daughter, chip of the old block, what! I never went back on a bit of good fucking, myself. Though her mother—oh, holy saints!"—he rolled his eyes to heaven. "But you warmed her up, oh, you warmed her up, I can see that. Ha-ha! My blood in her! You set fire to her haystack all right. Ha-ha-ha! I was jolly glad of it, I can tell you. She needed it. Oh, she's a nice girl, she's a nice girl, and I knew she'd be good going, if only some damned man would set her stack on fire! Ha-ha-ha! A gamekeeper, eh, my boy! Bloody good poacher, if you ask me. Ha-ha! But now, look here, speaking seriously, what are we going to do about it? Speaking seriously, you know!"

Speaking seriously, they didn't get very far. Mellors, though a little tipsy, was much the soberer of the two. He kept the conversation as intelligent as possible: which isn't saying much.

"So you're a gamekeeper! Oh, you're quite right! That pretty sort of game is worth a man's while, eh, what? The test of a woman is when you pinch her bottom. You can tell just by the feel of her bottom if she's going to come up all right. Ha-ha! I envy you, my boy. How old are you?"

"Thirty-nine!"

The knight lifted his eyebrows.

"As much as that! Well—you've another good twenty years, by the looks of you. Oh, gamekeeper or not, you're a game cock. I can see that with one eye shut. Not like that blasted Clifford! A lily-livered hound with never a fuck in him, never had.—I like you, my boy. I'll bet you've a good cod on you; oh, you're a bantam, I can see that. You're a fighter. Gamekeeper! Ha-ha! by crikey, I wouldn't trust my game to you!—But look here, seriously, what are we going to do about it? The world's full of blasted old women—"

Seriously, they didn't do anything about it, except establish the old free-masonry of male sensuality between them.

"And look here, my boy, if ever I can do anything for you, you can rely on me. Gamekeeper! Christ, but it's rich! I like it! Oh, I like it! Shows the girl's got spunk. What?—After all, you know, she has her own income, moderate, moderate, but above starvation. And I'll leave her what I've got. By Gad, I will. She deserves it, for showing spunk, in a world of old women. I've been struggling to get myself clear of the skirts of old women for seventy years, and haven't managed it yet. But you're the man! You're the man, I can see that."

"I'm glad you think so. They usually tell me, in a sideways fashion, that I'm the monkey."

"Oh, they would! My dear fellow, what could you be but a monkey, to all the old women—"

They parted most genially, and Mellors laughed inwardly all the time, for the rest of the day.

The following day he had lunch with Connie and Hilda, at some discreet place.

"It's a very great pity it's such an ugly situation all round," said Hilda.

"I had a lot o' fun out of it," said he.

"I think you might have avoided putting children into the world until you were both free to marry and have children."

"The Lord blew a bit too soon on the spark," said he.

"I think the Lord had nothing to do with it.—Of course Connie has enough money to keep you both—but the situation is unbearable—"

"But then you don't have to bear more than a small corner of it, do you?" said he.

"If you'd been in her own class—"

"Or if I'd been in a cage in the Zoo—"

There was silence.

"I think," said Hilda, "it will be best if she names quite another man as co-respondent, and you stay out of it altogether."

"But I thought I'd put my foot right in—"

"I mean, in the divorce proceedings."

He gazed at her in wonder. Connie had not dared mention the Duncan scheme to him.

"I don't follow," he said.

"We have a friend who would probably agree to be named as co-respondent—so that your name need not appear," said Hilda.

"You mean a man?"

"Of course!"

"But she's got no other—?"

He looked in wonder at Connie.

"No no!" she said hastily. "Only that old friendship—quite simple—no love."

"Then why should the fellow take the blame? If he's had nothing out of you?"

"Some men are chivalrous—and don't only count what they get out of a woman," said Hilda.

"One for me, eh?—But who is the johnny?"

"A friend whom we've known since we were children in Scotland—an artist."

"Duncan Forbes!" he said at once, for Connie had talked to him. "And how would you shift the blame on to him?"

"They could stay together in some hotel—or she could even stay in his apartment—"

"Seems to me a lot of fuss for nothing," he said.

"What else do you suggest?" said Hilda. "If your name appears, you will get no divorce from your wife, who is apparently a quite impossible person to be mixed up with."

"All that!" he said grimly.

There was a long silence.

"We could go right away," he said.

"There is no right away for Connie," said Hilda. "Clifford is too well known."

Again the silence of pure frustration.

"The world is what it is. If you want to live together without being persecuted, you will have to marry. To marry, you both have to be divorced. So how are you both going about it?"

He was silent for a long time.

"How are *you* going about it for us?" he said.

"We will see if Duncan will consent to figure as co-respondent: then we must get Clifford to divorce Connie: and you must go on with your divorce: and you must both keep apart till you are free."

"Sounds like a lunatic asylum."

"Possibly! And the world would look on you as lunatics: or worse."

"What is worse?"

"Criminals, I suppose."

"Hope I can plunge in the dagger a few more times yet," he said grinning. Then he was silent, and angry.

"Well!" he said at last. "I agree to anything. The world is a raving idiot, and no man can kill it: though I'll do my best. But you're right. We must rescue ourselves as best we can."

He looked in humiliation, anger, weariness and misery at Connie. "Ma lass!" he said. "Th' world's goin' to put salt on thy tail." "Not if we don't let it," she said.

She minded this conniving against the world less than he did.

Duncan, when approached, also insisted on seeing the delinquent gamekeeper, so there was a dinner, this time in his flat: the four of them. Duncan was a rather short, broad, dark-skinned, taciturn Hamlet of a fellow with straight black hair and a weird celtic conceit of himself. His art was all tubes and valves and spirals and strange colours, ultra modern, yet with a certain power, even a certain purity of form and tone: only Mellors thought it cruel and repellant. He didn't venture to say so, for Duncan was almost insane on the point of his art; it was a personal cult, a personal religion with him.

They were looking at the pictures in the studio, and Duncan kept his smallish brown eyes on the other man. He wanted to hear what a gamekeeper would say. He knew already Connie's and Hilda's opinions.

"It is like a pure bit of murder," said Mellors at last: a speech Duncan by no means expected from a gamekeeper.

"And who is murdered?" asked Hilda, rather coldly and sneeringly.

"Me! It murders all the bowels of compassion in a man."

A wave of pure hate came out of the artist. He heard the note of dislike in the other man's voice, and the note of contempt. And he himself *loathed* the mention of bowels of compassion. Sickly sentiment! Mellors stood rather tall and thin, worn-looking, gazing with flickering detachment that was something like the dancing of a moth on the wing, at the pictures.

"Perhaps stupidity is murdered—sentimental stupidity," sneered the artist.

"Do you think so? I think all these tubes and corrugated vibrations are stupid enough for anything, and pretty sentimental. They show a lot of self-pity and an awful lot of nervous self-opinion, seems to me."

In another wave of hate, the artist's face looked yellow. But with a sort of silent hauteur he turned the pictures to the wall.

"I think we may go to the dining-room," he said.

And they trailed off, dismally.

After coffee, Duncan said:

"I don't at all mind posing as the father of Connie's child. But only on the condition that she'll come and pose as a model for me. I've wanted her for years, and she's always refused." He uttered it with the dark finality of an inquisitor announcing an *auto da fé*.

"Ah!" said Mellors. "You only do it on condition, then?"

"Quite! I only do it on that condition." The artist tried to put the utmost contempt of the other person into his speech. He put a little too much.

"Better have me as a model at the same time," said Mellors. "Better do us in a group, Vulcan and Venus under the net of art.—I used to be a blacksmith, before I was a gamekeeper."

"Thank you," said the artist. "I don't think Vulcan has a figure that interests me."

"Not even if it was tubified and tittivated up?"

There was no answer. The artist was too haughty for further words.

It was a dismal party, in which the artist henceforth steadily ignored the presence of the other man, and talked only briefly, as if the words were wrung out of the depths of his gloomy portentousness, to the women.

"You didn't like him—but he's better than that, really. He's really kind," Connie explained as they left.

"He's a little black pup with a corrugated distemper," said Mellors.

"No, he wasn't nice today—"

"And will you go and be a model to him?"

"Oh, I don't really mind any more. He won't touch me. And I don't mind anything, if it paves the way to a life together for you and me."

"But he'll only spit on you on canvas."

"I don't care. He'll only be painting his own feelings for me, and I don't mind if he does that. I wouldn't have him touch me, not for anything. But if he thinks he can do anything with his owlish arty staring, let him stare. He can make as many empty tubes and corrugations out of me as he likes. It's his funeral.—He hated you for what you said: that his tubified art is sentimental and self-important. But of course it's true—"

CHAPTER XIX.

"Dear Clifford, I am afraid what you foresaw has happened. I am really in love with another man, and I do hope you will divorce me. I am staying at present with Duncan in his flat. I told you he was at Venice with us. I'm awfully unhappy for your sake: but do try to take it quietly. You don't really need me any more, and I can't bear to come back to Wragby. I'm most awfully sorry. But do try to forgive me, and divorce me and find someone better. I am not really the right person for you, I am too impatient and selfish, I suppose. But I can't ever come back to live with you again. And I feel so frightfully sorry about it all, for your sake. But if you don't let yourself get worked up, you'll see you won't mind so frightfully. You didn't really care about me personally. So do forgive me and get rid of me——"

Clifford was not *inwardly* surprised to get this letter. Inwardly, he had known for a long time she was leaving him. But he had absolutely refused any outward admission of it. Therefore, outwardly, it came as the most terrible blow and shock to him. He had kept the surface of his confidence in her quite serene.

And that is how we are. By strength of will we cut off our inner intuitive knowledge from our admitted consciousness. This causes a state of dread, or apprehension, which makes the blow ten times worse when it does fall.

Clifford was like a hysterical child. He gave Mrs Bolton a fearful shock, sitting up in bed ghastly and blank.

"Why Sir Clifford, whatever's the matter?"

No answer! She was terrified lest he had had a stroke. She hurried and felt his face, took his pulse.

"Is there a pain? Do try and tell me where it hurts you. Do tell me!"

No answer!

"Oh dear oh dear! Then I'll telephone to Sheffield for Dr Carrington, and Dr Lecky may as well run round straight away."

She was moving to the door, when he said in a hollow tone:

"No!"

288

She stopped and gazed at him. His face was yellow, blank, and like the face of an idiot.

"Do you mean you'd rather I didn't fetch the doctor?"

"Yes! I don't want him," came the sepulchral voice.

"Oh but Sir Clifford, you're ill, and I daren't take the responsibility. I *must* send for the doctor, or *I* shall be blamed."

A pause: then the hollow voice said:

"I'm not ill.—My wife isn't coming back."—It was as if an image spoke.

"Not coming back? You mean her ladyship?" Mrs Bolton moved a little nearer to the bed. "Oh, don't you believe it. You can trust her ladyship to come back."

The image in the bed did not change, but it pushed a letter over the counterpane.

"Read it!" said the sepulchral voice.

"Why—if it's a letter from her ladyship, I'm sure her ladyship wouldn't want me to read her letter to you, Sir Clifford. You can tell me what she says, if you wish."

But the face with the fixed blue eyes sticking out did not change.

"Read it!" repeated the voice.

"Why if I must, I do it to obey you, Sir Clifford," she said.

And she read the letter.

"Well I *am* surprised at her ladyship," she said. "She promised so faithfully she'd come back!"

The face in the bed seemed to deepen its expression of wild, but motionless distraction. Mrs Bolton looked at it and was worried. She knew what she was up against: male hysteria. She had not nursed soldiers without learning something about that very unpleasant disease.

She was a little impatient of Sir Clifford. Any man in his senses must have *known* his wife was in love with somebody else, and was going to leave him. Even, she was sure, Sir Clifford was inwardly absolutely aware of it, only he wouldn't admit it to himself. If he would have admitted it, and prepared himself for it; or if he would have admitted it, and actively struggled with his wife against it: that would have been acting like a man. But no! he knew it, and all the time tried to kid himself it wasn't so. He felt the devil twisting his tail, and pretended it was the angels smiling on him. This state of falsity had now brought on that crisis of falsity and dislocation, hysteria, which is a form of insanity. 'It comes,' she thought to herself, hating him a little, 'because he always thinks of himself. He's so wrapped up in his own immortal self, that when he does get a shock he's like a mummy tangled in its own bandages. Look at him!'

But hysteria is dangerous: and she was a nurse, it was her duty to pull him out. Any attempt to rouse his manhood and his pride would only make him worse: for his manhood was dead, temporarily if not finally. He would only squirm softer and softer, like a worm, and become more dislocated.

The only thing was to release his self-pity. Like the lady in Tennyson, he must weep or he must die.

So Mrs Bolton began to weep first. She covered her face with her hands and burst into little wild sobs.—"I would never have believed it of her ladyship, I wouldn't, I wouldn't!" she wept, suddenly summoning up all her old grief and sense of woe, and weeping the tears of her own bitter chagrin. Once she started, her weeping was genuine enough, for she had had something to weep for.

Clifford thought of the way he had been betrayed by the woman Connie, and in a contagion of grief, tears filled his eyes and began to run down his cheeks. He was weeping for himself. Mrs Bolton, as soon as she saw the tears running over his blank face, hastily wiped her own wet cheeks on her little handkerchief, and leaned towards him.

"Now don't you fret, Sir Clifford!" she said, in a luxury of emotion. "Now don't you fret, don't, you'll only do yourself an injury!"

His body shivered suddenly in an indrawn breath of silent sobbing, and the tears ran quicker down his face. She laid her hand on his arm, and her own tears fell again. Again the shiver went through him, like a convulsion, and she laid her arm round his shoulder.—"There, there! There—there! Don't you fret, then, don't you! Don't you fret!" she moaned to him, while her own tears fell. And she drew him to her, and held her arms round his great shoulders, while he laid his face on her bosom and sobbed, shaking and hulking his huge shoulders, whilst she softly stroked his dusky-blond hair and said: "There! There! There! There then! There then! Never you mind! Never you mind, then!"

And he put his arms round her and clung to her like a child, wetting the bib of her starched white apron, and the bosom of her pale-blue cotton dress, with his tears. He had let himself go altogether, at last.

So at length she kissed him, and rocked him on her bosom, and in her heart she said to herself: 'Oh Sir Clifford! Oh high and mighty Chatterleys! Is this what you've come down to!'—And finally he even went to sleep, like a child. And she felt worn out, and went to her room, where she laughed and cried at once, with a hysteria of her own. It was so ridiculous! It was so awful!—such a come-down! so shameful! And it *was* so upsetting as well.

After this, Clifford became like a child with Mrs Bolton. He would hold her hand, and rest his head on her breast, and when she once lightly kissed him, he said: "Yes! Do kiss me! Do kiss me!" And when she sponged his great blond body, he would say the same: "Do kiss me!" And she would lightly kiss his body, anywhere, half in mockery. And he lay with a queer, blank face like a child, with a bit of the wonderment of a child. And he would gaze on her with wide, childish eyes, in a relaxation of Madonna-worship. It was sheer relaxation on his part, letting go all his manhood, and sinking back to a childish position that was really perverse. And then he would put his hand into her bosom and feel her breasts, and kiss them in exaltation, the exaltation of perversity, of being a child when he was a man.

Mrs Bolton was both thrilled and ashamed, she both loved it and hated it. Yet she never rebuffed or rebuked him. And they drew into a closer physical intimacy, an intimacy of perversity, when he was a child stricken with an apparent candour and an apparent wonderment, that looked almost like a religious exaltation: the perverse and literal rendering of: "except ye become again as a little child."—While she was the Magna Mater, full of power and potency, having the great blond child-man under her will and her stroke entirely.

The curious thing was that when this child-man which Clifford now was—and which he had been becoming for years—emerged into the world, it was much sharper and keener than the real man he used to be. This perverted child-man was now a *real* business-man; when it was a question of affairs, he was an absolute he-man, sharp as a needle, and impervious as a bit of steel. When he was out among men, seeking his own ends, and "making good" his colliery work-ings, he had an almost uncanny shrewdness, hardness, and a straight sharp punch. It was as if his very passivity and prostitution to the Magna Mater gave him insight into material business affairs, and lent him a certain remarkable inhuman force. The wallowing in private emotion, the utter abasement of his manly self, seemed to lend him a second nature, cold, almost visionary, business-clever. In business he was quite inhuman.

And in this Mrs Bolton triumphed. "How he's getting on!" she would say to herself in pride. "And that's my doing! My word, he'd never have got on like this with Lady Chatterley. She was not the one to put a man forward. She wanted too much for herself—"

At the same time, in some corner of her weird female soul, how she despised him and hated him! He was to her the fallen beast, the squirming monster. And while she aided and abetted him all she could, away in the remotest corner of her ancient healthy womanhood she despised him with a savage contempt that knew no bounds. The merest tramp was better than he.

His behaviour with regard to Connie was curious. He insisted on seeing her again. He insisted, moreover, on her coming to Wragby. On this point he was pale and absolutely fixed. Connie had promised to come back to Wragby, faithfully.

"But is it any use?" said Mrs Bolton. "Can't you let her go, and be rid of her?"

"No! She said she was coming back, and she's got to come."

Mrs Bolton opposed him no more. She knew what she was dealing with.

"I needn't tell you what effect your letter has had on me," he wrote to Connie to London. "Perhaps you can imagine it if you try, though no doubt you won't trouble to use your imagination on my behalf.

"I can only say one thing in answer: I must see you personally, here at Wragby, before I can do anything. You promised faithfully to come back to Wragby, and I hold you to the promise. I don't believe anything nor understand anything until I see you personally, here under normal circumstances. I needn't tell you that nobody here suspects anything, so your return would be quite normal. Then if you feel, after we have talked things over, that you still remain in the same mind, no doubt we can come to terms—"

Connie showed this letter to Mellors.

"He wants to begin his revenge on you," said he, handing the letter back.

Connie was silent. She was somewhat surprised to find that she was afraid of Clifford. She was afraid to go near him. She was afraid of him as if he were evil and dangerous.

"What shall I do?" she said.

"Nothing, if you don't want to do anything."

She replied, trying to put Clifford off. He answered: "If you don't come back to Wragby now, I shall consider that you are coming back one day, and act accordingly. I shall just go on the same, and wait for you here, if I wait for fifty years."

She was frightened. This was bullying of an insidious sort. She had no doubt he meant what he said. He would not divorce her, and the child would be his, unless she could find some means of establishing its illegitimacy.

After a time of worry and harassment, she decided to go to Wragby. Hilda would go with her. She wrote this to Clifford. He replied: "I shall not welcome your sister, but I shall not deny her the door. I have no doubt she has connived at your desertion of your duties and responsibilities, so do not expect me to show pleasure in seeing her—"

They went to Wragby. Clifford was away when they arrived. Mrs Bolton received them.

"Oh, your Ladyship, it isn't the happy home-coming we hoped for, is it?" she said.

"Isn't it!" said Connie.

So this woman knew! How much did the rest of the servants know or suspect?

She entered the house which now she hated with every fibre in her body. The great, rambling mass of a place seemed evil to her, just a menace over her. She was no longer its mistress, she was its victim.

"I can't stay long here," she whispered to Hilda, terrified.

And she suffered going into her own bedroom, re-entering into possession as if nothing had happened. She hated every minute inside the Wragby walls.

They did not meet Clifford till they went down to dinner. He was dressed, and with a black tie: rather reserved, and very much the superior gentleman. He behaved perfectly politely during the meal, and kept a polite sort of conversation going: but it seemed all touched with insanity.

"How much do the servants know?" asked Connie, when the woman was out of the room.

"Of your intentions? Nothing whatsoever."

"Mrs Bolton knows."

He changed colour.

"Mrs Bolton is not exactly one of the servants," he said.

"Oh, I don't mind."

There was tension till after coffee, when Hilda said she would go up to her room.

Clifford and Connie sat in silence when she had gone. Neither would begin to speak. Connie was so glad that he wasn't taking the pathetic line, she kept him up to as much haughtiness as possible. She just sat silent and looked down at her hands.

"I suppose you don't at all mind having gone back on your word?" he said at last.

"I can't help it," she murmured.

"But if you can't, who can?"

"I suppose nobody."

He looked at her with curious cold rage. He was used to her. She was as it were embedded in his will. How dared she now go back on him, and destroy the fabric of his daily existence? How dared she try to cause this derangement of his personality!

"And for *what* do you want to go back on everything?" he insisted.

"Love!" she said. It was best to be hackneyed.

"Love of Duncan Forbes? But you didn't think that worth having, when you met me. Do you mean to say you now love him better than anything else in life?"

"One changes," she said.

"Possibly! Possibly you may have whims. But you still have to convince me of the importance of the change. I merely don't believe in your love of Duncan Forbes."

"But why *should* you believe in it?—You have only to divorce me, not to believe in my feelings."

"And why should I divorce you?"

"Because I don't want to live here any more. And you don't really want me."

"Pardon me! I don't change. For my part, since you are my wife, I should prefer that you should stay under my roof in dignity and quiet. Leaving aside personal feelings, and I assure you, on my part it is leaving aside a great deal, it is bitter as death to me to have the order of life broken up, here in Wragby, and the decent round of daily life smashed, just for some whim of yours."

After a time of silence she said:

"I can't help it. I've got to go.—I expect I shall have a child."

He too was silent for a time.

"And is it for the child's sake you must go?" he asked at length. She nodded.

"And why? Is Duncan Forbes so keen on his spawn?"

"Surely keener than you would be," she said.

"But really? I want my wife, and I see no reason for letting her go. If she likes to bear a child under my roof, she is welcome, and the child is welcome: provided that the decency and order of life is preserved. Do you mean to tell me that Duncan Forbes has a greater hold over you? I don't believe it."

There was a pause.

"But don't you see," said Connie, "I *must* go away from you, and I *must* live with the man I love."

"No, I don't see it! I don't give tuppence for your love, nor for the man you love. I don't believe in that sort of cant."

"But you see, I do."

"Do you? My dear madam, you are too intelligent, I assure you, to believe in your own love for Duncan Forbes. Believe me, even now you really care more for me. So why should I give in to such nonsense!"

She felt he was right, there. And she felt she could keep silent no longer.

"Because it isn't Duncan that I *do* love," she said, looking up at him. "We only said it was Duncan, to spare your feelings."

"To spare my feelings?"

"Yes!—Because who I really love—and it'll make you hate me—is Mr Mellors, who was our gamekeeper here."

If he could have sprung out of his chair, he would have done so. His face went yellow, and his eyes bulged with disaster as he glared at her. Then he dropped back in the chair, gasping, and looking up at the ceiling.

At length he sat up.

"Do you mean to say you're telling me the truth?" he asked, looking gruesome.

"Yes! You know I am."

"And when did you begin with him?"

"In the spring."

He was silent, like some beast in a trap.

"And it *was* you, then, in the bedroom at the cottage?"

So he had really inwardly known all the time.

"Yes!"

He still leaned forward in his chair, gazing at her like a cornered beast.

"My God, you ought to be wiped off the face of the earth!"

"Why?" she ejaculated faintly.

But he seemed not to hear her.

"That scum! That bumptious lout! That miserable cad! And carrying on with him all the time, while you were here and he was one of my servants! My God, my God, is there any end to the beastly lowness of women!"

He was beside himself with rage, as she knew he would be.

"And you mean to say you want to have a child to a cad like that?"

"Yes! I'm going to."

"You're going to! You mean you're sure! How long have you been sure?"

"Since June."

He was speechless, and the queer blank look of a child came over him again.

"You'd wonder," he said at last, "that such beings were ever allowed to be born."

"What beings?" she asked.

He looked at her weirdly, without answer. It was obvious he couldn't even accept the fact of the existence of Mellors, in any connection with his own life. It was sheer, unspeakable, impotent hate.

"And do you mean to say you'd marry him?—and bear his foul name?" he asked at length.

"Yes! That's what I want."

He was again as if dumbfounded.

"Yes!" he said at last. "That proves that what I've always thought about you is correct: you're not normal, you're not in your right senses. You're one of those half-insane, perverted women who must run after depravity, the *nostalgie de la boue*."

Suddenly he had become almost wistfully moral, seeing himself the incarnation of good, and people like Connie and Mellors the incarnation of mud, of evil. He seemed to be growing vague, inside a nimbus.

"So don't you think you'd better divorce me and have done with me?" she said.

"No! You can go where you like, but I shan't divorce you," he said idiotically.

"Why not?"

He was silent, in the silence of imbecile obstinacy.

"Would you even let the child be legally yours, and your heir?" she said.

"I care nothing about the child."

"But if it's a boy, it will be legally your son, and it will inherit your title, and have Wragby."

"I care nothing about that," he said.

"But you *must*!—I shall prevent the child from being legally yours, if I can. I'd so much rather it were illegitimate, and mine: if it can't be Mellors'."

"Do as you like about that."

He was immovable.

"And won't you divorce me?" she said. "You can use Duncan as a pretext. There'd be no need to bring in the real name. Duncan doesn't mind."

"*I* shall never divorce you," he said, as if a nail had been driven in.

"But why? Because I want you to?"

"Because I follow my own inclination, and I'm not inclined to."

It was useless. She went upstairs, and told Hilda the upshot.

"Better get away tomorrow," said Hilda, "and let him come to his senses."

So Connie spent half the night packing her really private and personal effects. In the morning she had her trunks sent to the station, without telling Clifford. She decided to see him only to say good-bye, before lunch.

But she spoke to Mrs Bolton.

"I must say good-bye to you, Mrs Bolton. You know why. But I can trust you not to talk."

"Oh, you can trust me, your Ladyship—though it's a sad blow for us here, indeed. But I hope you'll be happy with the other gentleman."

"The other gentleman!—It's Mr Mellors—and I care for him. Sir Clifford knows. But don't say anything to anybody. And if one day you think Sir Clifford may be willing to divorce me, let me know, will you? I should like to be properly married to the man I care for."

"I'm sure you would, my Lady! Oh, you can trust me. I'll be faithful to Sir Clifford, and I'll be faithful to you, for I can see you're both right in your own ways."

"Thank you! And look! I want to give you this—may I?—"

So Connie left Wragby once more, and went on with Hilda to Scotland.

Mellors went into the country and got work on a farm. The idea was, he should get his divorce, if possible, whether Connie got hers or not. And for the six months he should work at farming, so that eventually he and Connie could have some small farm of their own, into which he could put his energy. For he would have to have some work, even hard work, to do, and he would have to make his own living, even if her capital started him.

So they would have to wait till spring was in, till the baby was born, till the early summer came round again.

"The Grange Farm.   Old Heanor   29 September.

"I got on here with a bit of contriving, because I knew Richards, the company engineer, in the army. It is a farm belonging to Butler and Smitham Colliery Company, they use it for raising hay and oats for the pit-ponies—not a private concern. But they've got cows and pigs and all the rest of it, and I get thirty shillings a week as a laborer. Rowley, the farmer, puts me on to as many jobs as he can, so that I can learn as much as possible between now and next Easter. I've not heard a thing about Bertha. I've no idea why she didn't show up at the divorce, nor where she is nor what she's up to. But if I keep quiet till March I suppose I shall be free. And don't you bother about Sir Clifford. He'll want to get rid of you one of these days. If he leaves you alone, it's a lot.

"I've got lodgings in a bit of an old cottage in Engine Row, very decent. The man is engine-driver at High Park, tall, with a beard, and very chapel. The woman is a birdy bit of a thing who loves anything superior—so I'm quite the superior, King's English and allow-me! all the time. But they lost their only son in the war, and it's sort of knocked a hole in them. There's a long gawky lass of a daughter training for a school-teacher, and I help her with her lessons sometimes, so we're quite the family. But they're very decent people, and only too kind to me. I expect I'm more coddled than you are.

"I like farming all right. It's not inspiring, but then I don't ask to be inspired. I'm used to horses, and cows, though they are very female, have a soothing effect on me. When I sit with my head in her side, milking, I feel solaced. They have six rather fine Herefords. Oat-harvest is just over—and I enjoyed it, in spite of sore hands and a lot of rain. I don't take much notice of people—but get on with them all right. Most things one just ignores.

"The pits are working badly—this is a colliery district like Tevershall, only prettier. I sometimes sit in the Wellington and talk to the men. They grumble a lot, but they're not going to alter anything. As everybody says, the Notts-Derby miners have got their hearts in the right place. But the rest of their anatomy must be in the wrong place, in a world that has no use for them. I like them, but they don't cheer me much: not enough of the old fighting-cock in them. They talk a lot about nationalisation, nationalisation of royalties, nationalisation of the whole industry. But you can't nationalise coal and leave all the other industries as they are. They talk about putting coal to new uses, like Sir Clifford is trying to do. It may work here and there, but not as a general thing, I doubt. Whatever you make you've got to sell it. The men are very apathetic. They feel the whole damn thing is doomed, and I believe it is. And they are doomed along with it. Some of the young ones spout about a Soviet, but there's not much conviction in them. There's no sort of conviction about anything—except that it's all a muddle and a hole. Even under a Soviet you've still got to sell coal: and that's the difficulty. We've got these great industrial populations, and they've got to be fed, so the damn show has to be kept going somehow. The women talk a lot more than the men, nowadays, and they are a sight more cock-sure. The men are limp, they feel a doom somewhere, and they go about as if there was nothing to be done. Anyhow nobody knows what should be done, in spite of all the talk. The young ones get mad because they've no money to spend. Their whole life depends on spending money, and now they've got none to spend. That's our civilisation and our education: brings up the masses to depend entirely on spending money, and then the money gives out. The pits are working two days, two-and-a-half days a week, and there's no sign of betterment even for the winter. It means a man bringing up a family on twenty-five and thirty shillings. The women are the maddest of all. But then they're the maddest for spending, nowadays.

"If you could only tell them that living and spending aren't the same thing! But it's no good. If only they were educated to *live* instead of earn and spend, they could manage very happily on twenty-five shillings. If the men wore scarlet trousers, as I said, they wouldn't think so much of money: if they could dance and hop and skip, and sing and swagger and be handsome, they could do with very little cash. And amuse the women themselves, and be amused by the women. They ought to learn to be naked and handsome, all of them, and to move and be handsome, and to sing in a mass and dance the old group dances, and carve the stools they sit on, and embroider their own emblems. Then they wouldn't need money. And that's the only way to solve the industrial problem: train the people to be able to live and live in handsomeness, without needing to spend. But you can't do it. They're all one-track minds nowadays. Whereas the mass of people oughtn't even to try to think—because they *can't*. They should be alive and frisky, and acknowledge the great god Pan. He's the only god for the masses, forever. The few can go in for higher cults if they like. But let the mass be forever pagan.

"But the colliers aren't pagan—far from it. They're a sad lot, a deadened lot of men: dead to their women, dead to life. The young ones scoot about on motor-bikes with girls, and jazz when they get a chance. But they're very dead. And it needs money. Money poisons you when you've got it, and starves you when you haven't.

"I'm sure you're sick of all this. But I don't want to harp on myself, and I've nothing happening to me. I don't like to think too much about you, in my head, that only makes a mess of us both. But of course what I live for now is for you and me to live together. I'm frightened, really. I feel the devil in the air, and he'll try to get us. Or not the devil—Mammon: which I think, after all, is only the mass-will of people, wanting money and hating life. Anyhow I feel great groping white hands in the air, wanting to get hold of the throat of anybody who tries to live, to live beyond money, and squeeze the life out. There's a bad time coming. There's a bad time coming, boys, there's a bad time coming! If things go on as they are, there's nothing lies in the future but death and destruction, for these industrial masses. I feel my inside turn to water sometimes—and there you are, going to have a child by me.—But never mind. All the bad times that ever have been, haven't been able to blow the crocus out: nor even the love of women. So they won't be able to blow out my wanting you, nor the little glow there is between you and me. We'll be together next year. And though I'm frightened, I believe in your being with me. A man has to fend and fettle for the best, and then trust in something beyond himself. You can't insure against the future, except by really believing in the best bit of you, and in the power beyond it. So I believe in the little flame between us. For me now, it's the only thing in the world. I've got no friends, not inward friends. Only you. And now the little flame is all I care about in my life. There's the baby, but that is a side issue. It's my Pentecost, the forked flame between me and you. The old Pentecost isn't quite right. Me and God is a bit uppish, somehow. But the little forked flame between me and you: there you are! That's what I abide by, and will abide by, Cliffords and Berthas, colliery companies and governments and the money-mass of people all notwithstanding.

"That's why I don't like to start thinking of you actually. It only tortures me, and does you no good. I don't want you to be away from me. But if I start fretting, it wastes something. Patience, always patience. This is my fortieth winter. And I can't help all the winters that have been. But this winter I'll stick to my little pentecost flame, and have some peace. And I won't let the breath of people blow it out. I believe in a higher mystery, that doesn't let even the crocus be blown out. And if you're in Scotland and I'm in the Midlands, and I can't put my arms round you, and wrap my legs round you, yet I've got something of you. My soul softly flaps in the little pentecost flame with you, like the peace of fucking. We fucked a flame into being. Even the flowers are fucked into being, between sun and earth. But it's a delicate thing, and takes patience and the long pause.

"So I love chastity now, because it is the peace that comes of fucking. I love being chaste now. I love it as snowdrops love the snow. I love this chastity, which is the pause and peace of our fucking, between us now like a snowdrop of forked white fire. And when the real spring comes, when the drawing together comes, then we can fuck the little flame brilliant and yellow, brilliant. But not now, not yet! Now is the time to be chaste, it is so good to be chaste, like a river of cool water in my soul. I love the chastity now that flows between us. It is like fresh water and rain. How can men want wearisomely to philander. What a misery to be like Don Juan, and impotent ever to fuck oneself into peace, and the little flame alight, impotent and unable to be chaste in the cool between-whiles, as by a river.

"Well, so many words, because I can't touch you. If I could sleep with my arm round you, the ink could stay in the bottle. We could be chaste together just as we can fuck together. But we have to be separate for a while, and I suppose it is really the wiser way. If only one were sure.

"Never mind, never mind, we won't get worked up. We'll really trust in the little flame, and in the unnamed god that shields it from being blown out. There's so much of you here with me, really—that it's a pity you aren't all here.

"Never mind about Sir Clifford. If you don't hear anything from him, never mind. He can't really do anything to you. Wait, he will want to get rid of you at last, to cast you out. And if he doesn't, we'll manage to keep clear of him. But he will. In the end he will want to spew you out as the abominable thing.

"Now I can't even leave off writing to you.

"But a great deal of us is together, and we can but abide by it, and steer our courses to meet soon. John Thomas says good-night to lady Jane, a little droopingly, but with a hopeful heart—"

A PROPOS OF
"LADY CHATTERLEY'S LOVER"

A Propos of "Lady Chatterley's Lover"

Owing to the existence of various pirated editions of *Lady Chatter-ley's Lover*, I brought out in 1929, this cheap popular edition, produced in France and offered to the public at sixty francs, hoping at least to meet the European demand. The pirates, in the United States certainly, were prompt and busy. The first stolen edition was being sold in New York almost within a month of the arrival in America of the first genuine copies from Florence. It was a facsimile of the original, produced by the photographic method, and was sold, even by reliable booksellers, to the unsuspecting public as if it *were* the original first edition. The price was usually fifteen dollars, whereas the price of the original was ten dollars: and the purchaser was left in fond ignorance of the fraud.

This gallant attempt was followed by others. I am told there was still another facsimile edition produced in New York or Philadelphia: and I myself possess a filthy-looking book bound in a dull orange cloth, with green label, smearily produced by photography, and containing my signature forged by the little boy of the piratical family. It was when this edition appeared in London, from New York, towards the end of 1928, and was offered to the public at thirty shillings, that I put out from Florence my little second edition of two hundred copies, which I offered at a guinea. I had wanted to save it for a year or more, but had to launch it against the dirty orange pirate. But the number was too small. The orange pirate persisted.

Then I have had in my hand a very funereal volume, bound in black and elongated to look like a bible or long hymn-book, gloomy. This time the pirate was not only sober, but earnest. He has not one, but two title-pages, and on each is a vignette representing the American Eagle, with six stars round his head and lightning splashing from his paw, all surrounded by a laurel wreath in honour of his latest exploit in literary robbery. Altogether it is a sinister volume, like Captain Kidd with his face blackened, reading a sermon to those about to walk the plank. Why the pirate should have elongated the page, by adding a false page-heading, I don't know. The effect is peculiarly depressing, sinisterly high-brow. For of course this book also was produced by the photographic method. The signature anyhow is omitted. And I am told this lugubrious tome sells for ten, twenty, thirty, forty dollars, according to the whim of the bookseller and the gullibility of the purchaser.

That makes three pirated editions in the United States, for certain. I have mentioned the report of a fourth, another facsimile of the original. But since I haven't seen it, I want not to believe in it.

There is, however, the European pirated edition of fifteen hundred, produced by a Parisian bookshop, and stamped: *Imprimé en Allemagne*: Printed in Germany.—Whether printed in Germany or not, it was certainly printed, not photographed, for some of the spelling errors of the original are corrected. And it is a very respectable volume, a very close replica of the original, but lacking the signature, and it gives itself away also by the green and yellow silk edge of the back-binding. This edition is sold to trade at one hundred francs, and offered to the public at three hundred, four hundred, five hundred francs. Very unscrupulous booksellers are said to have forged the signature and offered the book as the original signed edition. Let us hope it's not true.

But it all sounds very black against the "trade." Still there is some relief. Certain booksellers will not handle the pirated editions at all. Both sentiment and business scruples prevent them. Others handle it, but not very warmly. And apparently they would all *rather* handle an authorised edition. So that sentiment does genuinely enter in, against the pirates, even if not strong enough to keep them out altogether.

None of these pirated editions has received any sort of authorisation from me, and from none of them have I received a penny. A semi-repentant bookseller of New York did, however, send me some dollars which were, he said, my 10% royalty on all copies sold in his shop. "I know," he wrote, "it is but a drop in the bucket." He meant, of course, a drop out of the bucket. And since, for a drop, it was quite a nice little sum, what a beautiful bucketful there must have been for the pirates!

I received a belated offer from the European Pirates, who found the booksellers stiff-necked, offering me a royalty on all copies sold in the past as well as the future, if I would authorise their edition. Well, I thought to myself, in a world of: Do him or you will be done by him,—why not?—When it came to the point, however, pride rebelled. It is understood that Judas is always ready with a kiss. But that I should have to kiss him back—!

So I managed to get published the little cheap French edition, photographed down from the original, and offered at 60 frs. English publishers urge me to make an expurgated edition, promising large returns, perhaps even a little bucket, one of those children's sea-side pails!—and insisting that I should show the public that here is a fine novel, apart from all "purple" and all "words." So I begin to be tempted, and start in to expurgate. But impossible! I might as well try to clip my own nose into shape with scissors. The book bleeds.

And in spite of all antagonism, I put forth this novel as an honest, healthy book, necessary for us today. The words that shock so much at first don't shock at all after a while. Is this because the mind is depraved by habit? Not a bit. It is that the words merely shocked the eye, they never shocked the mind at all. People with no minds may go on being shocked, but they don't matter. People with minds realise that they aren't shocked, and never really were; and they experience a sense of relief.

And that is the whole point. We are, today, as human beings, evolved and cultured far beyond the taboos which are inherent in our culture. This is a very important fact to realise. Probably, to the Crusaders, mere words were potent and evocative to a degree we can't realise. The evocative power of the so-called obscene words must have been very dangerous to the dim-minded, obscure, violent natures of the Middle Ages, and perhaps are still too strong for slow-minded, half-evolved lower natures today. But real culture makes us give to a word only those mental and imaginative reactions which belong to the mind, and saves us from violent and indiscriminate physical reactions which may wreck social decency. In the past, man was too weak-minded, or crude-minded to contemplate his own physical body and physical functions, without getting all messed up with physical reactions that overpowered him. It is no longer so. Culture and civilisation have taught us to separate the word from the deed, the thought from the act or the physical reaction. We now know that the act does not necessarily follow on the thought. In fact, thought and action, word and deed are two separate forms of consciousness, two separate lives which we lead. We need, very sincerely, to keep a connection. But while we think we do not act, and while we act we do not think. The great necessity is that we should act according to our thoughts, and think according to our acts. But while we are in thought we cannot really act, and while we are in action we cannot really think. The two conditions, of thought and action, are mutually exclusive. Yet they should be related in harmony.

And this is the real point of this book. I want men and women to be able to *think* sex, fully, completely, honestly, and cleanly. Even if we can't *act* sexually to our complete satisfaction, let us at least think sexually, complete and clean. All this talk of young girls and virginity like a blank white sheet on which nothing is written, is pure nonsense. A young girl, and a young boy is a tormented tangle, a seething confusion of sexual feelings and sexual thoughts which only the years will disentangle. Years of honest thought of sex, and years of struggling action in sex will bring us at last where we want to get, to our real and accomplished chastity, our completeness, when our sexual act and our sexual thought are in harmony, and the one does not interfere with the other.

Far be it from me to suggest that all women should go running after gamekeepers for lovers. Far be it from me to suggest that they should go running after anybody. A great many men and women today are happiest when they abstain and stay sexually apart, quite clear: and at the same time, when they understand and realise sex more fully. Ours is the day of realisation rather than of action. There has been so much action in the past, especially sexual action, a wearying repetition over and over, without a corresponding thought, a corresponding realisation. Now our business is to realise sex. Today, the full conscious realisation of sex is even more important than the act itself. After centuries of obfuscation, the mind demands to know and know fully. The body is a good deal in abeyance, really. When people act in sex, nowadays, they are half the time acting up. They do it because they think it is expected of them. Whereas as a matter of fact it is the mind which is interested, and the body has to be provoked. The reason being that our ancestors have so assidu- ously acted sex without ever thinking it or realising it, that now the act tends to be mechanical, dull, and disappointing, and only fresh mental realisation will freshen up the experience.

The mind has to catch up, in sex: indeed, in all the physical acts. Mentally, we lag behind in our sexual thoughts, in a dimness, a lurking, grovelling fear which belongs to our raw, somewhat bestial ancestors. In this one respect, sexual and physical, we have left the mind unevolved. Now we have to catch up, and make a balance between the consciousness of sex and the act of sex, the thoughtful consciousness of the body's sensations and experiences, and these sensations and experiences themselves. Balance up the consciousness of the act, and the act itself. Get the two in harmony. It means having a proper reverence for sex, and a proper awe of the body's strange experiences. It means being able to use the so-called obscene words, because these are a natural part of the mind's consciousness of the body. Obscenity only comes in when the mind despises and fears the body, and the body hates and resists the mind.

When we read of the case of Colonel Barker, we see what is the matter. Colonel Barker was a woman who masqueraded as a man. The "Colonel" married a wife, and lived five years with her in "conjugal happiness." And the poor wife thought all the time she was married normally and happily to a real husband. The revelation at the end is beyond all thought cruel for the poor woman. The situation is monstrous. Yet there are thousands of women today who might be so deceived, and go on being deceived. Why? Because they know nothing, they can't think sexually at all, they are morons in the respect. It is better to give all young girls this book, at the age of seventeen.

The same with the case of the venerable schoolmaster and clergyman, for years utterly "holy and good": and at the age of sixty-five, tried in the police courts for assaulting little girls. This happens at the moment when the Home Secretary, himself growing elderly, is most loudly demanding and enforcing a mealy-mouthed silence about sexual matters. Doesn't the experience of that other elderly, most righteous and "pure" gentleman, make him pause at all?

But so it is. The mind has an old, grovelling fear of the body and the body's potencies. It is the *mind* we have to liberate, to civilise on these points. The mind's terror of the body has probably driven more men mad than ever could be counted. The insanity of a great mind like Swift's is at least partly traceable to this cause. In the poem to his mistress Celia, which has the maddened refrain: "But—Celia, Celia, Celia shits!" we see what can happen to a great mind, when it falls into panic. A great wit like Swift could not see how ridiculous he made himself. Of course Celia shits! who doesn't? And how much worse if she *didn't*. It is hopeless. And then think of poor Celia, made to feel iniquitous about her proper natural function, by her "lover." It is monstrous. And it comes from having taboo words, and from not keeping the mind sufficiently developed in physical and sexual consciousness.

In contrast to the puritan hush! hush!, which produces the sexual moron, we have the modern young jazzy and high-brow person who has gone one better, and won't be hushed in any respect, and just "does as she likes." From fearing the body and denying its existence, the advanced young go to the other extreme and treat it as a sort of toy to be played with, a slightly nasty toy, but still you can get some fun out of it, before it lets you down. These young people scoff at the importance of sex, take it like a cocktail, and flout their elders with it. These young ones are advanced and superior. They despise a book like *Lady Chatterley's Lover*. It is much too simple and ordinary for them. The naughty words they care nothing about, and the attitude to love they find old-fashioned. Why make a fuss about it? Take it like a cocktail. The book, they say, shows the mentality of a boy of fourteen. But perhaps the mentality of a boy of fourteen, who still has a little natural awe and proper fear in face of sex, is more wholesome than the mentality of the young cocktaily person who has no respect for anything, and whose mind has nothing to do but play with the toys of life, sex being one of the chief toys, and who loses his mind in the process. Heliogabalus indeed!

So, between the stock old puritan who is likely to fall into sexual indecency in advanced age, and the smart jazzy person of the young world, who says: "We can do *anything*. If we can think a thing we can do it"—and then the low uncultured person with a dirty mind, who looks for dirt—this book has hardly a space to turn in. But to them all I say the same: Keep your perversions if you like them—your perversion of puritanism, your perversion of smart licentiousness, your perversion of a dirty mind. But I stick to my book and my position: Life is only bearable when the mind and the body are in harmony, and there is a natural balance between the two, and each has a natural respect for the other.

And it is obvious, there is no balance and no harmony now. The body is at the best the tool of the mind, at the worst, the toy. The business man keeps himself "fit," that is, keeps his body in good working order, for the sake of his business, and the usual young person who spends much time on keeping fit does so as a rule out of self-conscious self-absorption, narcissism. The mind has a stereotyped set of ideas and "feelings," and the body is made to act up, like a trained dog: to beg for sugar, whether it wants sugar or whether it doesn't, to shake hands when it would dearly like to snap the hand it has to shake. The body of men and women today is just a trained

dog. And of no-one is this more true than of the free and emanci-
pated young. Above all, their bodies are the bodies of trained dogs.
And because the dog is trained to do things the old-fashioned dog
never did, they call themselves free, full of real life, the real thing.

But they know perfectly well it is false. Just as the business man
knows, somewhere, that he's all wrong. Men and women aren't
really dogs: they only look like it and behave like it. Somewhere
inside there is a great chagrin and a gnawing discontent. The body
is, in its spontaneous natural self, dead or paralysed. It has only the
secondary life of a circus dog, acting up and showing off: and then
collapsing.

What life could it have, of itself? The body's life is the life of
sensations and emotions. The body feels real hunger, real thirst, real
joy in the sun or the snow, real pleasure in the smell of roses or the
look of a lilac bush; real anger, real sorrow, real love, real tenderness, real warmth, real passion, real hate, real grief. All the emotions
belong to the body, and are only recognised by the mind. We may
hear the most sorrowful piece of news, and only feel a mental
excitement. Then, hours after, perhaps in sleep, the awareness may
reach the bodily centres, and true grief wrings the heart.

How different they are, mental feelings and real feelings. Today,
many people live and die without having had any real feelings—
though they have had a "rich emotional life" apparently, having
showed strong mental feeling. But it is all counterfeit. In magic, one
of the so-called "occult" pictures represents a man standing, apparently, before a flat table-mirror, which reflects him from the waist to
the head, so that you have the man from head to waist, then his
reflection downwards from waist to head again. And whatever it
may mean in magic, it means what we are today, creatures whose
active emotional self has no real existence, but is all reflected
downwards from the mind. Our education from the start has *taught*
us a certain range of emotions, what to feel and what not to feel, and
how to feel the feelings we allow ourselves to feel. All the rest is just
non-existent. The vulgar criticism of any new good book is: Of
course nobody ever felt like that!—People allow themselves to feel a
certain number of limited feelings. So it was in the last century. This
feeling only what you allow yourselves to feel at last kills all capacity
for feeling, and in the higher emotional range, you feel nothing at all.
This has come to pass in our present century. The higher emotions
are strictly dead. They have to be faked.

And by higher emotions we mean love in all its manifestations, from genuine desire to tender love, love of one's fellow-men, and love of God: we mean love, joy, delight, hope, true indignant anger, passionate sense of justice and injustice, truth and untruth, honour and dishonour, and real belief in *anything*: for belief is a profound emotion that has the mind's connivance. All these things, today, are more or less dead. We have in their place the loud and sentimental counterfeit of all such emotion.

Never was an age more sentimental, more devoid of real feeling, more exaggerated in false feeling, than our own. Sentimentality and counterfeit feeling have become a sort of game, everybody trying to outdo his neighbour. The radio and the film are mere counterfeit emotion all the time, the current press and literature the same. People wallow in emotion: counterfeit emotion. They lap it up: they live in it and on it. They ooze with it.

And at times, they seem to get on very well with it all. And then, more and more, they break down. They go to pieces. You can fool yourself for a long time about your own feelings. But not forever. The body itself hits back at you, and hits back remorselessly, in the end.

As for other people—you can fool most people all the time, and all people most of the time, but not all people all the time, with false feelings. A young couple fall in counterfeit love, and fool themselves and each other completely. But alas, counterfeit love is good cake but bad bread. It produces a fearful emotional indigestion. Then you get a modern marriage, and a still more modern separation.

The trouble with counterfeit emotion is that nobody is really happy, nobody is really contented, nobody has any peace. Everybody keeps on rushing to get away from the counterfeit emotion which is in themselves worst of all. They rush from the false feelings of Peter to the false feelings of Adrian, from the counterfeit emotions of Margaret to those of Virginia, from film to radio, from Eastbourne to Brighton, and the more it changes the more it is the same thing.

Above all things love is a counterfeit feeling today. Here, above all things, the young will tell you, is the greatest swindle. That is, if you take it seriously. Love is all right if you take it lightly, as an amusement. But if you begin taking it seriously, you are let down with a crash.

There are, the young women say, no *real* men to love. And there are, the young men say, no *real* girls to fall in love with. So they go on falling in love with unreal ones, on either side. Which means, if you can't have real feelings, you've got to have counterfeit ones: since some feelings you've *got* to have: like falling in love. There are still some young people who would *like* to have real feelings, and they are bewildered to death to know why they can't. Especially in love.

But especially in love, only counterfeit emotions exist nowadays. We have all been taught to mistrust everybody emotionally, from parents downwards, or upwards. Don't trust *anybody* with your real emotions: if you've got any: that is the slogan of today. Trust them with your money, even, but *never* with your feelings. They are bound to trample on them.

I believe there has never been an age of greater mistrust between persons than ours today: under a superficial but quite genuine social trust. Very few of my friends would pick my pocket, or let me sit on a chair where I might hurt myself. But practically all my friends would turn my real emotions to ridicule. They can't help it: it's the spirit of the day.—So there goes love, and there goes friendship: for each implies a fundamental emotional sympathy. And hence, counterfeit love, which there is no escaping.

And with counterfeit emotion, there is no real sex at all. Sex is the one thing you cannot really swindle: and it is the centre of the worst swindling of all, emotional swindling. Once come down to sex, and the emotional swindle must collapse. But in all the approaches to sex, the emotional swindle intensifies more and more. Till you get there. Then collapse.

Sex lashes out against counterfeit emotion, and is ruthless, devastating against false love. The peculiar hatred of people who have *not* loved one another, but who have pretended to, even perhaps have imagined they really did love, is one of the phenomena of our time. The phenomenon, of course, belongs to all times. But today it is almost universal. People who thought they loved one another dearly, dearly, and went on for years, ideal: lo! suddenly the most profound and vivid hatred appears. If it doesn't come out fairly young, it saves itself till the happy couple are nearing fifty, the time of the great sexual change—and then—cataclysm!

Nothing is more startling. Nothing is more staggering, in our age, than the intensity of the hatred people, men and women, feel for one another when they have once "loved" one another. It breaks out in the most extraordinary ways. And when you know people intimately, it is almost universal. It is the charwoman as much as the mistress, and the duchess as much as the policeman's wife.

And it would be too horrible, if one did not remember that in all of them, men and women alike, it is the organic reaction against counterfeit love. All love today is counterfeit. It is a stereotyped thing. All the young know just how they ought to feel and how they ought to behave, in love. And they feel and they behave like that. And it is counterfeit love. So the revenge will come back at them, tenfold. The sex, the very sexual organism in man and woman alike accumulates a deadly and desperate rage, after a certain amount of counterfeit love has been palmed off on it, even if itself has given nothing but counterfeit love. The element of counterfeit in love at last maddens, or else kills, sex, the deepest sex in the individual. But perhaps it would be safe to say that it *always* enrages the inner sex, even if at last it kills it. There is always the period of rage. And the strange thing is, the worst offenders in the counterfeit love game, fall into the greatest rage. Those whose love has been a bit sincere are always gentler, even though they have been most swindled.

Now the real tragedy is here: that we are none of us all of a piece, none of us *all* counterfeit, or *all* true love. And in many a marriage, in among the counterfeit there flickers a little flame of the true thing, on both sides. The tragedy is, that in an age peculiarly conscious of counterfeit, peculiarly suspicious of substitute and swindle in emotion, particularly sexual emotion, the rage and mistrust against the counterfeit element is likely to overwhelm and extinguish the small, true flame of real loving communion, which might have made two lives happy. Herein lies the danger of harping only on the counterfeit and the swindle of emotion, as most "advanced" writers do. Though they do it, of course, to counterbalance the hugely greater swindle of the sentimental "sweet" writers.

Perhaps I shall have given some notion of my feeling about sex, for which I have been so monotonously abused. When a "serious" young man said to me the other day: "I can't believe in the regeneration of England by sex, you know," I could only say: "I'm sure you can't." He had no sex, anyhow: poor, self-conscious, uneasy, narcissus-monk as he was. And he didn't know what it meant, to have any. To him, people only had minds, or no minds, mostly no minds, so they were only there to be gibed at, and he wandered round ineffectually seeking for gibes or for truth, tight shut in inside his own ego.

Now when brilliant young people like this talk to me about sex: or scorn to: I say nothing. There is nothing to say. But I feel a terrible weariness. To them, sex means just plainly and simply lady's underclothing, and the fumbling therewith. They have read all the love literature, *Anna Karenin*, all the rest, and looked at statues and pictures of Aphrodite, all very laudable. Yet when it comes to actuality, to today, sex means to them meaningless young women in expensive under-things. Whether they are young men from Oxford, or working men, it is the same. The story from the modish summer-resort, where city ladies take up with young mountaineer "dancing-partners" for a season—or less—is typical. It was end of September, the summer visitors had almost all gone. Young John, the young mountain farmer, had said goodbye to his "lady" from the capital, and was lounging about alone. "Ho, John! you'll be missing your lady?"—"Nay!" he said. "Only she had such nice under-clothes—"

That is all sex means to them: just the trimmings. The regeneration of England with that? Good God! Poor England, she will have to regenerate the sex in her young people, before they do any regenerating of her. It isn't England that needs regenerating, it is her young.

They accuse me of barbarism: I want to drag England down to the level of savages. But it is this crude stupidity, deadness, about sex which I find barbaric and savage. The man who finds a woman's underclothing the most exciting part about her is a savage. Savages are like that. We read of the woman-savage who wore three overcoats on top of one another to excite her man: and did it. That ghastly crudity of seeing in sex nothing but a functional act and a certain fumbling with clothes is, in my opinion, a low degree of barbarism, savagery. And as far as sex goes, our white civilisation is crude, barbaric, and uglily savage—especially England and America.

Witness Bernard Shaw, one of the greatest exponents of our civilisation. He says clothes arouse sex and lack of clothes tends to kill sex—speaking of muffled-up women or our present bare-armed and bare-legged sisters: and scoffs at the Pope for wanting to cover women up; saying that the last person in the world to know anything about sex is the Chief Priest of Europe: and that the one person to ask about it would be the chief Prostitute of Europe, if there were such a person.—

Here we see the flippancy and vulgarity of our chief thinkers, at least. The half-naked woman of today certainly does not rouse much sexual feeling in the muffled-up men of today—who don't rouse much sexual feeling in the women, either—but why? Why does the bare woman of today rouse so much less sexual feeling than the muffled-up woman of Mr Shaw's muffled-up eighties? It would be silly to make it a question of mere muffling.

When a woman's sex is in itself dynamic and alive, then it is a power in itself, beyond her reason. And of itself it emits its peculiar spell, drawing men in the first delight of desire. And the woman has to protect herself, hide herself as much as possible. She veils herself in timidity and modesty, because her sex is a power in itself, exposing her to the desire of men. If a woman in whom sex was alive and positive were to expose her naked flesh as women do today, then men would go mad for her. As David was mad for Bathsheba.

But when a woman's sex has lost its dynamic call, and is in a sense dead or static, then the woman *wants* to attract men, for the simple reason that she finds she no longer does attract them. So all the activity that used to be unconscious and delightful becomes conscious and repellant. The woman exposes her flesh more and more, and the more she exposes, the more men are sexually repelled by her. But let us not forget that the men are *socially* thrilled, while sexually repelled. The two things are opposites, today. Socially, men like the gesture of the half-naked woman, half-naked in the street. It is *chic*, it is a declaration of defiance and independence, it is modern, it is free, it is popular because it is strictly a-sexual, or anti-sexual. Neither men nor women *want* to feel real desire, today. They want the counterfeit, mental substitute.

But we are very mixed, all of us, and creatures of many diverse and often opposing desires. The very men who encourage women to be most daring and sexless complain most bitterly of the sexlessness of woman. The same with women. The women who adore men so tremendously for their social smartness and sexlessness as males, hate them most bitterly for not being "men." In public, *en masse*, and socially, everybody today wants counterfeit sex. But at certain hours in their lives, all individuals hate counterfeit sex with deadly and maddened hate, and those who have dealt it out most perhaps have the wildest hate of it, in the other person—or persons.

The girls of today could muffle themselves up to the eyes, wear crinolines and chignons and all the rest, and though they would not, perhaps, have the peculiar hardening effect on the hearts of men that our half-naked women truly have, neither would they exert any more real sexual attraction. If there is no sex to muffle up, it's no good muffling. Or not much good. Man is often willing to be deceived—for a time—even by muffled-up nothingness.

The point is, when women are sexually alive and quivering and helplessly attractive, beyond their will, then they always cover themselves and drape themselves with clothes, gracefully. The extravagance of 1880 bustles and such things was only a forewarning of approaching sexlessness.

While sex is a power in itself, women try all kinds of fascinating disguise, and men flaunt. When the Pope insists that women shall cover their naked flesh in church, it is not sex he is opposing, but the sexless tricks of female immodesty. The Pope, and the priests, conclude that the flaunting of naked women's flesh in street and church produces a bad, "unholy" state of mind both in men and women. And they are right. But not because the exposure arouses sexual desire: it doesn't, or very rarely: even Mr Shaw knows that. But when naked women's flesh arouses no sort of desire, something is specially wrong. Something is sadly wrong. For the naked arms of women today arouse a feeling of flippancy, cynicism and vulgarity which is indeed the very last feeling to go to church with, if you have any respect for the church. The bare arms of women in an Italian church are really a mark of disrespect, given the tradition.

The Catholic Church, especially in the south, is neither anti-sexual, like the northern churches, nor a-sexual, like Mr Shaw and such social thinkers. The Catholic Church recognises sex, and makes of marriage a sacrament based on the sexual communion, for the purpose of procreation. But procreation, in the south, is not the bare and scientific fact, and act, that it is in the north. The act of procreation is still charged with all the sensual mystery and importance of the old past. The man is potential creator, and in this has his splendour. All of which has been stripped away by the northern churches and the Shavian logical triviality.

But all this which has gone in the north, the Church has tried to keep in the south, knowing that it is of basic importance in life. The sense of being a potential creator and law-giver, as father and husband, is perhaps essential to the day-by-day life of a man, if he is to live full and satisfied. The sense of the eternality of marriage is perhaps necessary to the inward peace, both of man and woman. Even if it carry a sense of doom, it is necessary. The Catholic Church does not spend its time reminding the people that in heaven there is no marrying nor giving in marriage. It insists: if you marry, you marry for ever!—And the people accept the decree, the doom, and the dignity of it. To the priest, sex is the clue to marriage and marriage is the clue to the daily life of the people and the church is the clue to the greater life.

So that sexual lure in itself is not deadly to the church. Much more deadly is the anti-sexual defiance of bare arms and flippancy, "freedom," cynicism, irreverence. Sex may be obscene in church, or blasphemous, but never cynical and atheist. Potentially, the bare arms of women today are cynical, atheist, in the dangerous vulgar form of atheism. Naturally the Church is against it. The Chief Priest of Europe knows more about sex than Mr Shaw does, anyhow, because he knows more about the essential nature of the human being. Traditionally, he has a thousand years' experience. Mr Shaw jumped up in a day. And Mr Shaw, as a dramatist, has jumped up to play tricks with the counterfeit sex of the modern public. No doubt he can do it. So can the cheapest film. But it is equally obvious that he can*not* touch the deeper sex of the real individual, whose existence he hardly seems to suspect.

And, as a parallel to himself, Mr Shaw suggests that the Chief Prostitute of Europe would be the one to consult about sex, not the Chief Priest. The parallel is just. The Chief Prostitute of Europe would know truly as much about sex as Mr Shaw himself does. Which is, not much. Just like Mr Shaw, the Chief Prostitute of Europe would know an immense amount about the counterfeit sex of men, the shoddy thing that is worked by tricks. And just like him, she would know nothing at all about the real sex in a man, that has the rhythm of the seasons and the years, the crisis of the winter solstice and the passion of Easter. This the Chief Prostitute would know nothing about, positively, because to be a prostitute she would have to have lost it. But even then, she would know more than Mr Shaw. She would know that the profound, rhythmic sex of a man's inward life *existed*. She would know, because time and again she would have been up against it. All the literature of the world shows the prostitute's ultimate impotence in sex, her inability to keep a man, her rage against the profound instinct of fidelity in a man, which is, as shown by world history, just a little deeper and more powerful than his instinct of faithless sexual promiscuity. All the literature of the world shows how profound is the instinct of fidelity in both man and woman, how men and women both hanker restlessly after the satisfaction of this instinct, and fret at their own inability to find the real mode of fidelity. The instinct of fidelity is perhaps the deepest instinct in the great complex we call sex. Where there is real sex there is the underlying passion for fidelity. And the prostitute knows this, because she is up against it. She can only keep men who have no real sex, the counterfeits: and these she despises. The men with real sex leave her inevitably, as unable to satisfy their real desires.

The Chief Prostitute knows so much. So does the Pope, if he troubles to think of it, for it is all in the traditional consciousness of the Church. But the Chief Dramatist knows nothing of it. He has a curious blank in his make-up. To him, all sex is infidelity and only infidelity is sex. Marriage is sexless, null. Sex is only manifested in infidelity, and the queen of sex is the chief prostitute. If sex crops up in marriage, it is because one party falls in love with somebody else, and wants to be unfaithful. Infidelity is sex, and prostitutes know all about it, wives know nothing and are nothing, in that respect.

This is the teaching of the Chief Dramatists and Chief Thinkers of our generation. And the vulgar public agrees with them entirely. Sex is a thing you don't have except to be naughty with. Apart from naughtiness, that is, apart from infidelity and fornication, sex doesn't exist. Our chief thinkers, ending in the flippantly cock-sure Mr Shaw, have taught this trash so thoroughly, that it has almost become a fact. Sex is almost non-existent, apart from the counterfeit forms of prostitution and shallow fornication. And marriage is empty, hollow.

Now this question of sex and marriage is of paramount importance. Our social life is established on marriage, and marriage, the sociologists say, is established upon property. Marriage has been found the best method of conserving property and stimulating production. Which is all there is to it.

But is it? We are just in the throes of a great revolt against marriage, a passionate revolt against its ties and restrictions. In fact, at least three-quarters of the unhappiness of modern life could be laid at the door of marriage. There are few married people today, and few unmarried, who have not felt an intense and vivid hatred against marriage itself, marriage as an institution and an imposition upon human life. Far greater than the revolt against governments is this revolt against marriage.

And everybody, pretty well, takes it for granted that as soon as we can find a feasible way out of it, marriage will be abolished. The Soviet abolishes marriage: or did. If new "modern" states spring up, they will almost certainly follow suit. They will try to find some social substitute for marriage, and abolish the hated yoke of conjugality. State support of motherhood, state support of children, and independence of women. It is on the programme of every great scheme of reform. And it means, of course, the abolition of marriage.

The only question to ask ourselves is, do we really want it? Do we want the absolute independence of women, State support of motherhood and of children, and consequent doing away with the necessity of marriage? Do we want it? Because all that matters is that men and women shall do what they *really* want to do. Though here, as everywhere, we must remember that man has a double set of desires, the shallow and the profound, the personal, superficial, temporary desires, and the inner, impersonal, great desires that are fulfilled in long periods of time. The desires of the moment are easy to recognise, but the others, the deeper ones, are difficult. It is the business of our Chief Thinkers to tell us of our deeper desires, not to keep shrilling our little desires in our ears.

Now the Church is established upon a recognition of some, at least, of the greatest and deepest desires in man, desires that take years, or a life-time, or even centuries to fulfil. And the Church, celibate as its priesthood may be, built as it may be upon the lonely rock of Peter, or of Paul, is in actual life established upon the fact of marriage. The Church really rests upon the indissolubility of marriage. Make marriage in any serious degree unstable, dissoluble, destroy the permanency of marriage, and the Church falls. Witness the enormous decline of the Church of England.

The reason being that the Church is established upon the element of *union* in mankind. And the first element of union in the Christian world is the marriage-tie. The marriage-tie, the marriage bond, take it which way you like, is the fundamental connecting link in Christian society. Break it, and you will have to go back to the overwhelming dominance of the State, which existed before the Christian era. The Roman State was all-powerful, the Roman father represented the State, the Roman family was the father's estate, held more or less in fee for the State itself. It was the same in Greece, with not so much feeling for the *permanence* of property, but rather a dazzling splash of the moment's possessions. The family was much more insecure in Greece than in Rome.

But in either case, the family was the man, as representing the State. There are States where the family is the woman: or there have been. There are States where the family hardly exists, priest States where the priestly control is everything, even functioning as family control. Then there is the Soviet State, where again family is not supposed to exist, and the State controls every individual direct, mechanically, as the great religious States such as early Egypt may have controlled every individual direct, through priestly surveillance and ritual.

Now the question is, do we want to go back, or forward, to any of these forms of State control? Do we want to be like the Romans under the Empire, or even under the Republic? Do we want to be, as far as our family and our freedom is concerned, like the Greek citizens of a City State in Hellas? Do we want to imagine ourselves in the strange priest-controlled, ritual-fulfilled condition of the earlier Egyptians? Do we want to be bullied by a Soviet?

For my part, I have to say No! every time. And having said it, we have to come back and consider the famous saying, that perhaps the greatest contribution to the social life of man made by Christianity is—marriage. Christianity brought marriage into the world: marriage as we know it. Christianity established the little autonomy of the family within the greater rule of the State. Christianity made marriage in some respects inviolate, not to be violated by the State. It is marriage, perhaps, which has given man the best of his freedom, given him his little kingdom of his own within the big kingdom of the State, given him his foothold of independence on which to stand and resist an unjust State. Man and wife, a king and queen with one or two subjects, and a few square yards of territory of their own: this, really, is marriage. It is a true freedom because it is a true fulfilment, for man, woman, and children.

Do we then want to break marriage? If we do break it, it means we all fall to a far greater extent under the direct sway of the State. Do we want to fall under the direct sway of the State, any State? For my part, I don't.

And the Church created marriage by making it a sacrament, a sacrament of man and woman united in the sex communion, and never to be separated, except by death. And even when separated by death, still not freed from the marriage. Marriage, as far as the individual went, eternal. Marriage, making one complete body out of two incomplete ones, and providing for the complex development of the man's soul and the woman's soul in unison, throughout a life-time. Marriage sacred and inviolable, the great way of earthly fulfilment for man and woman, in unison, under the spiritual rule of the Church.

This is Christianity's great contribution to the life of man, and it is only too easily overlooked. Is it, or is it not, a great step in the direction of life-fulfilment, for men and women? Is it, or is it not? Is marriage a great help to the fulfilment of man and woman, or is it a frustration? It is a very important question indeed, and every man and woman must answer it.

If we are to take the nonconformist, protestant idea of ourselves: that we are all isolated individual souls, and our supreme business is to save our own souls; then marriage surely is a hindrance. If I am only out to save my own soul, I'd better leave marriage alone. As the monks and hermits knew. But also, if I am only out to save other people's souls, I had also best leave marriage alone, as the apostles knew, and the preaching saints.

But supposing I am neither bent on saving my own soul nor other people's souls? Supposing Salvation seems incomprehensible to me, as I confess it does. "Being saved" seems to me just jargon, the jargon of self-conceit. Supposing, then, that I cannot see this Saviour and Salvation stuff, supposing that I see the soul as something which must be developed and fulfilled throughout a life-time, sustained and nourished, developed and further fulfilled, to the very end; what then?

Then I realise that marriage, or something like it, is essential, and that the old Church knew best the enduring needs of man, beyond the spasmodic needs of today and yesterday. The Church established marriage for life, for the fulfilment of the soul during life, not postponing it till the after-death.

The old Church knew that life is here our portion, to be lived, to be lived in fulfilment. The stern rule of Benedict, the wild flights of Francis of Assisi—these were coruscations in the steady heaven of the Church. The rhythm of life itself was preserved by the Church hour by hour, day by day, season by season, year by year, epoch by epoch, down among the people, and the wild coruscations were accommodated to this permanent rhythm. We feel it, in the south, in the country, when we hear the jangle of the bells at dawn, at noon, at sunset, marking the hours with the sound of mass or prayers. It is the rhythm of the daily sun. We feel it in the festivals, the processions, Christmas, the Three Kings, Easter, Pentecost, St Johns Day, All Saints, All Souls. This is the wheeling of the year, the movement of the sun through solstice and equinox, the coming of the seasons, the going of the seasons. And it is the inward rhythm of man and woman too, the sadness of Lent, the delight of Easter, the wonder of Pentecost, the fires of St John, the candles on the graves of All Souls, the lit-up tree of Christmas, all representing kindled rhythmic emotions in the souls of men and women. And men experience the great rhythm of emotion man-wise, women experience it woman-wise, and in the unison of men and women it is complete.

Augustine said that God created the universe new every day: and to the living, emotional soul, this is true. Every dawn dawns upon an entirely new universe, every Easter lights up an entirely new glory of a new world opening in utterly new flower. And the soul of man and the soul of woman is new in the same way, with the infinite delight of life and the ever-newness of life. So a man and a woman are new to one another throughout a life-time, in the rhythm of marriage that matches the rhythm of the year.

Sex is the balance of male and female in the universe, the attraction, the repulsion, the transit of neutrality, the new attraction, the new repulsion, always different, always new. The long neuter spell of Lent, when the blood is low, and the delight of the Easter kiss, the sexual revel of spring, the passion of midsummer, the slow recoil, revolt, and grief of autumn, greyness again, then the sharp stimulus of winter, of the long nights. Sex goes through the rhythm of the year, in man and woman, ceaselessly changing: the rhythm of the sun in his relation to the earth. Oh what a catastrophe for man when he cut himself off from the rhythm of the year, from his unison with the sun and the earth. Oh what a catastrophe, what a maiming of love when it was made a personal, merely personal feeling, taken away from the rising and the setting of the sun, and cut off from the magic connection of the solstice and the equinox! This is what is the matter with us. We are bleeding at the roots, because we are cut off from the earth and sun and stars, and love is a grinning mockery, because, poor blossom, we plucked it from its stem on the tree of Life, and expected it to keep on blooming in our civilised vase on the table.

Marriage is the clue to human life, but there is no marriage apart from the wheeling sun and the nodding earth, from the straying of the planets and the magnificence of the fixed stars. Is not a man different, utterly different at dawn, from what he is at sunset? and a woman too? And does not the changing harmony and discord of their variation make the secret music of life?

And is it not so throughout life? A man is different at thirty, at forty, at fifty, at sixty, at seventy: and the woman at his side is different. But is there not some strange conjunction in their differences? Is there not some peculiar harmony, through youth, the period of childbirth, the period of florescence and young children, the period of the woman's change of life, painful yet also a renewal, the period of waning passion but mellowing delight of affection, the dim unequal period of the approach of death, when the man and woman look at one another with the dim apprehension of separation that is not really a separation: is there not, throughout it all, some unseen, unknown interplay of balance, harmony, completion, like some soundless symphony which moves with a rhythm from phase to phase, so different, so very different in the various movements, and yet one symphony, made out of the soundless singing of two strange and incompatible lives, a man's and a woman's?

This is marriage, the mystery of marriage: marriage which fulfils itself here, in this life. We may well believe that in heaven there is no marrying or giving in marriage. All this has to be fulfilled here, and if it is not fulfilled here, it will never be fulfilled. The great saints only live, even Jesus only lives to add a new fulfilment and a new beauty to the permanent sacrament of marriage.

But—and this *but* crashes through our heart like a bullet— marriage is no marriage that is not basically and permanently phallic, and that is not linked up with the sun and the earth, the moon and the fixed stars and the planets, in the rhythm of days, in the rhythm of months, in the rhythm of quarters, of years, of decades and of centuries. Marriage is no marriage that is not a correspondence of blood. For the blood is the substance of the soul, and of the deepest consciousness. It is by blood that we are: and it is by the heart and the liver that we live and move and have our being. In the blood, knowing and being, or feeling, are one and undivided: no serpent and no apple has caused a split. So that only when the conjunction is of the blood, is marriage truly marriage. The blood of man and the blood of woman are two eternally different streams, that can never be mingled. Even scientifically we know it. But therefore they are the two rivers that encircle the whole of life, and in marriage the circle is complete, and in sex the two rivers touch and renew one another, without ever commingling or confusing. We know it. The phallus is a column of blood, that fills the valley of blood of a woman. The great river of male blood touches to its depth the great river of female blood, yet neither breaks its bounds. It is the deepest of all communions, as all the religions, *in practice*, know. And it is one of the greatest mysteries: in fact, the greatest, as almost every apocalypse shows, showing the supreme achievement of the mystic marriage.

And this is the meaning of the sexual act: this communion, this touching on one another of the two rivers, Euphrates and Tigris, to use old jargon, and the enclosing of the land of Mesopotamia, where Paradise was, or the Park of Eden, where man had his beginning. This is marriage, this circuit of the two rivers, this communion of the two blood-streams, this, and nothing else: as all the religions know.

Two rivers of blood, are man and wife, two distinct eternal streams, that have the power of touching and communing and so renewing, making new one another, without any breaking of the subtle confines, any confusing or commingling. And the phallus is the connecting link between the two rivers, that establishes the two streams in a oneness, and gives out of their duality a single circuit, forever. And this, this oneness gradually accomplished throughout a life-time in twoness, is the highest achievement of time or eternity. From it all things human spring, children and beauty and well-made things, all the true creations of humanity. And all we know of the will of God is that he wishes this, this oneness, to take place, fulfilled over a life-time, this oneness within the great dual blood-stream of humanity.

Man dies, and woman dies, and perhaps separate the souls go back to the Creator. Who knows? But we know that the oneness of the blood-stream of man and woman in marriage completes the universe, as far as humanity is concerned, completes the streaming of the sun and the flowing of the stars.

There is, of course, the counterpart to all this, the counterfeit. This is counterfeit marriage, like nearly all marriage today. Modern people are just personalities, and modern marriage takes place when two people are "thrilled" by each other's personality: when they have the same tastes in furniture or books or sport or amusement, when they love "talking" to one another, when they admire one another's "minds." Now this, this affinity of mind and personality is an excellent basis of friendship between the sexes, but a disastrous basis for marriage. Because marriage inevitably starts the sex activity, and the sex activity is, and always was and will be in some way hostile to the mental, *personal* relationship between man and woman. It is almost an axiom, that the marriage of two *personalities* will end in a startling physical hatred. People who are personally devoted to one another at first end by hating one another with a hate which they cannot account for, which they try to hide, for it makes them ashamed, and which is none the less only too painfully obvious, especially to one another. In people of strong individual feeling the irritation that accumulates in marriage increases only too often to a point of rage that is close akin to madness. And apparently, all without reason.

But the real reason is, that the sympathy of nerves and mind and personal interest is, alas, hostile to blood-sympathy, in the sexes. The modern cult of personality is excellent for friendship between the sexes, and fatal for marriage. On the whole, it would be better if modern people didn't marry. They could remain so much more true to what they are, to their own personality.

But marriage or no marriage, the fatal thing happens. If you have only known personal sympathy and personal love, then rage and hatred will sooner or later take possession of the soul, because of the frustration and denial of blood-sympathy, blood-contact. In celibacy, the denial is withering and souring, but in marriage, the denial produces a sort of rage. And we can no more avoid this, nowadays, than we can avoid thunder-storms. It is part of the phenomenon of the psyche. The important point is that sex itself comes to subserve the personality and the personal "love" entirely, without ever giving sexual satisfaction or fulfilment. In fact, there is probably far more sexual activity in a "personal" marriage, than in a blood-marriage. Woman sighs for a perpetual lover: and in the personal-marriage relationship she gets him. And how she comes to hate him, with his never-ending desire which never gets anywhere or fulfils anything!

It is a mistake I have made, talking of sex I have always inferred that sex meant blood-sympathy and blood-contact. Technically, this is so. But as a matter of fact, nearly all modern sex is a pure matter of nerves, cold and bloodless. This is personal sex. And this white, cold, nervous, "poetic" personal sex, which is practically all the sex that moderns know, has a very peculiar physiological effect, as well as psychological. The two blood-streams are brought into contact, in man and woman, just the same as is the urge of blood-passion and blood-desire. But whereas the contact in the urge of blood-desire is positive, making a newness in the blood, in the insistence of this nervous, personal desire the blood-contact becomes frictional and destructive, there is a resultant whitening and impoverishment of the blood. Personal or nervous or spiritual sex is destructive to the blood, has a katabolistic activity, whereas coition in warm blood-desire is an activity of metabolism. The katabolism of "nervous" sex-activity may produce for a time a sort of ecstasy and a heightening of consciousness. But this, like the effect of alcohol or drugs, is the result of the decomposition of certain corpuscles in the blood, and is a process of impoverishment. This is one of the many reasons for the failure of energy in modern people. Sexual activity, which ought to be refreshing and renewing, becomes exhaustive and debilitating. So that when the young man fails to believe in the regeneration of England by sex, I am constrained to agree with him. Since modern sex is practically all personal and nervous, and in effect, exhaustive disintegrative. The disintegrative effect of modern sex-activity is undeniable. It is only less fatal than the disintegrative effect of masturbation, which is much more deadly still.

So that at last I begin to see the point of my critics' abuse of my exalting of sex. They only know one form of sex: in fact to them there *is* only one form of sex: the nervous, personal, disintegrative sort, the "white" sex. And this, of course, is something to be flowery and false about, but nothing to be very hopeful about. I quite agree. And I quite agree, we can have no hope of the regeneration of England from such sort of sex.

At the same time, I cannot see any hope of regeneration for a sexless England. An England that has lost its sex seems to me nothing to feel very hopeful about. And nobody feels very hopeful about it. Though I may have been a fool for insisting on sex when the current sort of sex is just what I *don't* mean and *don't* want, still I can't go back on it all and believe in the regeneration of England by pure sexlessness. A sexless England!—it doesn't ring very hopeful, to me.

And the other, the warm blood-sex that establishes the living and re-vitalising connection between man and woman, how are we to get that back? I don't know. Yet get it back we must: or the younger ones must. Or we are all lost. For the bridge to the future is the phallus, and there's the end of it. But not the poor nervous, counterfeit phallus of modern "nervous" love. Not that.

For the new impulse to life will never come without blood-contact, the true, positive blood-contact, not the nervous negative reaction. And the essential blood-contact is between man and woman, always has been so, always will. The contact of positive sex. The homo-sexual contacts are secondary, even if not merely substitutes of exasperated reaction from the utterly unsatisfactory nervous sex between men and women.

If England is to be regenerated—to use the phrase of the young man, who seemed to think there was need of *regeneration*—the very word is his—then it will be by the arising of a new blood-contact, a new touch, and a new marriage. It will be a phallic rather than a sexual regeneration. For the phallus is only the great old symbol of godly vitality in a man, and of immediate contact.

It will also be a renewal of marriage: the true phallic marriage. And still further, it will be marriage set again in relationship to the rhythmic cosmos. The rhythm of the cosmos is something we cannot get away from, without bitterly impoverishing our lives. The early Christians tried to kill the old pagan rhythm of cosmic ritual, and to some extent succeeded. They killed the planets and the zodiac, perhaps because astrology had already become debased to fortune-telling. They wanted to kill the festivals of the year. But the church, which knows that man doth not live by man alone, but by the sun and moon and earth in their revolutions, restored the sacred days and feasts almost as the pagans had them, and the Christian peasants went on very much as the pagan peasants had gone, with the sunrise pause for worship, and the sunset, and noon, the three great daily moments of the sun: then the new holy day, one in the ancient seven-cycle: then Easter and the dying and rising God, Pentecost, Midsummer Fire, the November dead and the spirits of the grave, then Christmas, then Three Kings. For centuries the mass of people lived in this rhythm, under the Church. And it is down in the mass that the roots of religion are eternal. When the mass of a people loses the religious rhythm, that people is dead, without hope.—But Protestantism came and gave a great blow to the religious and ritualistic rhythm of the year, in human life. Nonconformity *almost* finished the deed. Now you have a poor, blind, disconnected people with nothing but politics and bank-holidays to satisfy the eternal human need of living in ritual adjustment to the cosmos in its revolutions, in eternal submission to the greater laws. And marriage, being one of the greater necessities, has suffered the same from the loss of the sway of the greater laws, the cosmic rhythms which should sway life always. Mankind has got to get back to the rhythm of the cosmos, and the permanence of marriage.

All this is glossary, or prolegomena, to my novel *Lady Chatterley's Lover*. Man has little needs and deeper needs. We have fallen into the mistake of living from our little needs, till we have almost lost our deeper needs in a sort of madness. There is a little morality, which concerns persons and the little needs of man: and this, alas, is the morality we live by. But there is a deeper morality, which concerns all womanhood, all manhood, and nations, and races, and classes of men. This greater morality affects the destiny of mankind over long stretches of time, applies to man's greater needs, and is often in conflict with the little morality of the little needs. The tragic consciousness has taught us even that one of the greater needs of man is a knowledge and experience of death, every man needs to know death in his own body. But the greater consciousness of the pre-tragic and post-tragic epochs teaches us—though we have not yet reached the post-tragic epoch—that the greatest need of man is the renewal forever of the complete rhythm of life and death, the rhythm of the sun's year, the body's year of a life-time, and the greater year of the stars, the soul's year of immortality. This is our need, our imperative need. It is a need of the mind and soul, body, spirit and sex: all. It is no use asking for a Word to fulfil such a need. No Word, no Logos, no Utterance will ever do it. The Word is uttered, most of it. We need only pay true attention. But who will call us to the Deed, the great Deed of the seasons and the year, the Deed of the soul's cycle, the Deed of a woman's life at one with a man's, the little Deed of the moon's wandering, the bigger Deed of the sun's, and the biggest, of the great still stars? It is the *Deed* of life we have now to learn: we are supposed to have learnt the Word, and alas, look at us. Word-perfect we may be, but Deed-demented. Let us prepare now for the death of our present "little" life, and the re-emergence in a bigger life, in touch with the moving cosmos.

It is a question, practically, of relationship. We *must* get back into relation, vivid and nourishing relation to the cosmos and the universe. The way is through daily ritual, and the re-awakening. We *must* once more practise the ritual of dawn and noon and sunset, the ritual of the kindling fire and pouring water, the ritual of the first breath, and the last. This is an affair of the individual and the household, a ritual of day. The ritual of the moon in her phases, of the morning star and the evening star is for men and women separate. Then the ritual of the seasons, with the Drama and the Passion of the soul embodied in procession and dance, this is for the community, an act of men and women, a whole community, in togetherness. And the ritual of the great events in the year of stars is for nations and whole peoples. To these rituals we must return: or we must evolve them to suit our needs. For the truth is, we are perishing for lack of fulfilment of our greater needs, we are cut off from the great sources of our inward nourishment and renewal, sources which flow eternally in the universe. Vitally, the human race is dying. It is like a great uprooted tree, with its roots in the air. We must plant ourselves again in the universe.

It means a return to ancient forms. But we shall have to create these forms again, and it is more difficult than the preaching of an evangel. The Gospel came to tell us we were all saved. We look at the world today and realise that humanity, alas, instead of being saved from sin, whatever that may be, is almost completely lost, lost to life, and near to nullity and extermination. We have to go back, a long way, before the idealist conceptions began, before Plato, before the tragic idea of life arose, to get on to our feet again. For the gospel of salvation through the Ideals and escape from the body coincided with the tragic conception of human life. Salvation and tragedy are the same thing, and they are now both beside the point.

Back, before the idealist religions and philosophies arose and started man on the great excursion of tragedy. The last three thousand years of mankind have been an excursion into ideals, bodilessness, and tragedy, and now the excursion is over. And it is like the end of a tragedy in the theatre. The stage is strewn with dead bodies, worse still, with meaningless bodies, and the curtain comes down.

But in life, the curtain never comes down on the scene. There the dead bodies lie, and the inert ones, and somebody has to clear them away, somebody has to carry on. It is the day after. Today is already the day after the end of the tragic and idealist epoch. Utmost inertia falls on the remaining protagonists. Yet we have to carry on.

Now we have to re-establish the great relationships which the grand idealists, with their underlying pessimism, their belief that life is nothing but futile conflict, to be avoided even unto death, destroyed for us. Buddha, Plato, Jesus, they were all three utter pessimists as regards life, teaching that the only happiness lay in abstracting oneself from life, the daily, yearly, seasonal life of birth and death and fruition, and in living in the "immutable" or eternal spirit. But now, after almost three thousand years, now that we are almost abstracted entirely from the rhythmic life of the seasons, birth and death and fruition, now we realise that such abstraction is neither bliss nor liberation, but nullity. It brings null inertia. And the great saviours and teachers only cut us off from life. It was the tragic *excursus*.

The universe is dead for us, and how is it to come to life again? "Knowledge" has killed the sun, making it a ball of gas, with spots; "knowledge" has killed the moon, it is a dead little earth pitted with extinct craters as with small-pox; the machine has killed the earth for us, making it a surface, more or less bumpy, that you travel over. How, out of all this, are we to get back the grand orbs of the soul's heavens, that fill us with unspeakable joy? How are we to get back Apollo, and Attis, Demeter, Persephone, and the halls of Dis? How even see the star Hesperus, or Betelgeuse.

We've got to get them back, for they are the world our soul, our greater consciousness lives in. The world of reason and science, the moon, a dead lump of earth, the sun, so much gas with spots, this is the dry and sterile little world the abstracted mind inhabits. The world of our little consciousness, which we know in our pettifogging *apartness*. This is how we know the world when we know it apart from ourselves, in the mean separateness of everything. When we know the world in togetherness with ourselves, we know the earth hyacinthine or Plutonic, we know the moon gives us our body as delight upon us, or steals it away, we know the purring of the great gold lion of the sun, who licks us like a lioness her cubs, making us bold, or else, like the red angry lion, slashes at us with open claws. There are many ways of knowing, there are many sorts of knowledge. But the two great ways of knowing, for man, are knowing in terms of apartness, which is mental, rational, scientific, and knowing in terms of togetherness, which is religious and poetic. The Christian religion lost, in Protestantism finally, the togetherness with the universe, the togetherness of the body, the sex, the emotions, the passions, with the earth and sun and stars.

But relationship is threefold. First, there is the relation to the living universe. Then comes the relation of man to woman. Then comes the relation of man to man. And each is a blood-relationship, not mere spirit or mind. We have abstracted the universe into Matter and Force, we have abstracted men and women into separate personalities—personalities being isolated units, incapable of togetherness—so that all three great relationships are bodiless, dead.

None, however, is quite so dead as the man to man relationship. I think, if we came to analyse to the last what men feel about one another today, we should find that every man feels every other man as a menace. It is a curious thing, but the more mental and ideal men are, the more they seem to feel the bodily presence of any other man a menace, a menace, as it were, to their very being. Every man that comes near me threatens my very existence: nay, more, my very being.

This is the ugly fact which underlies our civilisation. As the advertisement of one of the war-novels said, it is an epic of "friendship and hope, mud and blood." Which means, of course, that the friendship and hope must end in mud and blood.

When the great crusade against sex and the body started in full blast, with Plato, it was a crusade for "ideals," and for this "spiritual" knowledge in apartness. Sex is the great unifier. In its big, slower vibration it is the warmth of heart which makes people happy together, in togetherness. The idealist philosophies and religions set out deliberately to kill this. And they did it. Now they have done it. The last great ebullition of friendship and hope was squashed out in mud and blood. Now men are all separate little entities. While "kindness" is the glib order of the day—everybody *must* be "kind"—underneath this "kindness" we find a coldness of heart, a lack of heart, a callousness, that is very dreary. Every man *is* a menace to every other man.

Men only know one another in menace. Individualism has triumphed. If I am a sheer individual, then every other being, every other man especially, is over against me as a menace to me. This is the peculiarity of our society today. We are all extremely sweet and "nice" to one another, because we merely fear one another.

The sense of isolation, followed by the sense of menace and of fear, is bound to arise as the feeling of oneness and community with our fellow-man declines, and the feeling of individualism and personality, which is existence in isolation, increases. The so-called "cultured" classes are the first to develop "personality" and individualism, and the first to fall into this state of unconscious menace and fear. The working-classes retain the old blood-warmth of oneness and togetherness some decades longer. Then they lose it too. And then class-consciousness becomes rampant, and class hate. Class hate and class-consciousness are only a sign that the old togetherness, the old blood-warmth has collapsed, and every man is really aware of himself in apartness. Then we have these hostile groupings of men for the sake of opposition, strife. Civil strife becomes a necessary condition of self-assertion.

This, again, is the tragedy of social life today. In the old England, the curious blood-connection held the classes together. The squires might be arrogant, violent, bullying and unjust, yet in some way they were *at one* with the people, part of the same blood-stream. We feel it in Defoe or Fielding. And then, in the mean Jane Austen, it is gone. Already this old maid typifies "personality" instead of character, the sharp knowing in apartness instead of knowing in togetherness, and she is, to my feeling, thoroughly unpleasant, English in the bad, mean, snobbish sense of the word, just as Fielding is English in the good, generous sense.

So, in *Lady Chatterley's Lover* we have a man, Sir Clifford, who is purely a personality, having lost entirely all connections with his fellow-men and women, except those of usage. All warmth is gone entirely, the hearth is cold, the heart does not humanly exist. He is a pure product of our civilisation, but he is the death of the great humanity of the world. He is kind by rule, but he does not know what warm sympathy means. He is what he is. And he loses the woman of his choice.

The other man still has the warmth of a man, but he is being hunted down, destroyed. Even it is a question if the woman who turns to him will really stand by him and his vital meaning.

I have been asked many times if I intentionally made Clifford paralysed, if it is symbolic. And literary friends say, it would have been better to have left him whole and potent, and to have made the woman leave him nevertheless.

As to whether the "symbolism" is intentional—I don't know. Certainly not in the beginning, when Clifford was created. When I created Clifford and Connie, I had no idea what they were or why they were. They just came, pretty much as they are. But the novel was written, from start to finish, three times. And when I read the first version, I recognised that the lameness of Clifford was symbolic of the paralysis, the deeper emotional or passional paralysis, of most men of his sort and class, today. I realised that it was perhaps taking an unfair advantage of Connie, to paralyse him technically. It made it so much more vulgar of her to leave him. Yet the story came as it did, by itself, so I left it alone. Whether we call it symbolism or not, it is, in the sense of its happening, inevitable.

And these notes, which I write now almost two years after the novel was finished, are not intended to explain or expound anything: only to give the emotional beliefs which perhaps are necessary as a

A Propos of "Lady Chatterley's Lover"

background to the book. It is so obviously a book written in defiance of convention that perhaps some reason should be offered for the attitude of defiance: since the silly desire to *épater le bourgeois*, to bewilder the commonplace person, is not worth entertaining. If I use the taboo words, there is a reason. We shall never free the phallic reality from the "uplift" taint till we give it its own phallic language, and use the obscene words. The greatest blasphemy of all against the phallic reality is this "lifting it to a higher plane." Likewise, if the lady marries the gamekeeper—she hasn't done it yet—it is not class spite, but in spite of class.

Finally, there are the correspondents who complain that I describe the pirated editions—some of them—but not the original. The original first edition, issued in Florence, is bound in hard covers, dullish mulberry-red paper with my phoenix (symbol of immortality, the bird rising new from the nest in flames) printed in black on the cover, and a white paper label on the back. The paper is good, creamy hand-rolled Italian paper, but the print, though nice, is ordinary, and the binding is just the usual binding of a little Florentine shop. There is no expert bookmaking in it: yet it is a pleasant volume, much more so than many far "superior" books.

And if there are many spelling errors—there are—it is because the book was set up in a little Italian printing-shop, such a family affair, in which nobody knew one word of English. They none of them knew any English at all, so they were spared all blushes: and the proofs were terrible. The printer would do fairly well for a few pages, then he would go drunk, or something. And then the words danced weird and macabre, but not English. So that if still some of the hosts of errors exist, it is a mercy they are not more.

Then one paper wrote pitying the poor printer who was deceived into printing the book. Not deceived at all. A white-moustached little man who has just married a second wife, he was told: Now the book contains such and such words, in English, and it describes certain things. Don't you print it if you think it will get you into trouble!— What does it describe? he asked. And when told, he said, with the short indifference of a Florentine: O! ma! but we do it every day!—And that seemed, to him, to settle the matter entirely. Since it was nothing political or out of the way, there was nothing to think about. Every-day concerns, commonplace.

But it was a struggle, and the wonder is the book came out as well as it did. There was just enough type to set up a half of it: so the half was set up, the thousand copies were printed, and, as a measure of caution, the two hundred on ordinary paper, the little second edition, as well: then the type was distributed, and the second half set up.

Then came the struggle of delivery. The book was stopped by the American customs almost at once. Fortunately in England there was a delay. So that practically the whole edition—at least eight hundred copies, surely—must have gone to England.

Then came the storms of vulgar vituperation. But they were inevitable. "But we do it every day," says a little Italian printer. "Monstrous and horrible!" shrieks a section of the British press. "Thank you for a really sexual book about sex, at last. I am so tired of a-sexual sexual books," says one of the most distinguished citizens of Florence to me—an Italian.—"I don't know—I don't know—if it's not a bit too strong," says a timid Florentine critic—an Italian. "Listen, Signor Lawrence, you find it really necessary to *say* it?" I told him I did, and he pondered.—"Well, one of them was a brainy vamp, and the other was a sexual moron," said an American woman, referring to the two men in the book—"so I'm afraid Connie had a poor choice—*as usual*!"

Appendix

Lady Chatterley's Lover and the landscape of the English Midlands

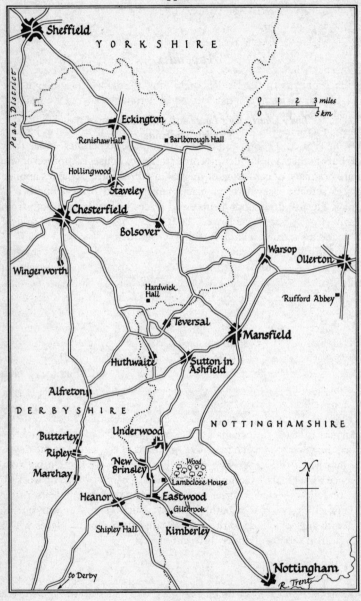

Map 1

More perhaps than any other of Lawrence's works, *Lady Chatterley's Lover* presents problems to the reader attempting to identify originals of the places it describes in the English Midlands. Although Lawrence continued his usual fictional practice of renaming and recreating actual places, yet in this novel – as in his short novel *The Virgin and the Gipsy*, written in January 1926 – he created a region full of real-life places, sometimes under their actual but at other times under invented names; of houses composed of two or more originals; of confusing or misleading directions; of names applied to places actually elsewhere; of places amalgamated from a number of originals. He also drew upon people and places he had known both from his early years in Eastwood (up to 1912), and from the early and middle 1920s. He thus created a kind of archetypal Midlands region.

In part this practice seems to have been deliberate; Lawrence's sense of the novel's sexual explicitness probably made him particularly careful to disguise some of its recognisable families and places, and their location. 'Wragby', discussed below, is an example; he had similarly disguised 'Breadalby' in *Women in Love*, in both cases using two quite distinct originals to create a composite fiction. But compared with his earlier novels and stories about the region – some of which are so accurate in their recreation of real places that one can effectively use the printed page as a gazetteer – these works of the later 1920s lack some of the old detailed recreation of Midlands life; they tend to turn the local and the particular into the mythical and the reminiscent.

Two maps are provided, of the Eastwood region and of Derbyshire, to show where many of the originals of fictional places are located. It must be stressed, however, that such maps are not maps of the action of the novel. They may assist the reader who wishes to study the connection between Lawrence's imaginative method and the landscape upon which he worked.

There follows below a brief account of some of the novel's major locations, citing references both to places which do not appear on the maps, with suggestions as to their composite nature, and to places which also appear in the novel under different guises.

'Wragby'

The name of the Chatterley home, 'Wragby Hall' (5:22), is probably taken from a village in Lincolnshire, 10 miles n.e. of Lincoln, which Lawrence may have remembered from trips to the east coast in his youth; he may well have passed through it on his car journey to Mablethorpe in August 1926, two months before he began the novel. The novel's 'Wragby' is situated near the mining village of 'Tevershall': beside it lies the wood, which is the other major focus of the book. For much of the novel, 'Wragby' is recognisably in the same location (and in the same relation to the village of 'Tevershall') as is Lambclose House, the home of the Barber family of Moorgreen, in relation to Lawrence's home township of Eastwood. Lawrence had previously described Lambclose House in his novels, notably as 'Highclose' in *The White Peacock* (ed. Andrew Robertson, Cambridge, 1983. Explanatory note on 9:10) and as 'Shortlands' in *Women in Love* (ed. David Farmer, Lindeth Vasey and John Worthen, Cambridge, 1987, Appendix III, p. 524); while in *Lady Chatterley's Lover* he makes a passing reference to the 'Duchess of Shortlands' (148:9). At other times, however, 'Wragby' is located elsewhere. Connie Chatterley explicitly drives 'south towards the Peak' (153:39) when she leaves it in chap. XI, for example, suggesting a location to the n. of the Peak District in Derbyshire. However, she arrives at Lawrence's recreation of Chesterfield on the same journey, so must have been driving well to the e. of the Peak District; and 'Wragby' then appears to be a recreation of Renishaw Hall, the home of the Sitwell family, which Lawrence visited in September 1926. Renishaw Hall is 1 mile s.e. of the mining village of Eckington and 6½ miles s.e. of Sheffield (which is once mentioned as close to 'Wragby', 27:8); Sheffield is also the location of a 'Palais-de-dance' (104:18). 'Wragby' also resembles Renishaw Hall and is quite unlike Lambclose House, which was totally rebuilt in the nineteenth century as a compact grey stone house. Wragby is 'a long, low old house in brown stone, begun about the middle of the eighteenth century, and added on to, till it was a warren of a place without much distinction' (13:5–7): Renishaw Hall was originally built shortly before 1627 but was much modified and extended in the late eighteenth century to become the 'long, rambling' brown stone building it is today (N. Pevsner, *Derbyshire*, 2nd edn, 1978, p. 302); its north front is exactly 300 feet long.

'Tevershall'

The village of 'Tevershall' – the name taken from the village Teversal in Derbyshire, itself only 3 miles s.e. of the great house of Hardwick Hall (see below) – also appears in two different locations, depending on the part of the novel being read. When Mrs Bolton describes it in chap. IX,

'Tevershall' recalls Eastwood, with some of its names disguised: 'Pye Croft' (102:7), with its bay-windowed houses (102:20), recreates the real-life (and bay-windowed) street Lynn Croft, where the Lawrence family lived 1905–11; 'Bestwood Hill' (102:9), using the name Lawrence employed for Eastwood in *Sons and Lovers* and elsewhere, corresponds to the Nottingham Road, which Mrs Bolton also calls 'Tevershall hill' (263:7); 'Kinbrook' (102:16) combines Kimberley and Giltbrook, 1½ miles s.e. of Eastwood. The Primitive Methodist Chapel (103:20) at Hill-Top and the Miners' Welfare (103:29) in Eastwood (see below) are not disguised: nor is 'Leiver's cab', Leivers' Garage, the successor of the pre-war Star Livery Stables, its yard located in Victoria Street (see note on 80:17), and probably where Field fills the car with petrol in chap. IX (152:34). 'Hanson's woodyard' (102:17) suggests the real-life Hanson's Brewery in Kimberley. Mellors describes working as a young man in 'Butterley Offices' (200:25): i.e. one of the local offices of the Butterley Colliery Co.; the company was based in Butterley (5 miles n.w. of Eastwood) but owned Plumptre Colliery, Eastwood, and had offices in Eastwood before World War I.

When Connie drives through 'Tevershall' in chap. XI, the only disguised name is that of the village itself; the narrator provides a detailed if slightly out-of-sequence recreation of Eastwood, reminding readers of the way that 'Bestwood' is such a recreation in *Sons and Lovers* and that 'Woodhouse' is in *The Lost Girl* and *Mr Noon*. Connie drives 'uphill' (152:7) along the Nottingham Road past the 'plaster-and-gilt horror of the cinema' (152:17) – the 'Empire Picture House', opened in 1913 at the corner of King Street and Nottingham Road. She sees 'the new big Primitive chapel' (152:18–19) on her right; the 'Wesleyan chapel, higher up' (152:20–1), down Victoria Street; and the 'Congregational chapel' (152:22) in the Nottingham Road, with its steeple. She also sees the 'Three Tuns' (visible across open space from Nottingham Road) – and, farther along, the 'Wellington' (also mentioned in Mellors's letter, 299:2) and the 'Nelson' (153:6) – i.e. the 'Lord Nelson'. The 'new school buildings' (152:24) which she sees are those of Devonshire Drive Schools, opened in 1910. On her left she views the post office, and 'the big but weary-looking drapers and clothing shops' (152:39–40) – for example, the massive building of 'London House', between Victoria Street and Market Place (see *The Lost Girl*, note on 3:4) – and comes out in the Market Place by 'the "Sun," that called itself an inn, not a pub' (153:1–2): i.e. the Sun Inn (or Hotel). 'Sam Black' (153:1) is Lawrence's name for the landlord, Sam Wood. On Connie's left, down Church Street, lies St Mary's Parish

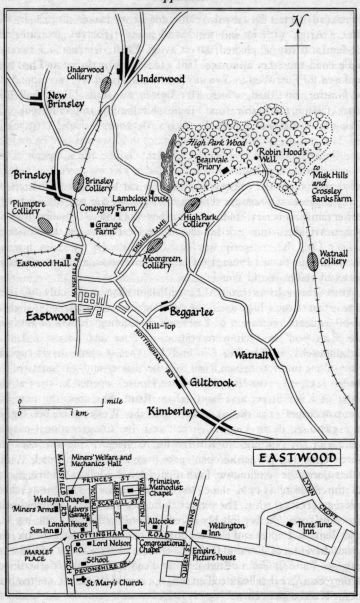

Map 2

church (153:4); but her car turns right, down the Mansfield Road past 'the Miners Arms' (153:5) and the 'Mechanics Hall' (153:7) of the old Mechanics Institute, erected 1863. George Chatterley (see note on 5:11) had been its secretary up to 1904; the Mechanics Institute itself had been used as a 'Miners Welfare' (153:8) centre from 1920.

However, as Connie's journey progresses, she is clearly 'travelling South' from n. Derbyshire; and 'Tevershall' appears to be a recreation of Eckington: see *Connie's journey in chap. XI* below.

The collieries

At several points the colliery company owned by Clifford Chatterley's family suggests the real-life company, Barber Walker & Co., run by the Barber family; it is recreated as the 'Tevershall Colliery Company' (81:10) in chap. VII, and as the 'Butler and Smitham Colliery Company' (298:12) in chap. XIX. The descriptions of 'Tevershall pit' and the burning 'Tevershall pit-bank' (13:9,22) are reminiscent both of Plumptre Colliery, owned by the Butterley Colliery Co. but closed in 1912, whose burning pit-bank (recreated in *Aaron's Rod*, ed. Mara Kalnins, Cambridge, 1988, 26:20–2) was a local phenomenon, and of Moorgreen Colliery, Eastwood, owned by Barber Walker & Co., which was near enough for its smells and sounds to penetrate Lambclose House, as the smells and sounds of 'Tevershall pit' infiltrate 'Wragby' in chap. II (13:25). In the early twentieth century, 'many inefficient collieries had to close' (Alan Griffin, *Mining in the East Midlands 1550–1947*, 1971, p. 232); in chap. IX, the Digby Colliery Co.'s 'New London' pit (105:13) is on the point of closing (though it stayed open until the late 1930s), while 'New England' pit (106:18), a name also used in *Sons and Lovers* – and perhaps another recreation of Plumptre Colliery, called 'New Brunswick Colliery' in *Aaron's Rod* – has already shut down. Another unidentified closed pit is 'Colwick Wood' (106:19), with its rusty railway lines (Colwick is a suburb of Nottingham); the Butterley Colliery Co. alone closed seven pits in the Midlands region between 1900 and 1914. The pit at 'Whiteover' (105:19), to which many 'Tevershall' men go, is probably a recreation of the Barber Walker & Co. pit at Watnall, 3 miles e. of Eastwood. Mellors's landlord in chap. XIX is an engine-driver 'at High Park' (298:24) – Barber Walker & Co.'s High Park Colliery – and lives in 'Engine Row' (298:23): Engine Lane linked Moorgreen and High Park collieries to Eastwood. 'Stacks Gate' colliery (42:17) is discussed below.

The wood

Just next to 'Wragby' lies the remnant of 'the great forest where Robin Hood hunted' (41:27); High Park Wood, next to Lambclose House, was commonly thought to be a remnant of Sherwood Forest (see *The Prussian Officer and Other Stories*, ed. John Worthen, Cambridge, 1983, note on 88:6); the main road from Eastwood to 'that once-romantic' (240:21) town Mansfield, associated with Robin Hood, goes 'round to the north' (41:30) of High Park Wood. Many of Connie's walks from Wragby Hall trace features of the landscape n. and e. of Eastwood which the young Lawrence knew intimately, though real-life names are mostly disguised. The 'spring called John's Well' (87:10), for example, recalls Robin Hood's Well in High Park Wood (see *The Prussian Officer*, note on 95:28). The keeper's hut 'made of rustic poles' (87:30–1) suggests the hut Lawrence saw in the wood in 1901 on his first visit (see *D. H. Lawrence: A Composite Biography*, ed. Edward Nehls, Madison, 1959, iii. 562), as well as the similar keeper's hut (with pheasant coops around it) which Lawrence described in his story 'The Shades of Spring' (see *The Prussian Officer*, 107:2). In chap. XVI the keeper's cottage – of dark red-brown sandstone – is situated at the end of a lane near a bridge passing over a railway; the line runs in a cutting through the wood. The colliery railway between High Park and Watnall collieries ran in a deep cutting through High Park Wood, and a bridge over the cutting led to Robin Hood's Well. No cottages were, however, ever situated there; nor did the road at the end of the lane go to Mansfield, as in the novel (240:12–13). 'Crosshill Road' (240:12), suggesting a road crossing the Misk Hills just n.e. of High Park Wood, is Lawrence's invention, as is 'Crosshill Village' (252:8), unless the latter is a recreation of Watnall; the name is perhaps influenced by Crossleigh Banks Farm, 1 mile n.e. A sandstone cottage (one of the two Shortwood cottages) to the e. of Beauvale Priory may have contributed to the scene, and may have been the cottage of the 'forest ranger' who 'used to beat his wife' which Lawrence pointed out to a friend in 1926 (Britton 108).

A single reference suggests that Lawrence also imaginatively located the wood in the neighbourhood of Renishaw Hall; when Connie and Hilda drive back from Mansfield to Mellors's cottage in chap. XVI, they take 'the other road, through Bolsover' (241:19), which – if Lawrence refers to the real-life Bolsover – shows that they are driving n.w. from Mansfield, through Bolsover towards Renishaw. This route provides, too, a lane-end and a bridge over a railway running next to the road, with a grassy lane leading to the east gate of Renishaw Hall (Britton 149).

When Connie takes a walk from 'Wragby' in chap. IX, '*not* towards the wood, but in the opposite direction' (129:17–18), she goes to 'Marehay' and 'Marehay Farm'. The names are borrowed from the real-life Marehay and Marehay Farm, 1 mile s.w. of Ripley, Derbyshire (Ripley being the home of Lawrence's sister Ada); but the novel's 'Marehay' is Lawrence's recreation of the real-life Coneygrey Farm, 1 mile n. of Eastwood, whose land borders the grounds of Lambclose House just as the land of 'Marehay' 'ran up to Wragby' (129:24–5). The tenants' name ('Flint') is identical with that of the real-life tenants (1908–28) of the nearby Willeywood Farm: it has been suggested that Mrs Flint (once a teacher) is a recreation of DHL's old Eastwood friend May Chambers Holbrook (Britton 115–16). Connie returns home via 'the warren' (see note on 131:31). Mrs Bolton, seeing Connie walking s.w. in the park, thinks she may be going to 'the rectory' (136:33): which suggests either Brinsley Vicarage, 2 miles w. of Lambclose House, or St Mary's Rectory in Eastwood.

Connie's journey in chap. XI

Lawrence, his sister Ada and her husband W. E. Clarke drove out into Derbyshire in the course of both his 1925 and his 1926 visits to the Midlands (they went to Renishaw in 1926); and much of the description of Connie's journey relates to what he saw on those two visits. When her car leaves 'Tevershall' and the part of the journey described above, Connie drives towards 'Stacks Gate'; she is 'travelling south' (153:40), and the land is rising (153:37). The reader may be puzzled, because Lawrence uses 'Stacks Gate' for two different locations in the novel. In chaps. V, IX and X, the new works and colliery of 'Stacks Gate' are 'not three miles' from 'Tevershall pit' (106:7) and are indeed within sight and hearing of 'Wragby' wood (42:17, 37); Mellors can hear the engines and see the lights from the wood (118:38–119:8), and is annoyed by 'Stacks Gate' colliers setting snares 'on the Marehay side' (143:13). This Nottinghamshire 'Stacks Gate' appears to recreate either Barber Walker & Co.'s colliery at Moorgreen or that at Underwood.

However, once in chap. IX (105:18) and continually in chap. XI, 'Stacks Gate' colliery is much farther away. Mrs Bolton assumes that Clifford has never seen it (105:19), and Connie's journey through the region confirms that the 'old Stacks Gate' (154:26) is Lawrence's recreation of the old Derbyshire colliery village of Staveley (3 miles n.e. of Chesterfield), and that the new Stacks Gate corresponds to the modern town and works of

Hollingwood (½ mile to the w.). In the late 1920s Hollingwood consisted of 'over 700 houses and a few shops, built by the Staveley Coal and Iron Company Limited' (*Kelly's Directory*, 1928, p. 404). The 'huge and gorgeous new hotel, the Coningsby Arms' (154:11–12), is Lawrence's recreation of the Hollingwood Hotel, in 'isolation off the road' to Chesterfield (154:13).

On her way towards the Derbyshire 'Stacks Gate', Connie can see 'on her left, on a height', the 'shadowy, powerful bulk of Warsop Castle' (154:1–2): although the name is borrowed from the Midlands town of Warsop, on the edge of Sherwood Forest and 14 miles e. of Chesterfield, 'Warsop Castle' is Lawrence's recreation of Bolsover Castle, clearly visible from the high ground around Staveley, with the 'newish' (154:4) New Bolsover Model Village (built 1891–3) and Bolsover Pit below it. The 'Duke' (154:6) of Portland (also Baron Bolsover) was lessor of the Pit.

Connie now drives s.w. from Staveley towards 'Uthwaite', which – with its 'pathetic little cork-screw spire of the church' (155:13) – is Lawrence's recreation of Chesterfield and the church of St Mary and All Saints, with its famous twisted spire. The town's 'old pharmacy' (155:32) and presumably 'Miss Bentley's shop' (160:11) are in the quarter of the old 'crooked streets' (155:31) between the church and the marketplace. 'Uthwaite hospital' (81:9) is elsewhere named as a place where Mrs Bolton has worked: although in the previous paragraph Chesterfield also appears under its own name (80:25).

On the way towards 'Uthwaite' Connie can also see 'Chadwick Hall, more window than wall, one of the most famous Elizabethan houses' (155:2–3): Lawrence's recreation of Hardwick Hall, 'more glass than wall', located 7 miles s.e. of Staveley, and visible when driving n. from Ripley towards Chesterfield or s. from it, as Lawrence did in 1926. Completed in 1597, the Hall is striking for its numerous tall windows; its picture gallery, extending the 166-foot length of the east front, boasts 27,000 panes of glass.

'Uthwaite', 'where the Chatterleys were still *the* Chatterleys' (152:1–2), has as one of its 'chief inns . . . the Chatterley Arms' (155:16); 'Uthwaite' thus also takes on features of Eckington, 1 mile n.w. of Renishaw Hall, with its Sitwell Arms public house. The real-life village of Huthwaite (3 miles s.w. of Mansfield) is perhaps the least important original of 'Uthwaite'.

The same might be said of 'Shipley' (156:38), to which Connie goes after stopping in 'Uthwaite' (she also visits 'Shipley' in chap. x). The real-life Shipley Hall, ½ mile s.w. of Heanor, hemmed in by collieries

(157:17) and unoccupied from 1924 (but not demolished until 1942), is only one influence upon Lawrence's creation, which he twice locates in n. Derbyshire, near 'Uthwaite'. 'Shipley Hall' also combines Rufford Abbey (6 miles n.e. of Mansfield), originally a Cistercian foundation and the seat of Lord Saville, Melbourne Hall (7½ miles s.e. of Derby), with its remarkable gardens and long yew alleys, and Barlborough Hall (4½ miles e. of Eckington), built 1583–4; the last being famous among other things for its corridors, 'softly curved and full of life' (157:15); it was owned in the 1920s by Godfrey Locker-Lampson (1875–1946). Lord Saville entertained Edward VII at Rufford on several occasions, but at least once Edward visited Alfred Edward Miller Mundy (b. 1849), known as Squire Mundy, at Shipley Hall. Squire Winter is seventy years old (149:25), and dies shortly after Connie's visit (158:25); Squire Mundy died in April 1920 at the age of seventy.

Connie observes, too, the demolition of 'Fritchley, a perfect old Georgian mansion' (156:19). Lawrence recreates Wingerworth Hall, 2½ miles s. of Chesterfield, home of the Hunloke family; completed in 1729, it was demolished 1924–7. Connie also ponders the loss of the Hall at 'Eastwood' (156:36): Eastwood Hall, the home of the Walker family, had been taken over as the Barber Walker & Co. Colliery offices in 1917.

Nottingham

Nottingham figures only briefly in the novel. It lies s. and e. when Connie is driving towards the Derbyshire 'Stacks Gate' (153:37); its 'Mikado' (104:31) at 39 Long Row was a well-known restaurant, and the Empire Music Hall in South Sherwood Street (by 1920, the Empire Theatre of Varieties) also appears under its own name (104:31). The Trent, upon which Nottingham stands, the chief river of the Midlands and the third largest in England, rises in Staffordshire and flows e. to the Humber estuary: it is described as dividing north from south (14:30).

Other place names

Mellors writes to Connie from 'Old Heanor' (298:10); Heanor is a village on the ridge 2 miles w. of Eastwood, but Lawrence is apparently recreating Brinsley or New Brinsley, 1½ miles n. of Eastwood. 'The Grange Farm' (298:10), where Mellors works, is probably Lawrence's recreation of the real-life Grange Farm, just e. of Brinsley. Matlock (153:21), a small holiday centre in Derbyshire which Lawrence visited with his mother in his youth (*A Composite Biography*, ed. Nehls, 1957, i. 54), and the hamlet of Beggarlee, just n.e. of Eastwood and mentioned by Mrs Bolton (263:10), appear under their own names: as does Ollerton, 8½ miles n.e. of Mansfield, which is mentioned in Mellors's account of his youth (200:19). The 'Peak' district of Derbyshire, lying to the w. of Sheffield, is located 'south' of it (153:39). The name of 'Lady Bennerley' (73:9) is perhaps taken from Bennerley Iron Works, 1 mile s.e. of Eastwood; 'Fillingwood' (150:10) is perhaps an allusion to Hollingwood (see above, *Connie's journey in chap. XI*).

Explanatory Notes

LADY CHATTERLEY'S LOVER

5:8 **Constance Chatterley ... Clifford Chatterley [5:11] ... twenty-nine [5:15]**   The name 'Chatterley' was common in DHL's native town, Eastwood: notable were George Chatterley (1861–1940), office manager at Barber Walker & Co. and its secretary from 1918–31, and his daughters Constance (1883–?) and Winifred (1886–?). The main action of the novel takes place from 1922–4. When injured in 1918, Clifford is 'twenty-nine' (5:15): but he was 'twenty-two' (10:4) in 1914 when the war started. Constance was 'eighteen' (8:21) in 1913 and 'twenty-three' (5:14) in 1918: but she is 'twenty-seven' (70:33, 71:12) early in 1924. Mellors, born like DHL in 1885, is 'Thirty-nine' (283:28) in August 1924; early in the year Connie had thought him 'thirty-seven or eight' (68:19).

5:13 **Flanders**   Area of northern France and a province of Belgium; the site of much conflict in the First World War and a symbol of the war in Europe.

5:23 **baronet**   A baronet ranks above a knight and below a baron. An hereditary title, Clifford's baronetcy would, if he had no son, go to the nearest male descendant of a former holder of the title. A baronet is conventionally addressed by his title and Christian name ('Sir Clifford'), his wife by 'Lady' and surname ('Lady Chatterley').

6:6 **Bond Street**   Street of expensive shops in London.

6:19 **R. A.**   Royal Academician; member of the Royal Academy of Arts, founded 1768.

6:20 **the cultured Fabians ... pre-Raphaelite days [6:21]**   The Fabian Society was founded in 1883 to promote moderate socialism ... The Pre-Raphaelites, a reforming group of English artists formed in 1848, emulated Italian painting of the 'pre-Raphael' period, especially its sharp detail and its immediate response to nature.

6:38 **Wandervogel songs**   The Wandervögel (literally, 'migrant birds' in German) were groups of hikers.

8:23 **L'amour avait passe par là**   Love had passed that way (French).

9:14–15 **lost a shilling and found sixpence**   A shilling had twelve pence. Popular saying to denote disappointment.

9:29 **Kensington**   Wealthy district of London.

9:38 **Westminster**   District of London containing the Houses of Parliament and government offices.

10:4 **Bonn**   German city; German universities offered the best technological education in Europe before 1914.

10:33 **Kitchener**   Field Marshal Horatio Herbert Kitchener (1850–1916) – immortalized during the First World War by a famous recruiting poster featuring his face and pointing finger above the caption 'Your country needs you' – became Secretary of State for War in 1914; he greatly expanded the British army.

11:14 **the Tommies . . . conscription** [11:15]   Term for British soldiers, short for Private Thomas Atkins, the full name used in sample forms for privates in the British army . . . In 1916 Britain introduced compulsory military service for all able-bodied men between eighteen and forty-one.

11:20 **mad hatter's tea-party**   The ridiculous confusion described in Lewis Carroll, *Alice's Adventures in Wonderland* (1865), Chapter Seven.

11:21 **over there . . . Lloyd George**   In France and Flanders, where the First World War (1914–18) cost millions of lives . . . David Lloyd George (1863–1945), a Liberal, dominated English politics from 1906–22 and often earned DHL's contempt.

11:35–6 **Horatio Bottomley**   Journalist, financier and Liberal Member of Parliament, Bottomley (1860–1933) accrued and lost vast sums of money by audacious speculations. Convicted of fraud in 1922, he was sentenced to seven years' penal servitude. He founded and edited *John Bull* (1906–29), a weekly journal that savagely attacked *Lady Chatterley's Lover* on 20 October 1928 and 19 January 1929.

13:22 **pit-bank**   Mounds of waste formed where coal was sorted and screened at the pit-head; they could ignite spontaneously and smoulder for years.

13:29 **manna**   The natural food God provided to the Israelites as they fled Egypt for the Promised Land (Exodus xvi). Biblical quotations are from the King James Bible.

15:1 **Mester**   See Glossary of Dialect Forms for this and dialect elsewhere.

15:11 **nonconformist**   Opposed to the Established Church; by extension, independent or radical.

18:14 *corpus delicti*   body of the crime (legal Latin); loosely, the victim's corpse in a murder case.

18:18 **demi-monde**   Socially not quite acceptable (French).

18:40–19:1 **Sufficient unto . . . evil thereof**   Matthew vi. 34.

21:1 **Mayfair**   Exclusive London district.

21:35 **The bitch-goddess . . . of Success**   Although later in the novel the narrator incorrectly attributes this phrase to the American novelist Henry James (see 62:29–30), his brother, the philosopher William James (1842–1910), coined the phrase to mean the power of money to breed 'moral flabbiness'.

24:30 **Renoir and Cézanne**   Pierre Auguste Renoir (1841–1919) and Paul Cézanne (1836–1906), French painters. See also note on 40:3.

25:25–6 the infant crying in the night   Tennyson, *In Memoriam* (1850), LIV, ll. 17–20: '. . . what am I?/ An infant crying in the night:/ An infant crying for the light:/ And with no language but a cry.'

29:30–31 Une immense espérance a traversé la terre   A great hope passed over the earth (French). From 'L'Espoir en Dieu', *Poésies Nouvelles* (1836–52), by Alfred de Musset (1810–57).

34:30–31 straight road . . . narrow gate   Cf. Matthew vii. 14.

34:31–2 English man of letters   Lord Morley edited a series of 67 volumes entitled *English Men of Letters* (1878–1919); inclusion implied classic status.

34:38 *hors de combat*   Out of action (French).

35:40 *arriviste*   One determined to get ahead (French).

36:22–3 Blest be . . . in kindred something-or-other   Tommy Dukes's adaptation of the opening lines of the hymn by the Rev. John Fawcett (1740–1817): 'Blest be the tie that binds/ Our hearts in Christian love:/ The fellowship of kindred minds/ Is like to that above.' See also 210:36, where Mellors completes line two 'in kindred love'.

36:32–3 Socrates in Plato . . . Protagoras [36:34] . . . Alcibiades [36:35]   The Greek philosopher Socrates (470?–399 BC) started the 'critical activity' (37:14) by posing questions to instruct his pupils. His student Plato (427?–347 BC) wrote several philosophical dialogues between Socrates and others: in the *Protagoras* dialogue appear both Protagoras (c. 485–c. 410 BC), the first and most famous of the Greek professors known as Sophists, and the Greek general Alcibiades (c. 450–404 BC).

36:40 Ye shall . . . its fruit   Cf. Matthew xii. 33.

37:17 *ex cathedra*   Literally 'from the chair' (Latin); from the seat of authority.

37:24 the ass had spoken   In Numbers xxii Balaam's ass suddenly addressed his master, rebuking him.

38:6 bolshevism   The Bolsheviks, an extremist group formed in 1903, advocated the violent overthrow of capitalism and in 1917 seized power during the Russian Revolution. DHL regarded Bolshevism as the Soviet form of communism.

40:2–3 Renoir said . . . his penis   According to his son Jean, Renoir made the remark when his hands were crippled with rheumatism.

40:10–11 If they . . . they be!   Cf. George Wither (1588–1667), 'A Lover's Resolution', ll. 7–8, 'If she be not so to me,/ What care I how fair she be?'

40:17 Hildebrand   Pope Gregory VII (1021–85) – who supported celibacy among priests – was originally a monk named Hildebrand.

41:25 riding . . . Robin Hood [41:27]   A track through a wood for horseback riders . . . the legendary medieval outlaw of Sherwood Forest (then about 16,000 acres) in Nottinghamshire.

44:11 Where are the snows of yesteryear?   From 'The Great Testament, Ballad of the Ladies of Bygone Times' by François Villon (1431–63?), French poet.

48:37 overhead smith A blacksmith working in the stables at the colliery's pit-head.

50:7–8 The colliers . . . a strike The General Strike in Britain began on 1 May 1926.

53:8 go off I.e. like a firework: 'go off' at 53:38 is colloquial for sexual climax.

53:20 my-eye-Betty-Martin 'All my eye and Betty Martin', slang for 'nonsense'.

58:12 Charlestoned The Charleston, a popular staccato dance introduced in 1923, featured swinging arms, kicking legs and pivoting toes.

58:15 as old as Methuselah A patriarch reputed to have lived 969 years; cf. Genesis v. 21–7.

60:40 blackleading Polishing iron-work such as stoves and grates with graphite.

62:24 *étape* after *étape* 'Station after station', or 'stage after stage' (French).

63:25–6 cock-a-whoopy Conceited, boastful, strutting like a cock. Cf. 'cockaloopy', a variant of 'cock-a-hoop', at 203:15.

64:28–9 'Go ye . . . find *a man*.' Connie adapts Jeremiah v. 1, 'Run ye to and fro through the streets of Jerusalem, and see now . . . if ye can find a man'.

64:32 C'est une autre chose! That's another matter! (French).

65:18 short time Less than a full shift, or not every day: see 299:28–9.

75:37 the cerebral stone Allusion to Luke xxiv. 2, linked to Dukes's preceding remark about 'the resurrection of the body'.

76:14 Carrara marble Italian marble, often snow-white, widely used by sculptors and monumental masons.

77:38 He ran to liver With a tendency to jaundice, by analogy with 'ran to seed' or 'ran to fat'.

78:31–2 Cannes . . . Biarritz Fashionable French resorts: Cannes on the Mediterranean, like Nice (79:1); Biarritz on the Atlantic coast.

80:30 butty Miner in charge of a small team working a section of coal face.

81:6 special ambulance I.e. training specifically for a nurse working with an ambulance team.

83:19–20 'Touch not . . . to loose.' Song (1840) by the Hon. Miss M. D., to words attributed to Sir Walter Scott (1771–1832).

85:14–15 'Seasons return . . . returns Spring——' Milton, *Paradise Lost*, iii. 41–2.

85:18 'Pale beyond porch and portal' 'The Garden of Proserpine' by Algernon Charles Swinburne (1837–1909), l. 49.

85:23–5 Ye must . . . bring forth John iii. 7; 'I believe . . . the body': from the Apostles' Creed; 'Except a . . . bring forth': paraphrase of John xii. 24.

85:33–4 'The world . . . thy breath.'   Swinburne's 'Hymn to Proserpine', l. 35, referring to Christ.

85:34 **Persephone**   Persephone (Proserpine), daughter of Zeus (Jupiter) and Demeter, was captured by Hades (Pluto) while gathering flowers and taken to his underworld kingdom. She was allowed to return to earth every spring.

86:3 **Absalom**   The third son of King David, Absalom organized a rebellion against his father; when it failed, he tried to escape on horseback, caught his long hair in the branches of a tree and was killed by the commander of David's forces. See 2 Samuel xiii–xix.

91:25 'Sweeter than . . . Juno's eyes,'   Shakespeare, *The Winter's Tale*, IV. iv. 121.

92:19–20 **the north-west frontier**   Mountainous area between India and Afghanistan; scene of frequent armed conflict.

92:25–6 **broad Derbyshire**   I.e. Derbyshire dialect.

93:14 'Thou still . . . of quietness,'   Keats, 'Ode on a Grecian Urn' (1820), l. 11.

100:1 *j'adoube*   Said by a chess player wishing to correct a piece's position without playing it; from 'adouber' (French), 'to set in place'.

100:37 **Mrs Gaskell . . . Miss Mitford**   Elizabeth Cleghorn Gaskell (1810–65) was the author of *Cranford* (1853), a portrait of village life; George Eliot (1819–80) recreated village life in *Adam Bede* (1859) and *Silas Marner* (1861); Mary Russell Mitford (1787–1855) wrote sketches of village life, collected in five volumes as *Our Village* (1824–32).

102:13–14 **chapel people**   The congregations of Methodist, Baptist, Congregationalist or Presbyterian chapels, as distinct from the Church of England. A class distinction is also implied. See note on 103:22.

102:28 **the pictures**   I.e. 'moving pictures', movies.

102:39 **wedding-present for Princess Mary**   In February 1922 the daughter of George V, Princess Mary (1897–1965), married Henry George Charles Lascelles (1882–1947).

103:2 **Swan and Edgars**   Well-known London department store.

103:20 **Primitive Chapel . . . Primitive Methodist** [103:22]   Breaking from the Wesleyan Methodists in 1811, the Primitive Methodists were notably revivalist and working class.

104:11 **the reds spouting**   The Communist Party of Great Britain, formed in 1921, supported the miners' struggle for higher wages, improved working conditions and nationalization of the mines.

104:18 **Palais-de-danse**   Dance hall (French): often 'the Pally', as at l. 20.

104:25 **Doncaster races, and the Derby**   The Derby at Epsom and St Leger at Doncaster are famous English horse-races.

104:31 **the Mikado . . . the Empire**   A well-known restaurant in Nottingham . . . the Empire Theatre of Varieties was an entertainment hall in Nottingham.

Explanatory Notes

106:3 **the old stocking-frames** Machines for making stockings; miners largely replaced 'stockingers' in nineteenth-century Eastwood.

106:25 **fan-wheels** Large, vaned wheels used to ventilate a mine.

109:10–12 **The new Achilles . . . lame him fatally** In Greek mythology, Thetis dipped her son Achilles in the river Styx to make him invulnerable, but missed the heel by which she held him and in which Paris wounded him fatally (hence the proverbial 'Achilles' heel').

111:39 **the great I-am!** In Jewish thought the name of God is so sacred it cannot be pronounced; hence phrases such as 'I AM THAT I AM' (Exodus iii. 14).

119:7 **winding-engines . . . turning down** [119:8] **. . . three shifts** [119:9] Engines that wind up and down the cages used to transport colliers and coal . . . winding down . . . the third shift was often used for safety checks and repairmen.

119:35 **Mammon** Heathen god symbolizing money-worship.

121:8 **'ca' canny' creed** Literally 'ca' canny' means 'call shrewdly'; i.e. 'go cautiously', or deliberately work slowly.

128:22 **King Edward** See note on 157:36.

131:30 **warren . . . gin close** [131:31] An enclosed area, often wooded . . . an enclosed field ('close') where rabbit traps ('gins') are set.

136:4 **a bacchante . . . Iacchos** [136:5] **. . . the Bacchae** [136:13] Bacchantes were women who worshipped the god of wine and ecstasy Bacchus (also called Dionysus and Iacchos). In a religious frenzy they could tear wild beasts – or men – to pieces: see Euripides' play *The Bacchae*.

137:5–6 **Sir Francis Drake** Drake (*c.* 1543–96) was the first Englishman to circumnavigate the globe.

137:35 **Racine** Jean Baptiste Racine (1639–99), neo-classical French playwright.

138:20–21 **'For hands . . . of hair—'** Swinburne, 'The Pilgrims', ll. 6–7, in *Songs Before Sunrise* (1871).

140:3 **'The lady loves her will.'** Cf. the traditional song 'The Four Loves': 'The Hart he loves the high-wood/ The Hare he loves the hill/ The Knight he loves his bright sword/ The Lady loves her will.'

140:14–15 **'Who knoweth . . . the angels—'** Cf. the epigraph to 'Ligeia' by Edgar Allen Poe (1809–49).

147:5 **cinquecento furniture** Cinquecento (Italian), short for 'mille cinque cento' or 1500; ornately carved furniture of the sixteenth century.

147:9 **Sir Edwin Landseer's . . . William Henry Hunt birds' nests** [147:10] Landseer (1802–73), popular painter of animals . . . Hunt (1790–1864), best known for still-life paintings of fruits, vegetables, birds and their nests.

148:28 **Ess.** Essence.

149:28 **bag wigs** Fashionable in the eighteenth century; the back hair was enclosed in an ornamental bag.

151:22–3 **the Gare du Nord: at Calais quay**   Trains carrying passengers
from England arrive at the northern railway terminal in Paris, via the
boat-train quay at Calais. Clifford imagines his embarrassment on this
journey.

152:27 **Standard Five**   Normally schoolchildren aged eleven or twelve.

156:12 **Queen Anne and Tom Jones**   Anne (1655–1714), reigned 1702–
14. Jones is the eponymous hero of the novel (1749) by Henry Fielding
(1707–54).

157:29 **Sandringham**   Royal residence in Norfolk bought in 1863 by
Edward VII (see next note).

157:24–5 **Queen Victoria's reign ... the then Prince of Wales**
[157:26–7] **... another King** [157:36]   Victoria (1819–1901) reigned
1837–1901 ... Edward, Prince of Wales (1841–1910), reigned as Edward
VII, 1901–10 ... he was succeeded by his son, George V (1865–1936),
who reigned 1910–36.

157:37 **soup-kitchens**   To provide food for the poor or unemployed.

160:19 **Nurse Cavell**   Edith Cavell (1865–1915), English nurse who helped
Allied soldiers escape from occupied Belgium to the Dutch frontier. In
October 1915 she was executed by the Germans.

160:26 **Saint George of Cappadocia**   Connie confuses the bishop of
Alexandria (d. 361) with St George, patron saint of England.

160:38 **Liptons**   The name of Glasgow merchant and tea salesman Sir
Thomas Lipton (1850–1931) was a household word.

160:39 *Roman de la rose*   An allegorical account of the wooing of a maiden
(represented by a rosebud) within courtly society, written first by Guil-
laume de Lorris *c.* 1225–40, then continued by Jean de Meun about 1280.

161:15 *au grand sérieux ... au très petit sérieux* [161:16]   Very seriously
... very *un*seriously (French).

161:38–9 'The fault ... are underlings.'   *Julius Caesar*, I. ii. 140–41.

179:23–4 **Plato never ... white steed**   In Book IX of the *Phaedrus*, Plato
compares the human soul to a charioteer driving a pair of winged horses,
one evil and one good: passions and desires are the black (or evil) steed.

181:4 **since Jesus and St. Francis**   See next note. Like Jesus, St Francis
of Assisi (1182–1226) renounced wealth and family to live a life of
poverty.

181:4–5 **take all ... give to the poor**   In Luke xviii. 22 Jesus tells the
rich man to 'sell all ... and distribute to the poor'.

182:35 **Nero's**   Born AD 37, Nero was Roman Emperor and tyrant from
AD 54 until his suicide in AD 68.

182:40 **Panem et circenses!**   Bread and games! (Latin), from Juvenal's
Tenth Satire, l. 81. Juvenal (*c.* AD 55–*c.* 127) believed that the Romans,
once world conquerors, cared in his time for nothing but spectacular
shows.

185:7 **Whither, oh weird ... course steering—**   Cf. 'A Passer-By' by

Robert Bridges (1844–1930), l. 1: 'Whither, O splendid ship, thy white sails crowding.'

190:16 *tableau vivant*   Living picture (French): a dramatic presentation by a motionless, posed group.

192:23 **Dieppe**   French port on the English Channel, about 100 miles from Paris.

193:24 *Noblesse oblige*   Rank imposes obligations (French).

194:1 **Schieber**   Profiteer, shyster (German).

194:26 **Proust**   Marcel Proust (1871–1922), French novelist, author of the seven-part *À la Recherche du Temps Perdu* (1913–27); the first volume of the English translation, *Remembrance of Things Past*, appeared in 1922.

195:24 **à la guerre ... la guerre**   Take the rough with the smooth (French).

200:27–8 **Persepolis and Timbuctoo**   Persepolis, the ancient capital of Persia, destroyed by Alexander the Great in 330 BC. Timbuktu, the ancient African city near the Sahara Desert.

201:22 **My Lord Duckfoot**   One who 'puts on airs' (English Midlands vernacular).

210:13 **John Thomas**   DHL wrote to Mabel Dodge Luhan (13 March 1928), 'John Thomas is one of the names for the penis, as probably you know' (*Letters*, vi. 318).

212:27 **a circulating library**   A commercial library that required payment for the use of its books.

214:6 **Retford ... Grantham** [214:8]   Stopping-places on the old Great North Road, the highway from Edinburgh to London.

214:31 **pontoon**   Card game popular among soldiers in the First World War.

217:5 **high game**   Gamebirds, once shot, are 'hung' for several days to soften the flesh. Because they smell, they are said to be 'high'.

218:14–15 **serpent swallows itself**   The serpent with its tail in its mouth is an image of eternity.

218:17 *te deum laudamus*   We praise thee, O God (Latin).

224:1–2 **Moses in the bull-rushes**   Exodus ii. 3.

227:8 **'Knight of the Burning Pestle.'**   Comic play (1607–8) by Francis Beaumont (1584–1616).

228:40–229:1 **'Good-bye my bluebell, farewell to you—!'**   The marching song 'Blue Bell', a great hit in 1904: 'Goodbye, my Blue Bell, farewell to you;/ One last fond look into your eyes so blue./ 'Mid campfires gleaming, 'mid shot and shell,/ I will be dreaming of my own Blue Bell.'

230:31–2 **alone and palely loitering**   Keats, 'La belle dame sans merci' (1819), l. 30.

233:10 **one of the latest scientific-religious books**   *Religion in the Making* (Cambridge, 1926) by Alfred North Whitehead (1861–1947). The last page is quoted.

237:31 **arcadian**   Of Arcady: pastoral, innocent.

238:3 **Minerva-like**   The Roman goddess of war, commonly identified with her Greek counterpart, Athena (238:11).

240:19 **Pall Mall**   Street in London's West End.

247:7 **Abélard . . . Heloïse** [247:8] **. . . passion** [247:9]   Celebrated lovers: he (1079–1142) a priest and theologian, she (*c.* 1098–1164) a student turned nun after their affair. Abelard wrote that 'no stage of love was omitted by us in our cupidity' (*The Letters of Abelard and Heloise*, 1925, p. 11).

253:10 *chair à plaisir*   Flesh at will (French), i.e. for him to have when he wants.

255:1 **flâneurs**   Loungers, loafers (French).

255:12 **the Bois . . . the Luxembourg gardens** [255:13]   The Bois de Boulogne, an extensive park in Paris located in a loop of the Seine . . . a public park in Paris renowned for its formal beauty.

255:17 **the Brenner . . . the Dolomites** [255:18]   The principal Alpine pass between Austria and Italy . . . mountains in north-eastern Italy.

256:12 **Mestre**   Mainland town in north-eastern Italy, 10 km. north-west of Venice.

257:22 **Chioggia**   A seaport 30 km. south of Venice, built on an island in the Venetian lagoon.

257:40 **Bucks**   Buckinghamshire, county in England.

258:28 **the Lido**   Island in the Venetian lagoon, with bathing beach.

258:34 **in Piazza . . . Florian's** [258:34] **. . . Goldoni plays** [258:35]   The Piazza San Marco, a centre of activity in Venice . . . a celebrated café on the south side of the Piazza . . . Carlo Goldoni (1707–93), prolific Venetian dramatist.

261:9 **When Jesus refused the devil's money**   See Matthew iv. 8–11 and Luke iv. 5–8.

261:32 **in puris naturalibus . . . in impuris naturalibus** [261:32]   In the purity of natural things (i.e. naked) . . . in the impurity of natural things (Latin).

261:34 **Venus . . . Apollo** [261:38]   Roman goddess of love and beauty . . . Greek god of the sun.

264:25 **Coty's**   Manufacturer of perfume and toiletries.

267:25–6 **as Benvenuto Cellini says, 'in the Italian way,'**   A reference to anal intercourse in *The Memoirs of Benvenuto Cellini* (written 1558–66).

267:38 **Rabelais**   François Rabelais (*c.* 1483–1553), French comic satirist, author of *Gargantua and Pantagruel* (1532–4), supposed advocate of permissive behaviour.

267:39 **Crippen**   Dr Hawley Harvey Crippen (1862–1910) poisoned his wife in 1910 and was hanged for her murder after a sensational shipboard arrest which involved the first use of radio in a police pursuit.

268:11–12 **Miller-of-the-Dee . . . for me!**   'The Miller of Dee', folk song

Explanatory Notes

from the ballad opera *Love in a Village* (1762) by Isaac Bickerstaff (*c.* 1735–1812), with refrain 'I care for nobody, no! not I, if nobody cares for me.'

268:16 **the Marquis de Sade** Donatien Alphonse François Comte de Sade (1740–1814), French writer of sexual fantasies, after whom sadism was named.

268:18–19 **Like Don Rodrigo ... most have sinned** From 'The Penitence of Don Roderick', printed in J. G. Lockhart's *Ancient Spanish Ballads* (1823): for penance after a sexual affair, Roderick must lie where a two-headed serpent eats his genitals with one head, his heart with the other.

269:37–8 **autobiography of the actress Judith** *My Autobiography* (1912) by the actress Julie Bernat (1827–1912), known as Madame Judith.

270:1 **the rector, Mr Burroughs** In spite of Mellors's syntax, the rector is different from Mr Burroughs, who is the doctor (see 268:33).

270:10 **Queen Mary** Victoria Mary of Teck (1867–1953), consort of King George V (see note on 157:36).

272:16 **the Orient Express** A famous luxury train connecting Paris and Constantinople; from 1919 it travelled via Venice.

272:20–21 **house-party for the grouse** Grouse-shooting begins on 12 August, when owners of shoots invite their friends to inaugurate the season.

280:15 **We mustn't ... you and I** In February 1913 DHL explained the current divorce law to Else Jaffe: 'in England, after the first hearing, the judge pronounces a decree *nisi* – that is, the divorce is granted *unless* something turns up; then at the end of the six months the divorce is made *absolute*, if nothing has turned up' (*Letters*, i. 514). See 285:33 below: 'you must both keep apart till you are free.'

281:4 **Charing Cross** London landmark (and railway station).

281:5 **Dahomey** Former name of Benin in West Africa.

281:12–13 **Colonel C. E. Florence ... soldier again** Colonel T. E. Lawrence (1888–1935), known as Lawrence of Arabia, served in the RAF as an ordinary aircraftsman 1922–5.

287:12 **Vulcan** The Roman god of fire, patron of blacksmiths; he caught his wife Venus with her lover Mars, and threw a net over them.

290:9–10 **Like the lady ... must die** See Tennyson's *The Princess* (1850), v. 532–5: 'Home they brought her warrior dead;/ She nor swoon'd nor utter'd cry./ All her maidens, watching, said,/ "She must weep or she will die." '

291:25–6 **'except ye ... little child.'** Conflation of Matthew xviii. 3 ('Except ye be converted, and become as little children, ye shall not enter into the Kingdom of heaven') and Mark x. 15 ('Whosoever shall not receive the Kingdom of God as a little child, he shall not enter therein').

291:26 **Magna Mater** Great Mother (Latin): the goddess who regenerated crops.

Explanatory Notes

296:30 *nostalgie de la boue*   Longing for mud (French), i.e. a longing to return to one's low origins; from Émile Augier's *Le Mariage d'Olympe* (1855).

299:4 **Notts-Derby**   Nottinghamshire and Derbyshire, counties in England.

300:8 **Pan**   Worshipped throughout the Greek world, Pan is a giver of fertility chiefly concerned with flocks and herds; represented with the horns, ears and legs of a goat.

300:25–6 **There's a bad ... time coming!**   A deliberate reversal of the words of the popular song 'The Good Time Coming' (1846) by Charles Mackay (1814–89): 'There's a good time coming, boys,/ A good time coming.'

301:1 **Pentecost ... forked flame** [301:2–3]   The Jewish Feast of Weeks celebrated on the fiftieth (the Greek is 'pentekostos') day after Passover; later the Christian feast of Whitsunday, celebrated on the fiftieth day after Easter to commemorate the Holy Spirit's descent on the Apostles 'in cloven tongues like as of fire' (Acts ii. 1–4).

301:28 **Don Juan**   From his first appearance in *El Burlador de Sevilla* (1630) by Gabriel Téllez (pseud. Tirso de Molina), through countless presentations since, Don Juan is the insatiable and impious seducer.

A PROPOS OF 'LADY CHATTERLEY'S LOVER'

305:2 **pirated editions**   For a description of these, see Jay A. Gertzman, *A Descriptive Bibliography of 'Lady Chatterley's Lover'* (Westport, 1989), pp. 35–9.

305:33 **Captain Kidd**   William Kidd (*c.* 1645–1701), notorious (and later romanticized) pirate; executed for piracy and murder.

306:26–7 **A semi-repentant bookseller of New York**   Terence Holliday sent DHL $180 on 31 January 1929.

306:38 **Judas ... a kiss**   Matthew xxvi. 48–9.

309:8 **the case of Colonel Barker**   In 1929 Lillias I. V. Smith was exposed as a woman masquerading as 'Colonel Barker' and sentenced to nine months in prison for perjury; she had 'married' Edith Johnson in 1923.

309:22 **the Home Secretary**   William Joynson-Hicks (1865–1932), Home Secretary 1924–9, nicknamed 'Jix'.

310:19 **Heliogabalus**   Born about AD 205, proclaimed Emperor of Rome in 218, Heliogabalus was slain in 222 when he affronted the state religion by exalting the Syrian sun-god Elagabalus as the chief deity of Rome.

311:25–8 **a man standing ... to head again**   One of the cards in the Tarot pack.

312:21–2 **you can fool ... all the time**   Cf. 'You can fool all the people some of the time, and some of the people all of the time, but not all of the people all of the time', attributed to Abraham Lincoln (1809–65) in a speech at Clinton, Iowa, 8 September 1858.

312:32–3 **Eastbourne to Brighton** Seaside resorts on the south coast of England.

315:4 *Anna Karenin* Constance Garnett's version (Heinemann, 1901) of the title of *Anna Karenina* (1878), novel by Leo Tolstoy (1828–1910).

315:5 **Aphrodite** Greek goddess of love and beauty; her Roman counterpart is Venus (see 261:36).

315:31 **Bernard Shaw ... chief Prostitute of Europe** [315:37] On 13 September 1929 George Bernard Shaw, addressing a London congress on sex reform, maintained that clothes enhance 'sex appeal' and that the 'chief Prostitute' should instruct the Pope.

316:13 **David was mad for Bathsheba** In 2 Samuel xi, David, captivated by Bathsheba's beauty, seduced her and arranged her husband Uriah's death in battle in order to marry her.

320:20–22 **Church ... built ... rock of Peter, or of Paul** Cf. Matthew xvi. 18.

321:12 **Hellas** Ancient name for Greece.

322:30 **rule of Benedict** St Benedict of Nursia (*c.* 480–*c.* 544), founder of the Benedictine monastic order; his Rule gave instructions for governing it.

322:30–31 **the wild flights of Francis of Assisi** St Francis (1182–1226) tried to reactivate his Church's missionary activity but often interrupted his travels to withdraw into solitude.

322:39–40 **Three Kings ... All Souls** Three Kings: Christmas celebration, see Matthew ii.1–12 ... Pentecost: see note on 301:1 ... St Johns Day: the Feast of St John, celebrated on 24 June ... All Saints and All Souls: feasts of the Church celebrated on 1 and 2 November respectively.

325:7 **the land of Mesopotamia** Literally, the land of the two rivers; at their source was (by convention) the Garden of Eden.

327:3 **katabolism** In a cancelled passage DHL defines 'katabolism' as 'a subtle breaking-down of the very substance of the blood itself'. See Cambridge edn, note to 328:38, for the full passage.

328:24 **Midsummer Fire** Fire-festivals were once held all over Europe on Midsummer Eve (23 June) or Midsummer Day (24 June).

329:19 **Logos** The word (Greek); especially as in John i. 1.

331:11 **Apollo, and Attis ... halls of Dis** Apollo: Greek god of the sun. Attis: a deity worshipped throughout the Roman Empire in conjunction with the Great Mother of the Gods. Demeter: Greek goddess of agriculture. Persephone (daughter of Demeter) and Dis (Hades): see note on 85:34.

331:12 **Hesperus ... Betelgeuse** The evening star (the planet Venus) ... a giant reddish star in the constellation Orion.

331:21 **hyacinthine or Plutonic** 'Hyacinthine' means 'hyacinth blue' but also recalls Hyacinthus, the youth whom Apollo loved and inadvertently killed, afterwards planting a flower where Hyacinthus died. 'Plutonic' describes igneous rocks formed beneath the earth's surface by solidified magma, but also recalls Pluto, king of the underworld: see note on 85:34.

Further Reading

The first two versions of the novel have also been published as *The First Lady Chatterley* (New York: Dial Press, 1944; London: Heinemann, 1972) and *John Thomas and Lady Jane* (New York: Viking; London: Heinemann, 1972).

Britton, Derek, *'Lady Chatterley': The Making of the Novel*, Unwin Hyman, 1988. (*A useful account of the novel's sources.*)

Daleski, H. M., *The Forked Flame: A Study of D. H. Lawrence*, Faber and Faber, 1965. (*A persuasive reading of the novel's male and female principles.*)

Gregor, Ian, 'The Novel as Prophecy: *Lady Chatterley's Lover*', in *The Moral and the Story*, ed. Ian Gregor and Brian Nicholas, Faber and Faber, 1962, pp. 217–48. (*An intelligent discussion of the novel's conflict between realism and fable.*)

Lawrence, D. H., *Lady Chatterley's Lover*, ed. Michael Squires, Cambridge University Press, 1993. (*Detailed discussion of the novel's genesis.*)

MacLeod, Sheila, *Lawrence's Men and Women*, Heinemann, 1985. (*An illuminating critique from a feminist viewpoint.*)

Millett, Kate, *Sexual Politics*, 1969, reprinted Avon Books, 1971. (*A biased but influential critical account; the first sustained feminist response to the novel.*)

Moynahan, Julian, *The Deed of Life: The Novels and Tales of D. H. Lawrence*, Princeton University Press, 1963. (*A judicious and thoughtful reading.*)

Sanders, Scott, *D. H. Lawrence: The World of the Five Major Novels*, Viking Press, 1974. (*A fine discussion of the novel's central themes.*)

Schorer, Mark, Introduction to *Lady Chatterley's Lover*, Modern Library, 1959. (*A perceptive early reading.*)

Spilka, Mark, 'On Lawrence's Hostility to Wilful Women: The Chatterley Solution', in *Lawrence and Women*, ed. Anne Smith, Vision Press, 1978, pp. 189–211. (*A balanced assessment of the novel.*)

Squires, Michael, *The Creation of 'Lady Chatterley's Lover'*, Johns Hopkins University Press, 1983. (*A study of the novel's evolution from first to final version; the appendices print some of Lawrence's drafts.*)

Weinstein, Philip M., 'Choosing Between the Quick and the Dead: Three Versions of *Lady Chatterley's Lover*', *Modern Language Quarterly* 43 (1982), pp. 267–90. (*A valuable analysis of the novel's three versions.*)

Glossary of Dialect Forms

Page and line references are to first occurrences only.

15:1	**Mester** Mister
58:32	**tha** thou (you)
58:39	**yo' mun ax 'er** you must ask her
59:6	**canna tell yer** can't tell you
61:9	**wheer** where
61:22	**fair a stranger** quite a stranger
62:19	**raggy** ragged
70:28	**glimpsey** glimmering, shining faintly
80:11	**bonny** plump, healthy
88:1	**Ah'm** I'm
88:1	**bods** birds
88:5	**'ere i' th' ut** here in the hut
90:7	**Not as Ah know on, the' isna** Not that I know, there
90:15	**'Appen** Perhaps
94:36	**Ah mun fend for t' bods some other road** I must look after the birds some other way
94:40	**pleece as'll du** place that will do
95:1	**yo' ll non** you'll not
95:1	**abaht a' t' time** about all the time
95:6	**thowt it *wor*** thought it *was*
95:8	**ta'e** take
95:9	**gi'e 't** give it
95:9	**t' stuff aht fust** the stuff out first
95:19	**iverythink as is** everything there is
95:20	**the 's bods ter set** there are birds to set (on eggs, to incubate)
95:21	**ned 'ardly come nigh t' pleece** need hardly come near the place
95:38	**wik's** week's
96:2	**ter yersen** to yourself
96:15	**Dunna** Don't
96:15	**niver meant nothink** never meant anything
96:16	**Ah sh' 'ave ter** I should have to

Glossary of Dialect Forms

96:20   **barrin'**   except that
103:37   **mysen**   myself
103:37   **Owt else'll**   Anything else will
104:8   **blether**   babble, talk nonsense
106:20   **coppy**   coppice, thicket of small trees and bushes
106:24   **that throng**   so busy
106:25   **stand**   stop
107:18   **he got his pecker up**   his spirits were roused
123:1   **dibbed about**   made little holes in the soil (cf. dibble)
162:31   **wezzle-brained**   hare-brained, thoughtless
162:39   **thysen**   yourself
162:39   **talk broad**   talk in dialect
164:17   **dool-owls**   spectres, hobgoblins
172:32   **dunna thee fret**   don't worry
172:37   **Ta'e th' thick wi' th' thin**   Take the good with the bad
176:36   **wider**   more
177:13   **naight**   night
177:13   **afore tha goos–sholl ter**   before you go–will you
177:20   **Yi**   Yes
177:22   **slaip**   sleep
177:33   **Coom**   Come
177:33   **mun**   must
177:35   **Maun**   Must
177:38   **Arena**   Aren't
178:3   **i'side**   inside
178:4   **on't**   of it
197:27   **nedna ... wouldna**   needn't ... wouldn't
201:14   **trolly**   trollop, whore
208:3   **Ma**   My
208:4   **Dunna let's niver**   Don't ever let us
210:11   **theer**   there
210:12   **nowt**   nothing
211:27   **a bit sin'**   a little while ago
212:10   **ba's**   balls
220:33   **get a turn**   experience a change in consciousness
223:18   **sees ter**   you see
229:13   **shimmy**   chemise
229:14   **be-out**   without
229:15   **tha bob-tailed young throstle**   you young thrush with short tail-feathers
237:10   **giving her man the go-by**   eluding her man
243:5   **ony cheer as yo'n a mind to**   any chair you want
243:11   **smite o' summat**   bit of something
243:24   **if Ah'n a mind to 't**   if I want to

364

Glossary of Dialect Forms

243:25	**If yo'n nowt** If you've nothing
245:12	**force-put** something unavoidable, compulsory
245:25	**crab** crab-apple
245:34	**doubt** fear
250:27	**twigged** suspected
251:6	*wae* woeful
257:38	**basta!** enough!
268:25	**clatfart** gossip
268:31	**cod atween** penis between
300:34	**fettle** get ready

Visit Penguin on the Internet

and browse at your leisure

- ◆ preview sample extracts of our forthcoming books
- ◆ read about your favourite authors
- ◆ investigate over 10,000 titles
- ◆ enter one of our literary quizzes
- ◆ win some fantastic prizes in our competitions
- ◆ e-mail us with your comments and book reviews
- ◆ instantly order any Penguin book

and masses more!

'To be recommended without reservation ... a rich and rewarding on-line experience' – Internet Magazine

READ MORE IN PENGUIN

In every corner of the world, on every subject under the sun, Penguin represents quality and variety – the very best in publishing today.

For complete information about books available from Penguin – including Puffins, Penguin Classics and Arkana – and how to order them, write to us at the appropriate address below. Please note that for copyright reasons the selection of books varies from country to country.

In the United Kingdom: Please write to *Dept. EP, Penguin Books Ltd, Bath Road, Harmondsworth, West Drayton, Middlesex UB7 ODA*

In the United States: Please write to *Consumer Sales, Penguin Putnam Inc., P.O. Box 999, Dept. 17109, Bergenfield, New Jersey 07621-0120.* VISA and MasterCard holders call 1-800-253-6476 to order Penguin titles

In Canada: Please write to *Penguin Books Canada Ltd, 10 Alcorn Avenue, Suite 300, Toronto, Ontario M4V 3B2*

In Australia: Please write to *Penguin Books Australia Ltd, P.O. Box 257, Ringwood, Victoria 3134*

In New Zealand: Please write to *Penguin Books (NZ) Ltd, Private Bag 102902, North Shore Mail Centre, Auckland 10*

In India: Please write to *Penguin Books India Pvt Ltd, 210 Chiranjiv Tower, 43 Nehru Place, New Delhi 110 019*

In the Netherlands: Please write to *Penguin Books Netherlands bv, Postbus 3507, NL-1001 AH Amsterdam*

In Germany: Please write to *Penguin Books Deutschland GmbH, Metzlerstrasse 26, 60594 Frankfurt am Main*

In Spain: Please write to *Penguin Books S. A., Bravo Murillo 19, 1° B, 28015 Madrid*

In Italy: Please write to *Penguin Italia s.r.l., Via Benedetto Croce 2, 20094 Corsico, Milano*

In France: Please write to *Penguin France, Le Carré Wilson, 62 rue Benjamin Baillaud, 31500 Toulouse*

In Japan: Please write to *Penguin Books Japan Ltd, Kaneko Building, 2-3-25 Koraku, Bunkyo-Ku, Tokyo 112*

In South Africa: Please write to *Penguin Books South Africa (Pty) Ltd, Private Bag X14, Parkview, 2122 Johannesburg*

READ MORE IN PENGUIN

Penguin Twentieth-Century Classics offer a selection of the finest works of literature published this century. Spanning the globe from Argentina to America, from France to India, the masters of prose and poetry are represented by the Penguin.

If you would like a catalogue of the Twentieth-Century Classics library, please write to:

Penguin Marketing, 27 Wrights Lane, London W8 5TZ

(Available while stocks last)

PENGUIN AUDIOBOOKS

A Quality of Writing That Speaks for Itself

Penguin Books has always led the field in quality publishing. Now you can listen at leisure to your favourite books, read to you by familiar voices from radio, stage and screen. Penguin Audiobooks are produced to an excellent standard, and abridgements are always faithful to the original texts. From thrillers to classic literature, biography to humour, with a wealth of titles in between, Penguin Audiobooks offer you quality, entertainment and the chance to rediscover the pleasure of listening.

You can order Penguin Audiobooks through Penguin Direct by telephoning (0181) 899 4036. The lines are open 24 hours every day. Ask for Penguin Direct, quoting your credit card details.

A selection of Penguin Audiobooks, published or forthcoming:

Tales from Watership Down by Richard Adams, read by Nigel Havers

The Brontës: A Life in Letters by Juliet Barker, read by Sian Thomas, Sean Barrett, Susan Jameson and Patience Tomlinson

Cleared for Take-Off by Dirk Bogarde, read by the author

An Ice-Cream War by William Boyd, read by James Wilby

Junky by William Burroughs, read by the author

Oscar and Lucinda by Peter Carey, read by John Turnbull

The Log by Craig Charles, read by the author

Excalibur by Bernard Cornwell, read by Tim Pigott-Smith

The Waste Land by T. S. Eliot, read by Ted Hughes

Ben Elton Live, performed by Ben Elton

10-lb Penalty by Dick Francis, read by Martin Jarvis

The Diary of a Young Girl by Anne Frank, read by Sophie Thompson

Jesus the Son of Man by Kahlil Gibran, read by Eve Matheson and Michael Pennington

My Name Escapes Me by Alec Guinness, read by the author

v. and Other Poems by Tony Harrison, read by the author

PENGUIN AUDIOBOOKS

Thunderpoint by Jack Higgins, read by Roger Moore
Tales from Ovid translated by Ted Hughes, read by Ted Hughes
A Mind to Murder by P. D. James, read by Roy Marsden
Wobegon Boy by Garrison Keillor, read by the author
One Flew over the Cuckoo's Nest by Ken Kesey, read by the author
Rachel's Holiday by Marian Keyes, read by Niamh Cusack
One Past Midnight by Stephen King, read by Willem Dafoe
The Black Album by Hanif Kureishi, read by Zubin Varla
Therapy by David Lodge, read by Warren Clarke
Rebecca by Daphne du Maurier, read by Joanna David
Amongst Women by John McGahern, read by Stephen Rea
How Stella Got Her Groove Back by Terry McMillan, read by the author
And when did you last see your father? by Blake Morrison, read by the author
Felix in the Underworld by John Mortimer, read by Michael Pennington
Into the Heart of Borneo by Redmond O'Hanlon, read by the author
Walking Lines by Tom Paulin, read by the author
The Queen's Man by Sharon Penman, read by Samuel West
The Bell Jar by Sylvia Plath, read by Fiona Shaw
Culloden by John Prebble, read by David Rintoul
A Peaceful Retirement by Miss Read, read by June Whitfield
The Marketmaker by Michael Ridpath, read by Samuel West
Perfume by Patrick Süskind, read by Sean Barratt
Kowloon Tong by Paul Theroux, read by Martin Jarvis
Jane Austen: A Life by Claire Tomalin, read by Joanna David
The Chimney Sweeper's Boy by Barbara Vine, read by Michael Williams
Victoria Wood Live, performed by Victoria Wood

READ MORE IN PENGUIN

A CHOICE OF TWENTIETH-CENTURY CLASSICS

Ulysses James Joyce

Ulysses is unquestionably one of the supreme masterpieces, in any artistic form, of the twentieth century. 'It is the book to which we are all indebted and from which none of us can escape' T. S. Eliot

The First Man Albert Camus

'It is the most brilliant semi-autobiographical account of an Algerian childhood amongst the grinding poverty and stoicism of poor French-Algerian colonials' J. G. Ballard. 'A kind of magical Rosetta stone to his entire career, illuminating both his life and his work with stunning candour and passion' *The New York Times*

Flying Home Ralph Ellison

Drawing on his early experience – his father's death when he was three, hoboeing his way on a freight train to follow his dream of becoming a musician – Ellison creates stories which, according to the *Washington Post*, 'approach the simple elegance of Chekhov.' 'A shining instalment' *The New York Times Book Review*

Cider with Rosie Laurie Lee

'Laurie Lee's account of childhood and youth in the Cotswolds remains as fresh and full of joy and gratitude for youth and its sensations as when it first appeared. It sings in the memory' *Sunday Times*. 'A work of art' Harold Nicolson

Kangaroo D. H. Lawrence

Escaping from the decay and torment of post-war Europe, Richard and Harriett Somers arrive in Australia to a new and freer life. Somers, a disillusioned writer, becomes involved with an extreme political group. At its head is the enigmatic Kangaroo.

READ MORE IN PENGUIN

A CHOICE OF TWENTIETH-CENTURY CLASSICS

Belle du Seigneur Albert Cohen

Belle du Seigneur is one of the greatest love stories in modern literature. It is also a hilarious mock-epic concerning the mental world of the cuckold. 'A *tour de force*, a comic masterpiece weighted with an understanding of human frailty ... It is, quite simply, a book that must be read' *Observer*

The Diary of a Young Girl Anne Frank

'Fifty years have passed since Anne Frank's diary was first published. Her story came to symbolize not only the travails of the Holocaust, but the struggle of the human spirit ... This edition is a worthy memorial' *The Times*. 'A witty, funny and tragic book ... stands on its own even without its context of horror' *Sunday Times*

Herzog Saul Bellow

'A feast of language, situations, characters, ironies, and a controlled moral intelligence ... Bellow's rapport with his central character seems to me novel writing in the grand style of a Tolstoy – subjective, complete, heroic' *Chicago Tribune*

The Go-Between L. P. Hartley

Discovering an old diary, Leo, now in his sixties, is drawn back to the hot summer of 1900 and his visit to Brandham Hall ... 'An intelligent, complex and beautifully-felt evocation of nascent boyhood sexuality that is also a searching exploration of the nature of memory and myth' Douglas Brooks-Davies

Orlando Virginia Woolf

Sliding in and out of three centuries, and slipping between genders, Orlando is the sparkling incarnation of the personality of Vita Sackville-West as Virginia Woolf saw it.

READ MORE IN PENGUIN

A CHOICE OF TWENTIETH-CENTURY CLASSICS

Collected Stories Vladimir Nabokov

Here, for the first time in paperback, the stories of one of the twentieth century's greatest prose stylists are collected in a single volume. 'To read him in full flight is to experience stimulation that is at once intellectual, imaginative and aesthetic, the nearest thing to pure sensual pleasure that prose can offer' Martin Amis

Cancer Ward Aleksandr Solzhenitsyn

Like his hero Oleg Kostoglotov, Aleksandr Solzhenitsyn spent many years in labour camps for mocking Stalin and was eventually transferred to a cancer ward. 'What he has done above all things is record the truth in such a manner as to render it indestructible, stamping it into the Western consciousness' *Observer*

Nineteen Eighty-Four George Orwell

'A volley against the authoritarian in every personality, a polemic against every orthodoxy, an anarchistic blast against every un-questioning conformist ... *Nineteen Eighty-Four* is a great novel, and it will endure because its message is a permanent one' Ben Pimlott

The Complete Saki Saki

Macabre, acid and very funny, Saki's work drives a knife into the upper crust of English Edwardian life. Here are the effete and dashing heroes, Reginald, Clovis and Comus Bassington, tea on the lawn, the smell of gunshot and the tinkle of the caviar fork, and here is the half-seen, half-felt menace of disturbing undercurrents ...

The Castle Franz Kafka

'In *The Castle* we encounter a proliferation of obstacles, endless conversations, perpetual possibilities which hook on to each other as if intent to go on until the end of time' Idris Parry. 'Kafka may be the most important writer of the twentieth century' J. G. Ballard

READ MORE IN PENGUIN

A CHOICE OF TWENTIETH-CENTURY CLASSICS

The Garden Party and Other Stories Katherine Mansfield

This collection reveals Mansfield's supreme talent as an innovator who freed the short story from its conventions and gave it a new strength and prestige. 'One of the great modernist writers of displacement, restlessness, mobility, impermanence' Lorna Sage

The Little Prince Antoine de Saint-Exupéry

Moral fable and spiritual autobiography, this is the story of a little boy who lives alone on a planet not much bigger than himself. One day he leaves behind the safety of his childlike world to travel around the universe where he is introduced to the vagaries of adult behaviour through a series of extraordinary encounters.

Selected Poems Edward Arlington Robinson

Robinson's finely crafted rhythms mirror the tension the poet saw between life's immutable circumstances and humanity's often tragic attempts to exert control. At once dramatic and witty these poems lay bare the tyranny of love and unspoken, unnoticed suffering.

Talkative Man R. K. Narayan

Bizarre happenings at Malgudi are heralded by the arrival of a stranger on the Delhi train who takes up residence in the station waiting-room and, to the dismay of the station master, will not leave. 'His lean, matter-of-fact prose has lost none of its chuckling sparkle mixed with melancholy' *Spectator*

The Immoralist André Gide

'To know how to free oneself is nothing; the arduous thing is to know what to do with one's freedom' André Gide. Gide's novel examines the inevitable conflicts that arise when a pleasure-seeker challenges conventional society, and raises complex issues of personal responsibility.

READ MORE IN PENGUIN

A CHOICE OF TWENTIETH-CENTURY CLASSICS

Enemies Isaac Bashevis Singer

Singer's first 'New York' novel is a bleak and brilliant love story, a study of people profoundly estranged from each other and from themselves. 'A brilliant, unsettling novel ... he works out a bizarre plot with perfect naturalness and aplomb' *Newsweek*

The Man Within Graham Greene

'One of our greatest authors ... Greene had the sharpest eyes for trouble, the finest nose for human weaknesses, and was pitilessly honest in his observations' *Independent*. 'No serious writer of this century has more thoroughly invaded and shaped the public imagination than Graham Greene' *Time*

Guilty Men 'Cato'

Published a month after the evacuation of Dunkirk, and conceived by three journalists, Michael Foot, Peter Howard and Frank Owen, this impassioned polemic singled out the leaders MacDonald, Baldwin and, above all, Chamberlain, who, through their policy of appeasement in the face of Hitler's aggression, had brought the country to the brink of disaster. 'A polemic of genius' Peter Clarke

The Victim Saul Bellow

Leventhal is a man uncertain of himself, never free from the nagging suspicion that the other guy might be right. So when a down-at-heel stranger accuses him of ruining his life, he half believes it, and cannot stop himself becoming trapped in a mire of self-doubt. 'A masterful and chilling novel' *The Times*

Wide Sargasso Sea Jean Rhys

Jean Rhys's literary masterpiece was inspired by Charlotte Brontë's *Jane Eyre*, and is set in the lush, beguiling landscape of Jamaica in the 1830s. 'A tale of dislocation and dispossession, which Rhys writes with a kind of romantic cynicism, desperate and pungent' *The Times*

READ MORE IN PENGUIN

A CHOICE OF TWENTIETH-CENTURY CLASSICS

The Prodigy   Hermann Hesse

Hesse's early novel *The Prodigy* is based on his own experiences of a narrow and uncaring education. Hans Giebenrath is a gifted child and the victim of provincial ambitions. Sent to theological school, the intelligent and imaginative boy is gradually driven to nervous collapse in a situation from which there seems to be no escape.

On the Road   Jack Kerouac

'*On the Road* sold a trillion Levis and a million espresso machines, and also sent countless kids on the road . . . The alienation, the restlessness, the dissatisfaction were already there waiting when Kerouac pointed out the road' William Burroughs. 'It changed the way I saw the world, making me yearn for fresh experience' Hanif Kureishi

Selected Poems 1947–1995   Allen Ginsberg

Chosen by Allen Ginsberg himself, this selection brings together nearly fifty years of experimental, intensely personal verse. 'No one has made his poetry speak for the whole man, without inhibition of any kind, more than Ginsberg' *The Times Literary Supplement*

The Temple of the Golden Pavilion   Yukio Mishima

'A fragment of contemporary Japanese life, with its roots still deep in the culture of the past, is presented not for our judgement but for our observation' Nancy Wilson Ross. 'Mishima achieved a fusion of thought, vision and expression that has been equalled by only a handful of writers this century anywhere in the world' *Sunday Telegraph*

Incest   Anaïs Nin

Spanning the years 1932–4, the material in *Incest* was considered too explosive to include when the journals were originally published. In it, Nin reveals her incestuous affair with her pianist father, and recounts other relationships, loves and desires.

READ MORE IN PENGUIN

D. H. LAWRENCE

NOVELS

Aaron's Rod
The Lost Girl
The Rainbow
The Trespasser
The Boy in the Bush
(with M. L. Skinner)

Lady Chatterley's Lover
Women in Love
Sons and Lovers
The White Peacock
Kangaroo
Mr Noon

SHORT STORIES

Three Novellas: The Fox/
  The Ladybird/The Captain's
  Doll
St Mawr and Other Stories
Selected Short Stories
The Complete Short Novels

The Virgin and the Gipsy
The Prussian Officer
Love among the Haystacks
England, My England
The Woman Who Rode
  Away

TRAVEL BOOKS AND OTHER WORKS

Studies in Classic
  American Literature
D. H. Lawrence and Italy

Sketches of Etruscan Places
Twilight in Italy
Apocalypse

POETRY

D. H. Lawrence: Selected Poetry
Edited and Introduced by Keith Sagar
Complete Poems

Penguin are now publishing the Cambridge editions of D. H. Lawrence's texts. These are as close as can be determined to those he would have intended.